*We request the pleasure of your company
this festive season to celebrate two winter
weddings. Enjoy these brand-new romances
packed so full of yuletide sparkle they'll
warm your heart on the coldest of
Christmas days…*

Lucy Monroe and **Louise Allen**
bring you two very special

Christmas Brides

*The perfect gift this Christmas
will be marriage!*

Lucy Monroe started reading at age four. After going through the children's books at home, she was caught by her mother reading adult novels pilfered from the higher shelves on the bookcase…alas, it was nine years before she got her hands on a Mills & Boon® romance her older sister had brought home. She loves to create the strong alpha males and independent women that people Mills & Boon® books. When she's not immersed in a romance novel (whether reading or writing it) she enjoys travel with her family, having tea with the neighbours, gardening, and visits from her numerous nieces and nephews. Lucy loves to hear from readers – e-mail her at LucyMonroe@LucyMonroe.com or visit her website: www.LucyMonroe.com

Louise Allen has been immersing herself in history, real and fictional, for as long as she can remember, and finds landscapes and places evoke powerful images of the past. She also writes for Mills & Boon® as one half of the Historical Romance™ writing partnership Francesca Shaw. Louise lives in Bedfordshire and works as a property manager, but spends as much time as possible with her husband at the cottage they are renovating on the North Norfolk coast, or travelling abroad. Venice, Burgundy and the Greek islands are favourite atmospheric destinations.

Christmas Brides

LUCY MONROE
LOUISE ALLEN

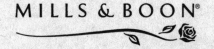
MILLS & BOON®

*MILLS & BOON and MILLS & BOON with the Rose Device
are registered trademarks of the publisher.*

*First published in Great Britain 2005
Harlequin Mills & Boon Limited,
Eton House, 18-24 Paradise Road, Richmond, Surrey, TW9 1SR*

CHRISTMAS BRIDES © Harlequin Enterprises II B.V. 2005

The publisher acknowledges the copyright holders of the
individual works as follows:

The Greek's Christmas Baby © Lucy Monroe 2005
Moonlight and Mistletoe © Melanie Hilton 2005

ISBN 0 263 84954 6

059-1105

*Printed and bound in Spain
by Litografia Rosés S.A., Barcelona*

CONTENTS

The Greek's Christmas Baby

by

Lucy Monroe

CHAPTER ONE

"She's coming out of it."

Eden heard the words, but didn't recognize the voice. Her eyelids felt glued together over a layer of sandpaper. It took a Herculean effort to force them apart and, at first, all she saw was white light and moving shadows.

There were more words, but they sounded like they were coming from under water.

Someone moved to her right. "Yes, Doctor."

Her eyes began to adjust, making recognizable interpretations of the light and shadows.

A young doctor bent over her, his pale blue eyes intent on her face. "Hello, Mrs Kouros. I'm Adam Lewis, the doctor on call when you were brought in. How do you feel?"

"Like I've been hit by a truck," she rasped. Her tongue felt parched and swollen.

"You were…or at least your car was."

Images flashed in her mind. Driving rain, a wet road, the sound of squealing tires. Headlights coming straight at them. The grating honk of a car's horn, long and penetrating. Aristide swearing in Greek and English. His arm coming out to shield her, the airbags rendering the gesture superfluous. Her brown hair swirling around her face, it and the airbag blocking everything else from view.

More distressing images bombarded her and her hand moved restlessly to cover her still-flat stomach.

Her gray eyes clung to the doctor's, begging reassurance. "My baby?"

The paramedics had said the tiny life inside her probably wouldn't survive the trauma, but she'd prayed desperately they were wrong. She didn't remember anything from that desperate prayer until waking up just now.

"You're still pregnant."

"Thank God," she said brokenly, relief pouring through her slight body.

"Unfortunately, you're spotting. The good news is that there is no amniotic fluid in the blood. However, the amniotic sac has disengaged from the wall of your womb in one place. We'll do everything we can to save the baby, but the next seventy-two hours are going to be critical. You must remain in this bed and stay calm."

She nodded and winced at the ache in her head. "Hurts…"

"Yes." He shone a small flashlight in her eyes and made a note on her chart. "You're suffering a minor concussion and have several small abrasions on your right arm from shattered glass."

Now that he mentioned it, her arm did sting, but her entire body felt like she'd been beaten.

Where was Aristide? Surely he wouldn't leave her to face this alone. He might not love her, but he adored being a father. Even after their argument, he would be by her bedside for the baby's sake.

"Where is my husband?"

The doctor laid his hand on her forearm. "You must remain calm, are we agreed on that?"

"Yes." She willed her emotions in check, despite fear trying to take a choke-hold on her. "Please tell me."

"Mr Kouros is in a room down the hall. His vitals aren't bad, but he hasn't come round yet."

"He's in a coma?"

"Yes."

She flinched as if the word had been a physical blow. She felt like it had been. Prior to the accident she'd convinced herself and told Aristide that she was ready for her marriage to end. She had believed there was no greater pain than loving a man she was certain cared for another woman, but she had been wrong.

The prospect of Aristide dying hurt much worse.

"Will he come out of it?" She could barely make herself ask the question, she was so terrified of the answer.

"There's no way to tell, but indications are good."

"I need to see him." If she could see him, it would be all right. It had to be all right.

"Not just yet. As I said before, moving you would be detrimental to your pregnancy. You must remain here."

"How can I stay here while Aristide is in a coma in another room?" She struggled to sit up.

He pressed gently against her shoulders, putting a halt to her feeble efforts. "Your husband will continue to live without you by his side, but, if you attempt to go to him, your baby might not. When he wakes up, we will bring him to you."

She appreciated the "when" rather than the doctor saying "if", but his promise was not enough. "Please…isn't there some way you can take me to him?"

"Your baby's life depends on you remaining calm and remaining flat on your back in this bed," the doctor said too firmly for her to ignore.

She gave up trying to move. "Seventy-two hours?"

"If he hasn't woken up by then and you are no longer spotting, we will arrange for you to be taken to his room to sit beside his bed."

She knew she had to be strong, but it was so hard. She just wanted everything to be the way it had been before she got married, when she thought Aristide was just poor at expressing his emotions toward her…before she'd decided he didn't have any.

The doctor squeezed her shoulder in comfort before stepping back. "Bed rest is the best chance you have of ensuring the viability of your pregnancy at this point, Mrs Kouros. I know it is difficult, *but you must stay here*. We will keep you apprised of your husband's progress. I promise."

"Thank you." She blinked away tears at the kind understanding she saw reflected in the doctor's eyes. "I need to make a phone call."

"Of course."

She called her mother-in-law. Phillippa was frantic at the news of the accident and Aristide's coma. Even so, she did not neglect to ask how Eden was doing.

"I'm fine. Some minor complications…a concussion…it will keep me on bed rest for a few days, though." The only family member who knew she was pregnant was Aristide and she had every intention of keeping it that way.

She'd found out very recently herself and the news had come as a total shock. She was still breast-feeding Theo, or had been, but her milk had stopped producing and she'd gone to her doctor to find out why. She'd been dumbfounded to discover she was pregnant again so soon after the birth of her first child. Theo was only nine months old.

Even if it had been a planned event, she would have hesitated to impart news of her pregnancy to her mother-in-law when there was a chance it would end in grief.

Her heart contracted at the thought and she sent yet another desperate prayer heavenward.

"I'm so glad Theo is staying with you."

"You must not worry about your son. All is well."

Eden actually managed a smile; thoughts of her son always gave her pleasure. "Thank you."

It had been murder leaving him behind and she went to sleep every night with images of his baby features, so like his father's, firmly fixed in her mind's eye. Theo shared Aristide's dark curly hair and olive complexion, but he had her gray eyes. She missed him like crazy, but she had intended this trip to New York to be an opportunity to cement her relationship with Aristide.

She had thought that by coming back to where they had met and been lovers, she could recapture the way things had been between them. However, the trip had been a dismal failure. She'd ended up playing second fiddle to Kassandra…again, and getting so mad about it, she'd asked Aristide for a divorce.

She could barely believe she'd done it. She'd been crazy in love with him from practically the moment they met. She'd thought he felt the same way. He'd certainly acted like it.

They'd bumped into each other in front of the Metropolitan Museum of Art. It had been a muggy day in summer and Eden was visiting her dad in the city. He was busy in a last-minute business meeting and had cancelled their plans for lunch. There was nothing new in that and she'd taken herself off to the museum as she'd done on so many occasions in the past.

Only this time, she'd never made it inside.

Busy thinking, Eden let her instincts guide her toward her destination. Now that Dad had cancelled lunch, she'd have time to meet with that new glass artist she'd heard about. Would he be open to showing his work in the upcoming "History of Glass in Art" exhibit at the small museum she worked for in upstate New York? Not all artists were open to museum exhibition.

There was little to no money in it for them, but the exposure was good.

She was composing her approach to the artist in her mind

when she hit what felt like a brick wall and bounced backward. Her gaze flew up as two strong, masculine hands grasped her shoulders and prevented her from falling.

Not a brick wall. A man. The most stunningly gorgeous male specimen she had ever seen. Easily six foot four, the dark-haired Adonis had eyes the color of blue lapis and a finely sculpted body encased in an Armani suit of perfect fit. He even smelled gorgeous. *Wow*. She thought maybe she mouthed the word, but wasn't sure.

He smiled down at her and she felt all the air go whooshing from her lungs while the blood rushed from her head. Dizzy, she could only be grateful he had kept his hold on her shoulders.

Those incredible blue eyes skated over her features with tactile intensity. "Excuse me, I did not intend to nearly knock you over."

But she knew, *just knew*, it had been the other way around.

"I wasn't watching where I was walking," she admitted with a grimace while she fought a totally inappropriate urge to reach out and touch the hard body so close to her own.

"And I was too busy watching you to notice the direction my steps took me." He spoke with a slight accent she could not place, his words infinitely more formal than the average American businessman.

She stared. "Did you really just say that?"

His smile grew to such sexy proportions, she was in danger of melting in a puddle at his feet. "You are unused to the men around you being honest in their attraction to you?"

"I'm not used to men like you being attracted to me at all." As soon as she blurted the words, she blushed so hotly she felt like her cheeks were on fire. She couldn't have been more gauche if she'd tried.

He didn't seem to notice. In fact, he was shaking his head,

his eyes speaking messages she had to be misinterpreting. "You are teasing me, no?"

"No. I'm not very good at that sort of thing."

This made him laugh. "You are charmingly honest."

"Whereas you are embarrassingly so," she muttered, not at all sure how to take this man's attitude.

He opened his mouth to speak, but his cell phone rang. He frowned. "Excuse me for a moment."

She went to move away, but he kept one hand firmly on her shoulder while flipping his phone open with the other. She had no trouble reading his expression then. He was silently telling her to stay right where she was and arrogantly assumed she'd do it as he turned his attention to his phone call.

Her heartbeat tripled at his continued nearness and the knowledge she didn't want to go anywhere.

He started speaking in another language, one she could not place any more successfully than she had placed the accent.

He didn't talk very long before hanging up the phone and then smiling at her once again. "I must apologize. It was my assistant."

"If you need to go…"

He shook his head. "No. I find my afternoon free. My hope is to spend it with you."

Totally unprepared for that claim, she shook her head, trying to clear it.

"You have another engagement?"

"No. I…" She swallowed. "A guy like you…you don't have free afternoons."

"A guy like me, *pethi mou*?"

"What does that mean?" she asked, diverted.

"*Pethi mou?* Loosely translated, it means my little one."

"In what language?"

"I am Greek."

"Oh," she sighed out. She should have realized. He was every bit as yummy as any statuary she'd ever seen of the Greek gods. More so, if she was honest with herself.

"Now, answer me…what do you mean by *a guy like me*?"

"A businessman…a corporate shark."

"You think I am a shark?"

She looked at his clothes, took in the familiar aura surrounding him, and then remembered the way he'd wielded his cell phone and how effectively he'd controlled her with a mere look. "Yeah."

"And do you have a lot of experience with guys like me?" Incredibly, he sounded jealous.

She almost laughed, but didn't think he'd appreciate the humor of the situation. "Not a lot, no. But my dad is one and I used to work for him."

"No longer?"

"No. I work for a museum in upstate New York now."

"So, you are not from the city?"

She shook her head. "I'm supposed to be visiting my dad, but something came up." And then, incredibly, she found herself telling him her other errand and he offered to go with her to see the artist.

It was mad, but she wanted desperately to say yes, to prolong this meeting between total strangers.

He read her hesitation and asked, "Your father is into big business?"

"Yes."

The gorgeous Greek handed her his phone. "Call him. Tell him that Aristide Kouros wants you to spend the afternoon with him."

His absolute assurance her father would know who he was and vouch for him surprised her, but maybe it shouldn't have. This guy was not lacking in confidence in any way.

"That's your name? Aristide?" she asked to put off making the call, trying to decide if she wanted to.

This man was dangerous, but so delectable she wasn't sure that was going to matter to her.

"Yes."

"My name is Eden."

Aristide's hand moved to cup her nape and his thumb brushed along her jaw. "That is a lovely name."

Her breathing fractured and she stuttered out, "Th-thank y-you."

He pressed the phone into her hand. "Call."

She did. Her father did indeed know who Aristide was and asked to speak to him. She couldn't tell much from Aristide's side of the conversation, but when she got the phone back, her father told her the other man was trustworthy.

"But he's out of your league, honey. Be careful."

"It's not safe to go with him?" she asked.

Aristide frowned, his body stiffening with offense, and she could just tell he wanted to grab the phone back from her and tell her dad a thing or two.

"I didn't say that," her dad was saying. "He's safe to your person, but your heart is another matter. He makes me seem like a tame pussycat."

That did give her pause. Her dad hadn't gotten serious with anyone since her mom, though he'd had numerous affairs, and the truth was, he hadn't been faithful to her mom, either. Was Aristide the philandering type?

One look into his burning blue gaze and she had to doubt that assessment.

Nevertheless, she was biting her lip when Aristide took the phone from her and flipped it shut.

She sighed. "He says I'm not in your league."

"You are in your own league, Eden. You are special."

"You don't know me, how can you say that?"

"Are you saying your reaction to me is like any you have had to another man?"

"No."

"Special."

"Yes."

"Do you think I make a routine practice of clearing my heavy schedule to spend time getting to know a woman I bump into on the street?"

Put like that… It should be impossible for something like this to happen so fast, but it *was* happening. "I guess I can accept that this is unique for you."

"*You* are unique for me."

And she had believed him, Eden thought as she lay in her hospital bed, memories washing over her. From that point on, he'd certainly treated her like she was special. They spent the day together and he didn't press to take her to bed that night. Honesty made her admit to herself that, if he had, she would have been a total pushover.

But he hadn't and she had stayed over in New York City for the weekend, which they spent together.

Then she had to go home.

She didn't know if she would see him again, but she had. He'd called several times that week and then surprised her by coming to see her in upstate New York. He'd wined and dined her, his every casual touch sending her libido to places it had never been. They talked for hours, discovering they liked the same foods, enjoyed the same movies and he was fascinated by her knowledge and interest in antiques.

When he took her home that night, he'd started making love to her and she'd gone under with all the buoyancy of a rock tossed into a stormy sea.

Remembering that first time made her heart palpitate even now.

Eden had waited in silence while Aristide unlocked the door to her apartment. The sexual tension in the air was so thick, it pressed against her like a physical force. He wanted her, but she wanted him too. More than she'd ever wanted another man…enough even to silence her clamoring nerves and internal worries that all of this was moving way too fast.

The look of dark promise in his deep blue eyes said he didn't think it was moving fast enough. "I like your place."

She looked around. Her home was the middle floor of a tri-story Victorian-era house that had been converted into three separate apartments. Carved wooden trim painted white and walls painted in deep rich tones gave her home an elegance that she had fallen in love with on first viewing the property.

She'd broken up the high gloss of the hardwood floors with antique oriental throw rugs in tones complementary to the walls. All of her furniture had an oriental motif, but it didn't feel modern. She'd scoured flea markets and antique stores all over the state to decorate with inlaid lacquer pieces and furnishings that gave the impression of the ancient culture of the Far East.

"I'm glad you like it. I do too."

He'd shut the door and locked it and now turned to face her, his hands divesting her of her jacket while his eyes devoured her. "I like you even more."

She licked her suddenly dry lips. "I like you too."

"I'm going to kiss you, *pethi mou*."

"All right."

But when his lips touched hers, it was unlike anything she'd ever known. Even with him. This kiss was claim-staking at its most basic. His hands curled around her waist and pulled her body into his while his tongue demanded entry into her mouth. She gave it to him.

From the first slide of his tongue against hers the passion he sparked in her burned through her body to singe every single, solitary nerve ending into sizzling life and she went up in flames. It was too much, but not enough, and she whimpered as she undulated against him in wanton abandon.

He groaned and one hand moved down to cup her bottom, massaging her and causing a burst of heated humidity between her legs. Their clothes fell away as if by magic and then she was standing naked in the circle of his arms.

Sudden fear had her breaking the erotic play of their lips together. "Aristide?"

"What, *pedhaki mou*?"

"This isn't just a one-night stand, is it? You won't disappear once we've made love?" She didn't know what made her ask the question, maybe her ongoing fear that this man was so far out of her league he belonged on another planet.

He stopped moving and held her still to meet his gaze, his expression so serious that she shivered. "I am making you mine, not preparing to notch a bloody bedpost."

She bit her lip. "Do you become mine too?"

"Of course."

She shuddered. "Okay."

It wasn't a promise of forever, but it was also not the age-old "no ties" out-clause of the commitment-shy male. He wanted more than a temporary slaking of physical need. She was glad because her feelings for him demanded it be more while at the same time making it nearly impossible to say no, regardless of what his intentions were.

They came together in a conflagration of need that broke through her virginal barrier with her barely even realizing it had occurred. The pain was minimal and incredible pleasure followed it almost immediately. Their lovemaking culminated in a completion so intense, she was insensate afterward.

She slowly became aware of him again as he kissed her all over her face and throat, saying over and over again that she was beautiful, passionate and *his*. The claiming lasted throughout the long night of her sexual awakening.

The next morning, he woke her with a kiss that was so tender it made her cry. He laughed when she explained her tears were because his lovemaking was so beautiful, his masculine arrogance basking in her overt approval.

And, as promised, their time together was in no way related to a one-night stand. He'd told her she was special and proved it. He had an even more demanding schedule than her dad, but he called her at least once a day. He spent almost every weekend with her, sometimes bringing her to New York City, but usually he came to her apartment despite it being a two-hour drive.

He treated her like a queen and made love to her like she was the most irresistible woman on the planet.

He willingly got to know her father. While they had actually met briefly in the business arena, they now became friends. She and Aristide were together months before she started to wonder about him introducing her to his family. The couple of times she had brought it up, he put it off, saying he wanted to keep her to himself and she believed him.

His life was so hectic, so high pressure that she got a charge out of being what he called "his oasis" in the desert of a life filled with the grains of sand that comprised his business and family commitments.

However, as the months grew to a year and he made trips back to Greece without ever once inviting her, she started to wonder about her role in his life. How necessary was an "oasis" and did him seeing her that way mean she was a mirage that would disappear from his life at some point in the future?

Unlike when he was living in New York, he rarely called her from Greece and never made any overt commitment to return to her when he left. But she knew if he did, she would be waiting. She loved him and her life, at least, was not complete without him. He left a huge void when he was gone and she felt like she walked around as half of a person until they were together again.

It gave her a frightening sense of vulnerability, one she was certain he did not share.

She discovered she was pregnant during one of the trips he took to Greece without her. She knew right away she was keeping the baby, but she was worried about telling Aristide. He'd been so careful about contraception and she couldn't help wondering if he would balk at her taking a more permanent role in his life…that of his child's mother.

She told him of the pregnancy his first day back. He'd come to see her straight from the airport and she took that as a good sign. They made love and were lying entwined in her bed when she told him about the baby.

She was curled into his side, sated and so filled with love for him, she was bursting with it. "I've got something I need to tell you."

He moved so he was leaning over her and met her gaze with his own, his eyes compelling her to honesty. "This sounds serious. What is it?"

"I'm pregnant."

He went completely still, the vibrant blue of his irises disappearing almost completely as his pupils dilated in shock. "But…"

"Contraceptives fail," was all she could think to say.

Then he was smiling brilliantly, the change in his demeanor happening so fast, she was stunned. "You are carrying my child? Why did you not call and tell me?"

"It's not something you say over the phone." Not to mention the fact she had never once felt comfortable calling him at his office in Greece or on his cell phone when he was abroad.

He nodded, his expression filled with blatant pleasure now. "I understand. This is amazing."

"I'm glad you feel that way."

"How else could I feel?"

"Trapped?" she suggested.

But he just laughed. "We'll get married as soon as possible."

As marriage proposals went, it lacked romance, but she was so relieved he wanted to spend the rest of his life with her, she didn't quibble. She loved him so much; regardless of the doubts that had plagued her over the last few months, he had to love her too.

He'd been too instantaneous in the marriage decision and for a guy like him to stay with one girlfriend so long had to be significant.

"All right. I'll marry you."

CHAPTER TWO

Eden moved restlessly in her hospital bed as she remembered her naïve assumptions. Aristide had moved her to Greece right after the wedding, introducing her to his family, a wonderful group of people who had accepted her without a qualm.

But the fairytale marriage situation ended there, because she saw less of her husband than she had of her lover. He spent as much time in New York as before, but now she was an ocean away. He called her frequently, but that did not assuage the lonely ache in her heart left by his absence.

At first, she had not traveled with him because of her morning sickness, but then he had told her he didn't want her uncomfortable, making the long flight in an advanced state of pregnancy. After the birth of their son, she had opted to breast-feed, which meant she went nowhere without Theo, and Aristide did not believe a tiny baby should make the long flight to the States.

In addition to the separations her new role in his life dictated, Kassandra had entered her life.

Kassandra and Aristide had grown up together and then the beautiful Greek woman had started working for his company. She'd been his personal assistant for the last five years. While Eden and Aristide were only lovers, Kassandra ignored Eden's existence, but that ended almost immediately after her marriage. Not that Eden had latched on to the change right away.

But looking back, she could see that Kassandra had begun enacting subtle ploys to undermine Eden's confidence and Aristide's time spent with her from the very first.

When Eden first began to suspect the other woman of manipulation, she had convinced herself she was imagining the other woman's malice. Everyone liked Kassandra. The family. The other people who worked with Aristide.

And Kassandra was so sweet to Eden on the surface that it had taken almost a full year before she realized the Greek woman really had it in for her marriage. Even then, she hadn't known what to do about it. She had not wanted to rock the boat in her relationship with Aristide, but the more convinced she became that her husband had married her simply for the sake of their son, the less quiescent she felt about Kassandra's machinations.

It had all come to a head in New York and Eden had complained for the first time about Kassandra. Bitterly and without pulling any punches. She now realized she'd been a fool to bottle it up for so long and not say anything. Her grievances had fallen on deaf ears because Aristide had thought she was out of her mind.

He trusted his assistant. Why shouldn't he? He'd known her for a lot longer than he'd known his wife and she'd never before shown this devious side to her personality.

But Eden had lost her ability to put up with Kassandra's manipulations when the other woman arranged to usurp Eden at Aristide's side for a Broadway performance they had planned to attend. Kassandra had turned the evening into a business event and Aristide had expected Eden to gracefully back out of attending the play with him.

She had been livid and refused and they had had the worst

fight of their marriage. She had accused him of being in love with the other woman. He had told Eden she was being both childish and selfish and flat-out refused to reconsider taking Kassandra to the play. Eden had rejected his peace offering of changing the entire seating arrangements to include one more person and had stayed in the hotel rather than go with them.

The following morning, they were driving upstate to spend the weekend away from his business pressures when Eden again voiced her grievances. Aristide had dismissed her complaints as if they were ludicrous. He had not taken her seriously at all and the more he stonewalled her, the angrier she became, until the rage inside her gave vent to a demand for a divorce.

In her desperation to be heard, she had believed they were the only words that might penetrate his stubborn Greek skull. She'd been right. He'd listened all right. He'd been shouting at her in rapid-fire Greek she couldn't begin to decipher when they were hit by the truck.

Eden now recognized how poorly she had handled the confrontation with her husband. She should have built up to it, pointing out Kassandra's undermining as they went along instead of hitting Aristide with it all at once in what he considered a fantastic claim. But if she'd messed up, so had he.

He had rejected her claims outright and had not taken her seriously at all…not until she said she wanted a divorce. He'd been paying attention then, and remembering his look of horror gave her a small measure of hope.

Aristide did not want their marriage to end. But she did not know if that was because he was a typically possessive Greek male who wanted to raise his children in a two-parent household, or if he personally could not stand the thought of losing Eden. It was a question she could no longer stand to go unanswered.

She was pregnant again, just like before, but this time she wasn't going to bury her head in the sand, making assumptions about his feelings based on his actions. She wanted the words. She had to know…one way or the other.

As scared as she was of both losing her baby and of Aristide's coma, she was also filled with determination. She was going to rock the boat on her marriage until her husband got seasick and sent the wicked witch flying off on her broomstick…or until he admitted he would rather have Kassandra in his life than Eden.

The accident had clarified a lot of things in her head. She wasn't giving up on her marriage, but she wasn't playing the doormat wife any more. She wasn't going through another pregnancy like the last one, where she got left behind in Greece "for her own good" while he worked in New York more than half the time.

Nor would she tolerate Kassandra's constant belittling of her, no matter how subtly the woman played it. She didn't think Aristide was sleeping with his assistant, but the other woman had too much of his loyalty. There was fidelity of mind as well as body and Eden was determined to have both from her husband.

Aristide was a wonderful father and there was nothing she wanted more than for him to be with her to raise their children, but he lacked in the husband department and it was time that changed.

She had lacked as a wife too, she saw now. She'd been too afraid to incur his anger to stand up for herself, too unsure of her place in his life to demand it fully. She wasn't going to be that way any more. She deserved better and so did he.

Marriage had changed her, she saw now. She'd wanted so desperately to gain Aristide's love and make it work that she'd become a woman she didn't always recognize or like any more. The change had begun during her time as Aristide's lover, but she didn't care what had made it start, she wanted it stopped.

She wasn't going to end up like her mother. *She wasn't.*

The next three days went by in a haze for Eden. Aristide did not wake up and every hour he laid in a coma in another hospital room, her heart bled a little more. She loved him so much and the thought of even trying to live without him sent her blood pressure skyrocketing, incurring a long lecture from the doctor.

His family had arrived and taken up residence in the hotel, but spent most of their time at the hospital. Phillippa had brought Theo and, thankfully, Rachel willingly cared for him with her own two children while at the hotel. She brought Theo in to visit Eden and that helped, but she could not forget for one second that her husband's life remained precarious.

She ached with the need to be by his bedside, but did her best to remain still and calm to retain the unstable hold she had on her baby.

Her father called from Hong Kong, where he was away on business. Once he learned her injuries were not life threatening, he made it clear he had no intention of flying home early on her account. She was hardly surprised by his lack of overt concern. As with Aristide, she had always taken a poor second to business with her father.

The doctor kept his promise and apprised Eden each morning and evening of Aristide's condition, no matter that she had frequent updates from his family. He was kind and she found his visits less stressful than Aristide's family. She did not have to hide her condition or worry for her baby from him and Adam Lewis turned out to be an unexpected friend.

* * *

Leaning heavily on Sebastian's arm for balance, Eden made her way slowly down the hall toward her husband's room. She'd refused to use a wheelchair, not wanting him to think the worst when he saw her and possibly suffer a setback because of it.

Adam had told her that Aristide had not asked about the baby, but that didn't mean he wasn't thinking about it. It was just like her strong husband to hide his worries, even from a doctor.

But her bleeding had stopped completely and the latest ultrasound had come back with good news. The doctor had assured her the short walk would not hurt the baby, but, due to her lingering concussion, she still wasn't supposed to be up and walking around a great deal.

Nevertheless, she'd taken a shower and washed her hair, leaving it to fall in a straight brown curtain around her shoulders. Aristide preferred that style and she was so happy he had woken from the coma, she wanted to please him. She had donned a set of pajamas that could pass for loungewear. She hoped Aristide wouldn't notice the IV shunt in her hand before she had a chance to tell him all was well with the baby.

No one had told him that she was in hospital as well and, according to his mother, he hadn't asked. Eden found that very odd, but then maybe he was still angry at her for bringing up divorce. She could see his pride balking at her temerity and she almost smiled.

They had a lot to discuss, but right now all she wanted to do was see the man she'd married and assure herself he truly was awake and going to be all right.

She walked into the room, her eyes hungry for the sight of the man she loved. She'd missed him so much during the hours of loneliness in her hospital bed while memories, both good and painful, filled her mind, reminding her just how much she would be giving up if she let her husband go.

Nothing could assuage the perpetual ache in Eden's heart left by her husband's absence. Which said a lot about the probability of her ever walking away from her marriage if there was *any* chance at making it work.

Aristide was sitting up in bed and tears of relief wet her eyes. She'd tried so hard to remain emotionally detached from his coma, but she'd been scared to death she would save her baby only to lose her husband.

His dark head was visible because of his height, but Kassandra Helios stood at the head of the bed, blocking Eden's view of his face.

She had always felt at a disadvantage next to the other woman and even more so now. Eden's looks were average, no matter what Aristide said in the midst of passion. But right now she knew her pale complexion could best be described as wan and her nondescript gray eyes were dull from her concussion.

The last thing she wanted right now was to face her nemesis. "I thought only family were allowed to visit critical-care patients."

The moment the words left her mouth, she regretted them. Too many people in this room considered Kassandra exactly that.

Kassandra turned, her smile imbued with so much false sympathy Eden had a sudden urge to be sick that could not be blamed entirely on morning sickness. "Surely I qualify. I've known him longer than any other woman in his life besides his mother…why, we're practically brother and sister."

Eden couldn't argue the claim, but she didn't buy it. The sly witch felt sisterly toward Aristide in a pig's eye. However, she bit back the retort she wanted to make. Now was not the time to take her stand against the enemy.

Before she had a chance to reply in any way, Kassandra

spoke again. "We are friends as well and I have been so worried," she said with an affecting break in her voice. "I have barely stirred from his side. It did not occur to me to make myself scarce now…that I would be unwelcome."

"Eden did not mean to imply any such thing," Phillippa said. "I'm sure she spoke merely out of surprise."

"We all know you have been a good friend to Aristide as well as an employee," Sebastian added in a soothing voice.

Eden felt like a monster, even though she knew it was all nothing more than a cleverly portrayed act. Kassandra's place within the Kouros clan was unassailable. No one saw her manipulations for what they were, but Eden was heartily tired of being wrong-footed by the Greek paragon.

Stubbornly determined not to apologize when she was not in the wrong, Eden inclined her head to Kassandra. The Greek woman made no effort to move, so Eden stepped around her in order to see Aristide properly. But she pulled up short at the total lack of recognition in her husband's brilliant blue eyes.

"Who are you and where do you get off censuring Kassandra for being here?"

The angry words whirled around in her head and she felt as if she'd taken a body blow. "W-what?"

He turned his irate gaze to his brother. "Who the hell is this, Sebastian? She's not Rachel and that's the only woman that should be hanging on to your arm like it's a lifeline."

Even sitting in the hospital bed having just woken from a coma, Aristide's powerful vitality emanated in waves from his tall, muscular body. His genuine lack of recognition was just as palpable a force.

"You don't know who I am?" she asked faintly.

"No. Should I?" he demanded. "I do not appreciate you coming into my room and upsetting my visitors."

Someone gasped. She thought it might have been Phillippa,

but she couldn't turn her head to find out. She was paralyzed with shock and reeling inside from a pain she'd never expected to feel. She swayed on her feet, her vision blurring as her skin grew clammy with shock.

"He doesn't remember me," she said to no one in particular, the words coming out in a whisper as her body sagged against her brother-in-law.

Strong hands stopped her fall, but that was the last thing she remembered until she woke in her bed some minutes later.

Phillippa was standing over her, worry etched in her beautiful Greek features. "Eden?"

"Why didn't you tell me he has amnesia?" she asked painfully. "I could have—" She bit off the words before revealing her pregnancy.

"We didn't know he did. He talked about Theo just as he always does…he knew all of us."

"So, it's only me he doesn't remember? That makes no sense. How can he remember his son and not the woman who gave birth to him?"

Adam put down her wrist after checking her pulse. "Apparently, it wasn't something he thought about until his family explained who you are."

That didn't ring true. Aristide wouldn't let that kind of inconsistency in his memory stand, but then he'd only woken from his coma forty-five minutes before she'd entered his room.

"He's confused."

"Yes."

"I'm sure he'll remember me now."

The doctor shook his head and Phillippa's eyes filled with tears. "He refused to believe us when we told him that you are his wife."

Eden couldn't breathe. She moaned, her head thrashing from side to side. "No…he *has* to remember me."

"Confusion and a temporary loss of memory are not un-common side effects with a head injury like he sustained in the accident." Adam gripped her hand with both urgency and reassurance, his kindness warming her. "And it's still not a good idea to allow *yourself* to become upset."

"My husband refuses to believe I am his wife and you expect me to stay calm?" she demanded, shaken to her soul by the implications of Aristide's memory loss.

"I'm sorry," the doctor said before insisting on giving her a pregnancy-safe sedative so she would sleep.

She woke the next morning, remembering the horror of being the only person her husband had forgotten.

When the doctor came in for rounds, he told her that Aristide's head injury didn't explain the selective amnesia. "It doesn't fit with any of the usual patterns for post-head-trauma amnesia."

"I see. Have you been able to convince him of who I am?"

"Your brother-in-law took that job on before I had a chance to tell him not to." The doctor looked less than pleased by that state of affairs.

"Why would you want to wait?"

"We don't know what's causing the lack of memory, but any emotional upheaval is risky for an amnesia patient."

"And did learning he has a wife he doesn't remember upset him?" she couldn't help asking.

"Not that we could tell." Adam sighed, as if realizing the news would be unwelcome to her. "Apparently, now that he's had time to think about it, the knowledge makes the existence of his son more sensible to him."

That sounded like Aristide.

"Does he want to see me?"

"He's trying to come to terms with his memory loss."

"What does that mean?" She couldn't take it in. "Are you saying he *doesn't* want to see me?" That was completely out of character for her husband.

He always wanted every piece of information concerning any situation. For him not to want to see her felt like the most directed of rejections, no matter what he could or could not remember.

"Not at present, no."

Pain coalesced inside her at the confirmation until there was a knot of it where her heart should be. "And Kassandra?"

"Do you mean Miss Helios?"

"Yes."

"She's a frequent visitor. I understand she is an old family friend who works for him."

The monitor beside the bed started beeping and Adam's pale gaze sharpened with concern. "You need to remain calm. The news is disconcerting, I know…but, given enough time, he will remember you. It may even be sooner than later. *You* are not out of the woods yet, though. You still have a concussion and your baby is doing well, but an emotional trauma on top of the physical one could be devastating to your pregnancy."

"I'm sure you are right." But she didn't know how to stop herself from being upset.

If she'd ever needed proof positive that Aristide didn't love her and had stayed in their marriage for their son's sake, she had it now. He remembered everyone but the wife he obviously wished he could forget.

Correction…*had* forgotten.

Three days later, Eden couldn't stand waiting any longer and decided to visit her husband in his hospital room even though he'd made no indication he wanted to see her.

She'd checked out of the hospital the day before with a

clean bill of health and been told that normal activity should not put her baby at risk. The doctor had even made the joke that a little stress wouldn't hurt the baby, so it was safe to go home and be a full-time mom to her nine-month-old again.

She hadn't been able to laugh. Her relief at her own restored health was heavily tempered by Aristide's continued memory loss.

She'd dressed with care for this meeting. Eden's slight curves did not lend themselves to the kind of sexy apparel that looked good on so many other women, but she had done her best with what she had.

She wasn't showing her pregnancy yet and, if it followed the path of the one she'd had with Theo, there would be very little outward evidence until her fifth month. So, she'd opted to don a figure-hugging dress in gray-blue cashmere with long sleeves and a skirt that stopped well above her knee. Aristide had said it was one of his favorites and she didn't get to wear it often in Greece. It was too warm.

Her shoes were basic black pumps, but their three-inch heels made her legs look longer. Five feet five might be average for a woman's height, but Eden often felt like a shrimp around the much taller Aristide.

She pushed his private room's door open without knocking and was greeted by a tableau to make any wife's heart catch in her chest. Kassandra sat on the bed, coaxing Aristide to eat his lunch.

Eden could not believe the pain she felt at the cozy scene. Aristide had not asked to see her, effectively banning her from his room by his silence, while Kassandra was not only welcome, but welcome to behave toward him with an intimacy that should have been reserved for his wife.

It should have been her sitting on that bed, but Aristide hadn't wanted her and the knowledge hurt beyond bearing.

Once again, she had been relegated to a secondary role in his life and knowing he didn't remember her only exacerbated the pain, not lessened it.

Even worse, he had forgotten the child she carried, as if the reminder of how inexorably their lives were linked was something he could not bear. She felt as if someone had taken a shredder to her emotions and she had no idea how to find any sort of happiness again.

They both looked up at her entrance, neither registering the slightest guilt, and anger washed over her. "I didn't realize your assistant's duties ran to playing nursemaid."

Aristide's blue eyes darkened with displeasure. "Why not? You certainly were not here to do it."

How dare he throw her absence from his hospital room back on her? If it had been up to her, she would have been here non-stop from the moment the doctor had said it was all right. *"You didn't ask for me."*

"And that stopped you from coming to the side of your husband's hospital bed?" he derided. "You are here now and still I have not asked for you."

Kassandra got up and walked toward Eden. "I think this is my cue to leave. I don't want to be the cause of another domestic disturbance."

She implied there'd been many, when in fact Eden had tolerated far too much in the name of harmony. She gritted her teeth to stop from saying so. Adam had made it clear that she was not to upset his patient, going so far as to instruct her unequivocally not to tell Aristide about the baby.

Bad enough Aristide had forgotten their child, but she must refrain from reminding him of the baby's existence. It was just another poisoned dart of pain that had found its way with the unerring accuracy of a bull's-eye to her heart. As kind as Adam had been to her, his concern for her husband was just as acute.

Kassandra's smug expression worried Eden and she couldn't help wondering what the poisonous witch had been telling Aristide. Eden waited until the other woman was less than a foot away before stepping aside to let her leave the room.

She turned and spoke in a low voice that would not carry to her husband's ears. "You get what you give, Kassandra."

The other woman's eyes widened, as if she couldn't believe Eden had dared to say anything in front of Aristide, then she smiled maliciously. "Oh, I will get what's coming to me all right. Just as soon as you let go of him."

It was the first time Kassandra had stated her intentions so blatantly, but they didn't surprise Eden, not by a long shot.

"That's not going to happen. I'm never letting him go. Not ever."

Kassandra smiled, her expression mocking. "I think you will. Besides, who said you would get a choice in the matter?"

Without another word, Eden spun on her heel and headed toward the bed and a husband that did not remember her, but whom she loved with every fiber of her being.

She wasn't letting Kassandra have him without a fight, but she couldn't help feeling she shouldn't have to fight for a man who had promised her a lifetime of fidelity. She'd kept her end of their marriage bargain, giving him a son and her heart.

She only hoped he had kept his. Ever since she'd come to the conclusion that he married her for the sake of their child, she had wondered if his feelings had never engaged for her because they were held elsewhere. Only, if he loved Kassandra, why had he made Eden his lover?

Was it a Greek thing? It was hard to believe, but maybe Kassandra was still a virgin. Aristide would not take her to bed without marrying her in that case. The thought she'd been nothing more than a sexual diversion gone wrong made bile rise in her sensitive stomach.

She stopped when her legs brushed the side of his bed. "The doctor said you would be released tomorrow."

He stared at her through eyes that had always had the power to mesmerize her, his expression impassive. "Yes." He shoved the tray of hospital food away. "I will finish the meetings here that the accident interrupted and then return to Greece."

Not *we*, but *I*. Looking for a distraction from the disturbing syntax, she focused on his hardly eaten lunch.

"Is that all you plan to eat?"

"Yes."

"Surely you shouldn't be skipping meals. You need to regain your strength."

"I am fine. And if you are so concerned about my health, perhaps you should not have been so quick to frighten off the woman convincing me to eat this tasteless mess."

Her frighten Kassandra? Not in this lifetime.

"Are you telling me you need someone to entice you to eat?" Eden mocked.

"Maybe I do. Are you prepared to take on the job?" His tone said he didn't see how *she* could cajole him into anything.

She'd been married to him for sixteen months and raising his son, who was very much like him, for nine of those months. He might not remember her, but she wasn't so handicapped. A woman who cared could learn an awful lot about her husband in that amount of time, and Eden cared...a lot.

She slipped her coat off and laid it over the chair beside the bed before taking the place Kassandra had vacated. Gritting her teeth at the scent of the other woman lingering around her, Eden reached out and touched his lips in a move he would have recognized as quite daring for her.

If he'd been able to remember.

"I know how to feed all of your hungers, darling." Her

voice was husky with a promise she hoped he would remember on an instinctual level.

His eyes turned a familiar midnight-blue and his jaw went taut like it did when he was trying to hold back desire.

She wasn't unaffected either. Even this small touch sent electric jolts of remembered intimacy throughout her body. It had always been like this—their reaction to one another had been cataclysmic and instantaneous from the first moment.

Without warning, Aristide jerked his head back, his eyes narrowing, the contempt in them unmistakable. "Is this how you trapped me into marriage? Using your body?"

CHAPTER THREE

The shock those words caused reverberated through her.

She let her hand drop. "I wasn't the one doing the seducing in our relationship."

"Kassandra implied you trapped me into marriage with the oldest trick in the book. Is that true?" he asked, sounding disgusted. "Did I marry you because you were pregnant with my child?"

So, Kassandra *had* been busy spreading tales. Eden wasn't surprised, but it hurt to think Aristide had listened with both ears open to the other woman's vitriol.

Eden gritted her teeth, wishing she could deny his accusation, but she couldn't. Not now that she herself had come to accept the truth. "Yes. You married me because I was pregnant with Theo. *But it was no trap.* I did not get pregnant on purpose."

Aristide frowned fiercely at her, his disbelief obvious. His attitude was far removed from that of the lover she had known for nearly three years. He had never once doubted her word before, not even when she told him she was pregnant with his baby. He could have accused her of seeing someone else while he was gone on his frequent and often extended business travels, but he hadn't.

He hadn't even implied it was a possibility.

He'd always treated her with respect, like she mattered. Maybe not as much as Kouros Industries, but more than an afterthought he couldn't be bothered to see while he was in hospital.

Had his patience toward her and proclaimed acceptance of her role in his life all been an act?

It was hard to believe anything else now.

"You love your son," she couldn't help saying, as if somehow that affection should reflect on her as well.

She knew it didn't. Hadn't she always known? But still there was a part of her that persisted in hoping. How stupid was that?

Aristide's expression hardened. "I am aware of it. *I remember him.*"

Well, that was telling her. Sharpened talons of pain clawed through her, piercing the barely inflated balloon of hope. "Yes, of course."

Her quiet acknowledgement seemed to make him uncomfortable and he shifted restlessly in the bed. "If nothing else, I owe you gratitude for giving me such a wonderful child."

His thanks was the last thing she could bear. She needed his love and now she didn't even have his memory. She stood up, unable to withstand any more. It had been a mistake to come here. One more in a long line of them, starting with her agreement to marry a man who had never once told her he loved her.

"You owe me nothing. I love our son every bit as much as you do." She grabbed her coat and started putting it back on.

But he seized her arm, stopping her from finishing the task. "Where do you think you are going?"

"Back to the hotel. It's obvious my company is surplus to requirements." She hated the weakness the catch in her voice revealed to him.

She had to get out of there.

"Like hell. You are my wife and this is the first time you have deigned to visit me in three days. You are not walking out after a perfunctory five minutes."

"You didn't want me to come." She could not stop hot tears from filling her eyes, but she tried to blink them back. "Y-you told the doctor."

"And that upset you?" he asked with a supreme lack of tact.

"Of course it did." How could he be so cruel? Even if he didn't remember her, was he totally insensitive to what a woman in her position would be going through right now? "*I love you.* How could this *not* upset me?"

"You love me?" he asked with derision she did not deserve. "The evidence is not in your favor. You were nowhere around when I was in a coma. No one told you to stay away then."

"I was in my own hospital bed."

"With minor complications. A concussion, I believe. If you loved me, would you not have had your bed and mine in the same room so you could be here, hoping for my awakening?"

She'd never once considered her absence from his bedside might affect him this way. Evidently, he'd taken it as proof positive she wasn't the wife she should be. And right at that moment, she could not make herself care. What difference did it make? He obviously had never wanted to be married to her in the first place.

But even as angry as she was, part of her wanted to exonerate herself by telling him of her pregnancy and the ordered bed rest. However, Adam had been very explicit…no revelations of that sort until Aristide regained his memory or they understood better why he'd lost it.

And she had to wonder if it would make a difference. He clearly had expected her to get a bed in his room for treating her concussion—would the reason for her bed rest make any difference to him? Probably not.

"It didn't occur to me," she admitted with pained honesty, just wanting to leave.

"Perhaps it should have."

"Apparently, but we aren't all brilliant tycoons with a penchant for solving logistics problems even while under sedation for our injuries."

"I do not appreciate your sarcasm."

"I'm sure you don't, but then you don't seem to appreciate anything at all about me now. And let's face it…you didn't exactly miss me. You forgot I even existed in your life."

"You act as if I did it on purpose."

"Didn't you?"

"Maybe I had reason."

"Is that what Kassandra said? That I'm some kind of monster wife who so tormented your existence you had to forget me?"

His silence said it all.

"And you believed her?"

"What other reason could there be for such selective amnesia? It only makes sense that I *wanted* to forget you. That you were the kind of wife a man like me would find intolerable." He didn't sound entirely convinced, but the words were damaging all the same.

"That's a pretty big assumption," she forced out between stiff lips, cold with the shock of his revelations.

"Not made without supporting evidence."

"Maybe you wanted to forget you had a wife at all," she said, voicing her own private suspicion. "Before I got pregnant with Theo, you weren't exactly keen on commitment."

"I am not so weak." And she could tell such an image of himself did not sit well.

"Maybe there's no reason for the amnesia. Maybe it's one of those inexplicable medical things that happens sometimes."

He shook his head, rejecting her no-fault excuse. "That is not likely. The doctor can find no physical reason for the selective amnesia."

"Did Adam say he thinks you wanted to forget me?"

"Adam?"

"Doctor Lewis."

"I find it odd my wife is on first-name terms with my doctor."

"You forget, he was my doctor as well. He's been very kind to me since the accident. He knew how much your coma upset me."

"Well, even your *good friend* the doctor believes my amnesia is psychological rather than physiologically triggered."

She let the "good friend" comment pass, not willing to be sidetracked from the point by something so insignificant. "But that doesn't necessarily follow that you forgot me because I was a bad wife. You're too smart to have married a woman that unsuitable. Surely you must see that."

She couldn't live with that possibility. Bad enough that he may have wanted to forget her simply because he had never really wanted to be married in the first place.

"I have to wonder if our marriage was the only way you would give me power in my son's life."

"You think I would use our child to blackmail you?"

He shrugged. "If that is the case, I am surprised I fell for it. After all, I had watched the Queen Piranha at work for years in her marriage to my uncle and, as you said, I am intelligent; however, love for a child may make a fool of the father."

Eden stumbled back and landed with a thump on the chair. *"You believe I'm like Andrea Demakis?"* she asked hoarsely, even more horrified by that than the idea he believed her capable of using Theo for her own ends.

There was no greater insult he could level at her.

She'd never known his uncle's wife. Both Matthias and Andrea had died in a car crash before Eden and Aristide met, but the stories about the woman were horrific. Aristide and the rest of his family had hated her. According to them, Andrea had been money-grubbing, irrational, unfaithful, entirely selfish and more egotistical than Narcissus.

The miracle was that such a woman could give birth to an incredible daughter like Rachel. Even more amazing was that Rachel had ended up married to Aristide's older brother, Sebastian Kouros. Having met her sister-in-law's father, Eden figured all the good genes had come from him. Vincent was a very special man, who had been capable of luring Phillippa from the isolation of her widowhood.

According to Aristide, their marriage was something like the eighth wonder of the world.

Adam walked in at that moment and frowned when he took in her tears and the look of frustrated anger on Aristide's face. "Eden, I was not aware your husband had asked for you."

She was beyond prevaricating, even with silence. "He didn't."

"My wife does not need to wait for an invitation to visit me." The glare Aristide gave the doctor should have singed his white lab coat. "Nor do I appreciate the familiarity of your address to her."

"I'm sorry it offends you. However, what concerns me the most is that this kind of upset isn't good for your condition," he said, indicating the two of them with a wave of his hand.

"My *condition* is a slight concussion and selective amnesia," Aristide said in a freezing tone he usually saved for the boardroom. "I fail to see how either could be hindered by a visit from my wife. Surely being in her company should jog my memory, not harm it."

"She is in tears."

"I noticed. If you leave, I can take care of that."

The doctor's brows rose at her husband's arrogance, but he nodded. "That might be best. This can't be an easy situation for either of you. I will come by later to discuss your release."

Eden scrambled to her feet, wiping her wet cheeks, embarrassed and still hurting so much she found it hard to breathe. "Don't leave, Adam. There's no need. I'm going."

She tried to pull her coat from Aristide's grip, but he wouldn't release his hold.

"Let go."

"I told you. I will not tolerate you leaving so quickly."

She'd had enough. He probably wanted the doctor to leave so he could berate her some more, but she wasn't sticking around for it. She let the coat go and rushed toward the door.

Aristide called her name in a voice heavy with frustration and demand. She ignored him and barreled out of his room, almost knocking Kassandra down in the process. The other woman had obviously been hanging around outside the door and eavesdropping.

Her smug expression said she liked what she'd heard too.

Considering how painful the interview had been for Eden, she saw red. Literally. A blood-red haze seemed to surround the tall Greek woman as Eden glared at her, incapable of making the movement that would separate them. Kassandra had done everything in her power to undermine Eden's marriage and now she was bent on destroying it completely.

But Eden wasn't going to let that happen. If she and Aristide failed in their bid to make a successful family, it would be because he didn't love Eden, not because Kassandra succeeded with her evil machinations. The woman was pure poison and it was not a poison Eden would allow to taint her marriage any longer. Desperate anger clawed at her insides. Whatever it took, she was going to fight for her marriage and for the man she loved.

"You ought to watch where you are going." Kassandra shoved her away, making no pretense of being polite or gentle and Eden fell against the wall.

Fear for her baby added to the cauldron of dark emotion boiling inside of her. "Don't ever do that again."

Kassandra appeared supremely unconcerned by Eden's anger. "Or what, Mrs Kouros? You'll tell Aristide? Do you really think he would care? I am his friend, *the woman he remembers*. He let me feed him, but he knocked you back," she said, confirming she'd been listening in on their conversation via the open door. "He doesn't mind my touch. *He trusts me*. Do you really think he'll care if I'm rude to you, or even believe you if you tell him so? He's already forgotten you. You're nothing to him. It won't be long before he's ready to kick you out of his life as quickly as he invited you into it."

Eden's mind seemed to screech to a halt at the viciously mocking words. She couldn't think. She could only feel and it was the blackest rage she'd ever known. No thought sparked her next action, just unadulterated fury. She slapped the other woman hard. The violence shocked her, but she didn't even begin to feel like apologizing.

Kassandra stumbled back, her expression stunned.

"You won't get away with it," Eden said when she could get her mouth to form words.

Kassandra's eyes narrowed. "You're wrong. I'm clever, much smarter than a woman who didn't even know enough to prevent an accidental pregnancy."

"You told him I got pregnant on purpose."

"He came to that conclusion on his own."

"But you led him there."

Kassandra's shrug said, *so what if she had?* "He should never have married you. You are not in his league and you never will be."

"One day he's going to remember. You know that, don't you?" Eden demanded. "Do not think for a minute he'll thank you for lying to him about what kind of wife I've been. Aristide's sense of honor is very important to him and he's going to be furious when he realizes you are directly responsible for him compromising it."

Kassandra smiled complacently, smug certainty of victory draping her like a cloak. "We were friends long before you met and we will be friends after you are gone. And believe me…you will be gone."

Eden stood very straight, letting all the disdain she felt for the other woman show. "*Friends* is the operative word. I was his lover and now I'm his wife and I'm not going anywhere."

If there was something to salvage of her marriage, she would save it. If not, she would walk away because it was the right thing to do, not because she'd been sent packing by the selfish manipulator in front of her.

"I may not be his wife, but what makes you so sure I am not his lover?"

"As I said…*my husband* is a man of integrity. He wouldn't take a mistress."

He had promised her and she had believed him. She wasn't sure Aristide didn't *want* Kassandra, but she refused to believe he had taken the other woman as a mistress. Without another word or opportunity for Kassandra to vent more of her malice, Eden stormed away.

She barely made it around the corner before she was rushing for a restroom where she was violently ill. Having committed the first act of violence in her adult life, combined with the knowledge that Kassandra was relying on Aristide's lack of memory to make it possible for her to play her cruel, destructive games more blatantly than ever before, was too much for Eden's pregnancy-sensitized system.

Aristide might not be able to remember his wife, but he knew he did not like seeing her cry. Even though he had every reason to believe she was all he despised in a woman, knowing her tears were his fault made him feel like a heel. And that made him angry.

He told everyone he could not remember her at all and in a sense that was true, but once he accepted he had a wife, an overwhelming sense of foreboding came over him every time he thought about his marriage. It centered on Eden, but he did not know what caused it or how to dispel it.

He knew only that something had been drastically wrong in his marriage and it was all too easy to believe his wife had been a carbon copy of the woman who had married his uncle.

Regardless, he got no enjoyment out of watching her walk away from him. It made him feel something very much like fear and he hated it. He feared nothing...particularly no woman. That way lay total destruction for the male of the species. He'd seen enough of it with his great-uncle.

Matthias Demakis had given his young wife way too much power in his life and she had repaid that gift by using and humiliating the old man. Both Aristide and Sebastian had learned a hard and painful lesson from Matthias's marriage to Andrea.

He glowered at the door Eden had gone through. Memory, or no memory, his wife would not bring him to his knees.

"That must have been some fight for her to go storming off without her coat. The temperature is below freezing out there and she didn't strike me as the sort of woman to storm anywhere."

Aristide's head snapped up at the sound of the doctor's voice. He didn't know how long he'd been staring at the closed door, half-expecting his wife to come back through. Though why he should, he had no idea.

"We were not fighting."

"You could have fooled me."

The tension inside Aristide increased another notch. "My relationship with my wife is not something you need to concern yourself with."

"That's not true. Your amnesia is almost certainly psychologically based, as we've discussed. I would say your relationship with Eden is key to your medical condition and your health is my responsibility."

Aristide clenched his jaw at the doctor's use of her first name again. No Greek doctor would be so familiar, but his wife and this doctor were both American. Common sense told him to leave it alone, but his male instincts shrieked for redress.

"Nevertheless," he said through gritted teeth, "I have no intention of discussing *my wife* with you."

"I cannot force you to, of course, but she's been through a lot since the accident. Your memory loss and refusal to see her has been hard on her. She's vulnerable right now. Try to remember that."

"I did not refuse to see her."

Doctor Lewis's blond brows rose. "You did."

"Once."

"You never asked for her after that."

"She is my wife. She should not require an invitation to visit my bedside."

"Perhaps someone should have told her that."

Aristide said nothing.

"Yes, well." The doctor lifted Eden's coat from where it had dropped, but Aristide still had hold of one sleeve. Doctor Lewis pulled gently. "Why don't you let me take this to her?"

Aristide forced himself to let go, an inexplicable twinge in his chest. Was the other man's interest merely that of a medical professional for a former patient, or was he attracted to Eden as a woman?

She was beautiful and if the aura of sweetness surrounding her was not genuine, she did a good job pretending. For most men, the combination would be irresistible. The thoughts spun in his head, making it ache as the doctor strode from the room, Eden's coat clutched in one hand.

A second later, Kassandra walked back in, her cheek red. Her dark brown eyes were filled with tears and her superbly glossed lower lip trembled.

"What happened?" he asked, feeling more irritation at her reappearance than concern.

Which wasn't fair to her. She'd been a good friend his entire life and loyal employee for many years. It wasn't her fault he had this damnable selective amnesia or a wife he couldn't figure out, but was instinctively wary of.

Kassandra shook her head, her hand going to cover her cheek in a protective gesture. "Nothing."

"Tell me."

"I would rather not," she said, averting her eyes. "Things are strained enough between you and Eden as it is."

"You are saying Eden hit you?" Astonishment coursed through him. As much as he had a bad feeling whenever he thought of Eden, she had not struck him as a violent woman.

"Your wife is upset I've been spending so much time with you."

"So, she slapped you?"

Kassandra nodded with obvious reluctance. "After issuing a rather strong warning to stay away from you."

Eden's vulnerability during their discussion must have been an act along with the façade of her gentle disposition. Kassandra had certainly implied that Eden was not the sweetness and light she appeared to be. The red mark on his assistant's face would seem to indicate she saw Eden more clearly than the doctor.

Yet…part of him refused to believe despite the evidence of his eyes. It made no sense. The dark feelings surrounding Eden in his mind should make it easy for him to believe, but it wasn't. It was as if he had a mental block and that made him feel helpless. He should have no problem trusting Kassandra and her loyalty to him. He knew nothing about Eden and everything about the woman who had been in his life so long.

If only he could remember.

His head began to pound in earnest.

"Are you all right?" Kassandra asked, her hand on his arm.

Funny…her touch did nothing for him. Whereas Eden standing within a foot of his bed had impacted his libido despite all his doubts about her and the lingering effects of a concussion.

"I should be asking you that."

She smiled bravely. "I am fine. I am sure she did not mean to do any lasting damage."

"She should not have hit you. I will speak to her."

"Don't. She is already…" Kassandra paused as if looking for the right word. "Volatile, or irrational rather. It is to be expected, I am sure. Any wife would have been severely taxed emotionally by everything you have gone through."

Left unspoken was the fact that Eden had shown little of that concern in staying away from his hospital room the past week. And yet she had expressed what he would have sworn was genuine hurt over his initial request she not come back in to see him immediately. Had apparently taken that as word one on her lack of welcome at his bedside…if the doctor's interpretation was to be believed.

Aristide closed his eyes against the pain in his head. He did not know what to think and he could not trust his own judgment. Not when it came to a woman he'd forgotten so completely.

There had to be a reason for that and he could think of no other than the one Kassandra had hinted at—that Eden was the kind of wife nightmares were made of.

CHAPTER FOUR

"Are you ready to go?"

Aristide turned at the sound of his wife's husky voice.

Eden had pulled her soft brown hair back in a French braid, leaving her face exposed to his view. However, her carefully controlled features and wary gray gaze told him nothing of what was in her mind, nor why she had chosen to come rather than sending his brother to see to his discharge.

She had called him last night too, ostensibly so he could tell Theo goodnight, but she had asked how Aristide was feeling and sounded genuinely interested in the answer. She had not rushed to get off the phone when he finished talking to the baby either, wanting to know what the doctor had had to say.

Aristide hadn't wanted to discuss Dr Lewis's visit, choosing instead to bring up Eden's altercation with Kassandra. When he told her how much her action displeased him, his wife's tone had gotten colder than the Arctic. She'd hung up quickly enough then after little more than a stilted goodbye.

He had not expected her to show up in his hospital room this morning.

She made no move to take her coat off, but stood ramrod straight by the door, as if ready to make a hasty exit if he made a wrong move. Either she was the best actress living, or underneath the avarice that had prompted their marriage, she was vulnerable in an unexpected way.

"I have been ready for the last hour."

She crossed her arms over her chest and tilted her chin at a defensive angle. "I'm sorry you had to wait. The doctor said ten-thirty."

Her body language screamed, *Do not touch me…stay out of my space.*

The hands-off attitude hit him on the raw, especially considering how he'd spent the morning stewing over the implied intimacy of his wife's relationship with the doctor. Aristide found himself crossing the room to pull her into his arms before he even thought about it.

He might not remember her, but this woman was his wife and no way was she going to hold back from him like he was some kind of pariah.

She gasped when their bodies collided. "What are you doing?"

She didn't sound nearly as composed as she had a moment ago and he was curiously satisfied by that reality.

His mouth hovered over hers. "Greeting my wife."

She opened her mouth and he closed his over it. He watched in fascination as her gray eyes widened and then slid shut, thick black lashes fanning her pale cheeks. He closed his eyes too, allowing sensation to take hold.

Their lips fit together with a perfection he had never known with another woman and she tasted as sweet as Christmas divinity. Not at all like a piranha wife with dollar signs in her eyes.

Her lips trembled under his and he deepened the kiss, claiming possession in a way that was wholly instinctual. She let him, her entire body trembling now as he explored the warmth of her mouth.

He closed his hands around her waist and lifted her against

him, his own body shuddering at the contact. It felt incredibly familiar when her arms locked around his neck and her tongue slid along his with tentative aggression. He couldn't believe the impact that one small touch had on him, but he was ready to toss her on the bed and make the sweetest kind of love to his forgotten wife.

Was in fact *aching* with the need to follow through on the promise of her pliant lips against his.

He broke the kiss. "You *taste* like I know you."

"I do?" She sounded so damn hopeful, he felt his first pang of guilt for forgetting her.

"Evidently my body knows you even if my mind does not."

She winced as if the words hurt her and maybe they had.

"I enjoyed it."

She let go of her hold around his neck, pressing against his chest as if she wanted him to release her. "Yes. Well, sex has never been a problem for us."

It was his turn to wince. She made it sound as if that was the only thing they got right and not like she thought that was all her fault. He had no way of denying it, but his pride smarted at the possibility.

He released her. She stepped away and, looking down, smoothed her coat. He let her get away with the small evasion, needing a moment to collect himself as well. He could not remember a simple kiss ever being so devastating to his senses. If their intimacy was always this explosive, his marriage made a lot more sense to him.

So did the birth of their son.

"I was expecting Sebastian this morning."

"He's waiting in the car."

"I did not expect you," he clarified.

"I didn't tell your family about our argument yesterday."

"So they expected you to do the honors?"

"Yes."

"Why not tell them?"

She looked at him then, her expression scornful. "You would prefer I shared our personal troubles with the others?"

She was right. He rarely revealed the most private parts of his life to anyone, even his mother and older brother. It was disconcerting to realize that while she was a complete mystery to him, she knew things about him even his closest friend wouldn't be aware of.

"No."

"I didn't think so."

"So you were doing as you thought I wanted?"

"Not really. Yesterday, I didn't particularly care what you thought."

He didn't know why, but he didn't believe her. "You did not?"

"No." She frowned at him like an evil genie and he almost expected to disappear in a puff of smoke. "I didn't buy it when the doctor said you were worried and sent him after me with my coat, either."

"He was being kind. It was his idea," Aristide said, feeling stung and conversely annoyed she was right that he had not been the one to think of her comfort.

He disliked even more the feeling of guilt that knowledge engendered in him.

She turned away, but not before he saw the look of hurt that crossed her features. "That's what I thought."

"So, why did you not tell my family if I made you so angry?"

"I didn't see any reason to increase their present turmoil." She took a deep breath and turned back to face him once more, this time her face as smooth as marble.

If her lips were not still red from his kiss, he would not be sure it had even happened.

"You Kouroses put a great store by strong marriages and family relationships. If your mother or brother thought we were having problems, it would worry them and I don't think they need any more worry right now. They've been upset enough by the accident and your loss of memory."

"Are you trying to say we should attempt a façade of the happy, loving couple in front of them?" If she knew him as well as a wife should, she would know that, though he was intensely private, he never lied to his family.

"That would be impossible, but I was hoping you would save open hostility for behind closed doors. Our son does not need to sense his mom and dad are at odds either. He's had a rough few days as well."

"Of course, but you are assuming we will continue to argue?"

"It's inevitable in the current situation."

"That does not sound like we have the most harmonious marriage."

"On the contrary. One of the reasons I'm hoping you will be reasonable about this is that neither your family, nor our son, are used to seeing us at odds. Until this trip to New York, we got along great, but my tolerance is at a very low ebb at the moment. I might even characterize it as nonexistent."

"Why is that, I wonder?"

"That isn't something I want to discuss until you've regained your memory."

"You are so sure I will challenge your tolerance?" She made it sound like he was the husband from Hades and that image of himself was not acceptable.

"As long as Kassandra Helios is in our lives, she'll do her best to instigate trouble between us. I'm no longer willing to ignore her machinations and, because of that, we're bound to fight. It's as simple as that."

"She is a long-term employee and a friend. You will not speak about her that way to me."

"Whereas I'm only your wife...that at least has not changed, memory or no memory."

Before he could answer the implied accusation in her words, the morning-shift nurse came in with a wheelchair.

"What is this for?" he demanded.

"Hospital policy," she said with a flirtatious smile that made his wife purse her lips cynically. "You have to be escorted downstairs."

Eden's eyes now glowed with provoking mockery, but she said nothing. It was obvious she knew how much he would hate the idea of being pushed in a wheelchair and found his predicament much too amusing for his liking. She obviously didn't mind his arrogance being taken down a notch, or two.

Aristide glared at her and then the nurse who had the effrontery to flirt with a married man. She'd been nauseatingly coy all morning.

"By all means, follow me with that thing and escort me, but I will not be sitting in it." He strode from the room to the sound of the nurse's anxious arguments and his wife's mocking laughter.

Eden sat in the backseat of the Mercedes and listened to Aristide and Sebastian talk business on the way to the hotel.

Aristide was every bit as savvy as he had ever been. This further evidence that he remembered everyone and everything but her added to the hurt roiling inside of her. Hurt that seemed to grow like a mushroom cloud after a nuclear explosion...out of control and with no end in sight.

Even the way he had so naturally projected the united front to his brother and the hospital staff that he had mocked in his hospital room gave her pain. He'd opened the door for her and helped her inside the car despite the fact he was the discharging patient. It had effectively made his position as her husband clear to the hospital staff and even Sebastian.

Knowing it had more to do with his pride than any real desire to align himself with her, the casual touches had nevertheless left her breathless. Her lips still tingled from his kiss as well, but she wasn't foolish enough to think that had been personal either.

She knew what that kiss had been about and it had nothing to do with undying love, or even a primal recognition that happened at a level deeper than the conscious mind. She wished she could believe it did, but she'd spent enough time in a fantasy world where her husband was concerned.

Reality was that though Aristide was a thoroughly modern man in some ways, he was as traditional as they came in others. He was also a competitive alpha male who would chase and conquer without conscious thought. He might not remember her, but he knew she was his wife. As such, he expected a certain openness from her toward him.

She'd known the mistake of her remote stance the minute that look of predatory intent came into his eyes. But she'd been angry at being taken to task over Kassandra, without ever once being asked for her own side. Eden was not a violent person. Aristide used to know that.

Telling herself he didn't remember didn't help. He never would have accused her of such a thing when they first met and were practically strangers.

So, she'd held herself aloof when she arrived in his room, only to regret her stance instantly. Only by then, it had been too late to stave off his natural instinct to establish his role as her mate. He'd kissed her and she had fallen into it like she always did, proving once again she had almost no self-protection where he was concerned.

It was not a pleasant revelation.

Phillippa cried as she hugged Aristide. "It is so good to see you out of the hospital, my baby boy."

"Hardly a baby, Mama."

"Always…until the day I die."

Eden couldn't help smiling at the exchange…she'd seen it so many times before. "I'm sure Aristide is happy to be out of the hospital as well. We all know how much he despises confinement of any kind."

Aristide looked at her, a strange expression on his face.

Rachel grinned and hugged her big husband. "It's a Kouros male trait."

"There is one notable exception, *agape mou*." Sebastian leaned over and brushed a kiss across her brow. "Don't you think?"

"What's that?" Eden asked with a smile for the other couple, despite the prick of envy in her chest.

Sebastian looked at her while tucking his wife close into his side. "Why, marriage, of course."

Eden lost her smile and noticed Aristide had too.

"Are you all right, Eden?"

She forced a smile for her mother-in-law. "Yes. Of course."

"It is good to have him out of the hospital, is it not?"

"Yes."

Then Phillippa grimaced as if she had only now realized that for Eden having Aristide "home" was not quite the same as it was for the others.

The sound of her son talking to himself in the other room told Eden that Theo had woken from his nap. She used the excuse of fetching him to get out of the suddenly laden atmosphere.

Theo was sitting up in his portacrib. His favorite purple dinosaur in his chubby little hands, he jabbered at the stuffed animal a mile a minute in baby talk.

Taking after his father's large stature, her sturdy son was already quite a handful and Eden groaned playfully as she lifted him. "You're such a big boy."

He grabbed her shirt and tried to stand in her arms. "Mama…Mama…Mama…"

Her son's repertoire of words was by no means extensive, but what he knew he used.

Taking a firmer grip on his squirming form, she cuddled him into her body and kissed his baby-soft cheek. "How is Mommy's little man? Hmm? You are such a good baby."

She kissed him again and he hugged her around her neck.

"Mama," he sighed with obvious baby delight.

She grinned at her name on her son's lips. This was one male she never had to wonder if he loved her. Her dad's love and Aristide's might be suspect, but not this precious bundle of joy.

"Is your diaper wet, honey?" she asked as she laid him on the makeshift changing table.

He grinned and kicked his feet.

She managed to get his PJ bottoms off without incident, but then he squealed and twisted with such glee he almost fell off the changing pad. "Da…da…da…da…"

Aristide's deep laugh alerted her to his presence close behind her and a second later his big body was so near, he surrounded her with his heat.

He reached past her to brush his fingers down their son's cheek. "Hello, *agape mou.*"

Theo squealed again and twisted toward his daddy. Aristide put his hand on the baby's strong little body and held him in place, talking to Theo in Greek while Eden finished changing him. It was like so many times before that, for a second, it was as if he'd never lost his memory.

Then he stepped back and allowed her to lift the baby from the table and the sense of closeness was gone.

"Let me take him." She nodded and handed the baby over, sucking in a pain-filled breath when her husband carefully avoided touching her.

Aristide walked into the bedroom, drying his hair with a towel, and stopped dead in his tracks. "You are sleeping in here?"

Eden adjusted the blankets over her nightgown-clad form. It was a new purchase, just as the pajamas she'd worn at the hospital had been. She hadn't worn nightwear to bed since becoming his lover, but something about sleeping naked with a man who didn't remember her left her feeling too vulnerable.

"Where else would I sleep?" she asked in genuine confusion.

"Shouldn't you be sleeping in Theo's room? As you said in the hospital, our son has been through a lot of upheaval this past week."

"I've slept in the room with him the last four nights and he's been fine." Not that Theo had noticed. Their son slept like a log. "Besides, your mom and Vincent are sleeping in there now that you are here."

"Wouldn't he be more comforted if he woke in the night to find you there?"

"Theo stopped waking in the night when he was four months old."

"But these are unusual circumstances."

"Not now they aren't."

"Because I am out of the hospital?"

"Because I am and have been for the past few days. Theo is used to his daddy being gone."

Aristide frowned. "I have a job."

"That comes before everything else. I know."

"And you do not like that?"

"What woman would?" She sighed, not willing to get into something that could have no resolution in the current situation. "Look, none of that matters right now."

"It is our marriage…I do not consider that of no import."

"You don't even remember getting married."

"Which does not equate to me dismissing my responsibilities as a husband."

"Look…it's a waste of time to discuss a past you don't remember. It's not as if you're going to take my word for the way things were."

He'd made that clear enough.

He shrugged, confirming her suspicions.

Then something occurred to her that probably should have earlier, but she had not even considered it. "Do you feel awkward about sleeping with a woman who is for all intents and purposes a stranger? Of course you do. I'm such an idiot not to have thought of it before. I'll move to one of the spare rooms."

"Do not be ridiculous. You are my wife."

"But still a stranger."

He didn't say anything, but his silence was all the answer she needed.

She couldn't believe she had been dumb enough to climb into their bed as if nothing had changed between them. She'd been so wrapped up in the shock of him seeing her as a villain that she hadn't realized his questions could be masking feelings of vulnerability. Aristide would rather be boiled in oil than admit weakness.

She climbed out of bed in the heavy silence, trying not to let her hurt from this additional rejection show on her face. After all, this situation was not his fault and it was time she stopped treating him like he had done it on purpose. He may have forgotten her because subconsciously he *wanted* to, but he had no way of undoing the damage now that it was done.

He grabbed her arm before she could leave the room. "Stranger or not, you are my wife. You sleep with me."

"It's all right, Aristide. Really."

"As you said, we do not wish to upset my family. My mother will not be pleased to find you in another room in the morning."

He had a point. "I could get up before she does."

"Good luck. Even I do not."

This was true. Phillippa required less sleep than her sons, which was superhuman in Eden's mind. She looked back over her shoulder. The bed was a king-size.

They could sleep the whole night without touching. "If you're sure you won't be too uncomfortable."

"You make me sound like a nervous virgin." And that was the last way he saw himself.

She actually laughed. "I can't imagine anything further from the truth."

She turned around and gasped inaudibly as he dropped his towel and climbed into the bed.

The thought of sharing even such a big bed with his naked body and not having the right to reach out and touch him sounded more like torture than restful sleep.

She went to the opposite side of the bed from him and slid beneath the covers. She stayed as close to the edge as possible, feeling lonelier than she ever had even when Aristide was gone on a prolonged business trip.

Eventually, she fell into a fitful sleep.

Sometime in the night she migrated toward his side of the bed, waking up in the pre-dawn hours with his body wrapped around hers.

She knew she should move, would be mortified if he woke and found her on his side of the bed, but it felt so good, so safe, that she stayed. She lay there almost not breathing, not wanting to end the small bit of heaven in a series of days that could only have been dreamed up in hell itself.

She leaned forward the tiniest bit so she could inhale his scent and found herself on her back being kissed to within an inch of her life without the slightest warning.

CHAPTER FIVE

It wasn't the first time this had happened.

Aristide didn't even need to be fully awake to begin making love to her, but this was the first time she wasn't absolutely positive she was the woman he was making love to in his head.

She couldn't seem to make that matter, though…not with his lips devouring hers and his big, familiar body warming every square centimeter of her skin.

She dove into the kiss with all the enthusiasm of a starving woman facing a feast. Her hands roamed over his naked back and torso, touching skin that was all satin strength and heat.

Oh, man, she needed this. Affirmation that on some level, at least, they still connected.

He divested her of the nightgown she'd donned earlier and closed one sure hand over her breast. Her nipple beaded immediately against his palm, throbbing with the need for his attention. She arched her back and he took the silent hint, breaking the kiss and tasting his way down her neck to her breast. He laved the soft flesh with his tongue, teasing her until she moaned with desire. He took the hard nipple into his mouth, pressing it against the roof of his mouth with his tongue and sucking hard all at once. It felt so good, so right, that tears filled her eyes.

She dug her fingers through his silky black hair. "Oh, Aristide...my love."

He released her nipple and blew on it, making it sting with a pleasurable ache. "Baby, you taste so good," he said against her breast. Then he said something low in Greek she didn't quite catch.

But baby? He'd never called her that, not once in all the times they had made love.

Her troubled thoughts splintered as his hand delved between her thighs. Long, talented fingers pleasured her most private flesh with knowing assurance. He might not remember her, but his body remembered how she liked to be touched.

She squirmed, reaching down to touch his hardness. He was big, but she knew he fit...that he felt perfect inside her. She wrapped her fingers around him, though the tips did not quite touch.

He groaned. "That's right, baby, touch me just like that."

She gritted her teeth, but in the end couldn't stop the question. "What's my name?"

His head came up, but she couldn't read his expression, not in the dark. "What?"

"Who am I?"

"My lover."

His mouth closed over hers, the kiss all consuming, but a small part of her refused to get lost in it. No matter how good his touch and lips felt devouring hers, she needed to know it was her he was making love to and not a phantom in his mind, or worse...another woman.

After several blissful moments, he broke the kiss and started trailing his lips down her neck toward her breasts again.

She forced herself to ask, "Who are you making love to, Aristide?"

He stopped with his lips over one aching and throbbing

nipple. He lifted his head as if trying to see her expression in the dark. Maybe he could. He'd always had better night vision than she did.

"What is this about, Eden?"

Relief surged through her. "Nothing. It's all right, now." He'd called her by name. He wasn't making love in his mind to some other woman.

He was still for a heartbeat. "What was the problem?"

"You called me *baby*."

"And this is not normal?"

The fact he had to ask pierced the haze of sensual pleasure. "No. It isn't."

"What do I usually call you?"

"Eden…or *yineka mou*." How she loved that endearment that labeled her both his wife and his woman, ever since the first time he'd told her what it meant.

"I cannot call you *my woman* when I do not remember you as part of my life."

Though spoken apologetically, the words were better at dousing her ardor than a bucket of cold water. "That's true… and how can you see yourself as my husband either?"

"I don't feel like a husband." He didn't sound like that bothered him all that much, but the words tore away the last remnant of the sensual blinders she'd been wearing since waking up feeling so secure in his arms.

She pushed against him. "I can't do this."

His finger brushed over her sweetest spot, eliciting a moan. "I think you can."

"I don't want to," she said desperately.

"Why not?"

"In your heart, we aren't really married."

"But we are in my head." He grabbed her hand and touched her wedding band. "This ring proclaims you are my wife."

She pressed against the spot on his chest where his heart resided. "But this tells you that I don't belong in your life."

"I want you."

"For sex."

"What is the matter with that? You were not always so scrupulous or we would not have a son, nor would we be married. But then maybe that was planned, sex for the big payoff. Have I been paying for your *affection* since then?"

"That's a terrible thing to say." He was comparing her to Andrea in his mind again and she couldn't stand it.

"Is it? The truth is not always pretty."

Her heart was breaking, but she wouldn't cry. Not now, with him. "Get off of me."

"Why should I? I'm sure we can come to some amicable arrangement. After all, I'm a rich man and I want you. Tell me, what did you get out of me the last time we had sex?"

She hit his shoulder with her fist. "Get off!"

He rolled away and she scooted off the bed, her body shivering uncontrollably, like she was standing naked in a blizzard. But the only ice bombarding her was the shards coming straight from his heart.

"You want to know what you gave me the last time we made love?"

"Yes," he ground out cynically.

"The knowledge that I was yours and you were mine. That you wanted *me*, not just a body. You gave me pleasure, but that pleasure wasn't about the way you touched me with your hands…though, heaven knows, you are an incredible lover. You gave me tenderness. I felt safe and appreciated, if not loved. Now, all I feel is dirty." The last words came out choked around the tears tightening her throat.

She rushed into the bathroom before he could answer.

* * *

Aristide sat up, his sexual frustration so acute, he was in pain. How dare she say he made her feel dirty?

He was her husband, not some stranger who had propositioned her. He might not remember her, but she remembered him, damn it. So, he did not feel married himself, that did not mean he wasn't. Damn illogical woman.

The sound of her sobs reached him.

Okay...so maybe he should not have goaded her that way. It wasn't as if he believed half of what he had said. No matter what kind of negative feeling hovered over him when he thought of his marriage, he knew himself well enough to know he would never stoop to paying for sex.

He felt like hell. Sexual frustration was lousy on his temper. She ought to know that, but then maybe she didn't usually tell him no. The thought made him ache.

What had he done in taunting her?

He wanted Eden, had woken up wanting her and had acted on that desire. But she had not liked him calling her *baby*. She claimed he usually called her *yineka mou*. That assertion did strange things to his insides—because, as he told her, he considered that endearment very personal.

Would he have used it on a wife he didn't want?

More importantly, why had he been so loathe to use it now? Two words and she would have let him into her body. He was married to her, those words should not be so hard to say, but they were. Impossible, in fact.

He'd never used them with a girlfriend, not once. He was a possessive guy, but *yineka mou* implied a level of possession he had never accepted reciprocally. He had only her word he had used the phrase, but why would she lie?

Her assertion that she could not make love to him when he did not consider himself married in his heart stood his view of her on its head. Unless it was some deep strategy on her part. The whole scenario made him question the wisdom of getting involved sexually with her.

He never lied to women, not in word or action. If he made love to her, would he be implying feelings he did not have?

His sense of integrity would not allow that, nor was he comfortable with the overwhelming nature of their intimacy. He'd lost himself and been tempted to lie to her just to get inside her body. That implied she had way more power over him physically than he had ever ceded to another woman and he wasn't sure he was willing to cede it to her.

"I don't understand why Theo and I can't stay here and return with you to Greece when you are done with your business."

Aristide frowned, unwilling to voice the key reason for his request that his wife and son fly back to Greece with the rest of his family the next day.

He feared his ability to refrain from making love to her. The longer he was in her company, the more he wanted her. It was an addiction he had no intention of feeding until he understood his marriage better. Hell, he wasn't sure even then he wanted to allow her the chance to wrap him up in a prison of her subtle sensuality.

He was confused enough with the holes in his memory; he could not afford to further cloud his thought processes with sex. Even if it was mind boggling, as he suspected it would be.

Besides, his wife had made it clear she would balk at sharing her body with him when he did not remember her. She had implied she thought his amnesia was subconsciously deliberate. He'd taken that to mean she acknowledged he had reason to do so.

However, that did not mean she liked being forgotten, or would want him touching her while he couldn't remember making her a Kouros…couldn't even remember the first time they met.

"A hotel room is not the most comfortable environment for a nine-month-old baby."

She glared up at him, her slight body stiff with displeasure. "Only in your rarified environment could someone label this two-bedroom suite a mere hotel room. Many people raise their children in apartments smaller than this."

"I am not one of those many people and there is no reason for my son to be cramped here when there is a perfectly good villa in Greece childproofed and arranged for his comfort."

"I'd planned to do more Christmas shopping while we were here."

Memories of his step-aunt's excesses bombarded him. "Surely the past four days have been sufficient time to buy all you were going to buy…even for the most voracious shopper."

Her lips pursed, as if his words had offended. "You might be surprised by this, but I've had too much on my mind the past few days to go shopping."

"You want me to believe you were so worried about me that you refrained from the delights of the shopping Mecca that is New York?"

"I don't expect you to believe anything good about me. You haven't so far." She turned away and started walking toward the door. "I'll fly home with your family. Heaven knows you didn't show a marked preference for my company before you forgot who I was and became convinced I am evil incarnate. It would be ludicrous to think you'd discover an untapped desire to be with me now."

He grabbed her shoulders and stopped her from leaving. Spinning her around to face him, he asked, "And why did I not like spending time with you?"

"I didn't say you didn't *like* to be with me."

"You said—"

"That you didn't show a *marked preference* for my company. It's not the same thing. Your business has always come first."

"You are sure it is not because I had a wife that made life away from home preferable to life at home?"

She twisted from his grip. "Believe what you like."

Damn it. Why did she have to sound so disheartened, like his awareness of her mercenary nature really hurt her?

She turned at the door to the bedroom, her eyes filled with sadness. "In answer to your question…I would say it's pretty obvious you found life at home boring or unpalatable, maybe even both. If you didn't, you would have spent more time there."

"You look pensive, Son. What are you thinking?"

Aristide looked up at his mother. Phillippa's beautiful brown eyes were fixed on him with obvious concern.

A striking woman, she was young enough to raise eyebrows when she announced the fact she was a grandmother. It was no surprise to him that she had finally remarried. The surprise had been that it had taken her so long.

She had been much younger than his father and still in her prime when Eugenios died. Yet, she had loved him so much that it had been more than a decade after his death before she accepted another man into her life. Aristide doubted she ever would have if she had not met Rachel's father. Vincent had been so obviously wounded by the years spent searching for his daughter that Phillippa's tender heart had been moved. First to compassion, and then to a love so genuine no one would ever deny its existence.

"I do not like this inability I have to remember my wife."

"No, of course not. Your amnesia is very difficult on both of you."

"So everyone keeps saying."

She reached out and squeezed his hand. "And we are all right. You hate to acknowledge weakness of any kind, but I know you must be very frightened by these holes in your memory."

He didn't want to dwell on his infirmity. He could not change it, therefore he would ignore it.

There were other matters of far more interest to him. "Was my marriage everything it should be?"

His mother's eyes widened in shock and then narrowed with an emotion he could not quite decipher. "Why would you ask me such a thing?"

"Doctor Lewis believes I had a reason for forgetting her. I am wondering if you know what it is."

"Eden is a good wife." His mother's staunch support of her daughter by marriage did not surprise him.

She was like a mama lion with her cub when it came to Rachel. He had no doubt that same attitude had prevailed with Eden upon his marriage, but he needed honesty, not platitudes given as a result of blind loyalty.

"Please, Mama, this is important."

Phillippa sighed, looking very uncomfortable and convincing him she knew more than she wanted to say. "Did you ask Eden?"

"She says she thinks I was not ready for marriage, that I forgot her because I never wanted the commitment to begin with."

"That is ridiculous." His mother's voice was laced with outrage. "No son of mine would be so weak!"

"I agree."

"But…" His mother's mouth drew down in a frown and she bit her lip as if trying to decide whether or not to remain silent.

"Tell me."

"Neither you nor Eden ever expressed dissatisfaction with your marriage. You must understand this."

"Your caveat is duly noted."

She accepted his words with a regal nod. "I am not certain how best to say this, but there were times I believed you were naïvely complacent."

"Me…not Eden?"

"Yes, you."

For some inexplicable reason the confirmation of his wife's unsuitability shocked him to the core, particularly coming from his mother. "What exactly are you saying?"

"You asked me if your marriage was all that it should be and I must tell you that many times I suspected it was not."

"Did I marry her to secure my place in Theo's life?"

"I often worried that was a larger part of your decision to marry than it should be. I had always hoped there was more genuine affection between you, but I did not pry."

"Did we seem affectionate?"

"You are a very private person, Aristide, even more so than your older brother. I have always found it difficult to read your emotions."

"In other words, there was no evidence of affection between the two of us."

"I did not say that. You men…you are always so literal and jump to conclusions all too easily. Your father was the same way."

Vincent arrived with a cup of tea for Phillippa and Aristide left off his questions. As she'd pointed out, he was private, too much so to discuss his marriage in front of the other man.

Eden waited for Aristide's plane to land, her nerves stretched so tight that she felt like a rubber band ready to snap. It had only lasted a few days, but this separation had been the worst one of her marriage—maybe because she had never felt less sure of what to expect upon her husband's return. Had he remembered anything of her at all? Surely he would have called to tell her if he had.

Beyond her uncertainty was a feeling of missing him that went bone deep. Unlike every other trip he'd taken away from her, Aristide had not called several times a day simply to connect and see how she and Theo were doing. She'd missed those calls terribly.

And it was as she realized just how aching her loneliness without him was that she asked herself how she could ever have contemplated divorce. How could she live the rest of her life without him when a mere three days without him had been such misery?

Would she have a choice?

The fear that she wouldn't was paramount.

He had not called at all except to say he would be flying in this evening. Apparently, he'd managed to wrap his meetings up with the help of his super-efficient assistant. She could only be grateful he had not delegated the telephone call to Kassandra.

Eden still smarted from the fact that he had sent her away and kept Kassandra by his side.

She thought maybe she understood his decision better after spending several sleepless hours analyzing the latest development in her marriage and coming to seriously regret her rejection of his sexual advances.

For Aristide, sex was as necessary as breathing, but he also had a strong sense of personal honor, not to mention a lion's dose of pride. Once she refused to make love to him, she should have realized he would see no recourse but to send her away. His desire for her was as strong as ever and he would have considered her too much of a temptation if she stayed. With the moratorium she had placed on sex, her presence in his bed would constitute a risk to both his pride and sense of self-control.

Eden wished she'd taken that into account before leaving the playing field wide open to her rival, but she hadn't been thinking all that clearly at the time. She'd been reacting.

Even more important than the fact that her denial had probably been what incited him to send her back to Greece ahead of time, she now wondered if he would regain his memory if she allowed him to make love to her. It was the one aspect of their marriage they always got right and, if they made love, it would have to prove to him that she was not the monster wife he suspected.

In addition, they communicated more between the sheets than anywhere else and she would have done well to remember that salient fact. It was the one place he never stinted on showing her affection or telling her how much he needed her. They'd been in bed together when he asked her to marry him. He'd told her about the effect of his father's death on him, how his uncle's painful marriage had impacted Aristide and the rest of the family and his pleasure in Phillippa's newfound happiness all during discussions post-coitus.

She couldn't believe she hadn't thought of it before, but by refusing to make love with him, she was denying the biggest catalyst she could give him for remembering her.

She'd decided to pick him up from the airport personally and planned to tell him she wanted to be a proper wife to him again on the drive home. Phillippa and Vincent were staying at the villa. Eden's best opportunity for a private, uninterrupted conversation with Aristide was now. Between Theo's needs, the servants who were ever present and a very concerned mother-in-law, her chances of being alone with Aristide were extremely slim.

Phillippa had told Eden that Aristide had asked his mother about their marriage. That showed more than anything that her husband was full of confusion and doubt. Acknowledging his own ignorance of their relationship would have been hard for the proud man she had married.

Interestingly, Phillippa had told her son that she thought he'd been blindly complacent in his marriage. Eden appreciated the sentiment. Aristide had assumed her love meant she would put up with anything.

He had never realized how much his lack of commitment to spending significant time with her had hurt her or taken stock of the damage it was doing to their marriage. Nor had he ever stopped to wonder why Eden frequently refused to attend social functions when she knew Kassandra would be present.

While they couldn't discuss any of these things until he remembered her, she was determined to do so as soon after he regained his memory as possible. Not only that, but she'd spoken to Adam on the phone just that day and the doctor had once again reiterated that it would be better to wait to tell Aristide of her current pregnancy.

In one respect, she had no problem with that. She wanted her husband's honest reaction to her and didn't think she'd get it if he knew she was pregnant again. Just as he had hidden his lack of any real desire to marry in the first place because of Theo. But in another respect, she desperately wanted to share news of the child growing inside her.

Sharing her first pregnancy with Aristide had been really special and there was a craven part of her that just wanted to go back to a time when he treated her so tenderly.

No matter what way she looked at it, his selective amnesia had effectively put their marriage on hold and the situation was intolerable. If it meant making love to a man who saw her as little more than a stranger so her husband could regain his memory and they could move forward, then she was prepared to do it.

* * *

"Eden. What are you doing here? Where is Aldo?" Aristide's tone was no more welcoming than his words, but she'd been expecting that reaction and forced herself not to take offence.

"I cancelled the car and came instead. You used to say you'd like it very much if I met you at the airport."

He'd implied he wouldn't mind making love in the limo on the way home because he was so hungry for her. She wasn't ready for that and she hadn't brought the limo, but she was hoping neither fact would matter since he would have no way of remembering his teasing.

"Did I?"

"Uh…huh. Anyway, I thought we could talk while I drove you home."

"I will do the driving," he said arrogantly.

"I hope you brought the Mercedes," Kassandra inserted from where she stood behind him. "After two weeks in New York, I have extra luggage."

Eden bit back a grimace, realizing her tactical blunder only at that moment. What an idiot she'd been. She'd been so wrapped up in thoughts of her marriage she'd actually managed to forget all about the other woman. Only Kassandra would of course have expected to ride home in the car chauffeured by Aldo as well.

"I'm surprised you didn't have your purchases shipped," Eden said by way of hiding her chagrin.

"There was no time." Kassandra smiled sweetly at her boss. "Aristide took me shopping and we didn't get done until a short time before takeoff."

Eden couldn't help flinching at the words, even knowing any sign of upset would give the Greek woman a great deal of satisfaction. She'd wanted to do her final Christmas shopping in New York with Aristide, but he'd turned her down, even though he clearly had found shopping with Kassandra no hardship.

"I brought the Jaguar." She bit her lip and looked at Aristide, mentally pleading for his understanding. "I thought you might insist on driving and you have always preferred it."

His frown said he wasn't impressed by her reasoning. "That's a small car to transport three people."

He was right. The car's backseat wasn't designed for luggage, it was miniscule, especially to a woman of Kassandra's height. The trunk wasn't much better. "Maybe Kassandra would be more comfortable taking a taxi to her apartment where there will be plenty of room for her bags."

The Greek woman made a moue of distaste. "If I had known you were going to change the transport arrangements I made, I would have had a car waiting to pick me up, but I suppose there's nothing for it than to wait in a taxi queue."

"Nonsense. Since Eden made the change, I am sure she will not mind waiting here while I run you home."

Eden opened her mouth to tell them both what they could do with their assumption that her needs always came last, but then snapped it shut. Kassandra was obviously hoping for just such a reaction and then she would undoubtedly offer to take a taxi again and Aristide would think Eden was acting the bitch.

Once again, she hadn't considered all the angles before acting. She had wanted to please Aristide by bringing his favorite car, but she had also wanted the increased intimacy in the atmosphere of the Jaguar over the Mercedes. She had completely forgotten about the need to see Kassandra home and thereby shot herself in the foot.

However, no way was she going to cool her heels at the airport while he and Kassandra took off together. "Don't be silly. You don't want to have to drive all the way back to the airport from Kassandra's apartment before going home. I'm small and will fit in the backseat, even with an extra piece of luggage or two."

She turned and headed toward the car before either of her nemeses could argue.

CHAPTER SIX

Eden was feeling slightly better after they dropped Kassandra off.

The other woman had attempted to cut Eden out of the conversation in the car, but this time it had been Aristide himself who foiled her ploy. He had asked numerous questions about Theo and the rest of the family that Eden answered with enthusiasm.

"Did the meetings go well?" she asked as he pulled away from Kassandra's home.

"As you heard."

So much for that topic. "I did a lot of thinking while you were gone."

"And did this thinking lead anywhere productive?"

"I believe so."

"Enlighten me."

"It occurred to me that I made a mistake refusing to make love to you in New York. I was being overly sensitive."

He tensed, his expression turning stoic in a way she'd always hated. It shut her out. "On the contrary," he said, "sex between us right now would be nonproductive."

"Nonproductive?" She couldn't believe what she was hearing.

His jaw set with granitelike hardness. "I've decided to move into a guest room for the time being."

"A guest room?"

"Do you plan to repeat everything I say from here on out?" he responded coldly.

"No." She forced her thoughts into working order so she didn't do it again, but flabbergasted didn't begin to describe the way she felt at his announcement. "Your mother and Vincent are staying at the villa."

"And?"

"Are you prepared to answer questions from her about why you are sleeping in a guest room?"

"I have no doubt she will understand."

"Before or after you explain it?" she asked helplessly.

"Does it matter?"

"No, I guess not." Not if he was willing to make the explanations. To her way of thinking, that little fact was as significant as the move itself. She shook her head, trying to clear it. He really was rejecting her sexually. She couldn't believe it. "But celibacy is not your style."

"I am not such a Neanderthal that I would insist on claiming my marital rights with a woman I do not remember marrying merely to satisfy my sexual urges."

"Maybe you plan to satisfy them elsewhere," she accused with pain-filled uncertainty. She knew only one thing for sure—her husband was less acquainted with sexual denial than he was with being poor.

"What the hell are you talking about?"

"You told me in New York that you didn't feel married. Does that mean you don't feel bound by your vow of fidelity? Not that you even said one," she rambled in confused shock, "the marriage ceremony in a judge's office is somewhat truncated."

"I do not intend to have sex with another woman."

"You expect me to believe you are willingly embracing celibacy for the indefinite future?"

"Why not? I travel quite a bit. I assume you would not have stayed married to a man who strayed." Sarcasm dripped off his tongue like acid.

"You assume correctly."

"I may not remember you, or our marriage, but I know myself and I would not have had sex with any woman but my wife."

"Are you sure about that? Kassandra's more than willing. She's made it clear to me that she's *eager* and, according to her, you're *already* lovers. Presumably, you would remember *that*, since you remember *her*."

"She told me you had jealous delusions about us."

"Did she?" Eden stared out the window, the darkened landscape not registering. "Which means what—you naturally assume I'm lying when I say she told me you two were lovers?"

She could feel him looking at her, but she refused to return his regard. She couldn't quite bounce back from a rejection she had never expected. The one thing she'd been certain of in her marriage to Aristide was his desire for her. She'd doubted his emotional attachment, but never his physical need. Now he was saying he didn't need her.

Was he having an affair with Kassandra? She had to contemplate the possibility his decision to move into a guest room reflected a turn of events she would have given almost anything not to face.

"When are you alleging Kassandra told you this?"

She tensed at his choice of words, a familiar sense of impotent anger surging up inside of her. "I'm not alleging anything. I'm stating a fact. She was waiting for me when I came out of your hospital room the day before you were discharged. We argued."

"And she told you we are lovers?" he asked, sounding disbelieving.

"Not exactly."

"Ah…"

She turned her head and looked at him then. His focus was on the road ahead, but she knew his peripheral vision was superior and she gave him a hot glare.

"Kassandra asked me point-blank if I was sure you weren't lovers. If that isn't an implication the two of you are having an affair, I don't know what is."

"Is that why you slapped her?"

"No." She opened her mouth to add more, but didn't know what to say.

Kassandra had been careful to lace her threats with innuendo. Repeating the conversation verbatim would not convince Aristide that Eden had been justified in her reaction. He would have had to have been there…and inside her heart, dealing with her pain to understand it.

And what were the chances Aristide would even begin to believe his precious Kassandra was intentionally undermining his marriage? Before the accident, they had been slim, but now that he didn't remember Eden or trust her at all, they were nonexistent.

Silence fell between them as she went back to looking out the window.

"Are you going to tell me why you did slap her?"

"I see no point in doing so."

"If it is something I need to discuss with her…"

"You've already made it clear who you blame for that altercation and it isn't your assistant."

"Maybe I did not have all the facts."

"It wouldn't make any difference if you did. You would still blame me because while you'll bend over backwards to give her the benefit of the doubt, you assume the worst about me and have done since waking up from your coma. I'm your wife, but you didn't stand by me and there's really nothing else to say in the face of that."

"Kassandra was there for me in the hospital when you were not. She is a devoted employee as well as a long-time friend. I would be a fool to trust the word of a woman I cannot remember over hers. After all, I did not wake from my coma having wiped *her* entirely from my brain. And I have to question why that was."

Pain ripped through Eden like a hurricane and she felt as ravaged as any debris-strewn coastline. She swallowed convulsively, her throat tight with tears. Because he hadn't just forgotten her, he'd forgotten their unborn baby as well. Somehow that made it ten times worse.

Not only had he obviously subconsciously wanted to wipe her existence in his life, but he'd also wanted to forget the tie an additional child between them would forge.

From the moment she had woken up in the hospital after the accident, she had been determined to fight for her marriage. Why? Because she loved Aristide so much she thought she might die inside without him. But he was tearing her heart to shreds and if she wasn't *dying* right now, she was certainly hurting.

Maybe it was time she faced that her love meant nothing in the face of his indifference.

What that meant for her future, for the future of her children and their life with her and their father, she didn't even want to contemplate. But one thing she knew—her hope was a dead weight in her chest, along with her leaden heart.

When they reached the villa, she left him to look in on Theo while she began moving his things from the master suite to a guest room down the hall. By the time he walked in forty-five minutes later, she and a maid had cleared out his dresser and most of his wardrobe.

He had his suitcase in his hand when he walked in. "What the hell is going on in here?"

"You're in the room at the end of the hall." She looked pointedly at his suitcase.

The maid came out of the walk-in closet carrying a big armful of his suits. Eden stepped out of the way so she could leave the room.

Aristide wasn't so obliging. "Where are you taking my things?" he asked in a dangerously soft voice.

The maid flinched, but Eden wasn't bothered by her husband's apparent anger. She was only doing what he wanted, after all.

"She's taking your suits to your new room."

"My new room?"

Now who was repeating words? "Yes. We're almost done moving you. I'll just transfer your things from our…I mean *my* bathroom and you'll be all settled in."

"I did not intend to move completely out of *our* bedroom."

"You'll be sleeping in another room, right?"

"For the time being."

"I'm sure you'll be more comfortable not having to go searching for your things between there and here…"

She'd never seen Aristide look lost for words, not in all the time she'd known him. She would have laughed if she wasn't hurting so much. He looked royally flummoxed now and that gave her a sense of grim satisfaction. He'd been standing her world on its ear since the day they met.

It was time she turned the tables a bit.

"If you will excuse me, I'll just collect your gear from the *en suite*."

"Damn it, Eden!"

"What is happening?" Phillippa stood in the doorway, her face creased with concern. "I saw the maid carrying Aristide's clothing into another room."

"Your son has decided he feels more comfortable sleeping elsewhere…for the time being. He seems to think you'll understand and no explanations are necessary. Should he be wrong, I suggest you ask him about it. He also made it clear he doesn't mind explaining if the need should arise."

Aristide watched as his wife spun on her heel and marched into the *en suite*.

His mother gasped. "Aristide?" she asked uncertainly.

"Yes?"

"Eden…"

"Has taken my desire to sleep in separate quarters at present to mean I no longer belong in our bedroom."

Her words to his mother had been filled with bitterness, but her eyes had reflected a pain that tore at something deep inside him. Did she think he didn't want her? Nothing could be further from the truth, but their relationship was too muddled as it was to confuse with sex. They both needed this time of adjustment.

From the expression on her face when she'd walked away, she didn't see it that way though. She was taking his desire to sleep in another bed as a form of rejection…one he had never intended. His usually superior brain had let him down when he assumed she would understand something he barely understood himself.

He cursed again and earned a censorious frown from his mother.

"You told her you wanted to sleep in a separate bed?" she asked, as if trying to take in a very shocking turn of events.

"*Ohi*," he affirmed.

She shook her head. "That was stupid."

"There is enough confusion in our situation right now. We do not need it clouded with sex."

She stared at him like she doubted his sanity or intelligence, or maybe even both.

This was not a conversation he wanted to have with his mother. "My decision is not up for discussion."

"Do not take that tone with me, Aristide."

"I apologize if my tone was disrespectful, but you must allow me to handle my marriage as I see fit."

"The problem is that you are not handling it, my son. You are undermining it when you can least afford to do so. Know this, Aristide—if you mess up your marriage, you will have no one to blame but yourself." With that, she turned and left the room.

Aristide felt like he'd stepped into an alternate dimension where everyone but him knew the rules. In New York, his mother had as good as said Eden wasn't the wife she should have been and now she was thrusting the blame for any failure in his marriage squarely on his shoulders.

His head began to ache again.

Eden came out of the bathroom, her arms laden with his toiletries. "I'll just drop these off in your bathroom."

Even though she had been the one to initially say she did not want to make love while he could not remember her, rejected hurt emanated from her every lovely pore. Clearly, she had changed her mind and did not appreciate the fact that he now questioned the wisdom of sharing a bed.

However, instead of arguing his decision to sleep elsewhere like he would have expected from her reaction, she was intent on removing every trace of his occupancy from their bedroom.

The sense of foreboding that hovered around the edges of

his marriage increased until he felt suffocated by it. "This is not necessary."

"I don't agree."

Desperation seared through him and fear clouded his thoughts until he was on the verge of recanting his desire to sleep in another bed. She didn't give him the chance, but marched from the room.

"Eden!" he called after her, that incomprehensible desperation lacing his voice.

Could she hear it? If she did, she ignored it as she continued down the hall as if he had never spoken.

He opened his mouth to demand she come back and then snapped it shut again. This was stupid. These feelings tormenting him were irrational and he would not be dictated to by them. He was stronger than that.

But he didn't feel strong…he felt like he was making a major tactical error here. Sleeping elsewhere had seemed so logical when he had been considering how to handle his aching desire for a woman he could not remember. He had to wonder if he'd been thinking straight.

Or was the problem that he was confused now? His usually superior brain felt like mush. His pride barely allowed him to acknowledge his possible mistake to himself, but no way could he admit it to *her*.

So there was nothing for it but to make his way to the guest room down the hall. It did not escape his notice that the bedroom was the furthest she could get him from the master suite without putting him in a different section of the villa entirely.

She walked out of the *en suite* as he entered the room. "You should be all set. Petra will unpack your case for you during dinner."

"Is that not a wife's job?"

"I don't think so," she mocked. "Besides, how can you have a wife if you don't feel like a husband?"

Eden hadn't been consciously baiting her husband, but as she watched the fireworks explode in his vibrant blue eyes, she realized this was exactly the reaction she'd been pushing for.

Something had snapped inside of her when he had told her so calmly that he wanted to sleep somewhere besides their bed. Coming from a man like Aristide, it was the ultimate rejection and she had been determined he feel at least the edge of its bite as well. And he had.

He didn't like having his things removed from their bedroom. It stung his pride and he deserved it. He'd lacerated hers along with her heart.

"Are you trying to imply you feel free to behave as if you are not married?" he asked in a deadly voice.

"No more than you do." He could take that any way he liked.

His eyes narrowed. He got it all right. "You do not think I take my vows seriously…you implied as much in the car."

She shrugged. "You said you weren't sleeping with Kassandra." Once. He'd said it once.

"But you do not believe me."

"I didn't say that."

Steel manacles masquerading as masculine fingers clamped down on her shoulders while rage vibrated around her. "But you think it, do you not? You believe I am having an affair with my assistant and for this reason, you think you have the right to similarly forget your promise of fidelity."

"We didn't make those promises at our wedding." And she was just now realizing how much she hated that, how she had felt slighted being married in a register office instead of a church.

"In Greece such promises are not part of the wedding ceremony. They are taken for granted."

"I wouldn't know. We had a ten-minute civil ceremony in New York. It was all the time you and my father could squeeze from your busy schedules."

"Surely not."

She sighed, the tension draining from her, leaving her exhausted in both body and spirit. "You left for a trip to England that night and he went back to the office after taking us out for a celebratory lunch."

"My mother would never have approved a register-office marriage."

"She didn't, but after you informed her I was already two months pregnant, she understood."

"I am sure she was ecstatic at the prospect of being a grandmother so quickly after our marriage."

"She made a few comments about neither of her sons seeming to get the whole 'first comes marriage and then comes babies' thing right, but, yes, she was very happy to have another grandchild on the way."

He was silent for a moment, seemingly letting go of his own nearly incandescent anger. "You did not realize you were pregnant immediately?" he asked, sounding wary.

"I figured it out within days of missing my period. I'm disgustingly regular in that department."

"Why did you wait to tell me?"

Funny how he just assumed she had, not that he had waited to marry her. It irked her that she could not fault him on that score. Right now, she wanted to fault him on everything, she was hurting so much.

"I didn't have a choice," she admitted. "You were in Greece and it wasn't something I was going to tell you over the phone."

"I spend more than half of my life in New York. You expected my imminent return," he correctly guessed. "We met there?"

"Yes. I was in town visiting my dad. We met outside the Metropolitan Museum of Art. I was planning to take in an exhibit while Dad was in a meeting and you were headed to lunch with someone else. You cancelled and spent the afternoon with me instead."

It had shocked and delighted her that he had acted as affected by her as she had been by him. It had taken her a while to realize her effect on him was mainly sexual while he had come to dominate her heart, her body and her thoughts.

"You said you were visiting your father? You did not live in New York?"

She shook her head. "I lived in a small town upstate. That's where we were headed when we were hit by the truck."

"You feel badly about this?"

He knew her better than he should, considering she was nothing but a stranger to him. "Yes. If we had stayed in the city, the accident would not have happened."

"These things happen. It was not your fault."

He was wrong. Her bombshell had been just that, even though she'd convinced herself that her asking for a divorce would hardly impact him. If he, or their baby, had died because of her poor timing, she would never have forgiven herself.

His vibrant blue eyes narrowed. "We live in Greece."

She knew what he was asking without him saying the words. Why not New York when he spent so much time there? "You wanted your children raised in your home country," she said.

His brow creased. "I've decreased my trips to New York in the last year or so."

Not enough, but, "Yes."

"I am *not* having an affair with Kassandra."

"But you have had." She'd always suspected, but he'd refused to discuss it.

Never once had he denied that the two had slept together,

but he'd been unwilling to talk about it if they had. And because she hadn't been sure that Kassandra was even sexually active, she hadn't pressed. Now she realized how silly she'd ever been to think the reason he had held himself back from the woman was because of her innocence.

Kassandra was as innocent as a viper.

"My relationships before I met you are not up for discussion."

"So you've said before, but are you so sure your relationship with *her* ended *before* we met?"

"When did we meet?"

"Almost three years ago."

The look of confused uncertainty on his face was like taking a rapier thrust to the heart.

"You were lovers, weren't you? And you can't be sure it ended before we met because the timing was that close, wasn't it?"

He let her go with the speed of a snake retreating and stepped back. "This conversation is pointless, you know I can't remember."

"How convenient."

"Do you think I do not want to answer you?"

"You said earlier that you know yourself well and that you would not sleep with a woman besides your wife, but your uncertainty now undermines that assertion, don't you think?"

He rubbed his forehead with his thumb and forefinger. "No, damn it. I know I would never respect myself if I had an affair when I was married."

"Which does not preclude you having her as your lover at the same time you were seeing me. After all, our relationship was hardly a committed one, no matter what daydreams I wove around you at the time."

"What do you mean?" he asked, his tension palpable.

"We were together well over a year before I got pregnant

and you never once asked me to Greece to meet your family. Heck, you didn't even invite me to have dinner with you and your brother when he was in town. There were times I felt like your dirty secret and the funny thing is, before I met you, I would have said I would give a guy a verbal kick in the teeth for treating me that way."

He'd certainly changed after their marriage, insisting she meet everyone from the receptionist at Kouros Industries' headquarters to his second cousin who lived in Turkey. But privately she'd always wondered if that had been for the sake of their baby, or for her. He had been so proud about his first foray into fatherhood.

"Your other lovers all took you home to meet their parents?" he asked cynically.

"There were no other lovers. Sex was never a casual thing for me. I planned to wait until I got married."

"Are you implying I seduced you?"

"Is it seduction when a woman has no thought of saying no?" She sighed. "This is getting us nowhere."

She turned and headed for the door. "I'll see you at dinner."

"Eden."

She stopped with her hand on the doorframe. "What?"

"You are my wife now."

"So the certificate in your study says."

"It is more than a piece of paper…*I am your husband.*"

She looked back over her shoulder, taking in his ferocious tension.

She indicated the room with a sweep of her hand. "As you said to me in the hospital…the evidence is not in your favor."

CHAPTER SEVEN

"I am surprised you let Eden stray so far from your side." The deep male voice belonged to Aristide's business associate and friend, Leiandros Kiriakis.

Aristide gritted his teeth against making an irritated retort and forced himself to face the other man with an expression of equanimity. "Leiandros, it is good to see you."

"You have recently returned from New York, have you not?"

"A week ago."

"Then I am doubly surprised Eden is more than six inches from your side. That is unlike you."

Was the other man implying that Aristide usually hung around his wife like a lost puppy? The image did not sit well and he frowned.

He had made the choice not to share his amnesia with anyone but family, so he could not expect a tactful handling of anomalies in his demeanor toward Eden. And, being honest with himself, he had to admit his annoyance did not stem from Leiandros noting the strange behavior anyway. It resulted from the fact that Eden had been *straying from Aristide's side* since the night she'd moved him out of their bedroom.

She had closed herself off from him, maintaining a definite emotional distance and going so far as to create a physical one when possible as well. She avoided sharing any meal but dinner with him and then she barely spoke to him. And she only tolerated his nightly presence during Theo's bath time because she wanted their son to maintain his sense of security. She had as much as told Aristide so.

He hadn't realized how much of herself she had left open to him until her manner had altered so significantly. Even having only the short time in New York and the drive from the airport to compare it to, her change toward him was so marked, he could not mistake it.

And while she was busy ignoring him, he was fully occupied trying to interpret the reaction of his family and others toward Eden. Their staff adored his rather quiet wife and, regardless of what she had implied about their marriage in New York, his mother treated Eden with a great deal of affection. It was nothing like the way she had reacted to Andrea Demakis. And Rachel was just as accepting of her sister-in-law.

Vincent and Sebastian's attitude toward Aristide's wife was one of warm indulgence. He would not have said either man was easily fooled, but Eden might be the consummate actress.

Not only that, but his own pride could well have spurred him to act like he was happy in his marriage no matter what had brought it about. Three irrefutable facts kept him wary toward his tempting little wife. One, even Eden admitted he had married her because she was pregnant. She claimed it had not been a trap, but she would hardly say anything else.

Two, he had forgotten her and all the research he had done on his condition pointed to the probability he had forgotten her because he subconsciously wanted or needed to. And three, she wielded power over his libido and emotions that no other woman ever had. That made her dangerous. Strong evidence of that fact was that, no matter how wary he felt toward her, Eden's current attempt to hold him at a distance really bothered him.

"Aristide?" Leiandros looked concerned.

Well he might. Aristide was staring across the room like a man in a trance. His pride balked at the picture he made.

"She is enjoying herself," he said, trying to explain his own apparently unusual behavior and save face.

She stood on the other side of the room, laughing with a group of *his* friends, yet they were people that knew her infinitely better than he did because of his memory loss. That knowledge brought him an unpleasant sensation of jealousy.

"No doubt, but I would say you are not, my friend." The knowing in Leiandros's eyes was as bad as being with his brother, Sebastian.

The shipping tycoon was older than both Aristide and Sebastian, but they'd been friends for years. There weren't that many men in the world, much less Greece, with the power, the wealth or the inner drive that all three possessed.

Even fewer that held and therefore practiced their particular stand on business ethics. It was no surprise the three men were friends despite the slight age difference, but the fact that they functioned so well in the business arena together shocked many.

"*I am fine.* Where is Savannah?" Aristide asked to change the subject.

His friend's features softened. "She and the children are shopping for my Christmas present. I am not allowed to see it, so I have been banished. She promised to join me here as soon as she settled the children with my mother."

"You didn't wait to come with her?"

"You know how it is…there are always business discussions at a gathering like this. I want to get them out of the way before my wife arrives, so she can command my full attention."

"You two are very devoted." There had been a lot of gossip when Leiandros married his cousin's widow, but even the most determined naysayers did not question the couple's deep and loving affection now.

"As are you and Eden."

"Do you think so?"

Leiandros's expression sharpened. "Definitely, but why would you ask such a thing?"

He shrugged. He could hardly tell the other man he couldn't remember his wife and therefore had no idea what sort of relationship they had before. From what Leiandros implied, either Aristide had been very good at putting on a front, or his relationship with Eden was not the unequal and unhappy union the facts of his present condition implied. He was fairly certain it had been nothing like the armed truce they were currently engaged in either.

Tired of that truce and the amalgam of unnamed needs that swirled through him constantly when it came to his wife, Aristide took leave of his friend.

He stopped beside Eden and laid his arm over her shoulders. It felt right and she smelled so damn good. It was a scent, like springtime after a rain, that he did not associate with anyone else. Her soft skin tantalized his fingertips and he could not help brushing his thumb along her exposed shoulder.

His friends apparently found nothing odd in this gesture of affection, none of them so much as blinking, but his wife went as stiff as a board beside him. She made a subtle effort to shrug off his hand, but rather than let her go, he pulled her closer. He knew it was a mistake the second he did it as a sexual charge leapt through his body and he became instantly aroused.

He had been an idiot to deny himself the pleasure of intimacy with his wife.

Doing his best to control a libido rapidly spiraling out of control, he smiled down at her. "Enjoying yourself?"

Her lips curved in an answering gesture that did not begin to reach her vulnerable gray eyes. "Yes, of course. I've been looking forward to this party for weeks."

The hostess, who was in the group surrounding Eden, looked pleased. "You did a lot to help me plan it."

The party was more than a gathering of friends for the holidays. It was a fund raiser for a worldwide children's organization. That much he remembered.

But Eden had helped plan it? That was hardly the action of a woman who had trapped him into marriage for mercenary motives.

"And you are pleased with the results?" he asked, his heart rate increasing as Eden's scent continued to tease his senses.

He could feel himself growing hard and changed his stance with Eden so she stood partially in front of him.

Apparently unaware of his predicament, the hostess nodded enthusiastically. "We raised over one hundred thousand dollars."

"That's fantastic!" Eden said, relaxing, her pleasure in the success of the evening blatant and clearly genuine.

He could not remember if he had donated anything beyond the door admission for him and his wife. Couldn't even remember buying the tickets. His mother and brother were here as well, but he didn't know if they had bought their own tickets. He hated these lapses of knowledge in his memory.

The hostess laughed. "How could it be anything else? You bought tickets for so many people here, Eden, it should be your name being bandied about tonight, not mine."

Well that answered one question…the one of who had bought the tickets. It was such a small thing, but there were so many little glitches like that in his memory banks, they were driving him crazy. His personal frustration aside, he could not fault a wife who had used his resources in such a fashion.

"Like I had anything else to do with my allowance," Eden said, sounding very American. "Aristide is so generous with me, I never have to buy anything for myself."

The unexpected approval in her voice warmed him. Until he remembered that approval was for the man he'd been before he lost his memory. She certainly wasn't as enamored of the man he was now…or at least the way that man treated her.

"I would happily double your allowance if this is how you would like to spend the money," he said honestly.

She looked up at him, her expression open and filled with pleasure for the first time in days. "Are you serious?"

"Very." He would triple it, if doing so would keep that expression on her face when she looked at him. "In fact, I will put you in charge of Kouros Industries' charitable contributions if you like."

Her expression closed up immediately and she looked away, all the relaxing her body had done disappearing in the blink of an eye. "That is Kassandra's domain."

"She has enough to keep her busy, she will be content to give that up, I am sure."

"Don't bet on it," Eden muttered.

"It does not matter. I am the boss, not she."

Eden's snort was followed by good-natured laughter from those around him. Clearly, the others thought she was teasing him, but he knew better.

He turned her to face him, his already overactive libido going into overdrive as he got a very nice view down the front of her slinky little dress. Damn it. Had other men seen her this way tonight? He could see the top swell of her breasts and it didn't take much imagination to picture her nipples a little further down.

His sex tightened and he had to bite back a groan. He wanted her with an obsessive ache that grew with every passing day.

"You mock me at your peril," he growled with a teasing look for the benefit of the others.

She gave him a saucy grin that went straight to his groin. "What are you going to do about it?"

He knew what he wanted to do about it, but making love to her in front of an audience was not exactly his thing. "Wait until we get home and see," he threatened.

Her eyes widened with mock trepidation and something else he could swear was very real anticipation.

Something flashed in his head…an impression, if not a clear memory. This type of teasing between them was not a new thing and it had been something he had enjoyed a great deal.

"The way you two carry on, it's hard to understand how you can stand to live apart as much as you do," their hostess said with a laugh.

The animation and anticipation drained out of Eden as if it had never been there. Reality flooded back. She stepped away before he could stop her. "You know what Aristide always says, it keeps our relationship fresh."

He didn't know how he had looked at things before, but more time spent together now would reveal her true nature faster than their current living arrangement. "Theo is older and he made the last trip to New York as if he was born to air travel. There is no reason you cannot travel with me now."

A mysterious shadow passed through her gray eyes, but all she did was shrug.

"You always said having your wife along would be too much of a distraction, Aristide." Kassandra joined their small group, her smile directed at him.

He did not miss the way she effectively cut his wife without making a point of doing so. Was she being protective? She had implied she felt he needed it when it came to his wife.

Even so, she could not be allowed to behave rudely toward Eden. He had chosen to marry her, and no matter how his loyal friend and employee felt about that, she needed to respect his decision.

"Maybe I have changed my mind."

"You no longer find Eden a distraction?" Kassandra asked, the barb so subtle he would have missed it but for the stone-like quality that took over his lovely wife's expression.

She was obviously very sensitive where his assistant was concerned. And he could not forget that she had accused the two of them of being lovers.

Kassandra had explained her remarks to Eden outside the hospital room, but his wife's ultra-sensitivity to the other woman would account for her taking them the opposite way they had been intended.

"On the contrary," he said for his wife's benefit, "I feel as if I've just gotten married for the first time again. If I can do my job while living with my wife in Greece, I fail to see how she would hamper me in New York or anywhere else for that matter."

Eden couldn't believe her ears. He was saying what she had thought for so long she almost pinched herself to see if she was in some bizarre dream.

"I do not know…I think marriage to a woman as delectable as your wife would be a constant distraction no matter where I lived and worked," an Italian man, who had joined their group just before Aristide, said.

She had never met him before, but the way he looked at her made her feel like crossing her arms over her less than generous curves.

"And you are?" Aristide asked with freezing cool that left no doubt what he thought of the other man's comment.

"Haven't you met Giuseppe?" their hostess asked, jumping in with an adroit maneuver meant to defuse the situation. "He's a great supporter of children's charities."

"Now that your husband is putting you in charge of corporate charities, we'll have to get together for lunch and talk over some of my pet projects." Giuseppe's sensual mouth curved in a smile that intimated he was interested in more than discussing their mutual interest in needy children.

She remembered someone saying once that all Italian men flirted, but she couldn't imagine most of them did it this blatantly. What did he see between her and Aristide that he thought he could get away with it or that she might possibly welcome it? Maybe it was the fact she had spent the first forty-five minutes of the party being virtually ignored by her tycoon spouse.

He wasn't ignoring her now though. Aristide looked ready to blow a gasket, but Kassandra's shocked gasp was audible to everyone.

"I thought you were happy with my management of that area of the company," she said, affecting a wounded attitude.

Eden nearly ground her teeth in frustration, certain Aristide's offer would be rescinded in days, if not hours. Kassandra was very adept at undermining Eden's progress with her husband.

"If you find you do not wish to alter your company's arrangements, I would be very happy to discuss Eden helping me with my efforts," Giuseppe said and Eden could have kissed him.

Their hostess smiled brightly, ignoring the undercurrents of the situation as any good society hostess would try to do. "What a wonderful idea."

"No, thank you," Aristide said to Giuseppe, shockingly talking right over their hostess's words. "My wife is sufficiently occupied. She does not have time to pursue outside endeavors of the type you are suggesting."

She should be used to having her sometimes arrogant Greek husband speak for her, but she wasn't and didn't plan to ever develop any real tolerance for it. "I think that is a decision I need to make, Aristide."

"Absolutely. You have got to remember, your wife is *American*." Kassandra said it like Eden was an alien species. "She prefers to remain independent in many ways. Playing the heavy husband will not go over well with her."

"When I need marital advice I will ask for it," Aristide said with a glacial look and more censure than Eden had ever heard him use toward his assistant.

Kassandra's big brown eyes filled with glistening moisture and her lip quivered. "Of course, I never meant… I know I am only your employee. If you will all excuse me." She spun on her heel and rushed toward the terrace.

Aristide cursed and, without consulting Eden, excused them both from the small group. He started tugging her toward the terrace, but she dug her heels in.

"Where do you think you're taking me?"

"I was rude and I need to apologize to her."

"You were honest."

"I hurt her."

"You hurt me, but I haven't received any heartfelt apologies."

The look of chagrin on his features said her words had hit their mark.

She pulled her arm from his grasp. "Go talk to her if you think you need to, but leave me out of it."

His hands fisted at his sides and his body went rigid with tension, but he nodded. "Perhaps that would be best."

Eden watched him walk away, her stomach churning and ended up making her own mad dash for the bathroom. Morning sickness that did not limit itself to the mornings was the pits. When she came out fifteen minutes later,

Aristide and Kassandra were just returning from the terrace together.

Eden walked in the opposite direction the couple was heading. She'd had enough of her husband's assistant's company for one evening. She spent the next hour avoiding them both, catching a glimpse of irritation on her husband's face more than once when she made herself scarce the minute he walked into a room. Well, too bad.

She'd warned him her tolerance level for Kassandra's game playing was at an all-time low. He should have listened, but, unsurprisingly, he had chosen to dismiss her concerns.

She was in an animated discussion about children's charities with Sebastian, Rachel and Giuseppe when she sensed Aristide's presence behind her. A scant second later his arm landed around her shoulder and it was all she could do not to throw it off, but she felt they'd caused enough of a scene tonight.

"Your wife has a real admirer here, little brother," Sebastian said with more warning than teasing.

Eden frowned at her brother-in-law.

He grinned back at her, unrepentant. "You're a lovely woman, Eden…it is no surprise my brother is not the only man to appreciate you so enthusiastically."

Giuseppe smiled as well, his eyes roaming over her like hands. "You are a very lucky man, Signor Kouros."

Aristide went rigid beside her, his hold on her shoulder tightening almost painfully. "I am well aware of my good fortune in my choice of a wife."

The words were born of his pride, not honesty, and that infuriated her. Not only had he *not chosen* her for his wife—nature had done that for him in allowing her to become pregnant—but he could in no way imply he currently wanted to be her husband in any shape or form.

Angry at his willingness to claim her for the sake of his

ego and not her heart, she twisted out of his hold. "I'm ready to go home."

"The evening is still young," Giuseppe said.

Almost as annoyed with the Italian as she was with Aristide, she smiled saccharine sweetly at him. "Then I suggest you find someone young to share it with you. As we say back home, I'm an old married woman. My baby son will wake me up bright and early no matter what time I go to sleep tonight."

She turned to Aristide. "You are welcome to stay. I can catch a taxi home with no trouble at all."

"We will drop you off," Sebastian said quickly. "Our little ones do not sleep much past dawn either, right, *agape mou*?" he asked, looking down at Rachel with love in his eyes.

Eden usually rejoiced in her in-laws' adoration for one another, but tonight it was like salt in a fresh wound. If she had to travel home, witnessing it at close proximity in the car, she would probably end up in tears and totally embarrassing herself.

"If you are ready to leave, I will of course accompany you," Aristide said with steel in his voice.

She had no desire to argue, but neither did she offer him any conversation once they were in the car. She could tell he was just sitting there stewing, his driving movement precise and indicative of tightly controlled anger.

They were almost to the villa when he broke the silence. "I do not appreciate my wife flirting with other men."

"I did not flirt."

"Giuseppe wants you."

"That's his problem."

"Is it?"

"Yes. I don't want him."

"Are you sure?"

"I'm a married woman, for heaven's sake, Aristide."

"But you do not feel like a married woman."

"That doesn't mean I'm going to jump in bed with the first beautiful Italian man who asks me." Giuseppe had been over the top and even a little smarmy in the way he looked at her, but he'd also been gorgeous.

His jaw clenched. "And if I asked you?"

"Asked me what?"

"To go to bed with me."

"After you disappeared on the terrace with your personal assistant?" She made a sound of disgust. "Forget it."

He said a very nasty American swear word. "She was upset. You told me to go to her. What did you expect me to do, ignore her distress?"

"Why not? You've done a very good job of ignoring mine on more than one occasion. And I didn't tell you to go to her. I made it clear I wanted no part of it, if you did."

"I'm sorry if my actions tonight offended you." It was a stilted apology at best.

"Celibacy starting to wear on you, is it?" she asked cynically, implying that was his only reason for saying he was sorry. And maybe it was.

"*Yes*, but my apology was sincere. It was not my intention to put Kassandra's feelings above your own. I did not seek her out merely to soothe her feelings, but also to make it clear I do not appreciate being the center of an emotional scene."

She could easily see him doing that, but it did not negate the other. "Her feelings do come first."

"I want *you*," he said in a driven tone.

It was quite the climb down for the man who had told her he didn't want sex clouding their relationship.

"What happened to sex between us being *nonproductive*?"

"I am fast learning that living together in the same house and not making love is impossible."

"So, I'm an addiction you can't break even if you don't re-member ever wanting anything more than my body?"

"I did not say that."

"Tell me, Aristide…who will be managing the corporate charitable gifts for Kouros Industries in the future?"

Two streaks of red slashed across the chiseled features of his face and she had her answer before he spoke. "I did not realize how attached to that aspect of her job Kassandra was when I made the offer."

"No, of course not."

"But you knew…apparently this has come up before," he had the gall to say with implied accusation.

Kassandra's effective negative publicity campaign at work again.

"Yes, it has, in fact—with the same results, I might add," she said defiantly. "Do remember who made the suggestion and that it was not me."

"The corporate charity fund is not the issue here and it has nothing to do with me wanting to take you to my bed."

"But it has a great deal to do with me not wanting to be there."

"I have got to hand it to you, Eden…you almost had me fooled. I was beginning to think there was not a mercenary bone in your body."

"And you see my desire to use my time promoting worthy charities as money grubbing?" she mocked, refusing to ac-knowledge the pain more accusations about her character caused her.

"No," he ground out. "I see you using your body as a bar-gaining chip in that light."

Was he really that dense? "Is that honestly what you think I'm doing, using my body for barter?"

"What else?"

"You don't think it might be natural for a wife to want nothing of intimacy with a husband who repeatedly puts his employee's wishes above her own?" Not to mention the fact he didn't remember her, but that was not the issue of paramount importance at the moment.

"That is ridiculous…the two do not coincide. Kassandra's pleasure in her job has nothing to do with your role as my wife. If you want to set up a charitable fund and administer it, I will be the biggest donor."

"If I said yes and invited you into my bed, then that really would make me the mercenary bitch you are so intent on believing me to be. No, thank you, Aristide. I would rather work with the somewhat smarmy Giuseppe."

"Do not try it." The deadly venom in his tone sent chills over her and she didn't argue the point.

She didn't want to work with Giuseppe anyway. The man might care about malnourished and undereducated children, but that couldn't make up for the fact he was so obviously interested in having an affair with a married woman.

Eden could never respect or be drawn to a man of that ilk, but she wasn't about to admit that truth to her husband. He deserved to sweat it out a little, like she'd been sweating his relationship with Kassandra since the beginning of their marriage.

CHAPTER EIGHT

Eden fed Theo his breakfast with a heavy heart.

Once again she was questioning her judgment in rejecting her husband. Had she made yet another mistake, or had she saved herself heartache? The last two weeks had been hard, but last night had been emotionally devastating.

Because for a very short time, it was as if she had Aristide back and that had both elated and frightened her. She was safe when her heart was locked away behind a cold wall built by his rejection, but when the wall started to crack, she realized she could still bleed.

She'd read somewhere that sometimes love was not enough. Her mother's love had been more of a handicap to her happiness than an emotion so powerful it could make up for her father's lack. Eden was beginning to think she had made the same mistake in marrying a man who did not love her the way she loved him.

But if love was not enough…if their marriage had to end, what did that say for Theo and the baby growing in Eden's womb? She shuddered at the thought of tearing them away from a father who would love them in a way her own father had never doted on her. Could she justify destroying their happiness for the sake of her own feelings?

She was so lost in thought, she did not hear Aristide come into the kitchen. Her first inkling he was there came when he leaned down and kissed their son's baby-round cheek. "Good morning, *agape mou*." He turned to her, his expression cooling several degrees. "Good morning, Eden."

He was still smarting from her sexual rejection, she could tell. There was an air about him that said he hadn't slept any better than she had either.

"Off to Kouros Industries already?" she asked, indicating his briefcase with a nod of her head.

It was barely seven.

"I have an early morning meeting."

"Did you remember that you promised to take your mother and Vincent out to lunch today before they leave?" The older couple planned to return to their home and then come back to the villa in time for a family Christmas.

"I am hardly likely to forget a lunch date we made yesterday."

"I didn't mean to imply that you would, but when you don't have something on your calendar, you've been known to remember it too late to be of any use." She said it softly, not wanting another slanging match this morning.

Neither she, nor her heart, were up to it.

He sighed, apparently accepting her explanation. "I will meet you at the restaurant at one."

"Okay."

He turned to leave and then stopped. "Speaking of engagements, my diary shows a dinner with you tomorrow night."

"Yes." Thinking about that dinner and the reason for it had been part of what kept her up the night before.

"We will have to do it another time."

"Why?"

"Something has come up."

"With Kassandra?"

"With my business," he said on another sigh. "Out of town colleagues will be here one evening only."

"That night." And she just knew who she could thank for arranging the timing on this one.

"Yes. That night. Surely you do not mind postponing the dinner. It is not as if we do not eat together several nights a week. I suppose this was supposed to be some sort of a date without Theo, but in our current situation that seems overkill, do you not think?"

Overkill? Probably so. And why should she mind? It was only the anniversary of the day they met, after all. He had contrived to make it special since the beginning, but he certainly would not remember that now.

"By all means, cancel the dinner."

"I did not say cancel, I said postpone."

She ignored his argument over semantics and went back to feeding their son. He was the one who said a date in their current situation was ludicrous.

Aristide stood there, smoldering in silence for several seconds.

He glared down at her and then swung out of the house, an angry panther deprived of its prey.

Aristide wasn't surprised to see his brother and sister-in-law with Vincent and Phillippa when he reached the restaurant, but he was surprised Eden was not present at the table.

"Where is Eden?" he asked after greeting his mother and sister-in-law with a kiss.

"I do not know. We have not seen Eden all morning. We have been Christmas shopping," his mother replied.

"She called and said she was running late." Rachel looked at Aristide as if wondering why his wife had chosen to call her instead of her own husband.

He had no answer for her, except that Eden no doubt planned to take avoiding him to new levels now that he'd cancelled their dinner date. His suspicion was confirmed when only minutes later his cell phone rang and it was Eden. She wasn't coming to lunch because Theo had just laid down for his afternoon nap and by the time she arrived it would be too late to eat with them.

She asked to speak to his mother and he passed the phone over, feeling gritty disappointment that he would not see his wife.

"Does she cancel like this often?" he asked after his mother flipped shut his mobile phone.

"Not at all, though I'm not surprised. If Theo needed her, she would not leave him. Eden has always been an exemplary mother and wife," his mother said with heavy-handed intimation.

"Has she?" he asked with bitter irony.

"What are you implying?" Sebastian demanded.

"If she was so wonderful, why did I forget her?"

Sebastian shook his head, clearly shocked by the question. "You were in a car accident…you had a concussion. That is excuse enough."

"Is it?"

"Oh, my heavens…you haven't voiced these suspicions to Eden, have you? That would devastate her," Rachel said, sounding worried.

Aristide thought silence the best defense at the moment.

His mother gave him a shrewd look and then shook her head. "You fool."

The condemnation was so aggravating, coming from his doting mother, that he turned on her. "You are the one who told me my marriage was not all it should be."

"But I never said it was Eden's fault."

"You thought it was mine?" he asked in total shock.

"Well…yes. I thought you took your wife for granted, that

you were naïvely certain her feelings for you would never change despite your neglect."

"I neglected her?" he demanded, one of his infernal headaches starting.

"Well, perhaps neglect is too strong a word, but you lived apart quite a bit. *By your choice*," she emphasized.

"Did you ever think that was because she was hard to live with?"

His entire family stared at him as if he'd lost his mind. Maybe he had. Maybe that is what losing one's memories did to one.

"Are you serious?" Sebastian demanded. "The only sweeter woman on the face of this earth than your wife is mine. Eden loves you so much, I almost pity her at times."

"Why the hell would you pity my wife?" Aristide asked in a near roar.

"Because she so obviously wanted to be with you and you seemed totally oblivious to how much your absences hurt her."

"Did you ever tell me this?"

"I tried." If looks could shrink a man, Sebastian's gaze would have turned Aristide into a Lilliputian. "You would not listen."

His mother was shaking her head at Aristide. "You are an idiot, my son. I am sorry to say it, but it is true. I thought you were smarter than your brother when you never doubted the parentage of your baby and married Eden right away." Sebastian grunted at this. "But I must say you are making up for that small act of wisdom with colossal stupidity now."

Lunch went downhill from there and by the time he got back to his office, Aristide felt attacked from all sides and his head hurt like someone was squeezing it in a vise.

Eden wandered down the hall of the spacious villa, feeling lost and disoriented. She was completely alone for the first time since discovering Aristide had forgotten her.

Phillippa and Vincent had left that afternoon and, because she and Aristide had planned to eat out tonight, the staff had the evening off. Theo was over at his Uncle Sebastian and Aunt Rachel's. When Eden had called to cancel their plans, Rachel had asked to have the baby anyway.

Her children had been looking forward to playing with their little cousin all week and were not at an age that they understood the changes wrought by their uncle's amnesia. Heck, she was a grown-up and she was struggling with comprehension.

She'd been clinging to her son since coming out of the hospital, needing the connection when everything had gone so terribly wrong with his father. Only it wasn't fair to the baby to keep him with her when he could be with his cousins having fun, so she'd let him go.

Without really understanding why she did it, she drifted into Aristide's room. There was nothing for her here. Just a tastefully decorated, tidy room that now housed her husband when once he had shared the master suite with her. The room's immaculate condition did not surprise her, but the sense of desolation that swept over her when she stopped beside the bed he now slept in did.

Emotions she had been holding in check since the accident fought to break free of the restraints she'd placed on them.

She shook her head against them, dropping to her knees beside the bed. His scent was there, on the carefully smoothed duvet, and she moaned as an ache that was both physical and soul-bruising slammed into her.

She'd tried to avoid physical proximity since his return from New York and moving into another bedroom. She refused to humiliate herself by letting him see how much she craved the comfort of his body. And she was afraid that if she let herself get too close, she would whimper like a pathetic, lost puppy, seeking her master's touch.

He still desired her. His telling her he wanted her had been proof of that, but climb down that it was from his position of separate beds, it had been hardly flattering.

So, he wanted to have sex with her. *That didn't mean anything.*

He still put Kassandra's feelings ahead of Eden's. Even if he didn't remember her, he knew she was his wife and she should be his first priority. A harsh bark of laughter erupted from her throat. What a joke that was.

Even when he'd remembered her, he hadn't put her first. She'd been a sexual convenience when they were dating, one he picked up and put down depending on his traveling schedule. At the time, she'd thought they had something special… just because he made an effort to spend time with her outside of bed. What a sap she'd been.

Their marriage had elevated her status in the eyes of others, but not his…she saw that now. Could not help seeing it. Even as the mother of his son, she'd only carried so much pull.

A whisper in the back of her mind tried to say it hadn't been that bad, but the pain roaring through her drowned it out.

She hit the bed with her fist, wishing it was him. His willingness to cancel their dinner in favor of sharing one with his assistant was the final straw. Okay…so he didn't know that it was a special night, but he did know he'd made a commitment to spend it with her and he'd broken that commitment.

Eden hit the bed again and then collapsed on the floor in a fetal ball. She was worse than a forgotten wife; she was the despised wife—unimportant to Aristide in any way. He didn't even need her physically, not like she needed him. He might want her, but he was surviving celibacy just fine.

He didn't lay in bed night after empty night, longing for her presence, wishing for warmth that was never there.

Misery clenched her insides as tears burned her eyes. She

couldn't fight it anymore and she stopped trying to. For once, it wasn't necessary. Everyone was gone and she was alone. She could cry out her grief without scaring her baby or having to explain herself to anyone.

She'd put on the brave front for Aristide's family, not wanting them to know how much his daily indifference hurt her. Not only for the sake of her pride, but for the sake of how they saw him. She'd even glossed over her emotional turmoil to her father when he called, wanting to know how she was doing now that she was back in Greece.

She refused to hurt her family by marriage and didn't trust her own father to understand or really care, so she'd carried the burden of grief alone. But it was too heavy and something inside her snapped under its weight.

She could hear her own racking sobs, but it was as if they were coming from someone else. She beat her fists against the floor over and over again until the sides of her hands were numb. It wasn't fair. She loved him. He didn't love her. She knew it. Wasn't that bad enough?

Why did she have to deal with the pain of being forgotten on top of it? Why? Her chest hurt from the violence of her tears and she didn't care. She lurched up and back on her heels screaming out, "Why? Why? *Why?*" between wrenching sobs.

She fell forward again, but something stopped her.

"Eden!" Aristide's hands were on her shoulders, their grip tight. "What is the matter?"

She shook her head and tried to pull away from him, unable to stand his touch. He wouldn't let go and she found herself pulled into his lap right there on the floor, his strong fingers pressing her face up so he could look in her eyes. "You must calm down, this kind of crying will make you sick."

"I—I…c-can't stop," she forced out between sobs.

"Yes, you can, baby. Hush," he soothed.

But she would not be comforted…he had called her baby again, a reminder she was not his wife…not really…not anymore. And that hurt so much, she would have doubled over with the pain of it if he had not been holding her so securely. An anguish-filled moan snaked out of her throat and her weeping increased.

He swore and started rubbing her back, talking to her in a gentle tone that barely penetrated her agonized mind. Eventually, however, a startling reality did manage to pierce her out-of-control grief—*Aristide was here with her, not at the dinner with Kassandra*. With a monumental effort, she forced herself to swallow back her sobs.

Hugging herself, she tried to keep her body from shuddering with more tears. "Y-you c-came h-home."

"I wanted to see Theo before he went to bed. Dinner is at seven-thirty." Aristide ruefully looked down at the tear splotches on his silk necktie. "It's a good thing I was already planning to change my suit."

The hope drained out of her. He had not come home for her…not even to see her before leaving again. He'd come for the baby. "He's not here," she said dully, too drained to even try to get off of his lap.

Aristide frowned, as if her tone bothered him. "Where is he?"

"At your brother's. It was already arranged and I didn't want to disappoint Rachel's children."

He nodded as if he understood that. "The staff are all gone too."

"They had the night off."

"Because of our dinner plans?"

"Yes."

His blue eyes filled with sensual speculation. "Presumably orchestrated so we would have privacy upon our return."

She just stared at him.

"Is that why you were crying? Because I had rescheduled our dinner?" he asked, sounding like he couldn't believe such a trivial matter could elicit her grief-stricken response.

"It doesn't matter."

It was his turn to simply look at her, his gentian blue gaze locked with hers for an eternity of seconds. "It will be all right, Eden."

She shook her head, the tears starting again, no matter how much she wanted to hold them back. "It won't be all right, not ever again. How can it be?"

He had married her for the sake of their unborn child—now, would she stay married to him for the sake of both Theo and the unborn child he had forgotten even existed? No joy there. No hope of a future happiness, just years stretching ahead loving a man who didn't even remember making her his wife.

"You have to trust me."

"Trust you?" she asked, the concept unbelievable in her current circumstances. "You're just like my dad. I didn't see it at first, but that's because I was blinded by my own love for you." She gave a brittle laugh. "Like mother, like daughter."

"What do you mean?"

"Dad hurt my mom because he didn't really care about her either. Oh, he took care of her when she had cancer…much like you make sure I have everything I need, I suppose. And he acted grief-stricken when she died, but if he had really loved her, he couldn't have continued having affairs like he did."

"I am not having an affair," Aristide ground out.

"But you will keep hurting me until there isn't anything left."

"You have drawn this conclusion because I rescheduled one dinner date?" he asked with disbelief.

"I came to this conclusion because it is our reality!" She hated that he couldn't remember, that he looked at her now with incredulity. "I made a really big mistake getting involved with you to begin with, but I compounded it by marrying you."

And there was no way out…but how *could* she stay married to a man programmed to hurt her because he could not love her?

She started crying again, collapsing against his chest from a pain too intense to be borne. He did not try to calm her down this time, but silently held her, as if he understood this awful pain inside of her and her need to get it out. He couldn't possibly, but knowing that didn't seem to matter. His arms were a strong haven in a world she had stopped being able to tolerate and she desperately needed him to hold her.

She wept until there were no tears left and her throat was raw from her hoarse sobs. Even after she quieted, he held her. His silence helped her calm down better than any empty words could have done. She didn't know how long her crying jag had lasted, but she felt utterly drained of emotion.

Eventually, she stirred. "I've soaked your shirt." She spoke against his chest, unwilling to look into his face.

"As I said, I planned to change." He sounded curiously subdued.

Perhaps having a hysterical wife that he couldn't remember crying all over him was too much for even Aristide's strong constitution.

Feeling uncomfortable in his embrace now that she had calmed down, she went to move off of his lap. "I guess you'd better get to it then."

"Not yet." His arms tightened around her so she could not move. "Tell me why you were crying."

She couldn't believe he couldn't understand. "Is it just you, or are all tycoons this dense when it comes to emotions?"

"I am not *dense*."

"As a London fog…oh, yes, you are."

"Why do you say that?"

"You asked me why I was crying." She sighed and let herself rest against him, too spent to fight or hide her peace at the contact.

He would push her away all too soon and she could go back to being a pregnant island in the hurricane of her life.

"And for this you believe I am stupid?"

"Yes."

He laughed harshly, the sound reverberating through her pliant body. "Were you always this unimpressed with me?"

"That's why I was crying."

"Because you think I am stupid and you are worried about the impact that will have on our son?" he teased, though his body was too tense for the words to come off as lighthearted as he obviously intended.

"Because you don't know how I felt before…because you forgot me. It was the final straw in a marriage that should never have happened to begin with."

The words hung between them for several seconds in utter silence. She could hear her heart beating, or was that his?

CHAPTER NINE

"I am sorry."

"Why? You're convinced I deserved it."

"No, I am not."

She wasn't buying it. He just didn't want her to start crying again. "Look, you'd better let me up. You've got things to do and so do I."

"What do you have to do?"

"Go dry off."

He laughed again; this time the sound was a little more natural. "I think we could both use a towel."

"Like you said, it's a good thing you planned on changing anyway. And speaking of…" she said, reminding him of his dinner engagement.

"You are making a habit of trying to send me away," he teased, making obvious reference to that morning as well.

Incapable of sharing his humor, she said sadly, "Usually, you are content to go."

He sighed as if acknowledging her mood. "Why did you not join Sebastian and Rachel this evening?"

"You're so sure they invited me?"

"Yes."

"That's quite an admission."

"What do you mean?"

"Well, that would imply that they like me a whole lot more than you do…which might mean you were wrong in your assessment of my character, wouldn't you say?"

"I have not said I do not like you…merely that I do not know you and am wary of our reasons for marrying."

He was slick at wiggling out of a tight spot, but she just shrugged. "If you say so."

"You did not answer my initial question."

And he wasn't going to let up until she did. "I didn't go with Theo to their house because I didn't feel like being around company tonight, all right?"

"You preferred to stay home and cry a river?"

"Something like that." She hadn't planned on the tears, but after all she'd been through recently, they were pretty much inevitable.

"I do not like seeing you cry." He sounded disgruntled by the admission.

"Don't let it worry you. It doesn't mean I'm anything special to you. You don't like seeing *any* woman cry."

"You are my wife. That is pretty special."

"You married me because I was pregnant with your son. That doesn't make me special, it only means I'm fertile."

"How can you make me laugh when my brain is telling me tragedy surrounds you like a shield?"

She shrugged. "Call it a gift."

He rubbed the top of her head with his chin, his arms wrapped tightly around her as if he could protect her from her pain. "I can't leave you like this."

"Sure you can."

"Do not tell me I have done so before."

"I'm not much of a cry baby."

"Which neatly sidesteps my question."

"I wasn't aware you asked a question. You made a statement. I didn't rebut it. You should be feeling vindicated in making it."

"Then why do I not?"

"I don't know."

"My family raked me over the coals at lunch today."

"Why?"

"Taking you for granted."

"They don't understand our marriage." And why she was making excuses for him when she agreed with his family, she didn't know.

He just sounded so bewildered by his family's censure. He wasn't used to it, that was for sure. She was pretty surprised herself. She'd never witnessed Sebastian, much less Phillippa, taking Aristide to task for anything.

"What is different about our marriage and that of my brother and his wife?"

"They love each other."

"And we do not?"

"I already told you that you don't love me."

"I told you this?"

"Not in so many words."

"I want you to stop being sad."

"I don't know if I can."

"Why?"

"Rejection isn't an easy thing to overcome. You, never having been the recipient of it, don't know that, but to put it delicately…it sucks."

He laughed again, the sound not exactly one of humor. "Are you saying I rejected you?"

"You forgot me. Isn't that the same thing?"

"No. As Sebastian reminded me today, I suffered a concussion…looking further for the cause of my amnesia is foolish."

"You don't want to sleep with me anymore."

"That is not true. I told you last night."

"But you don't need *me*."

"I do."

He meant physically, but her battered heart would take comfort where it could.

"You don't stay awake at night aching—" She cut herself off, but not before she had revealed more than she wanted to.

"Do you?"

"If I say yes, will your Greek pride be satisfied?"

"If I tell you that you are wrong, that you are not the only one who aches with a need that is not wholly physical, will your feminine pride be gratified?"

Not wholly physical? Did he mean it? "Are you saying that?"

"Yes, I am. And you?"

"Yes."

He tipped her chin up and pressed a soft, claiming kiss to her lips. "If I cancelled my dinner…if I stayed home and made love to my wife tonight, would you like that? Would you allow it?"

"Your dinner is too important…"

He pressed his finger against her lips. "No, Eden, it is not. I do not pretend to understand why our dinner date meant so much to you, but I hurt you when I broke it and I am sorry."

"It's the anniversary of the night we met."

Aristide heard the words without them registering at first. Kassandra had said she thought the dinner date with Eden was no big deal. He had believed her, trusting his long-time friend and personal assistant to know.

"You always contrived to make it a very special evening and canceling just reminded me how much we have lost." She made it sound like they were on the brink of divorce.

He wasn't going there. "You are still my wife."

But even if he was as dense in the emotional department as she had accused him of being, he was in tune with her enough to realize she wasn't looking at their marriage as an uncontested permanent part of her life.

He kissed her again, this time with all the hunger in his predator's soul. He could taste her tears and that did something to him, twisting his insides with unfamiliar pain. This woman was his wife and she was wrong about what that meant. *It did make her special.*

He kissed her until they were both breathing heavily, until she moaned with need and he ached with it.

He stood up with her in his arms and then carried her into their bedroom.

He laid her down in the center of their bed. "This is where we both belong."

She said nothing.

"I will not be leaving it again and neither will you."

"Are you sure about that?"

"Absolutely sure."

"Okay, then." She arched her back, the invitation to touch unmistakable.

He groaned, his sex so hard already, he thought he might explode before he got his clothes off. He tore out of his suit, ripping his soggy tie and shirt off with more impatience than finesse.

"You're certainly in a hurry," she said softly, the feminine laughter in her voice seducing his senses.

"I do not want you to change your mind." He said it jokingly, but part of him was very serious.

When she had turned him down the night before, he had felt a desperation he had not understood and liked even less.

She shook her head from side to side, her hair spreading out around her head like a silky brown halo. "Not a chance."

"That is good to know."

She smiled, Eve bent on seduction. "Take off your pants."
The look in her eyes said this wasn't the first time she'd made
such an order and he knew, from the response of his body, he'd
liked it when she'd done so before.

She was not an aggressive woman, so for her to make sexual demands would be the most erotic form of lovemaking.

He stepped out of his shoes, before toeing off his socks.
Then peeling his slacks away, he pushed his boxers down with
them. He stood completely naked before her, his body throbbing with the need to join with hers.

She stared at him, her chest rising and falling with shal-
low pants. Her pretty gray eyes were so dark with passion they
were almost black as her gaze moved over him like a hot caress. "You are so beautiful, Aristide."

He felt a twinge in the region of his heart. No other woman
had ever called him that. Sexy, yes. Masculine. Buff, even, but
never beautiful. He liked it, though he would never admit it
out loud.

She kicked her shoes off, but when she went to pull her
shirt off, he shook his head. "Stop."

Stilling, her eyes wide, she asked, "Why?"

"I want to unwrap you like a present."

She swallowed and hope flared in her eyes, making them
shine with silver lights. "You used to say that to me all the
time."

He didn't want to think about before, the time he couldn't
remember. He only wanted to think about now. In a rush that
made her gasp, he came down over her. His entire being jolted
with pleasure as they made contact. The layer of her clothes
could have been gone for all the notice his body took of the
barrier.

"Aristide…what is it?" she asked, her voice catching as he

settled himself between her legs and rubbed the apex of her thighs with his iron-hard sex.

"No more talking," he growled and then devoured her lips with his own, his kiss primal and hungry, demanding a response.

When she opened her lips on a small moan, he swept inside, claiming the warm wetness as his. He could not remember making this woman his own, but tonight she would know without doubt she belonged to him in the most primitive and binding way a woman could belong to a man.

She locked her legs behind his hips and arched into him.

He shuddered with pleasure and could not help pressing down, increasing the friction—though it undermined his control.

She felt so small beneath him and yet so womanly, more tantalizing than any woman had ever been. Her tiny curves drove him to madness and he cupped her breast, glorying when her nipple peaked instantly. He did not have to remember to get her to react to his touch…to be a husband in every sense of the word.

He played with the rigid bud through her top, realizing immediately that she was not wearing a bra. The knowledge made him desperate to touch the bare skin he knew waited for him under the cotton of her snug-fitting T-shirt.

Aristide's hand slipped under the hem of her top and glided up her ribcage, the light touch of his fingertips against her skin giving Eden chills. He stopped below the curve of her breast, his thumb brushing back and forth in a teasing caress that made her whimper into his mouth with need.

She ached for him to touch her breasts the way he'd touched them so many times before.

But would it be like it had been before? Or would it be different because she was a stranger to him?

It didn't matter. She remembered him and wanted him. She needed this confirmation of her importance to him. His hand made contact with her breast and her thoughts exploded in a maelstrom of feeling. The caress was familiar and yet it wasn't. It had a tentative quality that hadn't been there since the first time they made love, as if he was trying to figure out what pleased her.

She could have told him it didn't matter. He had never touched her in a way that did not wring pleasure from her. But she was too busy kissing him to say anything, not to mention too busy reveling in the deep concentration he gave to the task.

He played with her breasts, squeezing them and then teasing their rigid peaks with knowing fingers. He didn't know she was pregnant and yet he instinctively did not press too hard on her ultra-sensitive skin. He was good at this, an expert.

She started to moan and thrash under him, finally tearing her mouth from his to beg for more.

But it was still several minutes of teasing foreplay before he began unwrapping her like a present as promised. Would he notice she was pregnant? She barely showed a difference in her waistline and he didn't remember what she'd looked like before, but the thought was tantalizing. To have all the secrets revealed, to be able to share her pregnancy with her husband.

He touched her in a way that sent all thoughts in her head exploding into space. He kissed every inch of skin he exposed, starting with her feet and then paying close attention to her already highly stimulated curves. He laved the turgid peaks like an ice-cream cone and she shivered with delight.

He growled against her skin, the sound so animal-like she shivered again…this time an atavistic fear mixed with her sensual pleasure.

He had left her panties on and slid his hand inside as if he knew she found this pseudo-secret touch highly erotic.

Maybe he did. Maybe part of him was trying to remember. Her insides melted at the thought. Wanting desperately for it to be the way it had been before, she responded to him with all the trust and joy she had ever given him and prayed that this time of intimacy would restore their marriage in more ways than one.

It wasn't hard to pretend she was as important to him as she needed to be, not when for the first time in their married life, he'd opted out of his business dinner to stay home and make love with her.

Even as she had the thought, his cell phone started ringing.

He reared back, saying a harsh Greek word she knew but had never used herself. "Give me thirty seconds, all right, *pethi mou*? Then we will be left in peace."

She bit her lip, hoping the interruption did not mean the end of their time of intimacy.

He cupped her cheek. "Trust me."

"Okay."

He smiled and then dove for the ringing phone still attached to the waistband of his trousers.

Forcing back her fear that Kassandra would get to him yet again, she sat up and watched his big, gorgeous body move. It was no hardship considering the excellent view she had of his very fine backside. He had muscles *everywhere*.

He flipped the phone open and turned to face her at the same time.

Noticing where her gaze had been directed, he grinned with masculine confidence and said, "Aristide here," into the phone.

"Where are you?" Kassandra was so agitated, Eden could hear her through the phone.

He looked down at himself and then at Eden with a droll expression. "Something has come up and I will have to forgo the dinner tonight."

Eden choked on her laughter at the *double entendre* and bit her fist to stop the sound from escaping her lips.

Aristide climbed back on the bed and leaned over Eden. She fell back into the pillows, mesmerized by the hot promises bombarding her from his blue eyes.

"I am sure you can handle it. You are my personal assistant for a reason."

He rubbed himself against Eden and she had to bite back a moan of delight as Kassandra said something else.

He went rigid. "Perhaps you have forgotten who the employer is in this relationship, but I do not require advice from you on how to order my priorities."

Eden stopped in the act of reaching up to kiss his flat male nipple and her gaze flew to his. She could just imagine how Kassandra would respond to the reprimand. The woman was a master manipulator.

Aristide shook his head as if he could read Eden's mind.

His mouth thinned in a frown and his eyes narrowed in obvious displeasure. "We will have to discuss that Monday morning, Kassandra. Until then, I am unavailable."

He switched off the phone, flipped it shut and tossed it on to the floor and then turned back to face her. "I think it is time I finished unwrapping my present."

Euphoria filled her. He'd dismissed his personal assistant for her. Not only that, he had turned off his phone. The last time he had done that she had been in labor with Theo.

Most importantly, *Aristide had stayed for her*.

Happy tears burned her eyes and she smiled. "I'd like that."

His brow creased and he brushed at a single tear that had escaped. "Is something wrong?"

"No, it's just so right, I can barely stand it."

"Ah…so, these are tears of happiness."

She nodded, her voice too choked to speak.

"I am glad." He slid down her body, his mouth wreaking havoc with her nervous system.

"Oh, Aristide…it's so perfect with you."

"It is you who are perfect. Perfectly shaped." He kissed each of her turgid peaks, nipping them and she gasped. "Perfectly responsive." He pressed his lips to each of her ribs and then slid his mouth along her hot skin to explore her belly button with his tongue. "Perfectly lovely. Ah…my Eden."

It wasn't *yineka mou*, but it was close, and she felt sure his memories were only a breath away as she arched helplessly against him.

When he used his teeth to effect the final unveiling, pulling her panties down her legs with sexy mastery, she just about fainted from the pleasure of it. And he wasn't even touching her most private flesh yet…

Then he spread her legs and kissed her with an intimacy she could only ever imagine sharing with this man.

She cried out as his tongue brought her to almost immediate fulfillment, her insides clenching with cataclysmic pleasure. He didn't stop, but kept pleasuring her until the ecstasy of his touch left her wrung out and limp.

Only then did he move up her body to press himself against the throbbing entrance to her feminine core. His eyes asked a question and she grabbed his hips, pulling him to complete his possession. It was a ritual as old as the very first time they made love…he always asked in some way for permission to enter her body and waited for her acquiescence.

Sometimes she used that wait to tease him until she thought he might take her without it, but he never did. He had more self-control than anyone she had ever known.

As he eased inside of her, she felt closer to him than she had in months and couldn't help crying out, *"I love you, Aristide."*

His mouth slammed down on hers as if taking possession of the words, the kiss so intense that she lost herself in it. He made love to her with driving passion until they came together in a hurricane of ecstasy.

Afterward, he rolled on to his back, keeping their bodies connected like he had so many times before. She settled her head against his chest, listening to his heartbeat and letting the precious intimacy soak into her every pore.

He took a deep breath and let it out. "That was amazing."

She couldn't help grinning against his chest. "Worth skipping your business dinner?"

"Definitely. And you…did it make this night special enough for you?"

"I would say that finding each other again is a very fitting way to celebrate our first meeting."

His arms tightened around her. "Was it this good before?"

She pushed up on to her forearms, tilting her head so they were eye to eye. "You don't remember?"

"No."

"But…"

"What?"

"You made love to me like you remembered. That wasn't the intimacy between strangers," she said helplessly.

He affected a small shrug under her as if it was of little importance. "Obviously, our bodies know each other."

Or he had made love to every woman before her like he did to her. She'd never considered the possibility before, having assumed that it was as special for him as it was for her. Her stomach churned with the possibility that what she took for tender intimacy was, in fact, well-developed technique.

"What is it? You are frowning."

"I thought if anything could jar your memory of me, it would be our lovemaking."

"Is that why you allowed me to touch you?" he asked, his voice no longer lazy and warm.

"No."

But something in her face must have given her away because he glared. "Tell me," he insisted.

"It was my plan when you came back from New York."

"So that was why you were upset I wanted to sleep in a separate bed. You hoped to bring back my memory with sex."

"That was part of it, yes."

If he'd gone rigid during his call with Kassandra, that was nothing compared to his reaction now. "And this..." He pressed her hips down with hard hands, deepening his entry in her body. "It was all just a test?"

"No." Horrified at his reaction, she shook her head vehemently. "We made love because we both needed to...didn't we?"

She'd told him she loved him. And like all the times she'd said the words before, he had not responded in kind. At the moment she'd said it, his lack of response had not bothered her, but now it stung like a thousand wasps attacking her heart.

He relaxed a little. "Yes, we both needed it."

But had he needed her, or only a body? She'd never stopped to consider how she would feel after making love to a man who did not know her. It wasn't good...even though they were married, even though she loved him, she felt shame because she couldn't be sure he'd been making love to her and not simply a body.

She pressed against his chest. "I need to get up now."

The last vestiges of his anger drained from his face and his eyes gleamed with sensual anticipation. "I am not finished."

"I am."

"Because I did not remember you?"

How could she answer that? "The simplistic answer is yes," she admitted, "but it's a lot more complicated than that."

"Explain it to me."

"Let me up."

Despite their near argument, he had never completely lost his arousal and now it was growing.

He tilted his pelvis up, sending shivers of sensation through her. "No. You want me. Your body betrays just how much with every tiny movement."

She couldn't deny it. Her nipples were hard and aching for his attention all over again and her most secret flesh was clinging to him with pulsing strength.

She said the only thing she could say…the only thing he might understand. "But you don't want me."

"Wrong."

"You don't. Not *me*," she said earnestly. "I could be any woman to you."

"But you are not *any* woman. You are my wife."

"You don't know me," she cried, frustration and hurt filling her.

"How well did I know you the first time we made love?"

She stopped trying to get away, her face heating with an instant blush. "We made love the first time on our second date."

His smile was triumphant. "Then I could not have known you any better then than I do now."

His logic left her speechless for several seconds. "It is not the same," she finally responded lamely.

"How is it different?"

"You wanted to know me then. You pursued me."

"Not very hard, if it was only our second date."

"I was an easy mark for you."

"You were and are the woman I want." He proved it by surging up into her, fully aroused and ready to make love again.

She averted her face. "I never intended to make love with a man who was not my husband."

"And yet you were my lover for over a year before we married."

"Yes," she whispered, the lingering disappointment in herself in her voice.

He tilted her chin toward her. "You knew that was the longest relationship I had ever had with a woman?"

"I wasn't even sure we had a relationship. You never introduced me to your family."

"I wanted to keep you to myself."

"How do you know?" she asked deridingly. "You don't remember."

"But as I have told you, I know myself. I know what would have motivated me in the situation you describe."

"I believed it was because I was not important to you."

"The fact you are now my wife proves that was not the case."

She refused to remind him again that he had married her for the sake of their unborn son. He seemed to forget it and she only wished she could.

Despite the physical response of her body to their continued intimacy, she felt numb inside as she realized the one hope she had to reclaim her marriage was gone.

"We have talked enough."

"Yes, I suppose we have."

Ignoring her melancholy, he began the seduction all over again. She had no defense against him and didn't want any. At least if they made love she would not feel this awful inner frozenness that seemed to be spreading from her heart outward.

CHAPTER TEN

Eden was sitting on the floor, her back to him and playing with Theo the next afternoon when Aristide walked into the large living room. She'd pulled her silky brown hair up into a casual ponytail that revealed the delicate column of her neck. The snug-fitting cotton top and jeans she wore only served to remind him of the night before and how much pleasure he had found in her delicious body.

His own tightened with need at the memory.

But, damn it, it had been more than a slaking of lust…she'd been right. They had not made love like strangers, so why did he feel more like one with her today than he had before returning to her bed?

"So you are back from shopping," he said.

She'd left that morning, refusing his offer to accompany her on the pretext she needed to buy his Christmas gift.

"Yes," she replied without turning.

"You have been home long?"

"Not really." Long enough to change her clothes and collect their son from the nursery.

She had not sought out Aristide upon her return, but there was no surprise there. She'd been like this since they got up that morning—even more distant from him than she had been

since his return from New York. It was as if she had completely cut herself off emotionally from him and after their
lovemaking, that was not an attitude he could live with.

"I have made dinner reservations for tonight." He had
called the restaurant, figuring she must like the place if they
had planned to eat there originally.

It had been a long time since he had done something so
mundane, but he doubted she would appreciate that fact.

She looked over her shoulder at him and smiled vacantly,
then turned back their son, her smile for Theo much more natural. She tickled his tummy, talking in baby talk to him.

"Did you hear me?"

She stiffened, but then seemed to force herself to relax. "Yes,
but it's not necessary. As you said the other day, we hardly have
a normal relationship. A date would be superfluous."

"I do not agree."

She shrugged and he saw red. She hadn't even spoken and
he was ready to blow his top. No woman got to him like
this...hell, no person got to him like this.

He took a firm grip on his unreasonable temper. "I think
we need to get to know each other."

"I already know you."

"Then I need to get to know you," he said from between gritted teeth. When she did not respond, he said, "We must accept
that my memory may never come back and plan accordingly."

Her body jerked in reaction to his words, but that was the
only response he got.

"I know it must hurt you to hear I may never remember
you," he said, feeling more hesitant than he ever had, "but it
has to be acknowledged."

Gurgled laughter erupted from his son's throat, startling
Aristide. The baby had grabbed one of his toys scattered on
the floor and begun playing with it. It was a jack-in-the-box

and Theo had mastered turning the handle until the clown popped out. The childish music filled the silence that felt like an oppressive weight around them.

Finally, Eden turned to face Aristide, her expression stoic. "So you want to get to know me and decide if I'm worthy of being your wife."

"I did not say that."

"Then, what is the purpose?"

"Is it so hard for you to understand me wishing to get to know my wife?"

"We don't need to go out on dates for you to do that. You can do so just as well here…when you are home."

"I want to take you out," he ground out, annoyed by the reminder of his many absences.

He intended to change that, but didn't make the mistake of telling her so. She was in no mood to take anything he said at face value.

She sighed. "You don't have to court me all over again. I'm already your wife."

"It does not sound like there was much of a courtship the first time around."

She flinched and he cursed his quick tongue.

"Whatever you call our relationship before, it's done and we're married. To coin one of your own phrases, dating now would be nonproductive."

"I do not agree."

She rolled her eyes. "Why is it such a big deal to you?"

"Why are you fighting it so hard?"

"Maybe I've finally decided to accept the status quo of our marriage."

For some reason, that sent a cold chill up his spine. "And maybe *I have not*."

"Why not?" she asked, the ice finally cracking to give him

a glimpse of the hurting woman beneath the brittle façade. "You've got everything a man like you wants out of marriage. A faithful wife who will provide you with children and warm your bed when you want it. It's all you ever wanted from me and I've finally accepted that, all right?"

Her voice was choked with tears, but she didn't let them fall. "You can keep right on working your terrible hours, traveling half the time and spending more after-office hours with your personal assistant than your wife."

He didn't know how to rebut her words without memories to back up his claims, so he said the one thing she could not deny. "As of Monday morning, I will no longer have a personal assistant."

Eden went paper-white and swayed.

He dropped to his knee beside her and grabbed her shoulders. "Are you all right?"

"Did you just say that Kassandra quit?" she asked in a frail and disbelieving voice.

"No."

Her eyes closed as if in pain. "I didn't think it could be—"

"I plan to fire her," he said before she could go on.

Eden's eyes flew open and she stared at him with a hope that hurt him to see. "Say that again."

"I will be firing Kassandra the first thing Monday morning."

"But you can't," she whispered, her voice thready.

Her reaction categorically told him his decision had been the right one. "I assure you, I can."

"But why would you?"

"She told me that last night was nothing more than a regular dinner date that you would not mind canceling."

"She was wrong, but I hardly see how that would lead you to fire her."

"As my personal assistant, there is no way she could be unaware of such a significant date. When I realized this, I had to ask myself what other lies she had told me about you. The more I thought about it, the more I realized there have been many. Since she seems to be the only person who believes you are anything like Andrea Demakis, it follows she lied about that as well."

He did not know why he had forgotten his lovely wife, but if she was the wife from Hades, he was Santa Claus.

Eden swallowed, blinking back more tears. "She was trying to destroy our marriage."

He could not doubt her view of events. Nothing else made sense in the circumstances. "For a long time?" he asked.

"Since the beginning."

"Why?"

"She wants you."

"I do not want her."

Eden looked unconvinced.

He could not fault her for that. He had taken Kassandra's part on more than one occasion since he woke from his coma. He did not know how to explain to Eden the vulnerability he had felt in a world where everyone around him knew a piece of the puzzle that remained a mystery to him…his wife. He had relied on a woman he thought he knew and could trust.

"I am sorry I let her influence me and hurt you."

"You believed she was your friend."

"Only she wanted more than friendship."

"According to her, you had it."

"Once…we had a very short affair about three years ago."

"Right around when we met."

"I broke it off. If it was before or after we met, I do not know, but I do know that I would not sleep with two women at the same time."

His wife nodded, though doubt still haunted her soft

gray eyes. "I'll talk to Rachel about leaving Theo with her for our date."

Relief that was out of proportion to her acceptance surged through him. "Surely we have someone who can watch him here."

"I prefer family and so does Rachel…it's worked out well for us in the past."

"You are saying you rarely leave Theo." He smiled, thoroughly approving.

"That's not what I was saying, but it is true."

"Sebastian told me that the trip to New York was the first one you accompanied me on. Was that your decision, or mine?"

"Yours."

His jaw clenched. That is what he had thought from everything that had been said, but he had to be sure. "I see. And you did not mind?"

She turned her head away. "I would rather not answer that."

"Why not?" Damn it, there was so much he did not know.

"It may not have occurred to you, but there is a lot of humiliation for me in our current situation."

"Why should you be humiliated?"

"You're brilliant…everyone says so. You figure it out."

Just then Theo demanded her attention by grabbing her shirt and lifting himself to stand in front of her.

She turned back to their baby. "You're going to be walking soon, aren't you?" she asked with a smile and her heart full of love for her beautiful son.

Frustrated by the interruption, but glad for the progress that had been made, Aristide said, "If he does, heaven help us."

She laughed, the sound not quite natural. "He is one energetic little bundle."

Remembering what it had been like at his brother's that morning when he had gone to pick up Theo, he said, "I cannot imagine having two like Sebastian and Rachel do. Not yet, anyway."

She went all stiff again. "You always said you wanted a half-dozen children."

"Spaced appropriately apart, it is my fondest wish."

Eden put her earrings on with trembling fingers. It took three tries to get the diamond teardrops in place. She was going on a date with her husband and more nervous than a teenager going to her first prom.

He was going to fire Kassandra.

She couldn't take it in. When Eden had criticized his P.A. in New York before he lost his memory, he had staunchly stood up for the other woman. Now, without any prompting from Eden, he was suddenly willing to give Kassandra the heave-ho…all because she had lied and Aristide realized it.

He had no memory of the importance of their anniversary dinner date, but he'd reasoned that Kassandra would. Eden smiled. He really did have a brilliant brain, even if he couldn't figure out why it would bother her to expose the depth of her feeling in contrast to his.

She wished she knew if he was getting rid of the other woman because she had hurt Eden, or because a liar could not be trusted. Eden hoped it was at least a little bit of the former.

Regardless, the wicked witch was being banished and Aristide showed every evidence of truly wanting to make their marriage work. Eden had not been able to accomplish so much in over a year of marriage.

She felt like dancing around the room in celebration.

Okay, so there was a strong possibility that Kassandra would talk her way out of being fired. The woman was a master at circumventing Aristide's good intentions, but Eden didn't want to dwell on that unpleasant possibility. Her husband was too smart to go on being taken in by his personal assistant, no matter how good a liar she was.

Eden went back to her preparations, but a sudden thought froze her in the act of applying a light coat of mascara. If he remembered her and their past together, would he go back to being the way he'd been before the accident? Would their marriage once again take a backseat to his business?

She would rather she remained the forgotten wife than have that happen.

Aristide took her to their favorite restaurant and regardless of how he had discovered which one it was, she appreciated the effort.

She smiled at him as they were seated at their usual table. "Thank you for bringing me here."

"Does it have special memories?" For once the reminder of his selective amnesia did not hurt.

"Yes. The man who owns it has a brother who migrated to New York. We ate at his restaurant on our first date and many times after. You brought me here the first time to celebrate seeing our baby through ultrasound. When you told me the relationship to the other restaurant, I cried like an idiot."

His sexy blue gaze melted her. "I bet I loved it."

She laughed. "As a matter of fact, you did. You hate unhappy tears, but seem to get a very perverse pleasure out of making me cry for sentimental reasons."

He reached across the table and took her hand. "Maybe I just like making you happy."

"Then why did you leave me behind when you traveled?" she asked in a voice laced with remembered hurt, then felt instant guilt.

No way could he know the answer to that one. If she didn't

watch out, she was going to ruin the present with pain from the past.

But he didn't look upset by her question. His face wore its usual expression of casual self-assurance. "I do not know. When we were in New York, you said you did not think I was ready for marriage and perhaps you were right. However, I am content to be married now."

"Does that mean you won't travel so much?"

"I have no desire to be separated from you and Theo for long periods of time."

Which wasn't a direct answer, but was a whole lot more promising than his former attitude. Only, how could he be content to be married now when he had been so intent on maintaining emotional independence before? He barely knew her...so what was the difference? Had there been something about her that he had been unable to connect to on an intimate level before? More importantly, would he rediscover that something the more time they spent together now?

"Suddenly you look terrified, *yineka mou*. Tell me what is frightening you. I do not think it is the prospect of spending more time with me," he said with teasing confidence.

"You called me *your woman*."

"*My wife, my woman*...you are both of these things, are you not?"

"Yes, but you said before that I didn't feel that way to you. That you did not feel like a husband."

"We made love," he said as if that should explain it all—and maybe for him, it did.

Men could be so basic and, for all his sophistication, Aristide had a primitive streak in his character a mile wide.

His thumb brushed her palm and he smiled with predatory intent. "Do not think you will sidetrack me from my question. What had you looking so afraid?"

She bit her lip, thoroughly seduced by this man who had showed more interest in her emotional condition in two days than he had the entire time they had been lovers and then married. "What if you change?"

"Why should I?"

When she told him her reasoning, he frowned. "I know you a lot better than you think I do. Whatever prompted my behavior before, it was not a flaw in your character I am yet to find."

"How can you be sure?"

"Because I have spent every day since waking from my coma trying to find flaws in you that are not there. All I have found is a woman I was smart to make my own and then marry."

His wording was odd, but then she realized with his primal view of sex, he probably considered her his from the moment they became lovers.

"I will not change my mind about you."

She hoped he was right because her heart would shrivel up and die if their marriage went back to being what it had been. It was an incredible thought considering how much she had wanted that very thing only twenty-four hours ago, but the kind of relationship he seemed to be offering now was everything her dreams were made of.

But if he was right and there was a chance he wasn't going to regain his memory, shouldn't she tell him about the baby? She knew she couldn't. And secretly she didn't want to. She wanted to know this time that he was staying with her for her own sake. She needed that assurance.

Besides, this time she doubted he would be as delighted with her pregnancy as he had been the first time. She was fairly certain he would not consider a year and a half *proper spacing*.

On the other hand, could she hold him accountable for a

throwaway remark made with no knowledge of his impending second time at fatherhood? He loved being a daddy and she doubted even his image of the perfectly spaced family could diminish his enthusiasm for the role a second time around.

She hoped.

Regardless, it was simply something she refused to bring into the equation of their marriage right now.

When the roses Aristide had ordered were delivered to their table, Eden gasped and then gaped when she saw the jeweler's box nestled in the center of the arrangement.

"Open it," he instructed.

Her hand trembled as she lifted the small black velvet box from the foliage and it was all he could do not to pull her around the table and into his arms. She was so damned vulnerable. Had he realized that before, or had she been better at hiding it?

She snapped the ring box open and gasped again, the sound almost a sob. "It's beautiful."

He had the anniversary ring delivered earlier that day while she'd been out shopping and then sent it to the florist to include in the bouquet.

He did not know what he had originally planned to give Eden to celebrate the anniversary of when they first met. He had searched through his diary to no avail. Kassandra probably knew, but he did not trust her to tell him the truth about it. More likely she would have encouraged him to get something that would cause Eden further pain or some level of embarrassment.

He did not know what caused a woman he had trusted as close as family to turn on his wife, but he was convinced Eden had not provoked it.

"Does it fit?" The jeweler had taken a guess based on the size of her ring finger.

She slipped the diamond anniversary band on and nodded, her lips quivering suspiciously.

"Do not start crying again."

"It comes with the territory right now."

He supposed she meant living through the trauma of being forgotten by her husband, but those were happy tears if he'd ever seen any.

She stretched her hand out to admire the ring, her rain-water eyes glistening. "It's really gorgeous."

"Not half as gorgeous as the woman wearing it, *yineka mou*."

Her gaze flew to his and something hit him straight in the gut. She had said he didn't need to court her again…that they were already married, but he realized he *wanted* to court her. He wanted her to feel good about being married to him, not stuck with a man who could not remember the first time they had met, much less made love.

His pride demanded it, but so did something powerful in the region of his heart.

Aristide pulled Eden into his arms to dance with a strong feeling of relief. He had wanted to hold her since looking across the table and seeing the vulnerable expression in her lovely gray eyes.

They had talked throughout dinner and she had shown a surprising understanding of business. She'd explained that she had worked for her father, an American business tycoon, before moving away from New York City to pursue her real loves…art and history. Apparently, she had been an assistant curator for a small museum in upstate New York when they met.

The job fit her and he wondered if she missed it, but when he asked her, she said she really loved full-time motherhood and her volunteer work with an Athens-based museum society fed her interest.

The more he learned of her, the more he realized his wife was a very special and precious woman.

Not to mention sexy. She felt so good against him—too good—and his body had a predictable response he made no effort to hide from her.

"We'd better stay out here a long time if you don't want to be embarrassed exiting the dance floor," she teased in a husky voice against his chest.

Instead of pulling away, as he'd half-expected from his rather shy wife, she snuggled up against him.

The feel of her soft stomach pressing against his hard flesh tormented him and increased his arousal tenfold. "We may not make it off the dance floor at all if you keep that up."

Her husky laughter sent jolts of pleasure zinging through him and it took all his self-control not to carry her off the dance floor and to some private spot to make love. This woman could seduce him with a look. Was the knowledge of that power what had made him hold himself apart from her?

It had certainly contributed to his wariness since the accident. It could very well be the source of the sense of foreboding he had had surrounding his marriage. Considering his family's past, it made sense that he would find it hard to trust a woman who could wield that kind of power over him.

However, he did not see keeping her at a distance the safe course of action now.

It was patently clear to him that he had been on the verge of losing her when he lost his memory…at the very least, their marriage had been in some real trouble. He'd handled a lot of things badly since coming out of his coma, but he could and would fix them.

Eden's body sang with desire as Aristide carried her into their bedroom and kicked the door shut. He turned to lock it, ensuring their privacy. He had insisted on carrying her from the car because he said he could not remember carrying her over the threshold and wanted that memory now.

How could she turn down such a romantic request, even if she wanted to? And she hadn't.

She had always loved being carried by him and if he could remember, he would know that he had made a habit of it.

But tonight it was even more special. He'd been the epitome of a romantic escort all evening—wining and dining her, and dancing with her in a way that was guaranteed to seduce her senses. There was no doubt he was intent on completing the seduction now and all she wanted to do was let him.

She still didn't quite trust him, but she loved this side to him and wanted to enjoy the benefits while it lasted. Heck, she loved him period and doubted that would ever change. She would grasp the moments of happiness as they came and worry about the future...well...in the future.

And if he really did get rid of Kassandra, maybe that future had a chance of being something truly wonderful.

Eden focused on the pleasure of her husband's mouth claiming hers.

He broke the kiss with a masculine groan of pleasure. "You taste so good, *agape mou.*"

He licked her lips, teasing along the seam with the tip of his clever tongue and applying gentle pressure for her to open up. She let her lips part, inviting him inside with a small foray of advance and retreat. He took the invitation, sliding his tongue along hers, possessing the interior of her mouth with tender mastery.

She ran her hands over his shoulders and chest and face, everywhere she could touch, imprinting the warmth of his body on her senses. He felt and smelled so good...so masculine...so much her husband...her mate. Craving bare skin, she started undoing buttons so she could get her hand inside his shirt.

They both moaned when her hand came into contact with his hair-roughened chest. He was so strong, his muscles so hard they felt like velvet-covered steel under her hand. She found his nipple and circled it with her forefinger, over and over again, until it was hard. She pressed the small nub between her thumb and forefinger, that special spot between her legs growing moist and throbbing when he groaned into her mouth and tightened his hold on her almost bruisingly.

She needed to feel the entire expanse of his naked chest. She attacked his jacket, maneuvering it off, one arm at a time. It was hard to do without breaking their kiss, but she managed it, her legs swinging down and locking around his waist when he let them go so she could finish removing his jacket. The tie came off with relative ease, but his shirt had to be untucked from his slacks. She got it out, unbuttoning the last few buttons, and pushed the garment off his broad shoulders.

When she had him undressed from the waist up, she went back to exploring his torso, this time her questing fingers making his big body shudder as he moaned out his pleasure.

She wanted naked skin against naked skin, but couldn't stop touching him long enough to get her own clothes off.

Clearly he had the same idea because he started tugging her dress up with one hand while holding her against him with the other arm. He succeeded in getting her dress over her head, only breaking the kiss once and leaving her in nothing but her thigh-highs and panties.

She hadn't worn a bra and was grateful for that fact now as she pressed her swollen breasts against his hard chest.

His mouth broke from hers and he hissed as if the touch burned him. Heavens, it probably did…it felt like it was burning her. Her nipples stung where they were in contact with the dark curls covering his chest and she rubbed herself against him, increasing the friction and the pleasure.

"You are so sexy, Eden."

She was too busy kissing along his jaw and down his neck to answer. She found the place where his neck met his shoulder and sampled that favorite spot with her tongue, reveling in the salty maleness of his skin.

His hand slipped down her back, under the silk of her panties and cupped her bare bottom. He started kneading her flesh, his fingers coming perilously close to the apex of her thighs, but never quite touching the place that needed his touch most.

She softly nipped at his neck and ground her sweet spot against the hard ridge hidden by his trousers.

The world shifted and she found herself lying on their bed while he tore out of his slacks for the second time in twenty-four hours.

She pushed her panties off, but when she went to roll her thigh-highs down, he said, "No…leave them on."

His guttural demand sent a shiver down her spine and she leaned back on the bed, remembering how much he loved her in thigh-highs and nothing else.

Reaching her hands out toward him, she widened her legs in a double invitation.

He came down over her in a sensual rush and pressed inside of her with one smooth, darkly intense movement. *"You are mine."*

"Yes, and you are mine." She arched up against him, the sensation so incredible she could barely maintain conscious thought.

He drove into her with an animal-like growl and they made love with a raw intensity unlike any they had shared in all the passionate encounters of their relationship.

She felt the pleasure spiraling inside her, tightening, tightening, tightening…until it exploded. It radiated outward on a wave of such intense ecstasy, she could not bite back a primal scream of joy—despite the last bit of her sanity telling her that tonight they were not alone in the villa.

Aristide's roar was no more controlled as his body went rigid with his release.

Afterward, he collapsed on top of her, his breathing every bit as ragged as her own. "*S'gapo, yineka mou*. I love you."

Everything inside her clenched in rejection of the words. "No…you can't…"

CHAPTER ELEVEN

He reared back and looked down at her, his expression grim and almost frighteningly primitive. "I do."

"You didn't before. It's just the sex…it overwhelmed me too. I'm still overwhelmed," she admitted with a panting breath.

He shook his head as if trying to clear it. "You told me you loved me last night. Do not deny it."

Ah…that explained it. "I won't deny it. I do love you, but you don't have to feel obligated to return the words in kind. You never have before."

"I am saying it now."

"You don't have to. Honestly. Please, don't worry about it, Aristide. I know you don't love me, but I've learned to accept it."

He jumped off of her with an angry movement and then stood beside the bed, vibrating with outrage. "I did not say I love you because I thought you were expecting it."

Those stupid pregnancy-driven hormones were making her eyes water again and she tried to blink the tears away. "I didn't mean to offend you." She swallowed, her insides hollow at how the most amazing experience of her life was being ruined by words. Words she had always wanted to hear, but knew could not be true. "It's just…I don't want you telling me you love me out of some misplaced sense of guilt."

"Of what do I have to feel guilty over?"

"Nothing…I…" She shook her head, unable to go on.

"Do not cry," he growled.

"I won't." She turned her head and sniffed, blinking furiously.

He swore and the bed dipped beside her. Then she was in his arms, his body wrapped around hers. "I love you, but since I supposedly did not love you before, you find it impossible to believe now. Is that not true?"

Eden tilted her head back, her gray eyes filled with wary uncertainty and Aristide wanted to curse again.

"Well, if you were going to love me, wouldn't you have discovered it before this? I mean, you were really happy when Theo was born, so proud, I thought you would burst, but you didn't tell me you loved me then."

And she had been hoping he would, just as she had hoped the night before that making love would reclaim his memories of her. He ground his teeth in an effort not to say anything damaging. His lack of memory was more bothersome now than ever before.

"I do not know why I did not tell you I loved you before," he gritted out, "but that does not mean I did not feel the emotion."

Only an idiot would not love this woman.

She took a deep breath and then her expression changed, a seductive light coming into her eyes.

She rose up on her elbow and pushed him backward, her mouth coming within a breath of his. "It's okay, Aristide, really. I don't want to think about before or how you can't remember me now. I just want to make love. I've missed you and last night didn't begin to make up for it."

No man could stand against such naked provocation. She kissed him and he responded with passion he had thought spent.

* * *

Eden lay awake as Aristide slept beside her. They had made love again, this time tenderly and for a very long time. He shouted love words in the midst of his release and she had returned them, but how could she believe his were real?

They had been lovers and then married for a total of three years as of yesterday and not once had a word even slightly resembling love crossed his lips. Tonight was the first time he had ever called her *agape mou* even.

Was it possible that he had truly fallen in love with her? What did that say of the time they had been together before? What if he regained his memory and with it knowledge that what he felt for her was not love?

The questions whirled through her brain, tormenting her thoughts with one unhappy scenario after another.

What if he was only insisting now that he loved her out of guilt? She'd latched on to the fact he wasn't proud of the way he'd treated her up to now, though he seemed too full of macho pride to admit that fact. Could love born of guilt last? Was it even real?

Everything was so confusing. How would she ever know the truth of his feelings when he seemed so intent on proving he was a better husband than her memories indicated?

He was even willing to fire Kassandra. Eden actually thought that might happen now. Aristide in guilt mode (even one he refused to acknowledge) was a fearsome prospect.

She didn't want him coming out of it before Kassandra was gone from their lives, but neither did she want to spend the rest of her life married to a man who stayed with her because he felt badly about the way he'd treated her at first. That was hardly more appetizing a prospect than being married for the sake of their baby.

* * *

Aristide walked into his office on Monday morning with an unshakeable sense of purpose.

He had grilled Eden the day before on Kassandra's behavior since the beginning of their marriage and he had no doubts about firing the woman. She had made Eden miserable with her subtle innuendo and manipulations and *he had let her*. That was his cross to bear, but he wasn't letting Kassandra's poison infect his life or torment his wife one more day.

The confrontation went much as he had expected it to after Eden's revelations. Kassandra attempted lies and further manipulations to keep her job and her place in his life, but he refused to be moved.

"You are fired, Kassandra. Security is waiting by your desk with your six months' severance check to walk you out. You no longer have clearance in any of the Kouros Industries buildings or computers."

"You cannot be serious. You can't fire me!"

"You are wrong."

"But you need me, not that American whore. She knows nothing of your business...she cannot even speak our language adequately! I belong by your side, not her!"

"Do not ever call my wife anything like that again... I can ruin you, Kassandra...completely. Do not ever do something that will make me think I have to."

She blanched and then glared, her hands curled at her sides like claws. "You would have loved me if she had not gotten in the way."

"You were never in the running."

"You made love to me."

"We had sex. Mutually consenting sex without commitment." A brief affair, nothing more. He realized why now. The woman had no heart and he now knew the difference between cold, calculated sex and making love.

Eden made love to him and, God willing, he would never know a time without that gift.

"How dare you? It was not like that. We both enjoyed it." Her anger had twisted her features into an ugly mask. "I am important to you. You need me."

"No, I do not."

The tears spilled over, but for the first time in memory the sight of a woman's distress moved him not one iota.

She stopped at the door and turned back to face him. "She was ready to leave you in New York. She wanted to file for divorce. Did your sainted little wife tell you that?"

Something exploded in his brain, like a wall collapsing into rubble. "You are lying."

"No. You only wish I were. This time I am telling the unvarnished truth. I heard your argument about our trip to the theater. She was so angry, she was spitting mad, but it was nothing like the way she went for you in the car on the way to upstate New York."

"You could not possibly know what was discussed in that car ride."

"Of course I can, I had you bugged." She gave him a pitying look and then affected Eden's American accent. "I can't take it anymore, Aristide. I want a divorce."

With one final glare, Kassandra exited the office, but Aristide barely noticed.

His brain was bombarding him with images. The first time he saw Eden outside the Metropolitan Museum of Art—she had been so beautiful, she entranced him. The first time they made love…the birth of their son…so many pictures flashed through his brain at supersonic speed. Then came the car ride Kassandra mentioned…before the accident.

And he knew exactly what had caused that sense of foreboding that had plagued him since discovering he had a wife he could not remember.

Not for the first time since starting the drive, Aristide wished he'd used his chauffeur-driven car. Eden was intent on having a relationship discussion and he couldn't focus on her and the road at the same time.

"What are you saying?" he asked, sure he must have misunderstood her last words.

"You have a choice to make. It's either your precious assistant or your wife. You can't have both."

He bit back a curse. Eden's hormone-driven irrationality had already spawned one major argument between the two of them; he was determined to avoid another.

She hadn't told him she was pregnant yet, but they shared the same bed and he could count. She hadn't had her menses last month and she'd stopped breast-feeding rather abruptly.

He didn't know why she hadn't told him unless she was saving it as a Christmas surprise, or actually didn't realize it herself yet. She might not have put two and two together as quickly as he had.

He remembered how easily she'd gotten distracted during her pregnancy with Theo. Her scatterbrained mentality had been really endearing, but he had never teased her about it because she had been overly sensitive then too.

"I know you do not mean that."

"And on what evidence do you make that assumption?"

"You love me. You are not going to walk away because you have gotten upset with Kassandra over some trivial thing."

"You consider her attempts to undermine the viability of our marriage trivial?" she asked, her voice colder than he had ever heard it.

Damn it. "I did not say that."

"But you don't believe she's trying to break us up?"

"Listen to yourself, *yineka mou*. Do you not think you are being even a tiny bit dramatic here?"

"No."

He sighed. "Well, you are," he said as gently as he could. He really did not want to upset her more than she already was.

"I am not being dramatic, but I'm beginning to see you're never going to believe me."

"Be fair. You have never once before this week complained about Kassandra and I have seen with my own eyes her attempts to make you comfortable in a foreign environment."

"Her attempts to show up my ignorance, you mean."

He gritted his teeth, not wanting to lose his temper, but getting angry against his will. "You are not being reasonable."

"What is unreasonable about me wanting my husband to get rid of the woman trying to destroy my marriage?"

"Why would Kassandra want to do that?" he asked, taking another tack. If he could get her to see she was looking at things from a completely illogical point of view, they could end this ludicrous discussion.

"She wants you."

"She is my employee, not my lover."

"She was once, or so she intimated."

Tension gripped him. He had to tread carefully here. He and Kassandra had been lovers once. Very briefly, right around when he met Eden, but once he met his wife, other women stopped existing for him. Kassandra had taken their break-up with the same sophisticated cool she responded to everything else. Neither her heart nor her pride had been particularly affected.

"No way would she say that to you."

"You are wrong."

"Eden…" he growled, his growing frustration making his voice harsh.

"Oh, I forgot, you don't believe anything I say about your precious employee."

"Stop calling her that. The only woman around here who is precious to me is you, even when you are being irrationally jealous," he said teasingly, trying to defuse the tension growing between them.

"I am not irrational and I accepted a long time ago I am not precious to you either."

"What the hell do you mean by that?" he asked in a near roar, losing his hold on his temper.

"Just what I said. I knew you didn't love me when we got married, but I thought my love would make it all right. I was wrong. I've found that being married for the sake of my child and tolerated for the sake of my talent in bed isn't enough. It hurts too much."

"This has gone far enough. You are completely without reason and perhaps your condition is at fault, but you will stop making these wild accusations immediately."

"You're not in the boardroom, Aristide. You cannot order me around like one of your directors." Then she went silent and stayed that way for several seconds.

Good. Maybe she was calming down.

"You know I am pregnant." She said it in a flat voice, void of the joy such an announcement should bring.

"I am sorry if I stole your thunder, but, yes, I know."

"Since when?"

"Since you missed your first period and started craving burnt toast for breakfast in the morning."

"So, when you invited me to come with you to New York, you knew?" Why did she sound so passionless, as if her emotions were in lock-down mode?

"Yes, I knew."

"That explains it. I had hoped… It doesn't matter. I was wrong."

"What did you hope?"

"That you had finally gotten tired of being apart from me, that you wanted our marriage to be a closer one. Isn't that a joke?" she asked with bitter cynicism he hadn't thought her capable of.

"I do not like being apart from you."

Once he realized she was pregnant again, he also realized he was tired of leaving her behind in Greece when he traveled. He had ordered one of the jets to be equipped for travel with infants so she could come with him, but he hadn't told her.

He had wanted to save it as a Christmas surprise…a sort of reciprocal gift for her new pregnancy.

She laughed, the sound strained and blackly amused. "Right. How could you possibly miss me when you've got super-Kassandra along for the ride?"

"She is not my wife."

"She would like to be."

"That is nonsense."

Eden didn't reply to that. In fact, she said nothing for several miles.

It started to rain and he turned on the wipers. "We should be there soon." As conversation gambits went it was not great, but he was leery of starting yet another volatile argument.

"I think it would be best if we separated," she said in a weary, dead voice. "I can move back to New York, or move into a separate residence near Athens if you still feel strongly about the children being raised in Greece. We can work out visitation either way."

He felt like someone had punched him straight in the chest and the air seized in his lungs. He turned to look at her, needing to know if she was serious, hoping with everything in him she was not.

Her eyes were filled with pain-filled determination. "I can't take it anymore, Aristide. I want a divorce."

He couldn't breathe. His chest hurt. She had gone from, "I think we need to separate," to "I want a divorce," in a heartbeat.

He started yelling at her, but it took several seconds of no response and a sideways glance that revealed her blank-eyed regard for him to realize he'd been doing so in Greek. He shouted the one English word he could get out, "No!"

But it was lost in her scream and his eyes snapped back to the road to see a truck had swerved into their lane.

He had no time to maneuver. She would be hurt. He could lose her. He flung his arm out to protect her even as he tried to avoid the unavoidable.

He woke up. Lying beside the road. His head hurt and he could make little sense of the sounds swirling around him.

"Doesn't look good…blood…nothing we can do…unlikely…survive…" He slipped back into unconsciousness, certain his wife and unborn baby were going to die.

Aristide sat at his desk, shaking and sweating.

His wife had survived the crash, but had his baby? He remembered she had not been at his bedside during his coma… Kassandra had convinced him it meant Eden did not really care about him. But she had been hospitalized herself…not merely for a minor concussion…but for a miscarriage as well?

He picked up the phone and asked to be put through to the hospital in New York in a voice weak from the horror of his memories. Some time later, he put the phone down again, relief coursing through him. She had not lost the baby, but once again she had not told him about it either. Why not?

Then he laughed derisively at himself and his obtuseness.

She'd told him he married her solely for the sake of their unborn son and she had believed it. She had kept the baby out of the equation this time because she wanted to be the deciding factor in the way he felt about their marriage now. Or did she?

According to the memories torturing his mind, his wife wanted a divorce.

Bile rose in his throat. He had never told her he loved her and she believed he didn't. She had spent their entire time together believing she was nothing special to him when she was the very air he breathed.

He had not said the words, but, damn it, how could she not have known? He needed her in a way he had never and could never need another human being.

She hadn't left him after the hospital. In fact, she had acted like she wanted to salvage their marriage. Did she, or was that an act born of her tenderhearted nature? Was she holding off leaving him because of his amnesia? If he told her he could remember, would she walk out?

She certainly hadn't believed him when he told her he loved her last night, so in her mind, nothing was changed between them. She still didn't trust him and why should she? He'd done little enough to earn that trust. But he had fired Kassandra.

That had to be good for something.

None of it mattered if he couldn't convince her that he loved her, though. His mind spun with possibilities and he thought he came up with just the way to do it, but first he had to finish the courtship he'd started the day before.

He picked up the phone again; this time, he called a florist.

Eden felt like laughing out loud as yet another delivery arrived.

The first had been a huge bouquet of scarlet roses. The card attached had read, "You have my passion forever."

Then every hour on the hour, a new delivery arrived, each of them an arrangement of six yellow roses in a crystal vase. The card with these all read the same thing: "Yellow roses are for everlasting love…these are tokens of mine."

He really wanted her to believe he loved her. She was beginning to think that, regardless of what he had felt for her for three years, he really did love her now…maybe even as much as she loved him.

At four o'clock, there was no ringing of the doorbell with another delivery, but at four-fifteen, Aristide walked into the living room.

She was playing with the baby like she did every afternoon, this time facing the hall. She had been waiting for him and only now realized it. Her hungry gaze took in his features with joy.

He was dressed in one of his custom-tailored business suits and carried a crystal vase filled with six yellow roses just like the others.

She surged to her feet like a puppet on strings, controlled by his presence.

He smiled at her. "*Agape mou*, you look beautiful."

She laughed. She couldn't help it. She was wearing a T-shirt and jeans like she usually did when playing with their rambunctious son. Not exactly beauty queen material.

Aristide presented her with the flowers.

She took them and immediately buried her face in the fragrant blooms. "They're wonderful."

"Yellow roses are for everlasting love."

She lifted her head. "So the cards all said."

"Each one represents a month I have felt that way about you."

Including this vase, that would make thirty-six…the total number of months since they met. "That's impossible. I told you—"

His finger pressed against her lips. "I know what you believed, but you were wrong, my precious Eden, so very wrong."

She stared at him...had he remembered? But, no, he would have said. "How can you be so sure?"

"Because I know myself and I know that I could not love you this much now and not have loved you at all before. That is quite impossible."

Could it be true? Had she misjudged her husband's feelings for her? Like she had told Aristide, he had never once told her he *didn't* love her, he had just never told her that he did.

She turned and put the flowers on a nearby table then turned back and threw herself in her husband's arms. "It doesn't matter, if you love me now. It doesn't matter."

But it did. Aristide wanted to tell his wife he remembered, but he didn't want to risk her walking away before he got a chance to convince her of his love. She needed to believe without a doubt that his love for her was genuine. He hoped the plans he had set in motion today would be sufficient evidence.

They were in bed that night when he told her about firing Kassandra.

"She said you were on the verge of divorcing me," he said, fishing for her feelings on the matter now.

Eden paled, but she nodded. "It's true."

"Do you still feel that way?" he asked.

She looked down at their entwined naked bodies pointedly. "What do you think?"

"I think you are very generous, but why did you stay with me?"

"The doctor said not to upset you, that it could be very risky to a concussed patient. I thought telling you that the wife you could not remember wanted a divorce fell under the label of upsetting news."

He hadn't considered that angle, but it supported his worry that she stayed out of concern for him, not desire.

"I love you."

A shadow passed through her gaze, but she nodded and then kissed him long and hard. She still wasn't sure of him, but she would be.

Eventually, she settled back against his arm. "How did Kassandra know about me asking for a divorce?"

"She placed a pen with a listening device in the rental car."

"That's deranged!"

"Or determined. I put security on it immediately. They discovered that she had purchased two such devices over the Internet a month before our trip to New York. The other one was found in her apartment when it was searched."

"She let you search?"

"She was facing major charges being filed if she did not."

"She wanted to marry you."

"Yes, but she did not understand that love cannot be replaced by sex and ambition. She does not and never did love me, but she wanted more power than she had as my personal assistant. She thought she deserved it because of our lifelong friendship."

"I still say that makes her sick."

"Probably. It also makes her virtually unemployable."

"You're not keeping it quiet? What if the press picks up the story?"

"She should have considered the possibilities before playing her ruthless games with my life."

"Greeks really do have a thing with revenge, don't they?"

"My father used to say that bad behavior is its own revenge. He was right. Everything happening to Kassandra right now, she brought on herself through her actions."

"I'm glad she's out of our lives."

"I am too."

She was silent so long it made him nervous. "What?"

"I just can't believe everything is so different now."

"Wait until Christmas and you will find out how different."

She sat bolt upright and demanded, "What kind of different?"

"You will have to wait and see."

She immediately started badgering him for answers and he laughed, reveling in his ability to remember this endearing trait. She couldn't stand knowing she had a surprise waiting for her…she wanted to know everything right now.

She had wanted to know the sex of their child before Theo's birth and had spent hours researching genetics trying to figure out what color of eyes and hair he would have.

In the end, the only way to stop her questions was to make love to her and it was no hardship.

CHAPTER TWELVE

They went to the island for Christmas. No one minded the change in plans, but Eden wanted to know if it had something to do with her surprise. Aristide refused to enlighten her.

Sebastian, Rachel and the children joined them, as did Phillippa and Vincent.

Eden was awed by how beautifully the small island church had been decorated for the holiday and thought they should make coming to the island for Christmas a tradition. Red, white and pink poinsettias were everywhere, along with yards and yards of green garland and holly. Gold silk draped the pews with green-and-red velvet ribbon accents.

She could not wait for the candlelight service on Christmas Eve.

Music outside her window woke Eden on Christmas Eve morning. It didn't sound like Christmas carols, but she wasn't familiar with all the Greek forms of the festive music. She reached for Aristide's warmth without opening her eyes and frowned when her questing hand found only an empty bed.

Her eyes slid open and she saw that their room was empty. The *en suite* door was open and the light off. So, he wasn't in there. She threw the covers back to get up and go looking for her errant husband when the door burst open.

Phillippa and Rachel came in, both of their arms overflowing with garment bags and shoeboxes. There was lots and lots of white and Rachel carried a bouquet of white poinsettias, Christmas greenery and gold ribbon in one of her hands.

A strange sensation came over Eden. She remembered her sister-in-law telling her about Sebastian's attempt at a surprise wedding and her throat constricted. Was the pile of white silk in Phillippa's arms what she thought it was?

"*Kalimera*, Eden." Phillippa grinned. "And happy Christmas."

"Good morning to you—what's going on?" she asked in a breathless voice she barely recognized.

"Aristide has arranged a small surprise for you."

"The small surprise comes with a wedding dress?"

Rachel nodded, her own lovely face creased in a happy smile.

Tears filled Eden's eyes. "Oh…I…"

"I trust you are going to take this news better than my other daughter by marriage took the news of her own upcoming wedding."

Rachel blushed, looking chagrined. "I screamed."

Eden shook her head, her throat tight, but she forced out words. "I won't scream. I'm overwhelmed."

"Good." Phillippa took over then.

Within two hours Eden had eaten a small, but wonderful breakfast and was dressed as beautifully as any bride in history. Her gown fit her to perfection, not only in size but in design.

She stood before the mirror. "I look like a fairy princess."

And she did. The dress shimmered with gems and the kerchief-style skirt floated around her legs and ankles in several layers of iridescent silk. The bodice emphasized her small breasts without making them look meager and the jewel-encrusted ribbons woven through her hair gave her a definitely ethereal appearance.

There was a knock at the door and butterflies filled her insides.

Phillippa grinned and Rachel opened the door.

Aristide stood on the other side, Sebastian beside him carrying Theo, his own two small children standing beside them.

She had eyes only for her husband. He was dressed in a white tuxedo with long tails and looked so happy she thought her own heart would burst.

He dropped to one knee and took her trembling hand in his own. "Eden Kouros, I have loved you from the first moment and I will love you into eternity. Will you do me the honor of promising yourself to me before my family?"

Before she could reply, his voice gruff, he said, "I really have loved you since the first."

"But…" Her voice trailed off as she noticed something different about his eyes.

It had been there for the past week, but she had thought it was just his newfound love for her.

"You remember," she choked out.

"Yes."

He had a lot of explaining to do…later.

"I would be honored to promise myself to you, Aristide. I love you so much."

His face shone with relief and it was only then that she realized he had been unsure of her answer, and he had asked her in such a public manner anyway.

He stood and put his hand out. She took it and he led her on the traditional walk to the church. Dozens of people joined along the way and she realized from the familiar faces that many of the Kouros and Demakis clans had come to the island for the festivities.

They stopped outside the church to observe the ritual of drinking from the same cup and then proceeded inside.

The tiara he placed on her head glittered with diamonds and her favorite mystic topaz, his simpler crown looked old and she remembered seeing it in his parents' wedding pictures. It was the one his father had worn to marry his mother. For some reason that struck her as even more wonderful than everything else and she smiled lovingly at him through a mist of tears she didn't even try to blink away.

The ceremony was beautiful and, as he had once told her, there was no vow of fidelity, but the promise was in his eyes and her heart reacted to it with joyous acceptance.

The reception was big and boisterous with dancing and a lot of celebrating, ending with the candlelight Christmas Eve service.

It was much later when the other guests had left that she and Aristide were allowed to go to their room in privacy. Theo had long since gone to bed.

"When did you remember?" she asked after he carried her inside and lowered himself into a chair, seating her in his lap.

"The morning I fired Kassandra."

The day he had sent her all the roses, saying he had always loved her. "Why didn't you say something then?"

"I wanted to be sure you knew I loved you first."

"But why?"

"You told me you wanted a divorce. How could I be sure you wouldn't ask for one again once you figured out I remembered?"

"That's stupid! Why would I want a divorce now?"

"I did not know why you wanted a divorce then," he reminded her in a voice that reflected the pain of the conversation in the car on that fateful day.

"Do you understand now?" she asked.

"Yes, but, damn it, how could you be so mistaken about me not loving you?"

She couldn't believe he had to ask. *"You never told me any differently."*

"That was an unquestionably imprudent oversight, but I loved you with my body every time we joined as you loved me with yours. I was besotted and I find it difficult to believe you could not see that. I lost sleep, skipped meetings and turned my schedule upside down to visit you in upstate New York as often as I could when we were lovers."

"I didn't know our time together was such a tremendous hardship on your schedule."

"I am the President of Oversees Operations for a huge company...do you really think I routinely had weekends free during those months?"

"I didn't take that into account..." But that wasn't true.

She *had* considered it at first and taken it as evidence she was someone special to him, but even knowing what she did about her father's schedule, she hadn't begun to realize what the time with her had cost Aristide.

And later, when she had begun to truly doubt his feelings for her, she had dismissed the importance of that time entirely. She had seen only that none of that time included the other people closest to him in his life.

"I married you, Eden...did you think that meant nothing?"

"You married me for Theo's sake."

"When did I ever say that?"

"You didn't ask me until I told you I was pregnant."

"But if I had not loved you, I would not have asked you then. Perhaps I did not call the emotion by its proper name at the time…even to myself, but it was there. Be assured of it. After the example of my uncle's marriage, I would never have risked marriage for anything less." He smiled, the expression going straight to her heart. "And before you start creating any more wild scenarios, I did not organize this wedding because of the new baby either."

"You know…?"

"I remembered everything. I had some pretty terrifying moments waiting for word from the hospital in New York however." He put his hand protectively over her womb. "I am very happy you are pregnant again."

"No concerns about a lack of proper spacing between our children?" she teased.

He looked blank for a second and then his gaze sharpened with understanding and his hand pressed possessively against her. "None whatsoever."

She was glad he knew about the baby and relieved he had thought to contact the hospital instead of worrying they had lost their child. She was even happier he was thrilled about the news, but had she really ever doubted that response?

"I concede you did not marry me this time for the child," she said with a smile.

"And that I loved you all along?"

"If you loved me, why did you leave me in Greece while you traveled so much?"

Dull color scored his cheeks. "I would like to say I had no choice and, in some instances, that was true. I really did worry about you traveling during your pregnancy…you were so sick at first. Then, later, I did not know how easily a baby would travel. Sebastian has been content to allow me to do most of the traveling for Kouros Industries since before his marriage to Rachel."

"You said you would like to say that was the reason…" She

already knew it wasn't entirely valid, not for all the trips, and he was smart enough to realize it.

"The truth is all those trips were me being stupid again. You were right, I was not entirely ready for the commitment of marriage, but not for the reasons you thought. I had committed to you in those ways from the first time we made love, but you have more power over me than anyone ever has."

"And you are used to absolute control."

"Yes."

"How was being apart supposed to make that better?"

"I thought I could keep a lid on it if I did not get too dependent on you. This thinking began when we were lovers and continued after our marriage, but every trip I took was harder to go on. Every time I left I wanted to come home more. Surely you noticed how short my trips had become."

"I was too busy being miserably certain you didn't love me and never would."

"I called you all the time…do you think I did that with any other woman? I do not even call my mother as often."

She laughed at that. "I didn't consider multiple phone calls evidence of life-long loving devotion."

"You should have."

She almost laughed, but he seemed so serious. "Maybe I should have, but you didn't introduce me to your family the whole time we were lovers."

This time the red in his cheeks was dark and anything but subtle. "I knew if my mother or brother knew of you, they would disapprove."

"They would think I wasn't good enough for you? Because I wasn't Greek?"

"Because it would be obvious to anyone after ten minutes in our company that I had seduced you into anticipating our wedding vows. My mother would have been ashamed of me. You should have seen her with Sebastian over Rachel. It was not pretty. At first I was not ready to get married and then I was too content keeping you all to myself. I knew as soon as I married you, I would have to share you with everyone…not just my family. And I knew if I shared you with my family, we would end up married very quickly."

"That's—"

"Heinously selfish, I know."

"Sweet, I was about to say."

He seemed to relax a little. "I am glad you see it that way." He took a deep breath. "I talked with Dr Lewis for over an hour when I called the hospital. I know why I forgot you."

Scared—even though her heart and the way he held her told her she shouldn't be—she asked, "Why?"

"I woke beside the road, after the accident. I was really out of it, but I overheard the paramedics saying something about not being able to do anything for you…I thought you were going to die."

"They were talking about the baby."

"That is what Dr Lewis said."

"How could Adam know? He wasn't there."

"He surmised from their report."

"Oh…"

"I do not like you calling him Adam."

She stifled a grin. "American doctors are not as formal as Greek doctors."

"So I noticed."

"So you forgot me because you thought I was going to die?"

"Doctor Lewis thinks that on top of the trauma of you asking for a divorce, that belief triggered my mind into forgetting in self-protection."

"You told the doctor what I said in the car?"

"Yes. I had to know why I would forget you and he insisted on knowing everything before helping me figure it out."

"Wow. You really did love me."

His eyes filled with deep, dark emotion. "I could not face life without you...I still cannot."

"You should have said."

"I will spend the rest of my life saying it a hundred times a day."

"At least."

They both smiled, the love between them so tangible she had to ask herself how she could have been so sure it did not exist before. But she knew.

"Remember, I told you my dad had had affairs."

"Yes. He is not the most devoted of fathers either. Business always comes first."

"I thought it did with you too, but I see now how I was coloring you with his behavior."

"I made mistakes, but you and our family mean more to me than anything, *yineka mou.*"

"I'm glad. You mean more than anything to me too." She snuggled into Aristide's lap. "My dad said he loved my mom and then had multiple affairs. She died of cancer when I was thirteen. He nursed her so carefully, so lovingly through it all, but all I could remember were the nights I could hear her crying when he was out with one of his women."

"You did not trust men."

"No."

"I am not your father."

"No, quite the opposite. You have been as faithful as a man can be, but did not tell me you loved me. I should have been okay with that, you know?"

"My refusal to say the words made you insecure. Kassandra's innuendos did not help."

She leaned back to look directly into his eyes, her own wet with happy moisture. "I'm sorry I ever accused you of having an affair."

"I am sorry for so much I cannot begin to say it all, but it will be different from now on."

"Yes, we'll both be smarter."

"We will love each other forever." He kissed her and they sealed their very personal vows in a very personal way.

They opened gifts Christmas Day, the children going first and then playing with their new toys on the floor amidst a pile of colorful paper while the adults opened theirs.

Phillippa and Vincent loved their trip of the most famous gardens of the world that the men and their wives had arranged.

"Eden did most of the arranging, I'm sure you won't be surprised to hear," Rachel said laughingly.

Phillippa's look of loving joy made Eden blush and duck her head before anyone saw the tears in her eyes. Pregnancy hormones were the pits sometimes.

When she opened her gift from Aristide, she didn't understand what she was looking at. "You bought me a plane?"

He shook his head and laughed. "I had one of the Kouros jets outfitted for family travel."

She looked more closely at the pictures in the flat gold box and sucked in a breath of joy. "You really aren't planning to leave me behind anymore, are you?"

"No. We will have to stop traveling the last month of your pregnancy, but other than that, nothing will hold us back."

The room erupted with news of the baby and it was a long time before she and Aristide had a moment alone with their son. They were tucking him into his crib for his nap and Aristide had his arms around Eden while she soothed their son to sleep.

"We are a family, *agape mou*."

"A loving family," she affirmed.

They quietly crept from the baby's room. He suggested taking a walk down to the small church and she gladly went, loving this new open rapport they shared…the security she felt in his feelings for her.

They stopped in front of the altar where many candles burned.

He turned to face her, his eyes suspiciously bright. "The first Christmas after we met, I came here and thanked God for the gift of the woman who would become my wife."

She opened her mouth, but nothing would come out.

He kissed her softly.

"That was only a few days after we met."

"Yes."

"You knew then that you wanted to marry me?"

"I knew then that I *would* marry you, that you would be the mother of my children. I made mistakes, but never doubt that you have had my love all along."

"I won't. I won't ever doubt you again, my love."

He took her into his arms and pressed his lips to hers, the smell of Christmas greenery surrounding them in the small church that had hosted their marriage born of true love.

* * * * *

Moonlight and
Mistletoe

by

Louise Allen

CHAPTER ONE

December 4th 1814

The inhabitants of Winterbourne St Swithin prided themselves upon their village. It was no mere rural backwater, no sleepy hamlet full of rustics and yeomen whose social hierarchy was topped off by a red-faced squire and whose amenities consisted of the church and a tavern or two.

Theirs, they boasted, was a bustling community straddling the post road to Aylesbury with a glimpse over the meadows to the waters of the new canal ordered by the crazy old Duke of Bridgewater, up in his mansion on the Chiltern crest. There was the Bird in Hand, a large coaching inn, to serve the stage and the mail and the carriages of the gentry going to and from London and Oxford. There was the fine Winterbourne Hall with the Nugents to preside over local society and half a dozen gentry houses in the vicinity to fill the pews of the grey stone church with the living, and the marble monuments with the dead.

And there was even a shop, a superior emporium selling haberdashery and lengths of cloth, the London and Oxford papers a day late and snuff, tea and Hungary water.

The life of the village centred around the church, the Bird

in Hand and the Green, the grassy heart of the community with its duck pond, decaying stocks, venerable oak tree and ring of fine houses and half-timbered cottages.

On a raw, damp Thursday morning three respectable housewives made their way around the Green, deep in discussion of new and fascinating intelligence. It seemed there was no doubt that the gentleman who had taken the Old Manor— the one architectural blot upon the village centre—was none other than an earl.

'Or, as it might be, a duke,' Mrs Thorne hazarded hopefully, lifting her skirts to negotiate a puddle. 'Whichever, 'tis a fine thing for Winterbourne. He'll bring down all his society friends, you mark my words, and he'll be hiring on staff and wanting eggs and milk and bacon.'

'If he wanted his society friends, what's he doing in Winterbourne in December?' her bosom enemy Widow Clare enquired tartly. 'The nobs are all off visiting, or at their big country houses. What's an earl doing hiring that old barn of a place? Outrunning his creditors, that's what. I tell you, ladies, it'll be cash on the nail for any eggs that household wants to buy from my hens!'

'Oh, and nobody's seen him,' Mrs Johnson squeaked, her eyes popping at the thought of an earl in the village, even one fallen upon hard times. 'I've seen his butler, mind—I thought it was his lordship himself for a minute, so grand and starched up he was—talking to poor Bill Willett. "I will trouble you, my man," he said, all frosty-like, "I will trouble you to remember that only the freshest milk and cream is fit for his lordship's table and that cream is fit only for the cat." And have you seen the horses?'

The other ladies nodded. Not only had they seen them arrive three days ago but had been bored to death at dinner by their husbands and sons carrying on about the splendour of his lordship's stable. But, to everyone's chagrin, it seemed that his lordship had driven himself down from London and had managed to arrive at the one moment of the day when not a single curious eye was focused on the Green, but instead was watching the spectacle of the Mail sweeping through.

'He'll have to come out sooner or later,' Mrs Thorne prophesied comfortably. 'Even if the bailiffs are after him.'

She broke off as a gig turned off the main road and was driven at a spanking pace around the far side of the Green. It was a modest but somewhat rakish vehicle—the sort that a sporting curate might favour, perhaps—drawn by a neat Welsh cob.

The ladies stared as best they could from the shelter of bonnets and hoods as the gig turned through the gates of the pretty little house that faced the red brick façade of the Old Manor.

'Well, did you see that?' the Widow demanded unnecessarily. 'That was driven by a female!'

'With a groom by her side,' Mrs Thorne added. 'And she's gone into the Moon House.'

'Then the rumours are true,' Mrs Johnson concluded, quite unashamedly craning her neck now. But the vehicle and its occupants had vanished through the gate posts and the house had resumed its air of empty neglect. 'Sir Edward *did* sell it before he died. But who is she?'

Fascinated, the three continued on their way to the end of the Green, but the high wall of the Old Manor defeated their avid stares on one side and the dirt-streaked, empty windows of the opposite house stared blankly back at them from the other.

With infinite slowness, another ivy tendril curled out to cover even deeper the carved crescent moon that crowned the front door of the little house, a single star caught in its horns.

In the muddy yard behind the house, Miss Lattimer accepted the hand her groom held out and hopped neatly down from the gig, quite oblivious to the puddles. Pushing back her veil with a careless hand she stared around her with proprietary interest. 'Here we are, Jethro. The Moon House!' It was hard to keep a grin of pure pleasure from her face despite the air of neglect the yard radiated. A home again. Her home and a new start.

The groom, a gangling, solemn-faced youth not much above sixteen, glanced dismissively around and observed, 'So we are, Miss Hester. And your hair's coming down at the back again.'

'Oh, bother.' Hester put up her hands and made an ineffectual attempt to push the brown curls back into their confining net. 'Never mind, there's no one here to observe it. Now, Jethro, you see to stabling Hector and have a look at the rooms over the stable. I understand from the agent they are suitable and should have a bed and other furniture but I am certain they'll need a good clean before you sleep there, and certainly a fire… What is it?'

'Hector, Miss Hester?'

'The cob. I thought I had better give him a name and Hector seems appropriate. It is a good name, do you not think?' She regarded the animal hopefully: she had never had to buy a horse before, but she felt confident that she had made a good choice two days ago.

The boy's solemn face grew longer behind its mask of freckles and the occasional pimple. 'I could not say, Miss Hester.'

Hester smiled suddenly, a flashing smile that gave her an unexpected air of pure mischief. 'Now do not practise your butler's voice out here, Jethro! In the house you can buttle as much as you like—when you are not being boot boy, kitchen hand and footman. Out here you are the groom and the gardener—if it ever stops drizzling. We are all going to have to learn to be many things—I, for example, am about to go inside and become the housekeeper.'

She reached into the back of the gig and lifted out a small portmanteau, her reticule and an umbrella, adding as she turned away, 'And cook too, unless a miracle occurs and Miss Prudhome and Susan arrive in time before dinner.'

'I doubt it, Miss Hester,' Jethro observed gloomily, beginning to unbuckle the cob's harness and lead it out of the shafts. 'I'll bring the hampers in a minute and get the range going.'

Hester doubted it too. Her companion suffered so much from motion sickness that the *chaise* could move only at the slowest speed the postilion could be held to; goodness knew when she, Susan and the light luggage would arrive. Hester would doubtless have to see to dinner tonight as well as making up the beds and fires and chasing the worst of the spiders out.

But these lowering considerations vanished as she drew the large key from her reticule and set open the back door of the Moon House. Hester stepped slowly over the threshold into a dim, chill room, a little knot of anticipation and excitement in her stomach as she relished the moment. The air was still, redolent of dust, of old ashes and, regrettably, of mice. Then, as she stood there letting her eyes adjust to the shadows, it seemed as though a faint zephyr of a warm breeze filled the space whispering of laughter, roses, happiness—and as suddenly was gone.

Hester smiled at her own fancy; it seemed that pure happiness could take tangible form. Oh, yes, this was a happy house—she had known that from just a few minutes' observation over a year ago. She had stood at the gate, staring entranced at the overgrown rose-filled garden, the ivy-hung façade, the felicitous arrangement of doors and windows, the ineffable, indescribable air of charm that hung over the neglected little house. And then she had hurried back over the

Green to the Bird in Hand and to John, her friend and protector, who was waiting patiently in the private parlour while she shook the stiffness from her limbs.

He should never have undertaken that journey to Oxford; it marked the sharp deterioration in his condition, which had led to its inevitable end three months ago. They had only been together eighteen months, yet she still ached for his company, for their friendship and intimacy. If he had not protected her, in the face of scandal and family opposition, goodness knows what would have become of her after her father's death.

Hester shook herself briskly. John had known how short a time he had—better to do what he wanted than to purchase a few weeks at the expense of inaction and boredom. That part of her life was over now and she must learn not to brood upon memories and to stand upon her own two feet. She had learned from it and it had left her a legacy in both experience and scandal, as well as just enough money for genteel independence.

She had never been inside the mysteriously named Moon House, never seen it again after that one brief encounter. All her lengthy negotiations had been undertaken by an agent and she had simply placed her trust in his diligence and her own instinct. Now she pushed the door shut behind her and saw she was in the kitchen. Well, that was just as described—equipped with an old range and pine table, some chairs and dressers, the dulled glint of unpolished copper catching the light from the cobwebbed window. The next job for Jethro would be trying to light the range, if the chimney could be persuaded to draw. Hester smiled wryly: she was beginning to suspect they might have to take themselves over to the Bird in Hand for dinner.

Hester dumped the portmanteau and umbrella unceremoniously on the table, pulled off her bonnet with scant regard for the further chaos it wrought with her hair and tossed her pelisse on the chair. A rummage in the portmanteau produced a shawl, which she tied around her shoulders, a voluminous apron, which she struggled into, and a handful of soft rags ideal for dusting or giving spiders the rightabout.

Setting herself to explore, she emerged through a green baize-covered door into an alcove formed by the gracious upwards sweep of the staircase—somewhat marred now by dangling cobwebs. Hester swiped at them, sneezed, rubbed her nose with the back of her hand, transferring a large smudge on to nose-tip and cheek in the process, and stepped out into the hall.

'Oh, *yes*.'

She was unaware of speaking aloud, only conscious of the airy proportions, the elegant staircase, the quality of the cold light filtering through the fanlight over the door, despite the curtain of ivy that hung across it.

The walls were dingy with dust, marked here and there with ghostly oblongs where pictures or mirrors had once hung. The marble floor, chequered in an unusual grey and white, was grimy—but she could see none of the faults. The feeling of welcome and of belonging swept over her again and Hester walked slowly down the hall, then turned to lean back against the deep-cut panels of the front door.

'This is mine,' she said aloud, her tone wondering, then more strongly, *'Mine.'*

The blow on the door behind her was so unexpected, so abrupt, it sounded like thunder. With a shriek Hester leapt away and turned gasping to face it. Effortfully she dragged a breath up from the depths and clasped her trembling hands together while she composed herself. Someone had knocked on the door, that was all. If she had not been mooning like an idiot instead of doing some useful dusting or lighting a fire, it would have sounded perfectly normal.

The knocker fell again. Hester scrabbled in her pocket where she had transferred the keys and found the largest. This must be for the front door. She turned it, struggled for a moment with the bolts and finally dragged the door open.

Guy Westrope tapped one foot irritably on the step and cursed himself for a sentimental fool. What the devil was he doing here when he could have joined Carew's party in Rutland? Now he was stuck in a muddy Buckinghamshire village in a hideous house, the target of every prying yokel and gossiping goodwife. He raised an impatient hand to the knocker again, then dropped it as the door began to open.

The dishevelled figure revealed by the part-open door regarded him silently. She was of medium height with an oval face, big brown eyes, a wide and solemn mouth and quantities of ill-controlled brown hair. The dirty smudge across the apparition's face and the voluminous apron indicated that this particular housemaid had been engaged in dusting, a supposition confirmed when she hastily thrust the hand holding a bundle of rags behind her.

Guy realised he was probably scowling and pulled himself together; his unfamiliar inner turmoil was no excuse for treating subordinates rudely. This particular one appeared to have been cowed into speechlessness by his appearance. For some reason he had an almost irresistible urge to lean forward and rub the smudge off her cheek. He clasped his hands behind his back.

'Good morning. Is your mistress at home?' Parrott had reported a woman arriving alone, save for a groom. Presumably he would be dealing with a widow.

Something he could have sworn was mischief flashed into the maid's eyes and was gone. Her voice emerged in a whisper. 'No, sir. Leastways, she's not receiving, sir.' She appeared to pull herself together a little. 'Would you be wishful of leaving a message, sir?'

Guy extracted a card and held it out. A remarkably delicate hand, the knuckles smeared with cobwebs, took it. 'Will your mistress be at home tomorrow?'

'Er…yes, sir…my lord, I should say.'

This was hard work. Was this brown-eyed girl afraid of him or just naturally shy? He tried a smile and saw her eyes widen a little. He entertained the sudden fancy that her thoughts showed in her eyes, but in a language he could not read. 'And at what time might it be convenient for her to receive me, do you think?'

'Three o'clock.' That was unexpectedly decisive, especially as it was not the conventional time of day to receive visitors.

'Very well, then. Please tell your mistress that I will do myself the honour of calling upon her at three tomorrow. Good day.'

'Yes, my lord. Um…good day, my lord.' There was the merest suggestion of a smile on that solemn mouth. It made the swell of the lower lip seem almost pouting.

The door swung shut before he had half-turned on the step. Guy walked slowly back down the overgrown path. A quaint little creature, that maid. Fetching brown eyes and the piquancy of that solemn mouth—it would be interesting to make her smile again. He shook himself briskly and quickened his pace. This would never do—two days in the sticks and he was already eyeing the servant girls. He would take the curricle and the new greys out this afternoon and give himself something to think about other than the Moon House and its present occupants.

In the silent hall Hester leaned against the closed door in the same position she had assumed before and regarded the card in her hand while her heartbeat returned to something approaching normal.

Guy Westrope, Earl of Buckland. Monks Grange, Buckland Regis, Wiltshire and an excellent London address. What on *earth* was an earl doing calling upon her, especially as he presumably had no idea who she was? Hester pulled herself together and ran into the room to her right to peer through the window. She could just see the top of his tall hat passing the wall of that hideous house opposite.

What was an earl, who one might well expect to be wintering at his own or his acquaintances' country estates, doing calling upon an unknown lady in a Buckinghamshire village? With the memory of those very blue eyes vivid in her mind, Hester indulged a moment's fantasy that he had followed her from London, infatuated by her beauty and charm, which he had glimpsed from afar. The thought of being pursued by someone that powerful, that masculine, made her heart race again.

With a laugh at her own foolishness, Hester rubbed her handful of dust cloths over a cracked mirror hanging by the window and peered into its mottled depths. The vision revealed there cut any thought of laughter quite dead.

'What a fright!' There was a dark smudge right across her nose and one cheek, her hair was coming down, her collar was marked and a hasty glance down at hands and apron confirmed the picture of a slatternly housemaid. 'Oh, my goodness.' That would teach her to entertain fantasies about strange men.

She gazed around what had obviously once been a delightful reception room in horror. Her suggestion that the earl might call at three the next day had assumed that it would be simple to produce a civilised room to receive him in by then, and that he might be no more than mildly surprised by the eccentricity of a lady who did her own dusting and pretended to be her own housemaid.

Now she could see they would have to labour all day to make this room and the hall decent—and what he would think of such an abandoned creature as she must have appeared did not bear thinking about.

'What does that matter?' Hester asked herself briskly, marching across the hall to see if the opposite room was any better. It was not. 'He is probably just an acquaintance of John's.' That was not much comfort. If that was so he must already regard Miss Lattimer as an abandoned hussy.

'I must stop talking to myself,' she chided, promptly ignoring her own advice as she made her way back to the stairs. 'Bedrooms next.' It would be as well to find out the worst about those before the day was much older. The agent's description of the house as 'partly furnished' was proving somewhat over-optimistic.

'And what do you care what some earl thinks about you, Hester Lattimer?' *Not much in general*, her inner self answered, *but that particular man...*

The first bedroom yielded a decent-enough-looking bedstead with dust sheets over the mattress, which appeared dry and mercifully free of mice. Hester peeped into three other rooms, each with bedstead and mattress, thank goodness, and then opened wide the door into the room overlooking the front garden.

'Oh! How lovely.' This room had two generous windows, each with a window seat. Silk draperies marred with dust hung at each casement and between them stood a *chaise-longue* with a little table beside it. The bed was a charmingly feminine confection with slim posts festooned with embroidered silk. Hester touched one fall carefully, hastily withdrawing her hand as some of the silk shattered where it had been folded for so long. Again, enough care had been taken to protect the mattress and the room appeared habitable, if dirty and bone cold.

This chamber would be hers and Prudy and Susan could

have their choice of the other rooms. Doubtless there were servants' rooms in the attic, but they had too much to do to contemplate putting those to rights for quite a while. Susan would be much more comfortable down here.

There was another door in the corner of the room. Hester crossed to it, pausing for a moment to look at the ugly house opposite. In the summer it would be screened for the most part by a spreading elm tree; now it showed gaunt through the bare branches. Several windows were visible on the first floor, but there were no signs of life. Who lived there? Would they make congenial neighbours? She flicked over the catch on the window and after a tussle managed to push up the lower sash. Sharp, clear air flowed into the musty room and she smiled, taking a moment to enjoy it.

There was the sound of voices opposite and a gate in the high wall to the rear of the house opened. A curricle drawn by a pair of dark greys turned sharply out and headed away from the Green and out of the village. Unmistakably it was the earl who was driving and her own front wall was low enough for Hester to have an uninterrupted view of Guy Westrope's profile.

Hester realised that she had been far too flustered to have more than a muddled impression of him from their encounter. Blue eyes, those she did recall, although at this distance they could not be discerned. She could not say what colour his hair was, but she remembered those eyes and the size of him—tall, broad-shouldered and powerful. To that she could now add the impression of a determined chin. He did not look like a man to be trifled with and the scowl with which he had greeted her, and the coolly polite tones he had used to address her, left her more than a little apprehensive over how he might react to discovering the deception she had practised on him. But when he had smiled, there was the glimpse of quite another man.

At least she now knew who her neighbour was, although congenial was hardly the word she would use to describe him. And it only added to the mystery: to find he was staying at the Bird in Hand while he conducted whatever business he had with her was one thing—but why was he staying here?

If she didn't stop idling about and get on with making this house fit to receive visitors, she'd lower herself even further in his estimation, she scolded herself mentally, getting to her feet and pushing open the remaining door.

It opened into a dressing room and on to a scene of violence. Hester halted, appalled, on the threshold. The shield-shaped mirror that had stood on the dressing table was face down upon the floor, its glass smashed into shards that still lay where they had fallen. The doors to the clothes-presses hung open with the empty shelves pulled out and the chair before the dressing table was thrown on its side. One curtain hung from its last two rings, seemingly dragged down by some clutching hand.

A mass of filmy cloth lay at her feet. Automatically Hester stooped and picked it up, shaking it out to reveal an outrageously pretty nightgown of Indian muslin. It had been ripped from neck to hem. She moved abruptly backwards and something skittered out from beneath her foot. Under the blanketing dust the floor was strewn with pearls, enough to have made a veritable rope when strung.

What had happened in this chamber? Abduction? Rape? Murder? The calmly happy atmosphere of the house seemed to freeze here into anger and fear. Behind her the curtains flapped as the outer door opened and the door at her back slammed shut with enough force to propel her into the desecrated room.

Hester swung round, suddenly afraid, her feet scrabbling

on the treacherous pearls, her grasp on the door handle hampered by the nightgown. Against her own hands it began to turn. Someone was outside.

CHAPTER TWO

'Jethro! You gave me such a fright.'

'I'm sorry, Miss Hester, but I brought in the hampers and I couldn't see you. I called, then I thought I'd better come and find you.' He glanced over her shoulder and went pale under the freckles. 'Gawd, Miss Hester, what's happened in there?'

'Do not blaspheme, Jethro,' Hester said automatically, turning to let him see in. 'I have no idea, but it does not look as if it were anything good.' She twisted up the nightrail in her hands. Jethro was only a lad for all his size and his growing awareness of girls, and she did not want him seeing that violated, intimate garment.

'That's blood, Miss Hester.' He was already into the room, his feet crunching on broken glass and leaving clear tracks through the undisturbed dust.

'Oh, no, please, not that.' Hester followed him more cautiously and stared at the brown splashes on the wall. 'It is not so very much. Perhaps it is red wine, or maybe whoever broke the mirror cut himself?'

'That'll be it, no doubt about it, Miss Hester,' Jethro said comfortably. He was not as innocent as his young mistress thought him and the images that came to his mind when he saw the room chimed very much with hers. 'It'll have been burglars, to be sure,' he continued, walking firmly out so Hester had to give way in front of him. 'Throwing all the doors open and knocking things around when they found the cupboards empty, I'll be bound.'

He shut the door. 'Will this be your room, Miss Hester?'

'Yes…' Hester heard the hesitation in her own voice and said firmly, 'Yes, it will, and Susan can have the one to the right at the top of the stairs. I expect Miss Prudhome will like one of the rooms at the back.'

The unconscious glance she cast at the dressing-room door was not lost on the boy. 'I'll sweep those rooms out then, shall I, after luncheon, and light the fires? Then I can bring the bags up without your things getting dusty.' And there was a pot of whiting in the stables, he could soon mix some whitewash up and cover that stain, she'd feel better about the room with that gone and the broken things tidied away.

'The rooms over the stables are right and tight, Miss Hester,' he continued, firmly leading the way downstairs. 'There's a pot-bellied stove, so I'll be snug as a bug in there.'

'That is good news, Jethro,' Hester said briskly. Everything was perfectly all right, except for that disturbing room. Try as she might, she could not believe Jethro's explanation of burglars. The thick carpet of dust had been even, as though it had been left undisturbed as a whole. Surely the intruders' footprints would have shown, even through the later falls? And why would burglars tear a nightgown or break a valuable string of pearls and leave them?

'I was going to run over to the inn to order a cask of ale, Miss Hester. Do you want me to wait until the others get here?'

'No, the ale is a good idea and you may as well go now. Goodness knows how long it will take them to get here from King's Langley if Miss Prudhome's persuaded the postilion to go slowly the entire way.'

He shot her an anxious look, but took the coins she handed him and went out. *Of course it is all right being here alone*, Hester told herself firmly. *What are you afraid of? Ghosts?*

Her stomach rumbled at that point, effectively putting paid to all thoughts of spectres or earls. What time was it? The old longcase clock in the kitchen had last been wound years ago, but her pocket watch said clearly that it was two of the clock and that breakfast at the inn at King's Langley where they had stayed overnight was many hours away.

Jethro had thoughtfully drawn a bucket of water, which stood in the slate-lined sink. Hester dipped some out into a bowl, found an ancient scrubbing brush on the window ledge and attacked the kitchen table. It would need hours' more work before it became white again, but at least they could eat luncheon off it without a qualm.

She spread a cloth from the top of one of the hampers, found bread, cheese, a jar of pickles and a packet of butter, then turned her attention to the contents of the kitchen cupboards.

Jethro returned after half an hour with a vast earthenware pitcher of ale, heavy enough to make him gasp with relief when he set it down on the table. 'That's a ploughman's pot, that is,' he remarked, mopping his brow. 'Part of the plough-man's wages is his daily ale and his lad goes to fetch it for him. Often as not he'll empty it down, then break it on the plough handles and send the boy back for another one with a cuff on the ear for being so careless.'

Hester put down the stack of plates she had been scouring in cold water and regarded him, head on one side. 'That is interesting, Jethro. How did you know that?'

'Don't remember,' he muttered, opening the other hamper and starting to lift things out. 'They'll send the cask over later today, but I thought we'd need some for now.'

Hester sighed. She had found him unconscious in the gutter in Old Holborn over a year ago, starved thin as a rake and with the marks of old beatings on his back. Taken back to the house in Mount Street, he had been quiet, polite and obdurately silent on anything but his name. He attached himself with dogged devotion to Hester and obeyed her in everything but the request to tell of his past. His accent had a burr, which had largely vanished under the influence of London speech and Hester's cultured tones, but she suspected country origins and that little story seemed to confirm it.

'Here is some cutlery.' She pushed it over the table, abandoning any thought of probing further. If and when he wanted to tell her he would do so. She had enough bad memories and secrets of her own not to pry into his.

Finally they sat down to eat in front of the range, which was slowly beginning to take the chill off the air. Hester put down her ale, which she was drinking out of an earthenware beaker for want of any more suitable vessel, and observed, 'I hope the glassware arrives safely with Susan. We are having a gentleman caller tomorrow and I must offer wine.'

'At least we've got some good wine,' Jethro remarked. The disturbing memory had faded, leaving him bright eyed and interested.

'Yes, and fortunately I put a few bottles of the Madeira and port into the baggage that is on the *chaise*. The rest will be coming with the carrier.'

Bless John for having left her his wine cellar. An unconventional thing to leave to a woman, but they had enjoyed a glass of wine together so often. Of course, it was only one of the numerous scandalous things that could be laid at her door. And his relatives had not hesitated to enumerate every one.

This time it was Jethro who pulled her out of painful reverie. 'What gentleman is it, Miss Hester?'

'No mere gentleman…an earl, no less.' Hester pushed the card across to him. Jethro read it, eyes wide.

'You won't have Susan answering the door, will you, Miss Hester? Not in the afternoon?'

'No, Jethro. A female servant in the afternoon? That would never do.' Hester repressed a smile. 'I shall require you to put on your best suit and be the butler.'

His wide grin was not in the slightest reduced by the intelligence that, as well as setting the bedchambers and kitchen to rights today, they must all work tomorrow to clean the hall and make one of the front reception rooms decent before their visitor arrived.

'It will take all the furniture we can find to furnish up the one room.' Hester bit her lip thoughtfully. 'The carrier's cart will not arrive tomorrow and what there is here is sparse, to put it mildly.'

'And old-fashioned.' Jethro's ambitions in life caused him to be surprisingly aware of such details.

'Good quality, though, and very feminine. Perhaps the last person to live here was an elderly single woman, or a widow.'

Further speculation was cut short by the arrival of the post *chaise* in the yard. Susan Wilmott—plump, good natured and just now looking delighted to have arrived—jumped down and held up her hands to assist an older woman. Miss Prudhome, Hester's companion of two weeks' standing, and decidedly green in the face, tottered from the vehicle and into Hester's arms. 'Never again, Hester dear, not if I have to walk a hundred miles! Never again in one of those yellow bounders.'

'There, there.' Hester patted her back while trying to ignore the postilion's rolling eyes. 'You made very good time considering,' she added placatingly to the man. 'Jethro, show the postilion where he can water his horses while we unload the *chaise*.'

Hester placed her companion firmly in a chair in the kitchen with a glass of water and joined her two staff to bring in the contents of the post *chaise*.

Susan dumped an armload on the table and looked around her with interest. 'Nice house, Miss Hester, but it's awful big for just two staff. Are you going to hire in anyone else?'

'I hope so, Susan.' Hester lowered her end of a hamper of house wares. 'But I need to find out how much I must spend to get the house in order first and then I will see what we can afford. Until then we will just keep the downstairs and three bedchambers in order.

'Now, you find yourself some luncheon and then we will decide what to do first.' She regarded Miss Prudhome dubiously. 'Do you think you could manage a little luncheon, Prudy?'

A pitiful groan greeted the question. Miss Prudhome was thin, forty-eight years of age and, Jethro was unkind enough to remark, closely resembled a hen. 'One of those worried-looking brown ones, you know, Miss Hester.'

Hester did know, and unfortunately could not get the image out of her head whenever she looked at her recently engaged companion with her pointed nose and anxious little eyes behind precarious *pince-nez*.

She was, in fact, a governess but, as Hester's limited budget had ruled out all the superior companions who presented themselves in answer to her advertisement, she was the only affordable candidate. Her halting tale of being dismissed from her employment of ten years because the youngest boy had gone to school wrung Hester's kind heart and she had accepted her application against her better judgement. She had even yielded to Miss Prudhome's wistful request that she call her 'Prudy'.

Jethro marched in, arms loaded with broom, mop and

bucket and clanked past. 'I'll just get the worst of the mess sorted upstairs, Miss Hester, and light the fires.'

By seven o'clock the four of them were collapsed in a semi-circle of chairs by the range, which Jethro had managed to keep going, although with an ominously smoky chimney. 'Full of nests, I guess,' he observed. 'I'd better find a sweep tomorrow and have all the fires done.'

'Never mind,' Hester said cheerfully. 'We each have a comfortable bed to sleep in and a clean kitchen to cook and eat in. And tomorrow we can see to the hall and front room.'

Prudy twittered nervously, Susan sighed gustily and even Jethro looked a little daunted, presumably at the thought of all the other rooms, to say nothing of the garden, the stable yard and the outbuildings. But Hester felt nothing but peace and a sense of home. If she had been a cat she would have turned round several times and curled up in front of the fire with her tail over her nose; as it was she got to her feet, rolled up her sleeves and reached for a saucepan.

'Dinner and bed for all of us. If we do not eat soon, we will be beyond it,' she said bracingly. 'You peel the potatoes, Jethro. Susan, shred some of that cabbage and slice the onions and I will fry up those collops of veal. Prudy, please lay the table and put some bricks in the lower oven to warm up for the beds.'

The meal was good, filling and savoury, and the eyes of her three companions were soon drooping. Hester sent Susan and Prudy to bed, each clutching a flannel-wrapped brick, assuring them she had no further need of them that night, and even Jethro was persuaded to take himself and his lantern off to his bed over the stables after faithfully checking the windows and front door.

Hester twisted the key in the back door after him, dragged the bolts across and gave the fire a final riddle before taking a chamber stick and making her way through the now-silent house.

The darkness closed in behind her softly like a velvet curtain as she climbed the stairs. There was no light from the other rooms. She hesitated on the threshold of her chamber, her eyes on the door leading to the dressing room. In the firelight it seemed to move.

The silence enclosed her, friendly no longer. 'No,' Hester said firmly. 'This is my room and I am not going to be frightened by some broken glass and a stain on the wall.'

She marched over to the table by the *chaise-longue* and lit the candles in the three-branched stick that stood on it. Her own face reflected in the panes of glass in the unshuttered windows. It was the dark of the moon and only lights from the houses and cottages around the Green punctuated the night.

As she tried to pull the silk curtains closed they crumbled in her hands, rotten from years of neglect. On one window the shutters unfolded and closed easily enough, but on the other they would not shift, even at the cost of a broken fingernail. Hester shrugged; she would undress on the screened side of the room.

In her nightrail and shawl she bent to blow out the branched candlestick and found herself staring at that door again. Was she going to sleep or was she going to lie awake, staring at it in the dark and imagining goodness knows what?

Slowly Hester walked towards it, the single chamber stick in her hand, and finally turned the handle. 'Oh, bless the boy!' Jethro had swept and dusted. The glass was gone, the stained patch of wall gleamed newly white. The pearls had been collected up into a bowl on the dressing table and the doors of the presses were shut. He had even opened the window an inch and the chill air had driven away the musty smell. It was an empty, unthreatening room once more. He was a good lad, sensitive beyond his years sometimes. Hester smiled, recalling John's doubts when she had returned home with her filthy waif. 'You will regret it,' he said, studying the lad with a cynical soldier's eye, but she never had.

She drifted back to bed, reassured and suddenly too tired either to plan or to remember. As she snuggled under the sheets her thoughts flickered to tomorrow's encounter. What would the earl think of her? she wondered. Strange that it was not his wife who had made the first call. Perhaps he was unmarried...

Hester slept. Across the road in the red brick house Guy Westrope stood in his dark bedchamber, the book he had strolled upstairs to fetch in his hand. He could see in the dark uncannily well and had not troubled to pick up the branch of candles from the landing table when he entered. Now he stood waiting to see whether that slender ghost of a figure in white would cross the room opposite his again. But the window in the Moon House went dark as a candle was extinguished.

Who was she? Not that quaint maid, not in what must be the best bedchamber. The lady of the house? Or simply a phantom of his imagination? No, not that, for the ghost he would expect to conjure up would have blonde hair, not a tumbling mass of brunette curls.

Cursing himself for a fool, not for the first time that day, Guy strode out of the room and downstairs to a solitary meal. The most entertainment he could hope for would be his attempts to catch his butler Parrott betraying by so much as a quiver his utter disapproval of the village, the house and the entire enterprise. His valet was far more vocal on the subject and on the ruination of his hopes of seeing his master outshining every guest at Major Carew's house party. Guy smiled grimly: he was an extremely generous and considerate employer, but he was not going to be criticised by his own staff for whatever whim he chose to indulge. In this particular case he could do that quite effectively himself.

At ten to three the next afternoon Hester called her household into the newly garnished reception room and surveyed both it and them. They had scoured the room clean and then stripped the house of suitable furnishings. The *chaise-longue* from her bedroom, a dresser from the other front chamber and side tables from all over dressed the room and a large, if smoky, fire blazed on the hearth. There were two imposing armchairs, which she placed one each side of the fireplace, and a chair set to one side for Prudy to sit upon. It looked a little like a rented room in an unfashionable part of town, but it would have to do.

At least she and her staff were suitably clad to receive a caller: Jethro in his best dark suit with horizontally striped waistcoat, his hair neatly tied back, Susan in a respectable dimity and Prudy looking every bit the governess in sombre grey with a black knitted shawl. For herself Hester had chosen a gown of fine wool in a soft old gold colour, with a fichu edged with some of the good lace she had inherited from her mother and her best Paisley shawl. Her hair was ruthlessly confined in its net at the back with just a few soft curls at the temples and forehead.

Hester gave her hem one last anxious twitch. 'I think we look admirably respectable,' she announced firmly. It was the impression she was striving for, the impression it was essential to convey if she was to hope to have any kind of social life in the village or nearby towns. It was odd enough for a young lady of four and twenty to live alone save for a companion, but to produce the slightest suspicion of anything 'not quite the thing' would be fatal.

The effort it had taken to transform the front room and the hall had succeeded in distracting her from the nagging feeling that she might already have sunk herself beneath reproach when she answered the door to the earl yesterday. But now it returned. Would he be very affronted when he realised who the maid was? Or, even worse, would he consider it a great joke to be spread around his acquaintance? Being thought to be eccentric was not Hester's ambition either.

He was most certainly prompt. Hester had hardly settled herself before the fireplace with a piece of embroidery in her hand when the knocker sounded. Jethro tugged down his coat, straightened his face and strode out.

There was the sound of voices in the hall, then Jethro reappeared. 'The Earl of Buckland, Miss Lattimer.'

Hester rose to her feet, put down her embroidery, looked up and felt her breath catch in her throat. Somehow she retrieved enough of it not to croak as she stepped forward with outstretched hand. 'Good afternoon, my lord. I am Hester Lattimer.'

How could she not have realised yesterday? Had she been so overwhelmed by the house, so frightened by his sudden knocking? The man standing in front of her was not just extremely attractive—quite simply, he was her ideal. She had no need to do more than to look into those dark blue eyes with their crinkle of laughter lines at the corners, the lurking mixture of intelligence, humour and frank admiration in their depths, to feel a surge of heat in her blood and an indefinable sense of recognition.

He took her hand and her pulse began to thud so that she thought he must have felt it as he touched her. Hastily she retrieved her hand. 'My lord, may I make known to you my companion, Miss Prudhome?' He inclined his head with a smile and Prudy produced a gawky curtsy and an unintelligible twitter. Hester sighed inwardly and gestured towards the other chair. 'Please, my lord, will you not sit down?'

Goodness, he was tall, and broad and…male. Not good looking, she decided, for his nose had definitely been broken, the planes of his face were strong rather than beautiful, his dark blond hair was too long…

'Harrumph.'

Hester started. How long had she been staring at her visitor? Not too long, surely, for he did not appear discommoded. Jethro was standing by the door, looking abashed. His intended quiet throat-clearing had emerged as rather more of a foghorn than a tactful signal from a butler.

'Ackland, please fetch us some refreshment. Would you care to take tea, my lord? Or perhaps some Madeira?'

'Tea would be delightful, thank you, Miss Lattimer.' She nodded to Jethro, who effaced himself silently.

The earl's voice exactly suited him, she decided. So often a voice was a sad disappointment, but his was deep, pleasant and carried a hint of authority. He was watching her with composure, those blue eyes resting on her face, betraying no sign that he recognised her from the day before. To refer to it or not? Suddenly Hester felt she would make herself ridiculous in his estimation if she was missish about this.

'I am sorry I could not receive you yesterday when you called,' she began. 'We had only just arrived and it was necessary to do more than I had anticipated to set the house to rights.'

'My sister frequently tells me that the servant shortage is a difficulty,' he observed urbanely. Yes, no doubt about it, he did recognise her as that dishevelled 'maid'.

'Oh, it is not that, my lord. I have chosen to bring only a skeleton staff from London and I will hire locally. But just now we are a small household.' Hopefully that sounded as though she was used to commanding a staff of four times the number.

'But, until then, it is intolerable to have to put up with cobwebs?' The corner of his mouth quirked and Hester could feel her own twitching in response. There was nothing for it but to be frank and trust to his goodwill.

'Indeed. It was most remiss of me to have opened the door without thinking. Goodness knows what you must have thought.' Now that was a foolish thing to have said, inviting him to agree with her.

'I thought that the new arrival in the village had excellent taste in domestic servants.' Now what did he mean by that? Surely not that he considered her attractive? She found she had no objection to the earl holding that opinion, but for him to say so was the outside of enough.

'I should have called my butler,' she said repressively.

'Your butler? Surely you do not mean that youth who showed me in?'

'But certainly, my lord. I should tell you that Ackland has the intention to become the best butler in England,' Hester retorted warmly as the door opened. 'Ah, thank you, Ackland, please put the tray here. I was just telling his lordship that you have great ambitions to rise in your profession.'

'To be the best butler in England, I understand.' The earl half-turned in his seat to regard the gangling youth, showing no sign he had noticed the freckles, the pimples or the fact that the coat sleeves were already half an inch too short. Hester, who had been holding her breath, expecting him to snub the lad and wishing she had kept her mouth shut, could have kissed him.

'Yes, my lord.' Jethro blushed, but managed to keep his face and voice in order.

'Well, Ackland, I have to tell you that the best butler in England is Mr Parrott and he is in my employ.'

'Here, my lord? In this village?' Now he sounded fourteen and not the seventeen Hester guessed him to be.

'Certainly he is here. I shall mention you to him; perhaps one day, when he is not too busy, he will unbend enough to give you some advice on your chosen profession.'

Jethro had gone so white Hester was certain he was about to swoon. 'That is most kind of his lordship, Ackland. You may go now.' Bless him, his feet would not touch the ground for a week.

'That *was* most kind of you, my lord,' she said as the door closed behind the youth. 'He is so very serious about this, despite his age. A single lady's household is no training ground for him and I suppose he should be seeking a footman's post as a start.'

'But you need him here,' the earl said with a smile. 'Let us see what Parrott advises.' He saw the question in her eyes and nodded. 'Yes, I will make sure he spends some time with the lad.'

Hester poured the tea and wondered when her visitor was going to broach the reason for his call. Surely it was not purely social? 'Is the countess with you, my lord?' she enquired, passing the tea cup.

'My mother died some months ago.' Her eyes must have flickered over the dark blue long-tailed coat he wore, for he added, 'She abhorred mourning, so after the first month we all left it off. I do not feel that wearing unrelieved black for months on end helps one remember the departed any more fondly.'

'No, indeed,' Hester agreed. 'I myself—' She broke off. This was one area she did not wish to explore.

'You have suffered a recent loss too?' His voice was sympathetic and she almost said more than she should.

'Yes. I was a companion to an invalid for almost two years. The end was not unexpected.' If that left the false impression that she had been the companion to an elderly lady, then so much the better.

'It does not lessen the loss.' He put down his cup and saucer and recrossed his long legs. 'That was most refreshing. Miss Lattimer, I cannot pretend that this is a social call; I wish to discuss with you a matter of business.'

'Business?' Hester made no effort to hide her surprise.

'Perhaps I should address myself to your man of affairs? If you would give me his direction, I will be happy to do so, although I feel this is a matter upon which he would immediately have to consult you in any case.'

'Then perhaps you can broach the matter and I will refer you to him if necessary.'

'Very well. Miss Lattimer, I wish to purchase your house.'

CHAPTER THREE

'You wish to purchase my house?' Hester echoed blankly. 'Which house?'

'Why, this one.' His lips quirked again. This time Hester felt no inclination to smile back. 'Do you have another?'

'No! And I have absolutely no intention of selling the Moon House. I have only just bought it myself and I have been resident in it but one night, my lord.'

'I am aware of that, which is why I have called so close upon your arrival. I have no wish to disrupt your life, but you will not have had time to grow attached to the place and, as your heavy luggage has not yet arrived, I imagine you are far from settled.' He sat back more comfortably into the chair, his hands clasped, a picture of ease.

Hester was beginning to move from bemusement to anger. He was keeping a close eye upon her movements indeed! 'I am firmly attached to this house, my lord, which is why I bought it.'

'I agree it is a very pretty place,' he acknowledged sympathetically. 'You show admirable taste in selecting it, Miss Lattimer.' Hester narrowed her eyes, she was not going to be charmed, patronised or cozened out of the Moon House, it was ridiculous for him to try. 'I will put another house at your disposal until you have decided where you want to live. I have houses in London—'

'I have just moved from London.'

'Or Oxford, if you prefer another town. Or I am sure my agents can find you a country home you would be charmed with.'

'But I am already charmed with this one, my lord. I have no need, no desire and absolutely no intention of moving from it.' Hester took a reviving sip of tea and set her cup down with emphasis. Why did she feel Guy Westrope would quite happily take root here in her drawing room and persist until she gave in out of sheer weariness? The flame of attraction she had felt for him was rapidly becoming quenched under a douche of puzzlement and irritation. And he was so uncompromisingly large and male it was very difficult to ignore him.

'I will naturally pay you well in excess of your purchase price to compensate for the inconvenience, and my agents will undertake all the arrangements for you.'

Lord Buckland was regarding her calmly as though he had not the slightest doubt that she would eventually agree with whatever he wanted. Presumably if one was a wealthy, titled, personable aristocrat with one's fair share of self-esteem, one normally experienced little difficulty in obtaining what one desired. It was time he learned this was not an inevitable state of affairs.

'My lord, I have said no, and no I mean.' That appeared to make no impression. 'Why do you want the Moon House so badly?' she asked abruptly and was rewarded by a sudden flash of emotion in those blue eyes. Ah, so he was not as unreadable as perhaps he liked to think.

'I am not at liberty to say, Miss Lattimer. Might I ask why you are so attached to a house you scarcely know?'

'I am perfectly at liberty to tell you that, my lord,' Hester said, matching her cool tones to his. 'But I have absolutely no intention of doing so.'

His expression this time was of amusement and, she thought, a grudging respect. '*Touché*. I shall just have to see if I can change your mind, Miss Lattimer. Doubtless some of the inconveniences of the house will become apparent over the next few days as the first charm wears off. All old houses have their…peculiarities.'

A little shiver went through Hester. The dressing room—could that be described as a peculiarity? To hide her sudden apprehension she continued to attack. 'And meanwhile you intend to camp out in that hideous barracks of a house opposite while you attempt to wear me down?'

'How do you know that is not a favourite family home?' he enquired, steepling his fingers and regarding her over the top of them. Hester could not help but admire their length and the restrained taste of the heavy gold signet that was their only adornment.

'Because I looked at your card and then I checked the *Peerage*,' she retorted tartly, dragging her eyes away from his hands.

He nodded in acknowledgement of her hit. 'Most wise of you, Miss Lattimer. But my hideous barracks has one great advantage.'

'And what might that be?'

'The view is so much better from my windows than from yours.' He got to his feet with the natural elegance of a very fit man. 'Thank you for the tea, ma'am. It was a pleasure meeting you.'

Exasperating man. How could she ever have thought him attractive?

Hester rose and reached out to tug the bell pull sharply. It resisted, then the whole thing came away in her hands, showering her with a light dusting of plaster and dead flies. Prudy gave a cry of alarm. Hester stood stock still, clutching the fraying rope and trying to resist the temptation to swipe at the dust covering her gown. It would be undignified and would most certainly make marks. Possibly the floor would open up and swallow her, but she doubted anything so helpful would occur.

The earl stepped forward, an immaculate white handkerchief in his hand. 'Please allow me, Miss Lattimer, you have plaster dust on your lashes. It will be most painful if it goes in your eye.'

It appeared that nothing was going to stop him. With a noise like an cross kitten Hester closed her eyes and let him flick the fragments away. She opened her eyes again cautiously, only to find him still standing close in front of her.

'Did you know your eyes change colour when you are angry?' he asked conversationally. 'It must be those gold flecks.'

Taken aback, Hester spoke without thinking. 'They also change when I am happy.'

'I am sure they reflect your every emotion,' his lordship rejoined. 'A fascinating phenomenon; I must watch out for it. Closely.'

A series of possible retorts ran through Hester's brain, each one censored by good manners. She was going to hang on to the character of a gentlewoman if it killed her. 'I am sure you would rapidly become bored, my lord. I imagine I have exhibited my full range of emotions this afternoon.'

'Do you think so, Miss Lattimer?' He regarded her quizzically. 'I so very much hope you are wrong. Good afternoon. Miss Prudhome, ma'am.'

Jethro must have been standing with an ear to the door, listening for approaching footsteps, for he whisked it open before the earl reached it. 'Your hat, my lord.'

The door closed and Hester plumped down in the chair, the unwise force raising a cloud of dust. 'Infuriating man!'

'Oh, Hester!' Prudy hurried over and looked nervously from Hester's stormy face to the white-spotted gown. 'Shall I fetch the clothes brush?' She hesitated. 'Was the earl *flirting* with you?'

'Yes, do please call Susan to fetch the clothes brush, but wait until his lordship has gone. And I am not sure *what* he was doing other than trying to throw me off balance so that I sell him this house. If he thinks he can do it by flirting, then he is in for a big surprise.'

'Well, I do declare!' Susan bustled in unsummoned as the sound of the front door closing reached them. 'Look at the state of you, Miss Hester.'

'Oh dear, oh dear!' Miss Prudhome was staring at Hester aghast, her *pince-nez* crooked. 'He was flirting with you and I should have stopped him, hinted him away. My first duty as a chaperon and I have failed!'

'The nerve of the man! And him an earl too—is he one of those London rakes they talk about, Miss Hester?'

'Probably,' Hester said vaguely. 'Fetch me the clothes brush, please, Susan. Prudy, do sit down and compose yourself, no harm has been done.'

The maid hastened out, leaving Hester regarding her own clasped hands. Slowly she raised them, bent at the wrists in a gesture to push away an unseen figure. He had been so close. Her palms tingled as though from the imagined friction of superfine cloth against skin.

Hester rubbed her palms together briskly. That cool, polite manner and then that moment of quite shocking intimacy as he had gazed into her eyes! His closeness—the implication of his words—if not his tone—was suggestive of his desire for even greater closeness. Hester shook herself; he had wanted to throw her off balance and he had succeeded, that was all. It was nothing she was not perfectly capable of dealing with. Why, then, did she feel so disturbed, so…apprehensive?

Jethro reappeared, looking pleased with himself, Susan at his heels. 'That was very good, Jethro. Your first member of the aristocracy and you carried it off well. Oh, thank you, Susan, I think it will brush away easily enough.'

'I didn't drop his gloves nor nothing.' Jethro met her eye and carefully corrected himself. 'Or anything. Do you think his lordship meant it when he said I could talk to his butler? I mean, that wasn't something he just said because he was making up to you, was it, Miss Hester?'

'That is a most unsuitable expression, Jethro. I am sure Lord Buckland will be a man of his word.' Again that ripple of apprehension lapped at her nerves. He had said that he wanted the Moon House and somehow that had seemed not a request, but a statement of what was going to happen. Surely he would not stoop to attempting to suborn her staff? Oh, if only Prudy would stop snivelling; she could hardly think.

Susan was whispering urgently to Jethro. When they realised she was looking at them they fell silent and regarded her apprehensively. Finally Jethro said, 'Are you going to sell the house to him, Miss Hester?'

'Certainly not. This is our home now and I am not going to be turned out of it by some town buck because he has a whim to own it.' Their relief was palpable: already they were beginning to put down roots here.

Lord Buckland's departure left a flat feeling of anticlimax behind it, but Hester could not find the energy to change her clothes again and tackle any more housework.

'We will take the rest of the day as a holiday from house-work,' she announced briskly. 'The heavy luggage should arrive tomorrow, so let us explore outside and look at the garden and yard. Yes, you too, Prudy, I know it is cold, but at least the rain has stopped. Some fresh air will do us all good.'

Susan ran for their bonnets and cloaks, Jethro swathed himself in a vast baize apron to protect his finery and they set to exploring the back yard.

Hector the cob watched them curiously over his stable door as they poked about in the outbuildings lining the yard, one or other of them emerging from time to time with a treasure from amidst the cobwebby jumble. A coal scuttle, a flower basket, a large bag of clothes pegs full of woodworm.

'It is too dirty to move anything, and it is getting dark,' Hester announced after they had investigated the last lean-to. 'I think we must definitely find a man to do the rough work and clear the garden and perhaps two women to finish the cleaning in the house. If they prove suitable, perhaps we can retain one of them as cook. I do wish the vicar would call, then I can ask his wife if she could recommend anyone.'

Jethro cleared his throat meaningfully and Hester turned to find a portly man in clerical black regarding her benevolently over the folds of a heavy scarf. He doffed his hat. 'Good day, madam, I trust you will excuse my calling without notice and at rather a late hour, but my parish duties have kept me somewhat occupied today. However, I could not let the sun set without welcoming a new parishioner to Winterbourne St Swithin. My name is Bunting, Charles Bunting, and I am the vicar of this parish.'

Hester spared one despairing thought for the state of her skirts after dragging the coal scuttle out, and held out her hand. 'Good afternoon, Mr Bunting, how very kind of you to call. I am Hester Lattimer, this is my companion, Miss Prudhome.'

She was aware of his quick downward glance at her ringless left hand as he took her right.

'Then welcome to St Swithin's, ladies. I do hope you will be able to join us in church on Sunday; I have taken the liberty of bringing a small pamphlet with our hours of service to which I have appended a few notes on the history and antiquities of the parish. Others have been kind enough to say they found it of interest.' Hester took the proffered leaflet with suitable expressions of thanks and assurances that her household would most certainly be attending services. 'And is there any other matter with which I may assist you, ma'am?'

'Well, yes, in fact there is. But please, do not let me keep you standing out here, Vicar, may I offer you refreshment? A cup of tea, perhaps?'

'No, no, Miss Lattimer, thank you. I must decline the pleasure today as I have a sick parishioner to visit shortly. In what way may I assist?'

'I was hoping that perhaps Mrs Bunting might recommend some reliable women for the heavy cleaning work and perhaps a man for clearing the grounds and outbuildings.'

'But of course! My wife will be most pleased to call with some names; there are many deserving families hereabouts who would welcome the work. And as for the outdoor duties, there is no one better than Ben Aston—he does odd jobs all around the village. I will send him along to see you. Good day to you, ma'am.' And with a neat doff of his broad-brimmed hat he was off into the twilight at a surprisingly quick pace for such a rotund gentleman.

As he reached the gate he stopped and hurried back. 'Forgive me for asking, Miss Lattimer, but are you quite comfortable in the Moon House? If you are taking on staff, I assume you intend to stay? I only ask because it has been empty for so long and, well—' He broke off in confusion. 'I should not have said anything, the villagers do gossip so. Good day, Miss Lattimer.'

'Well,' Susan said roundly as he vanished from view, 'and what did he mean by that, other than to make us all uncomfortable?'

'I have not the slightest idea.' Hester's brow wrinkled. 'I think he spoke without thinking, then realised that the direction he was taking led to something he could—or should—not discuss.'

'But you *are* staying, Miss Hester?' Jethro persisted. 'I mean, you said you weren't sure yet whether we could afford any staff?'

Hester suppressed a smile at Jethro's unconscious use of 'we': he and Susan were 'family' indeed. 'Certainly we are,' she said firmly, marching towards the back door. 'I do not care whether I can afford the extra help or not; I intend demonstrating to my lord the earl that I am here to stay and an increased household will make that point very plain.'

CHAPTER FOUR

'No good, Miss Hester, this dratted stuff won't shift. I'll need a longer stepladder and some shears.'

Jethro jumped down from the folding steps set somewhat askew on the flags before the front door and glowered up at the mass of ivy, which obscured half of the façade of the house. 'Why don't we wait until that chap Vicar said he'd talk to comes round? I 'spect he's got his own ladders.'

Hester stood beside him, hands on hips, head tilted back to regard the frosted green tangle. 'Ben Aston? Yes, he can do all of the rest of the front, I just want to see what is over the door. There is something, you can just glimpse the odd bit of carving.'

She had woken that Saturday morning with a restless urge to imprint herself on the house that even the prospect of the heavy luggage arriving did not satisfy. Prudy had agreed to venture into the village with a shopping list of considerable length (looking as though she was setting forth for deepest Africa, as Jethro whispered to Susan). Susan had set to with a broom to sweep the front path and then polish the brass knocker and door handle and Hester had put Jethro to cutting back the mass of dead foliage that overhung the path and crowded the front door. With that clear, the weight of ivy over the transom was even more apparent.

Of course, finishing off cleaning inside and deciding where everything should go was far more important than getting cold and dirty in the wintry garden, but there was something very satisfying about being here in plain view of passers-by—whoever they might be—making it quite clear she intended to stay.

Hester had spared not a single glance at the house over the road, had ignored the creak of the gates opening earlier and even disregarded the sound of trotting hooves. Two horses, her sharp ears told her. The earl and a groom or two grooms out exercising his hacks?

If she were his lordship, she would stay well away from the Moon House for a day or so, build up the suspense over what his next tactic would be. Being able to see this so clearly was surprisingly no help in suppressing that suspense. When would the earl call, and what would his approach be? And how was she going to react to him if he tried to flirt with her again? She was annoyed that she was looking forward to the prospect. Doubtless it was simply the anticipation of an intellectual battle of wits.

'Do you want me to try and find some shears, then, Miss Hester?' Jethro was still waiting patiently, the tip of his nose red in the cold.

'Yes, please.'

'I'll likely be some time.' Jethro made off round the side of the house, leaving Hester trampling briskly on thoughts of Lord Buckland. She stepped closer to the door to try to see what peering up from beneath would reveal. Yes, there was definitely a carving.

Without thinking, Hester hitched up her skirts and climbed the first two steps of the ladder. With outstretched arms she could catch hold of some trailing strands of ivy, but not enough; all that happened when she pulled was that it broke off short. With a mutter of irritation she climbed one step higher to the top of the ladder and reached up again.

'That's better!' Now she could get a good double handful. Hester gripped, tugged and suddenly a mass about a foot square came away in her hands. The stepladder rocked on the uneven flags, she teetered, gripped harder on the ivy and felt it give way as she did so.

Should she jump? Or lean forward? Or… The ivy gave completely and she fell backwards to be caught neatly and lowered to the ground, her back to her rescuer.

Hands still gripped her securely, but gently, around the waist and Hester stood stock still. She could feel the man's body steadying her—his thighs were hard against her and his hands were warm even through her clothing. To wrench away would be undignified. Mysteriously she had not the slightest doubt who it was who had rescued her. In a moment he would release her, but for the moment it was wonderful to be held and supported, for she was utterly breathless, no doubt from shock. It seemed a very long time since anyone had held her.

Hester's hands went to her waist, overlapping the large ones that encircled it. This really had to stop—at any moment someone might pass.

'My lord!'

She was freed and spun round to face him, mingled indignation and embarrassment on her face. What was she thinking of? She should have freed herself instantly, not stood there letting him take liberties. No, that was not fair, all he had done was hold her steady.

A rangy bay was standing at her gate, the reins carelessly tossed over the gatepost. The earl was attired for riding—cream buckskins, boots, a heavy dark coat carelessly open—his hat, gloves and whip were lying on the path where he must have dropped them as he saw her start to fall.

In the open air he was even more attractive than inside, she decided, still searching for the right words to thank him and at the same time convey that his behaviour had overstepped the mark. His hair was ruffled by the wind, his skin was more tanned than she had realised, the riding clothes flattered his broad shoulders and long legs.

'Thank you, my lord, but really...' What was she going to say if he asked her how she had known it was him? That she just sensed it?

'Really you would have preferred to break your head on the flags? Good morning, Miss Lattimer. It is naturally delightful to see you in the garden, but surely that lad of yours would be better suited to removing the ivy than you?'

'I know,' Hester agreed with a rueful shrug. He was quite right, she had been very foolish and extremely undignified. It seemed she was fated to present a thoroughly unladylike impression every time they met. 'Jethro has gone for the shears. But there is something carved over the door and I wanted to see what it was.'

Lord Buckland stepped past her and looked up at the wall where the ivy was partly torn away. 'You are quite right, but was it so urgent?'

'When I want something, I am afraid I am usually somewhat impetuous,' Hester admitted.

One dark brow quirked upwards and Hester was left with the flustered impression that she had said something provocative. 'Very well, let me see what I can uncover.' Before Hester could protest she found herself holding his coat while the earl stood on the top step and investigated the ivy.

His balance was really extremely good, she thought, staring absently at the play of muscles in his thighs and back as he shifted his weight to allow for the unstable steps. Then she realised what she was doing, blushed hectically and fixed her eyes on his hands instead. With a hard downwards yank a whole curtain of ivy and root came away, revealing the bare stone behind.

Unmistakable, despite the marring remnants of stem and birds' nests, was an oval panel carved with a crescent moon, a solitary star caught on its lower horn.

'The Moon House! Oh, how charming.' Hester stared entranced at the carving. It was a simple thing, but somehow elegant and feminine like the little house itself.

'Yes, work by a good carver.' There was something in the earl's voice that made Hester look sharply at his profile, but she could read nothing there besides interest as he ran a hand lightly down the curve of the moon. 'Someone took pains with this house.'

'I know, it feels loved,' Hester remarked as he climbed down, tossing the armful of ivy to one side. 'Goodness, look at the state of your clothes, my lord. I will go and get a clothes brush, I will not be a moment.'

She had thrust his coat into his arms and whisked inside before Guy could argue, leaving him on the doorstep. *Somewhat impetuous!* Yes, that was certainly one way to describe Miss Lattimer. And determined with it. Not that he could criticise either trait; it was impetuosity that had brought him down here and stubborn determination that was keeping him. That, and a speaking pair of golden brown eyes.

The newly polished door knocker caught his attention and he raised a hand to it. It was an unusual design: a bow, pivoted at the top and hung so that it would strike against a quiver of arrows at its base.

A crescent moon and a hunting bow—Diana's symbols.

The cry from the casement above his head was sudden and short, cut off on a choking gasp. Guy took a rapid step backwards to stare up, but the window was almost closed and there was nothing to be seen. The silence that followed was almost as alarming and he shouldered his way through the door and took the stairs two at a time without conscious thought.

The room above the door was a bedchamber and to his relief Hester was there, alone and on her feet. She was staring through an open door, her clasped hands raised to her mouth as if to push back any further sound.

He reached her side and looked past her into a perfectly normal-seeming dressing room. 'Miss Lattimer? Hester, what is it? What scared you?'

'The pearls,' she said with some difficulty. She unclasped her hands and pointed at the floor, which was strewn with small white globes.

'You have broken your necklace,' Guy soothed. Hers seemed a disproportionate reaction, it must be a much loved heirloom. 'They will easily be restrung, there is no harm done. Let me call your maid to gather them up.'

'She has gone to the nearest farm for eggs,' Hester said stiffly. 'I did not break it. I found it on the floor, broken, the first night we were here. The pearls were picked up and put in that bowl there.' She pointed at a delicate china bowl on the dressing table. 'That has not moved. How did they come to be spilt again?'

'Perhaps your maid knocked them over this morning and neglected to replace them.' She was shivering with reaction. Concerned, Guy put out a hand and touched her shoulder.

'No, she came downstairs when I did, then went out without coming back up.'

'Young Ackland? Your companion?'

'He would not come into my chamber without asking first, whether or not I was here, and I know Miss Prudhome has not been upstairs since before breakfast.'

Guy looked at the window, closed almost to the top. No breeze stirred the heavy curtains; besides, what flapping curtain could scoop the pearls from a bowl, but leave it untouched?

'Have you a cat?'

'No.' He felt her shoulder move under his palm, almost as though she was bracing herself. 'I must pick them up.' She took a step forward, then stopped on the threshold and froze.

To hell with the proprieties. Guy swept her off her feet, heeled the dressing-room door closed and took her to the *chaise* where he sat down, Hester on his knee, and demanded, 'What was all that about? You are quite safe now.'

For answer there was a muffled hiccup from the region of his shoulder where she had buried her face. 'I am not crying, and I am merely very cross with myself for being a ninny.'

'No, of course you aren't crying.' Guy knew better than to agree with remarks about being a ninny. He had a sister.

Then, more clearly, 'I am such a coward, I was *not* going to let it prey on my mind and at the first little thing I go to pieces.'

Now what to say? If he agreed that the pearls were a little thing, he was agreeing with her own self-criticism. If he said that, in fact, it was a mystery—and apparently a disturbing one—that would only frighten her more. It might suit his purpose for her to take a dislike to the house, but this was not the way to achieve it. Guy contented himself with gently rubbing her shoulders and murmuring, 'There, there.'

It was a curiously pleasant occupation. Hester Lattimer fitted very nicely on his lap, her weight a positive thing. She was not heavy, but not frail either. His free arm tightened slightly around a slender, strong frame. She must ride, or walk a lot, he decided. Against his thighs and his chest she was deliciously soft and her hair tickling his nose smelt of rosemary.

With a sudden defiant shake she sat up straight and met his

eyes. 'I am sorry, my lord, you must think me a poor thing indeed, and a foolish one at that, starting at shadows.'

'You know, Hester, once you have reached the stage of sitting on a gentleman's knee, I do feel the time for formality is past. Will you not call me Guy?'

She looked startled, producing yet another shade of gold in those fascinating eyes. 'I could not possibly!'

'Well, you *are* sitting on my lap. I think calling me by my given name is a minor informality compared to that.'

'So I am! My lord…Guy…please let me go.'

'But of course.' He opened his arms wide and added wickedly, 'A pity, I was enjoying it.'

Hester, on the point of scrambling to her feet with more haste than dignity, caught his eye and twinkled back. 'So was I. What a truly shocking thing to admit, but you know, it was so nice to be looked after again, just for once.'

Guy found himself smiling as she sat down again next to him, arranging her skirts primly around her legs as she did so. She was enchanting. That frankness, the mischievous look in her eye. But she was, he would stake a thousand sovereigns on it, no hoyden or flirt. She was simply honest, impetuous and had sustained an unpleasant shock. Now was not the time to pursue that remark about being looked after, but he stored it away for later thought.

Her hands moved convulsively in her lap before she made an obvious effort to still them and sit calmly. 'Thank you for running to my rescue twice in one morning, my lord. Guy.'

'It is my pleasure. Will you not tell me what frightens you so much about that room?'

She hesitated, then said calmly, 'I had better begin with a little history.'

'You know the history of the house?' Guy prided himself on his self-control, but the sharp question was out of his mouth before he could stop it and he cursed inwardly at the surprise on Hester's face.

'No, not at all. I was only going to explain that it has been empty, unoccupied for about fifty years. I was surprised, for it has been well kept up in all the essentials—the roof is sound, the windows have been cleaned from time to time and, from the evidence of the hearths, regular fires have been lit to keep the damp at bay. But no one has lived here—which I do not understand.'

'Were you given no explanation when you bought it?'

'None.' She shook her head, a little line of puzzlement between her dark brows. 'Sir Edward Nugent was ailing when he agreed to sell and my man of business dealt entirely with his agent. We asked, of course, but the reply was that he had chosen not to sell it, yet could not find a suitable tenant.'

'That did not make you curious?' It would have made him as suspicious as hell.

'A little, but by all reports Sir Edward was somewhat reclusive and eccentric, so I assumed that accounted for it. And anyway, I wanted the house too much to be put off, despite the length of time the negotiations took.'

Damn it, he had only just missed buying it. If only he had known sooner what those old papers revealed. 'Go on,' Guy prompted, enjoying the concentration on Hester's face as she recounted her story.

'We were therefore not at all surprised to find the house in such a state. There was dust everywhere and an odd assortment of old-fashioned furniture.'

'I suspect I saw most of it yesterday.'

'Indeed,' Hester agreed ruefully. 'So much for attempting to look respectably established for callers! Anyway, although it was dirty, the house was tidy, with everything in its correct place. Except for that room.' She nodded towards the dressing room door and Guy saw her go a little pale.

'What did you find?' He took her hand. Hester appeared not to notice. Under his light grip her pulse fluttered and raced.

'It had been ransacked. The doors of the presses stood open with the drawers pulled clean out. A chair was over-turned and the mirror smashed on the floor. A curtain was part torn down, as though by a clutching hand. The pearls were strewn everywhere and there was a torn nightgown by the door. And...' Her voice trailed away.

'And what?' Guy pressed gently.

'There was blood on the wall.'

It was not until his fingers closed tight on her wrist that Hester realised that Guy had been holding her hand. Now she had told the most shocking part of her tale she felt curiously better, half-expecting him to say it must have been some other stain, wine perhaps. She was not prepared for the sud-denness with which his eyes went hard and the colour ebbed under his skin.

'My lord?'

'I am sorry. That must have been an unpleasant discovery indeed. Whereabouts is the stain?' He released her and got to his feet, apparently recovered from whatever shock she had dealt him.

'Jethro whitewashed over it. We put the room to rights and I have used this bedchamber for two nights now. I had thought myself quite sensible about it, certain there must be some in-nocent explanation. Until now.'

'I am sure there is.' Guy Westrope smiled at her. Surely it was only her overheated imagination that made it seem that the curve of his lips found no reassuring echo in his eyes. 'Are you sure you are feeling all right now? I had better remove myself from your bedchamber before your companion returns and reads me a lecture on propriety.'

'She would certainly do that, and me too, quite deservedly.' Hester got up and joined him in the doorway. 'Jethro is probably back with the shears and a proper ladder and wondering what on earth a horse is doing tethered at the gate and a gentleman's hat and gloves lying on the path.'

'An apparent mystery with a perfectly rational explanation, as I am sure the pearls will prove to have,' Guy remarked, following her down the stairs and out of the front door. 'No, no sign of your very junior butler; I may make my escape unremarked. Good day, Miss Lattimer.'

Hester watched as he bent to pick up his belongings from the path, put on his hat and gloves and led the patient horse across the road, then looked around her for some distraction from her disordered thoughts and emotions, none of which she had the slightest desire to examine just now.

'Jethro! Where has the boy got to?' Hester walked through the house to the back door, only to see him coming across the yard struggling under the weight of a long ladder with a pair of somewhat rusty shears pinned under his arm.

'There you are,' she said mildly. 'Whatever kept you?'

'Gentleman called.' Jethro grounded the ladder with a grunt of relief. 'He rode over from the fields and through the back gate into the yard. Said he was passing and wanted to know if you were receiving. I said not today because of the heavy luggage arriving, but I thought you might be at home after that. Was that all right, Miss Hester?'

'Yes, of course. Who was he?'

'Sir Lewis Nugent of Winterbourne Hall.'

'He must be the son of Sir Edward who sold me the house and died soon afterwards.'

'Must be, Miss Hester, he was wearing mourning. Good

tailor,' Jethro added critically, 'but not as good as the earl's. Mind you, his lordship has the figure for it.'

'And doubtless the money,' Hester retorted tartly. The less she thought about Guy Westrope's admirable form, the better it would be. Quite how he had managed it she was not sure, but in the space of two days he had inveigled his way into her bedroom, had established first-name terms between them and had succeeded in mystifying her about his character and motives. The sooner she widened her social circle the better; perhaps Sir Lewis and his family would prove the means.

'Jethro, you have not been in my dressing room this morning, have you?'

'Certainly not, Miss Hester. Why, is something amiss?'

'Those loose pearls are all over the floor again, but the bowl is still exactly where it was on the dressing table.'

She had been hoping that Jethro would immediately produce some convincing explanation, but all he did was stare at her, wide eyed. Eventually he said, 'That's strange, Miss Hester.'

'Could anyone have got in? Perhaps a chance thief found his way up there, picked the pearls out of the bowl, then dropped them when he heard something.' It was the only explanation she could think of other than the supernatural.

'Suppose so.' Jethro wrinkled his nose in thought. 'Back door was open and Susan and Cluck…I mean, Miss Prudhome are out. Someone could have come in the back way while we were out the front.'

'It would be a bold thief to do that. Oh dear.' Hester sighed. 'It seemed such a nice village. Now we will have to be suspicious and lock our doors. I must speak to Susan about it.'

CHAPTER FIVE

Miss Prudhome arrived back at the same time as the vicar's wife called, so Hester had no opportunity to ask her about the pearls before she greeted her visitor. Mrs Bunting was as well rounded as her husband and equally as welcoming to the new-comers to her parish.

She settled in the front room in a rustle of skirts and beamed cheerfully on Hester and Prudy once the initial ex-change of introductions and greetings was done with. 'Now, my dear Miss Lattimer, I understand you require some re-spectable women to do the rough cleaning. I can thoroughly recommend Mrs Dalling and Mrs Stubbs. They are both wid-ows; decent women who are bringing up their families by thrift and hard work.'

'Then by all means I must follow your recommendation. May I offer you tea, Mrs Bunting?'

'Thank you, Miss Lattimer. I will speak to both women when I leave you and ask them to call this afternoon, if that is convenient. I am glad to be able to say that the inhabitants of this village are as honest and hard-working as may be found anywhere. You have certainly found a most pleasant place to settle and I hope you find it so.'

Hester smiled back, delighted to have found approval from

the vicar's wife. She would go a long way to establish Hester's credit in the neighbourhood. 'I am so glad to hear that, Mrs Bunting. I had been somewhat concerned, for it seemed that someone had made their way into the house this morning.'

Prudy gave a squeak of alarm, then subsided with a nervous glance at Hester. Hester sighed inwardly; somehow she was going to have to teach Prudy to be a more self-assured companion and not keep nervously in the background as a proper governess must.

'Oh dear, surely you are mistaken?' Mrs Bunting looked quite amazed. 'No one here would behave in such a way and I would have heard if there were any tramping fellows about. The churchwardens are very alert for that sort of thing, you know. The last thing they want is any vagrant settling in and attempting to claim parish support.'

'Oh, it is a relief to have you say so.' It was anything but. A sneak thief was a familiar London nuisance that could be guarded against. Now she was left with no explanation again—and no defence.

'What made you think something was amiss?' Mrs Bunting asked.

'Perhaps it was nothing after all. It was just that some pearls that had been in a dish were scattered all over the floor and I could think of no other explanation,' Hester said lightly.

'Oh.' Mrs Bunting looked both thoughtful and somewhat disturbed. 'How very…odd. Has anything else out of the ordinary occurred?'

'No.' Hester was not going to describe the state of the dressing room again. 'Nothing.'

'Well, that's all right then.' The vicar's wife looked relieved. 'There will be a perfectly rational explanation.' She sipped her tea, then added vaguely, 'I never think it a good idea to listen to village gossip.'

Hester decided to ask right out. 'Mrs Bunting, is there some rumour circulating about this house? Only the vicar said something that made me wonder, and now you mention village gossip.'

The older woman looked distressed and flustered. 'My foolish tongue! It is inexcusable of me to alarm you. The villagers will talk so, but I am sure it is only because this house has been empty for so long. They tell a silly tale of blighted love or some such nonsense concerning the lady who last lived here. But that was such a long time ago.' She fanned herself with her lace handkerchief and took another sip of tea. 'There is a local story of the scent of roses—although how anyone could know I have no idea because Sir Edward Nugent never allowed anyone in except for his agent and the occasional workman.'

Hester shivered. She had smelt roses as she had entered the house for the first time—roses on a warm breeze in a cold airless room. 'The garden is full of them, quite untamed and half-wild. There are even a few now with a flower or two despite the season. It is no wonder that the scent is noticeable here.'

'A very sensible observation, my dear Miss Lattimer,' Mrs Bunting remarked. 'My husband and I have only been in the parish for four years so we know little of the earlier history. However, there has been talk of lights being seen here at night, quite recently. That seems to be a new rumour. I think it would be sensible to check all the window catches, just in case someone has started using it as a shelter. Although with you in occupation they would soon be scared away, I am sure.'

'Yes,' Hester said slowly. 'That would be a wise precaution. How recently were the lights seen?'

Mrs Bunting cocked her head on one side and thought. 'Two or three days before you arrived, that I heard of. But it will have been some tramping fellow I am sure, now long gone—or imagination.'

Hester turned the conversation and began to talk about the garden and her plans for it. In Mrs Bunting she found she had another enthusiast for horticulture and was soon overwhelmed by offers of plants and cuttings in the spring. 'Thank you so much, ma'am, but I had better not accept anything until I have the front garden under control somewhat or I will have no-where to put the plants. I suppose I should be concentrating on plans for the house, but I confess that I look to the garden to distract my eye from the Old Manor opposite.'

'Hideous, my dear, I quite agree. And such a pity when one considers how perfectly charming the rest of the houses around the Green are. Even the humblest cottage has some picturesque merit to it.'

'I wonder that a gentleman should wish to take it at such a time of year,' Hester said, hoping that she was not sound-ing too interested.

'Indeed!' Mrs Bunting settled more comfortably into her chair, reminding Hester of a broody bantam sitting snugly on her nest. 'After Boxing Day for the hunting, perhaps—but now? The villagers will have it that the earl is avoiding his creditors, but that must be nonsense, one only has to look at his horses to see he does not want for money.'

Hester thought of the casual way he spoke of not only buy-ing her house, but resettling her wherever she wanted to go. No, Lord Buckland was not in want of a fortune. Naturally she could not tell Mrs Bunting this.

'How long has he been here?' She poured tea and placed the biscuits within reach.

'Why, not much longer than you have yourself, Miss Lattimer. Three or four days before, I cannot quite recall.' She began to tick off on her fingers. 'He was not in church last Sunday, that I know. Mr Bunting called on him on Wednesday I think, in very heavy rain. Yes, I recall now. He arrived on Monday.'

Hester put her cup down with a little clatter. Lord Buckland had been in the village three days before she had arrived and during that time mysterious lights had been seen in the Moon House for the first time. She racked her memory for signs that anyone had been there, but the floors had been roughly swept in all the main rooms and there had been no betraying footprints in the dust. The dressing room had been unswept, of course. That had certainly not been entered—the dust had lain unmarked like grey snow.

Could he have been in the house? To what end? If, as it seemed, his purpose for staying in Winterbourne St Swithin was to persuade her to sell the Moon House, why should he need to enter it clandestinely and prowl about by candlelight? She did not like feeling this suspicion, it went against her instinctive liking for him.

Mrs Bunting was speaking again and Hester hastily composed her mind and her face and listened attentively. '…a small afternoon party only, you understand. Just the intimate circle of ladies in the village. We do not have a large social group actually *in* the village, although when one includes all the families in outlying houses and estates there is a not inconsiderable throng whenever someone holds a dance.

'However, I am keeping it small because I hope to persuade Miss Nugent to attend. She is still in mourning, of course, it is only two months since her father died, but it will do her good to enjoy a little feminine company.' She beamed at Hester. 'Will you and Miss Prudhome be able to join us?'

'Thank you, we would be delighted to. Um…which day did you say, I am afraid I did not quite catch…?'

'Wednesday next week. At three. You cannot miss the vicarage, it is just up the lane next to the church.'

* * *

Shortly after she departed, leaving Hester prey to some very mixed emotions. It was excellent that she had been invited to Mrs Bunting's At Home, for the sooner she met and began to mix with the local ladies, the sooner she would find her feet in this small community. And some more callers coming and going would certainly help to make visits by Lord Buckland less conspicuous. But the prospect of such an exclusively feminine society was somewhat daunting. She had become so used to male company. But repining about that was pointless. She had needed a new home, a home of her own, and it was up to her to make this a success and to learn to put the dangerous pleasures of masculine company out of her mind.

Prudy hovered anxiously, wringing her hands. 'Oh, Hester dear, has there really been a burglar?'

'I have no idea,' Hester responded briskly. 'But if there was, he's gone now. We must just be careful of the doors.' Prudy was still looking wretched. 'What is it, Prudy?'

'Did...did Mrs Bunting truly invite me as well?'

'Yes, Prudy,' Hester said firmly. 'You are my lady companion, it is only proper that you go about with me. We will look at your gowns, I am sure one of the afternoon dresses we bought will do admirably.'

'Thank you, Hester,' the little woman responded, looking terrified.

What was I thinking of, employing her? Hester wondered, then reproved herself. A chaperon, however ineffectual, was essential; without one she would be socially unacceptable, and she knew only too well what that was like. 'You will soon become familiar with local society,' she said kindly. 'And I would be so grateful if this afternoon you could look over the hampers of linen and make me an inventory. I am sure you will do a much better job of it than Susan,' she added mendaciously, rewarded by the tremulous smile she received.

Once alone, there was nothing to distract her from her imaginings. Hester carried the tea tray out to the kitchen with an abstracted air, trying to convince herself that her qualms about his lordship were simply because of his mysterious desire to buy her house and not because she believed for a moment that he had been creeping about the place at night.

There was also the complication that he showed an alarming tendency to flirt with her and that she showed an even more worrying susceptibility to that flirting. She had even allowed herself to be held on his knee, for goodness' sake! Only…he was so very attractive, and there was something in his expression when he looked at her that made her want to trust him. And he had only taken her on his knee to comfort her, hadn't he?

'Oh, bother men!' She set the tray down with more force than judgement, setting the fragile cups jumping.

'And so say I, Miss Hester.' Susan emerged backwards from a cupboard on one side of the wide fireplace, tugging at a large wicker hamper by its rope handle. 'I don't know how many times I've asked Jethro to drag this out so I can use this cupboard for my brooms and brushes, but he's off setting the china to rights in the dining room, which is *much* more important than me trying to get this dratted kitchen straight.'

'What is in it?' Hester enquired, deciding from long experience it was not worth getting in the middle of one of Susan and Jethro's periodic fallings-out.

'Just old pots and pans and some cloths. I'll have a look later and see what is any use.' Susan gave the hamper a last vicious shove into a corner of the kitchen and attacked the now empty cupboard with her broom.

Hester dodged the cloud of dust that emerged and opened the door on the other side of the hearth. It appeared to be the mirror image of the one Susan was attacking and was quite empty. Why on earth she could not use that one for her brushes Hester could not imagine, unless, once she had asked him, she was determined that Jethro must empty the first one. But it was dark and dank and a large spider was sitting firmly in the middle of the floor. Hester shuddered, shut the door and went in search of Jethro.

She found him in the other front reception room, which he had decided should be the dining room. It was now graced with Hester's dining table, four chairs and a dresser, giving an effect she was more than pleased with. Jethro was unpacking the good china, rinsing it in a bowl of water, drying it and setting it on the dresser.

'Jethro, I wish you would give Susan a hand for a little while, I found her dragging the most enormous hamper out of a cupboard in the kitchen.'

'Yes, ma'am.' He put down his cloths obediently and got to his feet. He showed Hester a willing face, but as she entered the kitchen on his heels he did not hesitate to continue the dispute that he and the maid had obviously been stoking all morning. 'What's wrong with the cupboard on the other side, then?'

'It's damp, I told you.' Susan looked up red-faced from her position hanging over the hamper. 'Must be a crack in the wall or something, letting the water in. This side's dry as a bone. Faugh!' She flapped a hand in front of her face. 'Look at the state of this cloth. Give me a hand to drag it into the yard, Jethro, it'll all have to be burned.'

Disinclined to chase spiders around the kitchen, Hester wandered back to the front of the house. 'Find something useful to do,' she castigated herself. 'Stop mooning around wondering about Guy Westrope's motives.'

As absolutely nothing was more absorbing than considering his lordship, ideas about helping with the inventory of the linen, doing some mending, creating a plant list for the spring garden or thinking about menus for the week paled into insignificance.

Hester found herself curled up on the sofa, chin in hand, brooding not unpleasurably on the sensation of sitting upon the earl's knee. It had felt safe…no, not safe, that was the wrong word. She had felt protected, but at the same time vulnerable and flustered. It was an intriguing feeling and when the knocker banged she grimaced with annoyance at the break in her train of thought.

She waited, but obviously Jethro and Susan were out of earshot. A glance in the glass was reassuring: at least this time she was not going to appear a complete hoyden, opening her own front door.

It was a footman, tall and dressed in a subdued livery suitable for country use. 'Good day, madam. His lordship asked me to deliver this. Would you wish me to wait for a reply?'

Hester took the proffered letter and gestured the footman into the hall as she broke the seal. 'A moment, please…yes, if you will wait.'

It was an invitation. Hester spread it open on her writing table.

Lord Buckland requests the pleasure of the company of Miss Lattimer and Miss Prudhome at dinner… It went on to give a time of seven on Monday evening. Hester's eyes widened at the fashionable hour; if she was invited for seven, it was unlikely they would sit down before eight, a daringly late hour for country society.

Across the bottom of the formal note, in a bold, less disciplined version of the same hand, he had written, *I have invited a most respectable company, so you need not be alarmed at an invitation to a bachelor's table. Tell your stickler of a butler that I will make sure a footman walks you home and bring your dragon of a companion.* The letter *G* filled the remaining corner of the sheet in an arrogant scrawl.

Should she go? Such short notice meant that the rest of the 'respectable company' might not be present to lend her countenance and poor Prudy was hardly a defence against an earl with a whim to flirt or worse. Then she smiled at her own naivety; everyone in the neighbourhood would be agog to be invited by such a host and her presence would fade into insignificance. Any previous engagements would be ruthlessly broken, she felt sure. Was it arrogance on his part, she wondered, or simply a shrewd knowledge of human nature? Probably the latter.

Without giving herself time to think, she pulled a sheet of paper towards her and dipped her quill in the standish. *Miss Lattimer thanks Lord Buckland for his kind invitation...Miss Lattimer and Miss Prudhome would be delighted...*

The footman took the finished note with a respectful bow and marched back across the street, leaving Hester prey to sudden qualms. Should she have done that? she wondered as she went back to pick up the invitation. What would local society say to an unmarried lady accepting—even if there were other guests?

'Did someone call, Miss Hester?' Susan popped her head round the door.

'Look, Lord Buckland has invited me for dinner on Monday. He says he has invited other people, so I suppose I should not concern myself, but do you think it will cause talk?'

'You being a single lady?' Susan came into the room, revealing that she was wrapped in a vast sacking apron. 'I was just about to start on that range,' she explained, seeing Hester's expression. 'Soot everywhere, I'll be bound. It wouldn't have mattered in Portugal,' she said, applying her mind to Hester's question. 'No one thought anything of it if you went out to dinner or dances when your papa was away. Don't know about London, though...'

'Neither do I,' Hester admitted. 'I was hardly in a position to go out into society when I was living with Sir John.' She pushed down the memory of the snubs and the scandal and focused on the present. 'I think I can risk it; after all, everyone is going to be so agog to receive an invitation that they will probably assume that I am just the same. Safety in numbers,' she added ambiguously.

'Oh, Miss Hester! You don't think he would…?'

'Certainly not,' Hester said, wondering guiltily what Susan would have said if she'd seen her cradled on his lordship's knee in her own bedroom. 'After all, Miss Prudhome will be with me. Now, what am I going to wear?'

'You've got several good gowns. Any of them would do.' Susan undid her apron strings. 'I'll just go and shake them out so you can decide. I'll need to press something for church tomorrow in any case.'

'You do not think they might be too fashionable for local society?' Hester worried out loud as they went upstairs. 'I would not like to seem forward.'

Although in her time living with Colonel Sir John Norton she had never been able to go out in public with him, he had liked her to dress well and enjoyed their evening meals together with her well gowned, her hair coiffed and with jewels at her throat. *Dear John*, she thought wistfully as they entered the bedroom. Marriage had been out of the question, she had finally made him accept that, but the venomous dislike of his distant relatives at his funeral and the scandal that had sent her fleeing from London still made her cringe inwardly.

'They'll be interested to see what's in vogue,' Susan prophesied. 'And in any case, all the ladies will be wearing their finest, I'll be bound. What about Miss Prudhome?' she added dubiously.

'Prudy!' Hester called down the landing. 'We are invited to dinner at his lordship's! Come and talk about gowns.' She exchanged a rueful smile with Susan at the sound of Prudy's shriek of dismay.

Sunday proved to be a welcome respite from housework, thoughts of Lord Buckland and lurid imaginings about the house. Even Prudy stopped working herself into a state worrying about her modest dinner gown, the fact that she would be expected to make conversation and the knowledge that she must guard Hester from the advances of a Dangerous Man.

They arrived in good time for matins, and Hester found herself escorted courteously to a pew by the verger. 'Here you are, Miss Lattimer, ma'am, the Moon House pew.'

And sure enough, there was the crescent moon carved on the panelled door of the highbox pew. Hester entered with Prudy on her heels, hoped that Susan and Jethro had found themselves suitable seating in the gallery and composed herself to pray.

When she resumed her seat she looked around with some interest. Most of the congregation were now in their places. Bonnets and an assortment of male heads could be glimpsed. Near the front she could see the jet-black rim of a heavily veiled bonnet next to a dark head: the Nugent brother and sister, possibly. On the other side there was one blond crown of hair she would recognise anywhere; his lordship was dutifully attending church. Hester felt her heart give an odd little skip and tightened her hands on her prayer book; it was unseemly to even think about a man under these circumstances.

After the service Hester waited, eyes modestly upon her prayer book, until the front pews had emptied before stepping out. Their occupants had vanished and she let out a sigh of relief. What if Lord Buckland had decided to renew his pressure on her to sell in such a very public place?

Mr Bunting greeted them warmly at the church door and received her compliments on the efforts of the choir with enthusiasm. 'One of my interests, you know, Miss Lattimer. It had been sadly neglected before my time, but I flatter myself it is as tuneful a gathering as any in the county now.'

He turned to the next parishioner and Hester made her way back across the Green, musing aloud to Prudy that they must embroider new pew-seat cushions and kneelers. The cushions were thin and offered little protection against hard old oak, the kneelers sagged under the weight of her knees, bringing them into contact with cold stone. That would be a most suitable occupation for a young lady, and one where she could exercise both her artistic sensibilities and also concentrate her mind upon suitably reverent religious symbolism.

Yes, entirely suitable and far more respectable than any of the ways she had been occupying her time recently.

CHAPTER SIX

The remainder of Sunday and the intervening night gave Hester more than enough time to wonder just what she was about, accepting the invitation to Guy's dinner. Sketching designs for the cushion and kneeler did little to distract her. She was a single lady attempting to establish herself in local society and here she was, agreeing to dine with a single nobleman, chaperoned or not. The lowering thought that she would probably not have been worrying about it if she were not so attracted to him did not help lift her anxieties.

'I am going to indulge in an absolute whirl of social activity,' she observed with assumed brightness to Susan as they retreated to the bedchamber for her to change. 'I forgot to say that the vicar's wife invited me to a ladies' afternoon tea party on Wednesday afternoon.'

Susan giggled. 'All the ones who weren't at tonight's dinner will be agog and jealous, and all those who were will be dying to brag about it, really, but wanting to appear unimpressed.'

Hester smiled back. 'I am afraid you are right. I confess to finding the idea of a party of ladies more intimidating than tonight's dinner.'

'That is not surprising.' Susan ran a critical eye over a gown of pale primrose silk. 'This has hung out rather well.'

She flicked at a piece of lint on the hem, then added, 'After all, you are more used to the company of gentlemen, aren't you, Miss Hester?'

'Yes, I may be,' Hester agreed drily, 'but I certainly do not want to give that impression! That is lovely, thank you, Susan. Please can you go and see if Miss Prudhome needs any help with her hair?'

Jethro kept a sharp eye on the arrivals across the lane and finally called up from the bottom of the stairs, 'Mr and Mrs Bunting have come, and a lady and gentleman I don't know.'

It was ten past seven and Hester decided it was time she left. She had wanted to avoid being first, but at the same time she did not want to make a late arrival, which could appear as though she was attempting to make an entrance.

She descended the stairs with Susan behind her, making last-minute attempts to stop her back hair falling down, and arrived in the hall feeling quite pleasantly fluttered.

'Oh, stand still, Miss Hester, do! Now, that should stay up,' Susan added doubtfully. She stood back and regarded her mistress from top to toe, head on one side, pin cushion in hand. 'Very nice, Miss Hester. About time you got all dressed up again.'

Jethro meanwhile picked up a stout walking stick from beside the door and stood by while Hester tied the strings of her heavy winter evening cloak.

'What on earth are you carrying that for, Jethro?'

'You're wearing the diamonds, Miss Hester,' the lad said, eying the cold blaze at Hester's throat and in her ears. Miss Prudhome produced a predictable gasp of alarm.

'I hardly think I am going to be beset by footpads in the village street,' Hester retorted with a chuckle. 'I do hope they won't seem ostentatious, but Papa did like me to wear them.'

'Now, stop worrying.' Susan urged her towards the front

door. 'Go and enjoy yourself.' She glanced at Jethro. 'We did wonder, Miss Hester…'

'You want to go out too? Yes, of course,' Hester agreed readily. 'Where to?'

'Only to the Bird in Hand. They have a skittle alley out the back.'

'And a local team who are playing the next village,' Jethro chipped in. 'Seeing as how I'm a dab hand with the skittles, I did wonder if I might get a chance to try my luck.'

Hester suppressed the remark that playing skittles in the local hostelry was hardly the recreation of choice of fashionable butlers and agreed. 'Just be back by ten, please, for I do not expect to be much later than that.' She stepped through the door and added, 'And do remember to lock up before you go out.'

A different footman from the one who had delivered the invitation opened Lord Buckland's front door to them. She entered, suppressing a flutter of nervous anticipation. It was simply the unfamiliarity of English social life, nothing else, she told herself, sending Prudy a reassuring smile. Where she had been so confident, mingling with Wellington's officers in Portugal, acting as a very young hostess at her father's side whenever he was home on furlough, now she had to learn how to act as a well-bred single lady in provincial England. She suspected it would place her under far more searching scrutiny than she had ever had to endure before.

Still, she must study to adapt quickly. London, or at least respectable society there, was closed to her now.

'Good evening, madam.' It was Guy's very superior butler, Parrott. Hester smiled, inwardly contrasting the gauntly correct figure with her Jethro. She wished now that Guy had not promised to speak to Parrott about the lad, he was sure to have forgotten and Jethro would be so disappointed.

The butler cleared his throat. 'If it would not be inconvenient, I had hoped to invite your man Ackland to call in the next day or so. His lordship mentioned that he might find it interesting to view our arrangements here.'

She had been wrong to doubt Guy; the warmth of pleasure touched her. 'Thank you, Parrott, I am more than happy for Ackland to call. He is an ambitious young man and will appreciate the opportunity to observe the running of a superior household.'

The butler inclined his head at the compliment and threw open a door. 'Miss Lattimer, my lord. Miss Prudhome.'

Guy turned from his conversation with Mrs Bunting and her bosom bow Mrs Redland to greet the new arrivals and almost stopped in his tracks. This could not be Hester Lattimer, the young lady with her hair half down her back or full of ivy stalks and dust. This was certainly not the impetuous harum-scarum miss who balanced on rickety ladders because she was too impatient to wait for help or who answered her own front door in an apron.

This was an elegant lady dressed in the first stare of London fashion, her hair coiffed, her jewels sparkling. As he reached her and bowed to her answering curtsy, Guy also recognised with what skill she had chosen her ensemble. The gown was modestly high across the bosom and relied more on cut and fabric than on ornamentation to make its impact. Her diamonds, though fine, were simple, and her skin and eyes were innocent of any aids to beauty.

She appeared exactly as she no doubt had fully intended—a single lady of respectable means, breeding and good taste. Nothing here to put up the backs of the local dowagers or scandalise the critical.

He was equally careful how he greeted her. Any hint of familiarity would set tongues wagging and scandal-broth brewing. He was aware of her sharp-nosed companion regarding him nervously.

'Miss Lattimer, Miss Prudhome. Good evening. Now, I believe not everyone here is yet known to you? Mr and Mrs Bunting you know, of course. May I introduce Mrs Redland, Miss Redland and Mr Hugh Redland of Bourne Hall? Major Piper and Mrs Piper of Low Marston.'

There were nods and greetings, then Mrs Bunting took Miss Prudhome firmly under her wing and drew her into a discussion about the village school.

Guy watched Hester without seeming to as she passed from one guest to another. Whoever this mysterious young woman was—and he was finding her an increasing mystery and contradiction with every encounter—her social skills were immaculate. She had a pleasant deference to the older guests, but without the slightest hint of shyness. With the Redland son and daughter she was warm and friendly.

Yet he felt a suppressed watchfulness about her, a wariness as though she was expecting to be challenged or snubbed. Was anyone else aware of it? It seemed not, the group was absorbing the newcomer comfortably. There was curiosity, certainly, and on the part of the gentlemen those subtle changes that come over any group of men in the presence of beauty.

Startled at his own thought, Guy shifted his position as he stood talking to the major so he could watch Hester. Indeed, she *was* beautiful. Not conventionally so—and he was sure she would deny any such description—but her skin was creamy, her hair soft and full of springing waves, her figure slender yet womanly. His own body stirred as he recalled the feel of her in his arms. Then she turned, smiling at something young Hugh Redland was saying and he saw the laughter in her eyes and with the movement caught a hint of her scent.

An unusual scent for a woman, he thought. Almost woody, or perhaps mossy with a hint of citrus. He had not noticed it before; in fact, if anyone had asked him to describe the scent of Hester Lattimer he would have replied, 'Plain soap and dust.' This fragrance suited her soft brown looks and the amber lights in her eyes.

She was becoming more of a puzzle the more he knew her. There were young ladies of his acquaintance who would have fainted rather than get dirt on their hands and others who thought nothing of saddling their own horses or going on long scrambling walks with muddy boots and tousled hair. But he was not used to young ladies who would knuckle down to cleaning the house alongside their servants and yet take the care to dress so exquisitely or choose their scent with such taste.

Hester Lattimer was becoming dangerously close to pre-occupying his thoughts and that was folly. To achieve his aim in coming to Winterbourne St Swithin she had to be removed from the Moon House, and soon. He was already spending too long on this obsession. So far it seemed her discomfort with the mysteries of the house were not sufficient to make her reconsider her vehement rejection of his more than generous offer. He must think again, adjust his tactics.

'Sir Lewis Nugent, my lord.' His last guest. Guy turned to greet the young baronet, not failing to notice that the attention of the ladies in the room had been instantly caught.

A personable enough young man he had thought on his first encounters with Nugent, but he certainly appeared to advantage in the formality of evening wear and Miss Redland was positively fluttering. Guy suppressed a smile, then saw Hester regarding the newcomer with well-bred interest. He wondered at the stab of irritation he felt. Of course, if she formed an attachment that would make it considerably harder to dislodge her from the neighbourhood. It would be necessary to distract her; not such a hard task for a man with his experience of women.

'Nugent, good evening! I am sure you know everyone except Miss Lattimer, perhaps? And her companion Miss Prudhome.'

Hester shook hands with the young man as Guy presented him, finding it hard to resist the look of admiration he directed at her. It would be a rare woman indeed not to be susceptible to those dark good looks or the frank admiration in his green eyes. Jethro had been right: Lewis Nugent did not possess Lord Buckland's fine physique, but then he was younger and perhaps had some filling out to do still. There was something faintly familiar about him; she sought for it, but it was gone.

She found her hand was still in his and withdrew it. 'I must offer my condolences on the loss of your father, Sir Lewis. I understand your sister does not go about much yet, although I have hopes of meeting her the day after tomorrow at Mrs Bunting's small gathering.'

'Thank you. We do both feel it very much still, my father was a man of considerable character. However, Sarah is gradually getting about more; in such a small and friendly community it is easier, although she does not feel yet that she should go to such a formal occasion as this. You must excuse us for not calling upon you.'

He hesitated, then asked, 'And are you comfortable at the Moon House? We wondered that anyone would buy it after it had stood empty for so long.'

Miss Redland had drifted across to join them. Hester admired the casual way she achieved it. 'Oh, yes, Miss Lattimer, are you not afraid of the ghost?'

Hester admired less her rather too obvious flutterings of mock-horror and they certainly did not seem to provoke the protective instincts she had hoped for in Sir Lewis. He frowned and said repressively, 'You should pay no attention to superstitious village gossip, Annabelle. Just because of a number of strange incidents, there is no need to build up some fantasy of hauntings.'

'So how do you explain them?' Miss Redland demanded, suddenly reduced from grown-up young lady to the girl who had doubtless played and argued with the Nugents all her childhood. 'You cannot, can you?'

'Just because I cannot explain something does not mean it is anything to be afraid of.' Sir Lewis was looking somewhat harassed. 'I am sure it is quite safe. But you must let me know if you are regretting your decision, Miss Lattimer: I would always repurchase the house. In fact, I feel it my duty.'

'Thank you, but I am perfectly comfortable,' Hester said firmly. 'I pay no attention to gossip—why, I am sure any house that is empty for some time attracts some such nonsense.' All the same, she did wish people would stop trying to reassure her about it—their very words seemed to conjure up phantoms where none had existed before.

Guy Westrope was within earshot and she realised he was watching her, his face serious. She seemed to read a warning in his eyes. Did he think there was something to be worried about? But in her bedchamber he had said he was sure there was a perfectly rational explanation for both the pearls and the state of the dressing room. Hester gave herself a little shake. Perhaps he was warning her about taking this nonsense too seriously. Which was generous of him, considering that nothing would suit him better than for her to decide to sell up and move. The creeping anxiety about him returned.

'Dinner is served, my lord.'

The small dinner party sorted themselves out with the ease of old acquaintances, despite being in the home of an unfamiliar host. Hester realised that Guy must have taken considerable pains to make himself known in the neighbourhood in a very short time. He had apparently asked Mrs Bunting to preside at the foot of the table while he took the head and Hester found herself being taken in by Major Piper and seated at Guy's left hand opposite the formidable Mrs Redland.

For the first remove she devoted herself to Major Piper as convention demanded. He was thin, apparently rather shy, which made him gruff, and, she estimated, in his fifties.

With patience she extracted the information that he was a major of Marines and had been invalided out of the service after receiving a bullet in the chest. He now devoted himself to breeding the perfect spaniel and the management of his small estate.

Hester realised she must have sounded more knowledgeable than she had intended whilst talking about military matters when the major enquired whether she had relatives in the armed forces. Cautiously she explained that her father had been a major in the Peninsular Army and had been killed in 1812.

Why she should have been aware of Guy listening to their conversation she could not say. His head did not turn and she was conscious of him maintaining a constant flow of small talk with Mrs Redland, yet somehow she was sure he was listening to what she was saying.

And what if he is? she scolded herself. *Nothing you are telling the major would arouse anyone's interest. England is littered with the orphaned offspring of military men.* To assume that anyone in this inward-looking community would have knowledge or interest about one disgraced young woman was to place her own importance far too high. And eligible, noble bachelors would certainly have not the slightest knowledge of the gossip surrounding insignificant young ladies. What did it matter anyway if a certain sector of society shunned her as the mistress of the late Colonel Sir John Norton?

As the staff cleared the first remove with silent proficiency, she acknowledged yet again that it did matter and that she had been left scarred and humiliated by the slurs of Sir John's relatives. Telling oneself over and over again that the opinion of such blinkered, uncharitable persons could not be regarded by a rational person of clear conscience seemed not to help at all.

Firmly fixing her social smile on her lips, Hester turned to Guy, only to find him watching her with such intensity that she had a sudden qualm that her back hair had escaped again.

'It hasn't, has it?' she hissed.

'What?' he hissed back, laughter suddenly lighting up his eyes.

'My hair—you were looking so…'

'I can assure you it is the picture of perfection, Miss Lattimer. Does it escape so frequently that it is the only reason you can think of why a gentleman might stare at you?'

Hester blushed, darting a quick glance at Mrs Redland in case she had overheard this blatant piece of flirtation. Fortunately she was intent on a spirited conversation with Mr Bunting about some detail of the church flowers with Miss Prudhome silently listening to their exchanges.

'It is the despair of my maid,' she admitted candidly, deciding to ignore the latter part of his question.

'Perhaps it is the outward sign of your impetuous nature,' Guy suggested, carving the wing from a capon and placing it on her plate. The glitter of laughter was there again and something else, which touched her skin as a flicker of warmth.

Suddenly breathless, Hester looked away and found diversion in thanking Major Piper for the offer of the timbale of rice. It was back, that shiver of recognition that this man was the embodiment of an ideal. It was insane to think like that;

it would be madness even if she was the possessor of an unspotted reputation. Not only was Lord Buckland a peer of the realm, far above her socially, he was also a man she knew she could not wholly trust, much as she wished she could.

Eventually she could find no excuse not to turn back and resume their conversation. 'Thank goodness the weather has turned drier, constant drizzle is so dispiriting, do you not think?' she enquired. She was not in the slightest interested in Guy's opinion of the weather, but it was the safest topic she could think of.

'Indeed,' he agreed with a gravity which told her he knew exactly what she was about. 'I did not know your father was in the army.'

'But why should you?' Hester replied, smiling to remove the sting from her brisk answer. Then her stomach performed an uncomfortable lurch—had he been having her investigated, all the better to dislodge her from her home? No, a moment's thought told her. He had been genuinely surprised to find a young single woman in possession of the Moon House. Aware that she was verging on being rude, she added, 'He was with Wellington in the Peninsula and was killed at Vittoria.'

Guy sent her a look of sympathy, which conveyed more than any amount of trite condolence could have, and said simply, 'You must be very proud of him.'

'I am,' Hester agreed. 'We were close. My mother died when I was fifteen and we had always followed him on campaign when we were able. I just continued doing so, for there were always officers' wives to chaperon me. I was in Portugal when he was killed.' She stopped somewhat abruptly, not wanting to go into any more detail that would lead him closer to her life in London.

'So what happened then?'

Hester glanced around, but both Mrs Redland and Major

Piper were absorbed in conversation with their neighbours. 'I
came back to England. My father had made arrangements
years ago in case anything happened to him, but of course by
then I had no need of a guardian. Fortunately I secured a position as a companion to an invalid very quickly.'

Guy gestured to a footman and they fell silent as the man
refilled their wine glasses and withdrew. 'Why did you not
need a guardian?'

'Because I was of age, of course.' Hester laughed and
picked up her glass. Perhaps one more sip, it was such a pleasure to drink good wine in a man's company again. She caught
the teasing twinkle and could not resist an answering smile.
'And do not look like that, my lord. You are not going to
cozen me into revealing my age. Suffice to say I had been out
and acting as Papa's hostess for *years*.'

'Years?'

'Years,' she said firmly. She was not going to tell him that
she had put her hair up on her seventeenth birthday and five
days later had been hostess at a dinner where two generals and
an admiral had been amongst the guests. Let him think her
older than her twenty-four years if it helped make her seem
less vulnerable.

Fortunately he asked her nothing about her late employer,
which was a relief, for Hester was unhappy at the thought of
lying. Dissembling as she was already made her uneasy.

'So how are you occupying your time, Miss Lattimer?
After London I should imagine that Winterbourne, however
delightful, has far less to offer in the way of diversion.'

'On the contrary, my lord, I was never in a position to
enjoy London diversions. I have my books and sewing, a
house and garden to restore, lovely countryside all around and
most congenial company.'

Conversation was becoming more general as dishes were

removed and replaced with sweetmeats and nuts. Mrs Redland had obviously overheard, for she turned with her somewhat glacial smile and remarked, 'I am glad to hear you say so, Miss Lattimer. So many young people despise country life, but here we have a most respectable yet active society. I hope I may interest you in some of my favourite charitable causes.'

'I am sure you can, Mrs Redland. May I enquire what they are?'

'There is the village school for the children of the labouring classes, the Society for the Relief of Limbless Servicemen Passing through the Parish, the Ladies' Sewing Circle—we produce shirts and infant clothes for the deserving poor—and…' she lowered her voice '…the Home for Fallen Women in Aylesbury.'

Two of those enterprises struck a distinct chord with Hester, but she felt it politic to mention only one of them. 'A most interesting collection of charitable aims, Mrs Redland. I feel great sympathy with the plight of the limbless soldiers, having spent time in the Peninsula myself, but naturally I will do my best to assist with all of them.'

Mrs Redland beamed and turned to inform the lower half of the table that she had secured a willing recruit to their charitable groups. Guy lowered his voice and remarked, 'Very worthy and a dead bore. I cannot imagine you sewing endless infant garments for the products of the Home for Fallen Women. Do you ride?'

Hester flashed him a reproving glance. 'One cannot blame the infants for the sins of their mothers.'

'No, indeed,' he said with such emphasis that she blinked. 'Nor the mothers, either, in most cases. You did not answer my question.'

'Yes, I ride, but I have had no riding horse since returning to England, only Hector the Welsh cob who pulls my gig. I have not ventured to put a saddle on his back—I doubt he is used to a side saddle in any event.'

'So you drive? But only a gig?'

'I will have you know that it is a most dashing vehicle, my lord,' Hester retorted.

'Could I tempt you to try a curricle?'

'Very easily indeed,' she replied frankly. 'But I should not.'

'Even with a groom up behind?'

'Single ladies have to be very careful of appearances, my lord.'

To her surprise, it was Major Piper who intervened. 'Our local ladies are very partial to driving, Miss Lattimer, I am sure there would be no question of censure. My wife is a most accomplished whip and Miss Redland also. Carriage picnics are an established summer recreation amongst us.'

At this point Mrs Bunting rose, collected the other ladies' attention and announced, 'We will leave the gentlemen to their port.'

The ladies followed the vicar's wife out, leaving behind them the scraping of chair legs as the men resumed their seats.

'How lucky you are, Miss Lattimer,' Miss Redland exclaimed as the door was closing. 'Fancy Lord Buckland offering to teach you to drive a curricle! Mind you, he is not so good looking as Sir Lewis.'

'Annabelle!' Her mother turned, clucking in disapproval, the sound finding an echo in Miss Prudhome's audible agitation.

'Well, I think it is most unfair of Miss Lattimer to arrive just when another eligible gentleman comes to Winterbourne,' Annabelle said with a joking air that Hester suspected was only partially genuine. 'And with such lovely London gowns as well.'

'Nonsense, child, you will give Miss Lattimer a most unfortunate impression of you.' Mrs Redland turned an approving eye upon Hester as they took their seats in the salon. 'I am sure Miss Lattimer's intentions are far removed from such frippery trifles as gowns and flirtations.'

Hester smiled back modestly, but with a sinking heart. It was going to be akin to walking a tightrope to maintain one's reputation in such a small society and with such ineffectual chaperonage. Especially when one's heart yearned to be seated beside Guy Westrope as his curricle bowled along the road with not a groom in sight.

CHAPTER SEVEN

Hester spent the next half-hour in a state of nervous suspense, negotiating the social minefield presented by a group of well-bred and curious ladies all intent on extracting as much information as possible about her and speculating upon their host.

She answered all their personal questions with modest reserve, but with as much frankness as possible, correctly judging that not to do so would create an air of mystery and draw unwanted attention. Fortunately Miss Prudhome knew next to nothing about her new employer's background. Hester told herself that if she could survive the first few weeks then she would cease to be a novelty and would feel much safer.

Apparently satisfied by her explanation that she found London noisy and unhealthy and yearned for a return to the rural life she had enjoyed in Portugal, the ladies moved on to genteel speculation about their host.

'Why do you think he is here, Miss Lattimer?' Mrs Piper enquired. 'You are his nearest neighbour, after all.'

'Perhaps he is looking for property in the area?' Hester suggested, snatching at a part-truth.

'Possibly,' Mrs Redland agreed. 'But why not send his agent?'

Eventually they speculated themselves to a standstill and moved on to discuss the arrival in Aylesbury of a *modiste* reputed to be lately of London. Hester took her part in the conversation, aware from movement outside that the gentlemen, or some of them, had gone out into the garden.

Why she could not imagine, for it was far too dark to walk around and must be decidedly cold, then she saw the glow of a cigarillo end and guessed that at least one of them was enjoying blowing a cloud before rejoining the ladies.

For a moment she glimpsed a flash of light from one of the Moon House windows; Jethro and Susan must have returned early. Although why they should have needed to go into the dining room…

'I do beg your pardon, Mrs Bunting. My attention was caught by something outside and I missed what you just said.'

'Only that I hope the village women I recommended are proving satisfactory, Miss Lattimer.'

'Indeed, yes,' Hester agreed warmly. 'They are making great inroads into the cleaning, which allows my people to concentrate on setting the rooms to rights. I have yet to decide on whether I will employ one of them as a cook.'

'I do hope you are not troubled by rats and mice, after the house has stood empty for so long,' Mrs Piper interjected. 'Horrid things—and the nearest reliable rat catcher is at Tring.'

Stepping into the room with his male guests, Guy caught the last sentence. 'Is anyone plagued with rats?' he enquired.

'Oh, no, my lord,' Mrs Piper assured him. 'I was just warning Miss Lattimer that should she be so troubled we do not have a rat catcher in the village.'

A flicker of an idea came to him and at the same moment he caught Hester's eye. Her level gaze said as plainly as if she had spoken, *And do not think of introducing them!* He smiled inwardly, enjoying the wordless exchange. He felt a sense of affinity with Miss Lattimer, which was rare in his acquaintance with women. It was a feeling both pleasurable and unsettling.

No, Hester Lattimer was too intelligent—something as simple as a few rats was not going to work. If Miss Lattimer was not going to be frightened away from the Moon House— and that might still happen—then she would have to be seduced away, and that before she became any more comfortable in the neighbourhood.

In fact, he decided, settling in a chair next to Mrs Bunting and appearing to take an interest in the drama of the choir-master's falling-out with the churchwardens, he was not at all sure he had not made an error in inviting her this evening. It was a gesture that cemented her social position in the village faster than perhaps anything else could have done and it brought her into all too close a proximity with young Nugent.

Eventually the clock struck ten and the party began to break up. In the hall Hester was helped into her cloak by a footman.

'If you will excuse me, Miss Lattimer, I will just fetch a lantern to light you across the road.'

The Redland family made their way out leaving Major Piper and the vicar waiting patiently whilst their wives recalled a matter that they simply had to discuss there and then. Hester looked up to find Guy by her side. 'Thank you, my lord. It was most kind of you to invite me—such a pleasant way to get to know my new neighbours.' His smile seemed somewhat wry, which was a puzzle. Hester saw the footman emerging from the back regions and held out her hand. 'Goodnight, my lord.'

To her surprise, instead of shaking it, he turned it and kissed the gap over her pulse just before the buttons began. His lips were dry and warm and she felt them curve against her skin as though in a smile. 'Goodnight, Miss Lattimer. I hope you will reconsider the driving. And my other suggestions.'

Flustered, Hester retrieved her hand, hoping that none of the other guests had noticed the unusual gesture. She did not know what to make of it, only that her pulse was fluttering in a shamefully pleasant manner.

'Goodnight,' she called to the others and went out with the footman, Miss Prudhome hurrying at her heels. Guy was flirting, of course, that was all; pursuing his course of trying to unsettle or charm her enough to agree to what he wanted. It would serve him right if she pretended to fall for his wiles and take him at face value. It might be amusing to flirt back and see him beat a hasty retreat at the thought of an ineligible young woman appearing to accept his advances.

Unless, of course, he assumed she would go as far as to accept a *carte blanche* from him. Hester flushed in the darkness: that would be too humiliating.

Another lantern was approaching around the edge of the Green, moving very fast. The footman slowed and positioned himself between it and Hester, but she had recognised the faces it illuminated and called out, 'Susan, Jethro, I thought you were home.'

Jethro came to a halt in front of her, his breath visible in puffs on the chill air. 'I'm sorry, Miss Hester. I got to playing and what with one thing and another I only noticed the time when the clock stuck the hour.'

Hester turned to the footman. 'Thank you. I will be all right now.'

'His lordship told me to see you to your door, ma'am,' the man responded stolidly. Hester sensed Jethro bristling.

'Very well, I would not wish to countermand his lordship's orders. And we are nearly there.'

Jethro made great play of producing the front-door key and ushering Hester and Susan in before nodding dismissively to the footman who towered over him by a good foot.

Hester suppressed a smile, then suddenly remembered why she had thought they were already home. 'I was sure I saw a light, some time ago. I assumed it was you returned from the inn.'

Jethro turned from lighting the hall sconces. 'No, Miss Hester. That's an odd thing.'

'Must have been the moon reflecting in the glass,' Susan said sensibly. 'Look.' And sure enough the thinnest sliver of new moon shone clearly through the transom glass over the door.

'Of course,' Hester murmured with relief; the thought of the mysterious lights seen in the Moon House before she had arrived had been unsettling. Perhaps reflected moonlight was the answer to those as well. 'Well, I am for my bed, you can tell me all about your adventures at the Bird in Hand tomorrow.'

Susan was agog to hear about Hester's experiences and sighed gustily at her description of exactly what had been served at dinner, the gowns of the other ladies and even what his lordship had worn.

'None of the gowns were as fine as yours, then,' she said with satisfaction as she untied Hester's stay laces. 'That Miss Redland sounds a bit worrying, though; her mama will be off ordering her new gowns before the week's out, I'll be bound.'

'Nonsense. You speak as though there was some sort of competition.' Hester met Susan's eye in the mirror and added, 'And that is ridiculous.'

'Yes, Miss Hester. Is there anything else?' Susan paused in the doorway of the dressing room and suddenly Hester's heart was in her mouth, but she only stooped to pick up a stray ribbon and continued in to fold away Hester's clothes without any further check.

Hester climbed into bed and blew out the candle as the door closed behind the maid. 'Foolish,' she chided herself as she lay back against the pillow. The new moon was clear through the glass on the unshuttered window and she made a mental note to remind Jethro to get the hinges mended.

But it was soothing to lie watching the slender white crescent in the dark velvet of the sky, the stars twinkling around it. Hester snuggled down, searching for the flannel-wrapped brick with her toes. She let her mind wander over the events of the evening, but all her treacherous memory would do was dwell on the sound of Guy's deep voice, the flash of humour in his eyes, the touch of his lips on the soft skin of her inner wrist.

The curtains stirred slightly in the breeze and the room was suddenly filled with the sound of rustling branches. Hester slept. In the darkness outside a pair of calculating eyes rested thoughtfully on her window.

She was halfway downstairs the next morning when Hester recalled the broken shutter. 'Susan, do remind me to ask Jethro to get that shutter in my bedchamber repaired.'

'You need new curtains too before the weather gets much colder,' the maid remarked. 'But fixing the shutter will be quicker. Jethro's in the drawing room, I think. I'll go and put the kettle on.'

Susan disappeared towards the kitchen, singing what seemed to Hester to be a new song. She just caught the tail of the chorus: 'Never say me nay, my lusty lad.' It hardly seemed a suitable ditty and was doubtless the result of an evening spent in the public bar of the Bird in Hand.

With an indulgent smile Hester looked round the drawing-room door: no Jethro. She crossed the hall and stepped into the dining room. Again it was empty, but on the table lay a dark, spiky bundle of something next to a chamber stick.

Puzzled, Hester approached the table and peered at the bundle. It was a bunch of roses. Dead roses. Cautiously Hester poked them with her finger tip and the bunch fell apart. They were very dead, brown and perfectly crisp. There seemed to be fourteen of them and beside them on the table an ordinary chamber stick with a burnt-out candle in it.

Hester took an involuntary step backwards, recalling the light she had seen the night before in this room. Not moonlight but the light of this candle placed on the table by whoever—whatever—had left the dead roses there.

She stopped her instinctive retreat by calling up all her rational good sense and made herself step forward again. The front door had been locked. So had the back door, for Jethro would certainly have raised the alarm if anything had been out of order when he left to go to his bed above the stables. And, reliable as the church clock, he made his rounds of all the windows before leaving every night.

Something had got in. Or it had already been inside. Hester realised she was scanning the corners of the room as if expecting some spectral presence to be lurking there. That was as terrifying a thought as her first assumption of an intruder.

She ran her tongue over lips that were completely dry. She could not leave that sinister bouquet there; she must move it before the others saw it. Cautiously Hester gathered it up, just as there was a brisk knock at the front door.

'I will get it!' It was Susan, running along the hall before Hester could slip out of the dining room door. 'Oh. Goodness…I mean, good morning, my lord. I'm not sure if Miss Lattimer is receiving yet.'

'I would not wish to disturb Miss Lattimer, only to return this handkerchief, which, from the initials, I believe must be hers.'

'Thank you, my lord, yes, it is Miss Lattimer's, I am sure

of it. Will you not step in and I will see if she—oh, there you are, Miss Hester.'

Left with no option but to put a good face on it, Hester stepped out into the hallway. 'Good morning, my lord, how kind of you to take the trouble.' Conscious of her unpleasant burden already crumbling into brown flakes in her hands she chatted on determinedly. 'Such a pleasant dinner last night; I meant to ask you if you had lured your London chef down to the country or whether you have been fortunate in finding local staff.'

It was hopeless. The blue gaze was fixed on the roses as he said lightly, 'I am glad you enjoyed it, I will tell Maxim; he insists on accompanying me, apparently in the belief that I would starve else. Not that that devotion to duty prevents him from moaning almost continuously about the conditions into which I have dragged him.'

'That must be very tiresome,' Hester said.

'It is not I who has to listen to him,' Guy responded. 'You appear to have an admirer with a very strange taste in flowers, Miss Lattimer.' Was it her imagination or was there an odd note in his voice?

'They are dead, my lord.'

'I can see that.'

'Flowers do die,' Hester stated briskly.

'*Let us crown ourselves with rosebuds, before they be withered,*' Guy murmured vaguely. 'I wonder where that comes from? The Bible, possibly. But flowers in water do not die like that; these are uniformly crisp and brown and have been deliberately set to dry, or possibly hung up.'

'These had been put aside and forgotten,' Hester retorted, knowing she was becoming flustered. 'Susan, take them, please, and throw them away.' She thrust the tattered bunch into her maid's hands and confronted Guy as Susan made her way down the hall, trying to keep the crumbing stems intact.

'As I was saying, my lord…'

'Guy. I thought we had agreed on Christian names when we were alone. Hester, those flowers have been dead a long time, in a house I know you have been turning out very thoroughly indeed—and you are afraid of something. Where did they come from?'

His voice was very gentle and his eyes concerned. Hester found herself being drawn in, taking one step towards him. She *was* a little frightened, it would be foolish to deny it. To tell him, to be held safely in those strong arms as he had held her in her bedchamber—the thought was powerfully seductive. And, after all, she knew where he had been all the time she had been out of the Moon House. It could not possibly be any doing of Guy Westrope's.

'I found them in the dining room just now…' she began hesitantly. Something sparked in that deep blue gaze and she realised that she did *not* know where he had been for every minute of yesterday evening; at least one of the men had been strolling in the darkened gardens after the ladies had retired. It would have taken a matter of minutes to cross the road in the glimmer of moonlight and leave the dead bouquet, provided you had access to the house. And someone had, of that she was increasingly convinced; thoughts of ghosts were absurd. Someone could come and go in the Moon House, just as they wished.

And no one else had any reason for wanting to scare her away. Something of her thoughts must have shown on her face, in her unfinished sentence. Guy's eyes narrowed and he said, almost roughly, 'If you will not confide in me, then take care, Hester. I do not like the symbolism of those roses.'

She gathered her tumbling wits, her voice cool. 'And I do not like attempts to scare me away from my home. I told you Guy, I will not be bought out, and I would tell whoever is behind this that I will not be scared away either.'

He caught up her meaning with a directness that astonished her. 'You think that I would attempt to frighten you away?' Those expressive blue eyes showed nothing but concern that she could misjudge him.

Flustered to be taken up so directly, Hester returned to the attack. 'I did not say so. But who else wants this house?'

'No one who has made their wishes clear, apparently.' His voice was dispassionate. 'But that does not mean they do not exist.' He had moved towards her slightly and Hester stepped back into the dining room. 'I would remind you that I made my intentions perfectly clear—and made you a generous offer of compensation.'

'Because you thought I was an elderly lady who might be cozened by a gentleman of your standing into complying with your desires,' Hester retorted. Her breath was coming very short and for some reason she felt quite uncomfortably hot.

Guy chuckled. 'I thought perhaps you would be a middle-aged widow,' he admitted. 'But as for my *desires*…' Hester knew she was blushing. Of all the foolish words to have used! 'Within one minute of seeing you I formed a strong desire to do this.' And he took her very firmly in his arms and lowered his mouth to hers.

Hester gasped, then realised her mistake, for he took instant advantage of her parted lips to deepen the caress. Her hands clenched against his chest and she realised faintly that she might as well be pushing against the wall. Without her conscious volition her fingers opened and her palms pressed against the fine broadcloth of his coat.

He seemed to consume every sense; the taste and the scent of him were novel and dangerously male. Her hearing was blurred by the sound of her own heartbeat, fast and excited. The feel of his mouth gently, but inexorably, roused her to trembling, yielding surrender in his arms. Her eyes fluttered open and she was hazily aware of the texture of his skin, the curl of his hair at the temple.

How long she might have stayed there in Guy's arms she had no idea. There was a crash from the kitchen region and a wail from Susan and the next thing she knew Hester was standing unsupported against the dining-room door frame. Guy regarded her with eyes that seemed to spark sapphire fire and she hastily dropped her gaze to find herself staring at his mouth. The sensual curve of that was even worse. Anger seemed the only way to retrieve the situation.

'My lord! That was outrageous!'

'I thought it delightful,' Guy remarked, taking a precautionary step backwards as Hester advanced towards him wrathfully.

'I know exactly what you are about, my lord,' she snapped, now too angry and flustered to be cautious. 'You think you can flirt with me until I become too befuddled to resist your proposals and agree to sell the Moon House to you. Or else until I compromise myself in the eyes of local society and *have* to sell.'

'Hester, I promise I would never do anything to compromise you. And if I were intending to seduce you into selling to me, I would not do anything so fatal to my chances as kissing you in your own front room. See how angry it has made you.'

'Oh, you are insufferable,' Hester stormed. 'Out!' She stood, elbows akimbo while Guy opened the front door and, with a slight bow, removed himself.

He stood for a moment on the doorstep, reviewing the last few minutes. So much for his idea of seducing Hester Lattimer out of the Moon House. He had thought that a discreet flirtation might awaken her to the idea that life in London would, after all, be pleasant. He had no idea what it was that had sent an attractive and well-bred young lady hastening into rural seclusion, but he had some confidence that talk of balls and parties, fashionable shopping and promenades, combined with flattering male attention, would persuade her to change her mind.

Guy jammed his hat on his head with some force and strode down the garden path. *And what did I do?* he demanded inwardly. *Kissed her straight out. Idiot.* 'Idiot,' he repeated out loud, fortunately to an empty street. No wonder she was angry, she was a virtuous young lady. And an enchantingly sensual and responsive one at that.

Guy turned and strode across the Green with no destination in mind, but a pressing need for action. That flash of feeling as his lips touched hers…as if her mouth was made for his. Angrily he kicked a stone out of the road. Dalliance with respectable young ladies was not in his plans.

And this particular respectable, sensual, angry young lady was also, he now realised, a very brave and stubborn one. Those roses had shaken her but she was not going to give into her fear—which was a dangerous choice to make. Money, fear, seduction had all failed: what did that leave? Kidnapping?

CHAPTER EIGHT

Hester retreated into the living room in a state of shock. 'You let him kiss you,' she scolded herself. Then, with unquenchable honesty, 'You kissed him back.' She had been unnerved by those roses, of course, but that was no excuse for positively wanton behaviour. What would Guy think of her now? She smiled grimly—that was all too easy to answer.

She had been kissed before by amorous young officers when she had been in Portugal. She had always found those hopeful advances both easy to repel and equally easy to forget; this was different. Her relationship with John had been, whatever his indignant family might choose to believe, entirely platonic and gave her no yardstick to compare Guy's caresses against. Trying to ignore the sensations that were assaulting her body, Hester forced herself to think about the dead flowers instead.

Someone was trying to frighten her and, she had to admit, they had succeeded. Now, with the distance of time and a shattering kiss between that first discovery and now, Hester was ready to believe that there was some human mind at work here. Resolutely she pushed all thoughts of the numerous Gothic novels she had read behind her and tried to concentrate on who might wish her out of the Moon House.

Lord Buckland—she refused to think of him more famil-
iarly—was the obvious, in fact the sole, candidate. Yet her instincts were telling her to trust him, if only in the matter of
the Moon House.

'Miss Hester—breakfast is ready. I called ten minutes ago.'
It was Susan, looking hot and flustered; so flustered, in fact,
that she was unlikely to recognise signs of agitation in her
mistress.

'Did you?' Hester asked vaguely. Her fingers were against
her lips; she removed them hastily. 'I did not hear you. I did
hear a crash.'

'I dropped the platter,' Susan admitted. 'Ham and eggs.
And it's the devil…I mean, it is very hard to get the grease
up off those flagstones.'

'I am sure it is,' Hester agreed, following the maid out.

Jethro and Miss Prudhome were already seated at the
kitchen table, but it was obvious that more was wrong than a
simple accident with the food. Miss Prudhome was sitting
poker-backed on her hard chair, obviously under the influence
of powerful emotion; her sharp nose was pink and her eyes
looked suspiciously damp behind their sheltering *pince-nez*.

Jethro was flushed and embarrassed and Hester's entrance
interrupted him in mid self-justification. '…mean to criticise
you, Miss Prudhome, I just said there was talk in the village.
I never meant you to overhear me.'

'What is going on?' Hester demanded. 'Susan, please pour
the coffee, it seems we all need it.' *Certainly I do*, she admitted inwardly, pressing her fingers to lips which she was sure
must be betrayingly red and swollen.

'I am a failure,' Miss Prudhome blurted out. 'I should never
have presumed to think I could be a fitting companion.'

'Nonsense,' Hester said, more robustly than she felt. In
truth, her heart was sinking; unsatisfactory as she was, Miss

Prudhome was all that stood between her and scandal, for no young unmarried woman could set up home without chaperonage. 'Now, drink your coffee while Jethro repeats whatever it was he said to start this.'

Jethro went redder, shot a sideways look at Hester and muttered defensively, 'Of course, you'd expect a bit of talk with a new arrival.'

'Yes?' Hester enquired with a sinking feeling. 'Talk you heard at the Bird in Hand, I suppose? Go on.'

'Just that…that it's odd a young single lady moving into a village like this and then…'

'And?' Hester persisted, a sick emptiness building inside her.

'And…his lordship moving in right opposite, like—at almost the same time.'

'What?' Hester found herself gaping at her young butler and shut her mouth sharply. She had expected some gossip at her arrival, but it had not occurred to her that Guy Westrope's presence might be linked to hers. She had expected to ride out any initial disapproval of her youth by a display of obvious respectability and to make acquaintances as fast as possible so that her character might be easily established and displayed. Guy's coincidental arrival had never struck her as a threat to her own good name—now their proximity seemed highly dangerous.

To give herself time to think, she took some rashers of ham and ate with an appearance of calm. 'Eat up, all of you,' she said steadily. 'We know this household is entirely respectable, it just requires us to act with confidence and these foolish rumours will soon die down. Prudy, you and I will discuss our tactics after breakfast.'

Miss Prudhome gave a worried squeak of agreement, which Hester registered absently. If she threw herself upon the confidence of Mrs Bunting—no, even better, Mrs Redland—

she could explain her anxieties and enlist that critical lady's support.

She pushed the plate away. Somehow she could not feel hungry; in fact, her inner equilibrium felt decidedly unsteady. Could she be sickening for something?

'I will talk about my predicament at Mrs Bunting's At Home tomorrow,' she decided out loud. 'I will be quite frank about my fears and the gossip and I will ask the more formidable matrons for advice.'

'A good plan.' Susan nodded vehemently. 'They will see you have nothing to hide and will feel sorry for you and flattered that you are deferring to their judgement.'

Pleased by this show of support, Hester relaxed, only to be jolted by Jethro. 'Where did those dead roses come from, Miss Hester?'

There was no point dissembling. 'I have no idea. I found them on the dining-room table this morning.' She looked at their startled faces and added, 'Next to a burned-out candle in a chamber stick.'

'But there was no one—'

'You saw a light before we got home!'

'What roses?'

They spoke over each other in a rush of realization, then fell silent. Jethro gnawed his lower lip. 'I locked up, all right and tight before we went out, Miss Hester, I'd take my Bible oath on it.'

'I know,' she assured him. 'And you checked again when we got home, I saw you.'

'We'll have to change the locks,' he announced. 'And I'll go all round outside and try to force the window catches, see if there are any that are loose.'

'What did his lordship have to say about the roses?' Prudy asked abruptly.

'He said he did not like their symbolism.'

Jethro's brow furrowed and Susan explained. 'Dead flowers. And roses, at that—like dead love, perhaps. Nasty.' She shivered.

'Well, we will do no good brooding on it,' Hester said briskly. 'Jethro, when you have brought in the coals for Susan and checked the windows, please take the gig into Tring and find a locksmith. Susan, you have plenty to do in the house. Prudy, could you spare me a moment, please?'

'Should we lock ourselves in?' Miss Prudhome enquired nervously.

'Certainly not.' Hester was brisk. 'Whoever it is, is trying to scare us away and I will not give them the satisfaction.'

She poured herself another cup of coffee, pretending she did not hear Jethro's muttered observation, 'Only one person we know of wants us out of here, and that's a fact.'

When the coffee was finished Hester felt she could put a difficult interview off no longer and bore Miss Prudhome away into the drawing room.

'What do the roses really mean?' the little governess asked, her voice quavering.

'I do not know, only that it appears that someone has access to the house without our knowledge.'

To her surprise Miss Prudhome did not throw a fit of the vapours that Hester had expected to be developing. Her thin lips narrowed and she sat up straighter. 'And do I understand that his lordship is under suspicion, Hester dear?'

'He is the only person we know of who wishes me to leave,' Hester admitted.

'I know my duty,' Miss Prudhome announced. 'It is to protect you.' Her voice shook again. 'I know I have not been strong enough, I have shrunk from standing at your side.'

'It is all so new to you, Maria,' Hester said, suddenly desperately sorry for the lonely little figure.

Miss Prudhome started. 'No one ever calls me by my Christian name; my pupils always called me Prudy…'

'But I am not a pupil,' Hester said gently. 'Was it so very difficult and lonely, being a governess?'

'Yes, but one expects it, you see,' Maria confided. 'One is neither one thing nor the other. It was difficult at first, when one was young, to know one's place, but one soon learns…'

No doubt one does, Hester thought grimly. *A few snubs from one's employers, a few turned shoulders from the upper staff. Yes, one would soon learn one's place.*

'Well, in this house you are my companion and an equal, for I need you very much and I have every confidence that you will help and support me,' she said bracingly. 'Now, tomorrow I would like you to wear your best afternoon gown and borrow my Paisley shawl and you must do your utmost to join in the conversation as an equal, which you are.' She watched the emotions chase across the plain face opposite her and leaned forward to pat Maria's hand. 'I am relying on you, Maria. Besides wishing to have your companionship, my reputation depends upon your chaperonage.'

The household had passed a jumpy day and night looking forward to the locksmith's promised arrival. Hester was conscious of not looking her best as she dressed for Mrs Bunting's At Home on Wednesday. She chose an afternoon gown of impeccable respectability, added a modest lace fichu and sallied forth with pelisse and umbrella and Maria at her side.

The Rectory was a bustle of feminine chatter by the time she arrived and Hester was grateful that she already knew the Redland ladies and Mrs Piper, as well as their hostess. She greeted her acquaintances, was introduced to the widowed Mrs Griggs and her plain niece Miss Willings and with Maria took an early opportunity to catch Mrs Redland alone.

'I wonder, ma'am, if I might presume to ask your advice about a sensitive matter?' She saw immediately it was the correct approach. The matron's eyes sharpened, but she inclined her head graciously, obviously gratified to be the recipient of such confidence. Hester launched into her carefully prepared speech.

'…so different from London—I was confident that in such a close and respectable society my age and single status would be compensated for by the kindly attention of my new acquaintance, and of course, by the presence of my dear Miss Prudhome.' This produced an understanding nod, so Hester forged on. 'But, ma'am, imagine my discomfort when I discover that my nearest neighbour is a bachelor and one with no established character in the district. And worse, one whose arrival so nearly coincided with my own.'

Mrs Redland's expression became positively avid. Hester hurried to reassure—and disappoint—her. 'Not that his lordship has behaved in any way that causes me in the slightest to doubt his gentlemanly instincts.' She crossed her fingers behind her back; she was as much to blame for that kiss as he and she had no intention of blackening Guy Westrope's name. 'But I hear from my staff there has been talk in the village—you can see why I am concerned.'

'Indeed I can.' Mrs Redland took Hester's arm and steered her towards the window seat. 'No one would think anything of your youth once they had made your acquaintance, my dear, and that of Miss Prudhome here.' The companion produced a gratified twitter. 'As you say, the country is a very different matter to the town. But I understand your scruples about the near proximity of a single gentleman to your establishment. Do not concern yourself—with your permission I will confide in the ladies of influence in our little circle. They will watch out for your welfare and at the same time provide you with any additional chaperonage or protection you may require.'

That was all Hester had hoped for and more. With expressions of gratitude, which Mrs Redland accepted with a gracious smile, Hester was setting about greeting old acquaintances and drawing Maria into conversation with new ones when Miss Nugent was shown in.

Hester regarded Sir Lewis's sister thoughtfully as her hostess brought her across the room to be introduced to the newcomers. Dark hair and large greenish hazel eyes like her brother, average height, a delightful figure and an expression of suffering bravely borne. Hester's immediate reaction was that this last was somewhat overdone, then she chided herself for a lack of charity. Everyone dealt with grief differently; just because she did not suffer from an excess of sensibility herself, it did not mean that no one else might.

'How do you do, Miss Lattimer?' The delicately gloved hand rested in hers for a moment, making Hester feel overlarge and clumsy.

'Miss Nugent. I am so glad to meet you and to have the opportunity of expressing my condolences. I was not acquainted with your father, but I know his loss is much felt hereabouts, and must be a great sadness for his family.'

'Thank you.' It was said with a brave sigh and a downward flutter of eyelashes, then Miss Nugent seemed to gather herself. 'And are you comfortable in the Moon House? For myself I wonder that you should care to live there; I know Lewis would never have sold it to a single lady—he says he wishes you would sell it back—but of course poor Papa was too unwell to consider that sort of thing.'

'What sort of thing?' Hester asked.

Miss Nugent waved her hands vaguely. 'Oh, the local stories, the lights and so on. Ghost stories are all very well, but one hardly wants to live in a haunted house, does one?'

'Well, no, one does not,' Hester said as briskly as she could manage. 'Not that I believe in ghosts and I do not for a moment believe the Moon House to be haunted.'

'You are so brave!' Miss Nugent exclaimed in a tone that suggested that she was too polite to say 'foolhardy'. 'All I know is that dearest Papa could never find anyone willing to remain in it—not after the first cycle of the moon.'

'What can you mean—?' Hester began, only to be interrupted by Annabelle Redland.

'Sarah darling! Are you telling Miss Lattimer all the dreadful stories about her house? Is she not intrepid?'

'You were saying something about the phases of the moon?' Hester persisted.

'Apparently the manifestations, if that is the right word, are linked to the moon, or so the family story goes. I will have to check the records,' Sarah said. 'But perhaps you are not sensitive to those sorts of things and so will not notice?'

Hester would not have admitted noticing anything now, even if a headless horseman had ridden through the kitchen. 'That must be it,' she said lightly. 'I have no sensibility.'

'You must come to dinner at the Hall,' Sarah said. 'Lewis can tell you all the stories.'

'Thank you,' Hester responded with every appearance of delight and a sinking feeling at the thought of learning any more disturbing tales. She was finding Miss Nugent far less sympathetic than her charming brother. 'If you will excuse me, I must just speak to Mrs Piper—'

She broke off as the door opened and Mrs Bunting's footman announced, 'Lord Buckland, ma'am.'

He strode into the room, a startling contrast with his height and his breeches and boots amidst the feminine gathering. 'You must excuse me, Mrs Bunting, but I need to find Miss Lattimer.'

Hester was conscious of every eye in the room turning to

her and of a turmoil of emotions pouring through her. Embarrassment at being singled out by Guy, a hard jolt of physical excitement at the sight of him, alarm at what this sudden arrival might portend.

'Your man Ackland has had a fall,' he said tersely. 'Your maid had the sense to run across to my house and seek help. Parrott has sent for the doctor. Will you come?'

'Yes, of course. Mrs Bunting…'

'Off you go, my dear,' her hostess urged. 'Let me know if there is anything I can do.'

Hester found herself outside the vicarage, her pelisse half-buttoned and Miss Prudhome chattering anxiously at her side. Guy's curricle with the greys in harness was at the gate, the groom at their heads. 'Cuttle, see Miss Prudhome safely home, please.' Guy handed Hester up and with a flick of the reins sent the greys away at a canter from a standing start.

Hester clutched the side of the seat with one hand, her bonnet with the other. 'How badly hurt is he?' She was aware, under her anxiety, of the skill with which Guy was handling the team along the twisting lane; the sight of his hands, strong and competent on the reins, was curiously comforting.

'I do not know. He was conscious, but his right shoulder seemed to be giving him a lot of pain. That's a long flight of stairs to go down and he fell from halfway.'

'Do you mean the stairs in the house—?' Hester broke off as Guy urged the greys round the last bend and they burst out on to the road around the Green. 'But Jethro isn't clumsy, how did he fall?'

'He slipped on something that had been left on the middle step,' Guy said. 'Look, that must be the doctor's gig.'

Hester scrambled down before Guy could reach her and ran up the garden path and through the front door.

The hall was empty save for a broken ewer on the marble

and one dead rose. The remains of the bunch were scattered, crushed, down the staircase, marking Jethro's tumbling fall.

'These roses have developed a much more dangerous character,' Guy said quietly behind her. 'I want you out of this house now.'

'I will not go,' Hester said equally quietly and found herself spun round to face Guy. He held her still, one hand cupping each shoulder.

'You are placing yourself, and your household, at risk.' The temptation to take a step forward, to lean into his sheltering, strong body was so overwhelming that Hester found herself swaying. 'You are not going to faint now, Hester.'

'I have no intention of fainting,' she retorted, jerking herself free of his hands and swinging round. 'Susan!' She turned back at the foot of the stairs. 'I want to see Jethro and I want to find out what is going on here. No one is going to drive me out of my home, my lord, and that includes you.'

'Here, Miss Hester.' Susan appeared at the top of the stairs. 'We've put him in the spare bedroom. Mind those roses, do,' she added as Hester gathered up her skirts and began to run up the stairs.

'Please can you pick them up, Susan?' She reached the top of the stairs, Guy at her heels. She could hardly turn him out now, but his presence was unsettling; it was hard to be close to someone into whose arms one longed to be gathered when one dare not trust their motives an inch.

Jethro was stretched out on the spare bed, looking frighteningly young and white. But he was conscious and in full possession of his faculties as his continuing argument with the doctor demonstrated.

'I can't lie here! I am quite fit to get up, sir, Miss Hester needs me.'

'Miss Hester needs you to get well. Ah, you must be Miss

Lattimer. Doctor Forrest at your service, ma'am. I am sorry we could not be introduced under happier circumstances, but this young man will be up and around in a week if he does as he is told and rests.'

'He will do that, I can assure you.' Hester smiled, switching to a severe look at Jethro, who had opened his mouth to protest. 'Doctor, may I introduce Lord Buckland, who was kind enough to fetch me here.'

She left the men exchanging courtesies and went to kneel by the bed. 'Jethro, does it hurt very much? Is your shoulder broken?' His right arm was swathed in a sling with bandaging right across his chest and shoulder.

'No, Miss Hester, the doctor says I dislocated it and I've wrenched the muscles and tendons. Hardly aches at all; I can get up.'

He was sheet-white under his freckles and Hester could see his left hand clenched to resist the pain. 'You will stay exactly where you are and do what the doctor orders,' she said, smoothing back his tumbled hair gently.

'But how'll you manage, Miss Hester?'

'Really, Jethro,' Hester said in rallying tones. 'As if three able-bodied women can't manage a little house for a week!'

'I'll send a footman over, Ackland,' Guy said from behind Hester. 'No, don't starch up on me, young man—he can take his orders from you.'

Jethro subsided just as a patter of footsteps on the stairs heralded the arrival of Miss Prudhome. Hester's heart sank, but to her surprise her companion came in, surveyed the sickroom with a competent eye and announced, 'You need more comfortable pillows, Jethro, and some lemon barley water. Now you just leave him with me, Hester, I am very used to sickroom nursing.'

Somehow Hester and Guy found themselves outside the

room while Miss Prudhome interviewed the doctor. 'What has come over your companion?' Guy regarded the door panels that had been firmly shut in his face with some incredulity. 'She wouldn't say boo to a goose and now…'

'Now she thinks she is back being a governess again. Doubtless she has seen numerous small boys through measles and broken limbs; Jethro is just going to have to resign himself to being treated as though he is seven again.'

Guy gave a snort of amusement, tucked Hester's hand under his arm and headed for the stairs. 'I think we had better talk to Susan about exactly what occurred.'

'I will most certainly do that, but you, my lord, need trouble yourself no further. I am very grateful for your assistance and for fetching me so promptly, but I can manage now.' She tugged, but her hand stayed firmly captured. 'My lord!'

'Guy. And if you think I am going to walk away and leave you in a house where someone can obviously gain admittance at any hour of the day and night and where a member of your staff has had a very lucky escape from breaking his neck, then you have obviously formed a most faulty idea of my character in the course of our short acquaintance.'

Hester decided that to struggle would only result in an undignified tussle and allowed herself to be steered into the kitchen where Susan was just thrusting the remains of the roses on to the fire. 'There was just twelve of them, Miss Hester,' she observed. 'Fourteen last time.' She hefted the kettle off the range and put it under the pump. 'I'll make tea, shall I?'

'Yes, please, and can you run upstairs and see if Dr Forrest would like some?'

But the doctor was already in the hall and Hester went out to shake his hand and enquire if there was anything she needed to do for Jethro.

'No, nothing at all, ma'am, beyond the instructions I have

given to Miss Prudhome. A most capable lady, she knows just what to do. Good day to you, ma'am, my lord.'

'I will take my leave of you too.' Guy gathered up his hat and gloves. 'I will send the youngest footman, which might help Jethro swallow his chagrin.'

'Thank you, my lord, but we can manage perfectly well, I assure you, and I will not need your footman. I would, however, be grateful if one of your grooms could look after my cob, if that would not be too much trouble.'

'You should not be unguarded at night. I will send a man over and he can sleep on a truckle bed in Ackland's room— I assume you will be keeping him in the house for the moment?'

'I will indeed, and I repeat, my lord, I do not need assistance, although naturally I appreciate your concern.'

'Hester, you will appreciate rather more than my concern if you do not stop this stubbornness.' He put his hands on her shoulders before she realised what he was doing. 'I do not know whether to shake you or…'

'Or what?' Hester looked warily into his narrowed eyes, trying to ignore the flutterings that the feel of his hands on her sent through her body.

'Or give into the very strong temptation to kiss you until you give in,' he replied grimly.

'Miss Lattimer?' The front door swung open and Mrs Redland swept through.

CHAPTER NINE

Hester felt ready to sink. Of all the people in Winterbourne St Swithin to have discovered her virtually in the embrace of the Earl of Buckland, it had to be Mrs Redland.

She had reckoned without Guy's considerable address. 'Ma'am, you are just the person to assist me,' he said warmly.

'I am?' Mrs Redland looked sharply from Hester's rosy cheeks to Guy, who had only that moment dropped his hands from her shoulders.

'Miss Lattimer, who is understandably distressed over the injury to her only male member of staff, was just refusing my offer to lend her a footman. I am sure you will agree with my anxiety that a household of ladies should not be without able-bodied male support.'

'Well…' Mrs Redland met Hester's imploring gaze and hesitated. Hester nodded meaningfully at Guy's back, then shook her head vehemently. Mrs Redland had obviously not forgotten their conversation earlier that day.

'That is a most generous suggestion, my lord. However, I cannot but feel that such an offer, whilst meant with the most chivalrous of intentions, might be misinterpreted in some quarters. A single lady, especially one of Miss Lattimer's years, cannot be too careful.'

Hester smiled at Mrs Redland, then rapidly composed her face when Guy swung round to look at her.

'Very well, Miss Lattimer, it appears I am overruled by wiser counsel. I will send a groom over daily to attend to your cob. Please feel free at any time to call upon my household for assistance; you have only to speak to my butler. Good day, Miss Lattimer, Mrs Redland.'

'Tsk!' Mrs Redland regarded the door, which his lordship had most carefully refrained from slamming, with some amusement. 'Not a gentleman used to encountering opposition to his will, that is obvious.' She allowed herself to be ushered through to the drawing room, but refused the offer of a seat. 'No, my dear, I merely called to enquire if there was anything I could do to help.'

'Thank you, ma'am, that is most kind. It is all very worrying.' Hester could not now believe that Mrs Redland had overheard anything compromising. 'However, the doctor has been most helpful and Miss Prudhome has extensive sickroom experience.'

'Very well, I will take my leave, but do let me know if there is anything I can do to assist or if, now Miss Prudhome has other calls upon her time, you require a chaperon.' She paused as Hester was opening the front door for her. 'I am sure his lordship's intentions are merely to be attentive and of use as a neighbour, but I commend your reticence, Miss Lattimer.'

More than a little relieved, Hester made her way back to the kitchen. What a narrow escape!

'There you are.' Guy was sitting at the kitchen table, a steaming mug of tea in his hands. He stood up as Hester entered and the look he exchanged with Susan was not lost upon her.

'I'll just see if Miss Prudhome needs any help.' The maid bustled self-consciously out of the door, wiping her hands on her apron as she went.

'I will thank you not to conspire with my servants behind my back, my lord!' She felt so angry that it was difficult to control her voice.

'I merely remarked to her that I wanted an opportunity for a word in private.' Guy gestured to the chair opposite. 'Will you not sit down? This is an excellent cup of tea and I am anxious to finish it.'

Hester sat down with some emphasis. 'Far be it from me to disoblige you, my lord. Please finish your tea at your leisure; I cannot imagine that we have anything else to discuss.'

The mug was grounded with enough force to splash tea on the scrubbed pine. 'Why do you not trust me, Hester?'

'Because someone is trying to frighten me out of this house and you are the only person with a motive for doing so.'

'You obviously never studied logic—I am the only person whose motives you are aware of. That does not mean that I am therefore the culprit.'

'Since society opposes scholarship for women, you are correct that I am untutored in logic. However, I have enough native wit to know when someone is hiding something. You will not tell me why you want the Moon House: you cannot therefore complain that I am suspicious of you. Tell me why you want my house and you may find I trust you.'

Guy ran one long-fingered hand over his mouth and chin, then shook his head decisively. 'It is not just my story to tell you.'

Hester shrugged. 'Then we have a stalemate.'

'Do you seriously think I would harm you?' That expressive hand reached across the table and captured hers. 'Do you?'

'No.' She found she believed it. Her hand lay passive under his, then turned, seemingly of its own volition, until their fingers interlaced. 'And neither do I think you, or anyone else, are tiptoeing about this house depositing roses personally. I am sure whoever is behind this is employing some agent and on this occasion they must have been frightened, put down the roses and left. It was pure accident that Jethro did not see them.'

'He could have broken his neck.'

Hester shivered at the thought. 'And so could any of us if Susan had not cleaned the flags in here thoroughly after spilling a pan of greasy cooking the other day. Accidents happen, my lord, and I would be foolish indeed if I trust everyone who appears well intentioned and friendly.'

'Then at least promise me you will take care.' He let go of her hand and she stifled a little murmur of protest.

'I can certainly promise you that. And I have had all the locks changed and the window catches checked. Whoever thinks they can come and go as they please will soon find they are mistaken.'

'If that is how they have been entering. They got in today, did they not?' Guy put down his empty mug and stood up, looking down at her with sombre eyes. 'Somehow I do not think you are dealing with someone who comes and goes by the front door, or even by a window.'

'Then you believe this to be a ghost story?' Hester laughed, wishing she felt as confident as she sounded. 'I could almost suspect you of reading Gothic novels, my lord.'

He was at the back door, but swung round with some irritation. 'No, I have not, Miss Lattimer, but I could wish that you had, they might produce some healthy fear in you. And for heaven's sake, stop calling me "my lord" in every other sentence. You sound like a simpering miss at Almack's.'

'As I have never had the good fortune to attend Almack's, *my lord*, I would not know how young ladies there sound. I have had to make my own way in the world and perhaps that has made me somewhat more independent than gentlemen like.'

His brows rose. 'I have no objection to your independence, Hester, I just wish it did not give you this foolhardy confidence.'

'I thought you were upset that I do not trust you?' she jibed, now thoroughly nettled. 'You should congratulate me on retaining a caution about anyone whom I have known for such a short time.'

'I see there is no reasoning with you. Good day, Miss Lattimer.'

'Good day, my lord.' The door shut behind him and she watched through the window as he strode across the yard to the gate. 'Guy.'

Five minutes later she realised she was still sitting at the kitchen table, staring into space. 'For goodness' sake, pull yourself together, Hester!' she exclaimed. 'You wanted him to keep a proper distance, that at least is now assured!' This should have been a comfort, but somehow her anxiously sought respectability and acceptance in the community seemed a hollow ambition now.

Hester got to her feet and took herself upstairs to see how Jethro did. Halfway across the landing she stopped, turned and ran downstairs to lock the back door, knowing as she did so that it was probably a futile gesture.

Thursday dawned bright and clear as Miss Prudhome announced when she met Susan and Hester in the kitchen. 'Lovely and sunny, despite all that rain last night.'

'Which is more than can be said for us,' Susan observed, banging down a coffee pot on the tray destined for Jethro's room. 'I didn't get a wink of sleep, and I dare say you didn't, either, Miss Hester—not judging by those dark circles under your eyes.'

'I am sorry,' Maria apologised, with a return to her old fluttering nervousness. 'I did try and creep about, but Jethro was very uncomfortable and needed a lot of attention.'

'It wasn't you, Miss Maria.' Susan seized the carving knife

and attacked the ham as though it had done her a personal injury. 'It's not knowing when that creature will get back in the house again. Pass me the butter, would you, Miss Hester?'

Hester pushed the crock across the table. It had not just been nervousness that had interrupted her sleep. Endless fantasising about exactly how she should have dealt with Guy the day before had not helped either. 'At least anyone outside would have seen Maria's candle moving from room to room upstairs and would have known they would be heard if they attempted to enter.' She tried, and failed, to stifle a cracking yawn. 'Oh dear, I think we should take it in turns to have a nap today. Until Jethro is better and we have seen the last of these strange incidents, I fear none of us will sleep well at night.'

She opened the door for Susan to pass through with Jethro's breakfast and drifted back to the table, regarding Maria's heavy eyes with concern. 'Is Jethro so very poorly, Maria? Perhaps we should send for the doctor again. Do you not think that perhaps some laudanum drops would help him sleep, then you can get some rest too?'

'No, it is only what you would expect,' Maria assured her. 'He is thoroughly uncomfortable, still somewhat shocked, and miserable that he cannot get up. Shall I coddle some eggs? I could just fancy egg and toast. Do we have a coddler, do you know?'

They scanned the shelves, but failed to see one. Maria opened one of the doors to the cupboards flanking the fireplace, peered in, shook her head and opened the other. 'Goodness, that's a dank, draughty hole.'

'I know, I think I must get a builder in to look at it. There must be a crack that the rain gets in, but I am certainly not going to investigate myself, last time I looked there was an enormous spider.'

Miss Prudhome shuddered and closed the door briskly. 'No coddler. Never mind, I can improvise with a small bowl.'

By the time Susan came down—'I thought I'd better cut up his ham for him'—Maria was spooning eggs over slices of toast and Hester had made a fresh pot of coffee.

'So what are we going to do today?' she enquired briskly. 'Other than all of us having a rest this afternoon? I think I might take the gig and drive into Tring to speak to a builder about that cupboard.'

'His lordship's groom's been and seen to the cob,' Susan volunteered. 'I saw him when I came down to make up the range. Do you need me to help get Hector hitched up?'

'Yes, please, Susan. Would you like me to fetch anything for either of you in town? I don't feel more than one of us should be away at a time.'

'If you could just find some darning wool for me.' Maria produced a basket from beside the hearth. 'I cannot match these stockings of Jethro's in the village shop.'

'And we are low on coffee,' Susan added, helpfully tucking one stocking into Hester's basket. 'Do you think you should be driving into town all by yourself, Miss Hester? His lordship would lend you a groom, I'm sure.'

'His lordship would probably tell me I shouldn't be driving myself, more likely,' Hester muttered under her breath. 'I will be fine, thank you, Susan.'

They had just finished backing a placid Hector into the shafts, and Susan was tickling him under the girth to make him breathe in so she could tighten it, when the sound of hooves on the cobbles made both women look up.

Hester's instinctive frown yielded to a smile at the sight of Sir Lewis Nugent astride a neat bay hack. 'Miss Lattimer!' He swung out of the saddle and came across to take over the last of the harness buckles from her. 'Sarah told me about the accident to your manservant and I came over to see if there was any way in which I might assist you. How is the boy?'

'Well enough, I thank you, Sir Lewis. Bruised and very shaken and sore, but he will soon mend with rest. The doctor has ordered him to stay in bed and I suspect the effort of keeping him there for a sennight will prove to be the main challenge.'

'Then there is nothing I might do to help?'

'You might recommend a builder to me if you will. There is a cupboard in the alcove of the kitchen chimney breast that is constantly damp. I assume there is a crack of some sort and I want to have it fixed before it damages the brickwork. I was just on my way to Tring to find someone to look at it for me.'

'Let me see.' Sir Lewis handed her Hector's reins and strode towards the mass of the chimney.

'The left-hand side, Sir Lewis. Oh, do take care of your boots, there is such a tangle of rubbish on that side.'

Nugent heeded her warning, stopping at the point where the cobbles were obstructed by a broken hurdle and a large, very mossy water butt.

'That will be your problem.' He gestured at the butt. 'It is overflowing, and possibly there is a cracked downpipe, or perhaps some damage to the wall. It needs emptying and the pipe diverting away from the corner. Then we can see whether it will dry out.

'My steward will send one of the estate workers down to have a look at it. Why do you not drive back with me to Winterbourne Hall and speak to him yourself? Then you can agree to a convenient time, and I am sure Sarah will be delighted to offer you luncheon.'

'Well, thank you, Sir Lewis.' It was a kind offer and very neighbourly and Hester scolded herself for the sinking feeling that the promise of some time spent with Miss Nugent produced. Sir Lewis, on the other hand, was much more pleasant company. 'I would be glad to do that if you think an unexpected visitor would not inconvenience Miss Nugent. Susan, expect me back after luncheon, and do make sure Miss Prudhome lies down for a rest later.

'I must not be away too long, Sir Lewis,' she explained as he helped her up into the driving seat. 'Ackland has had a very restless night and Miss Prudhome was up at all hours nursing him.'

The baronet swung up on to his mount and fell in beside the gig. 'If you turn left out of your gate, it is straight on for about a mile. Restless, you say? Why not try a sleeping draught? I used one when I had a broken arm and I found it answered wonderfully; there is nothing like a good night's sleep to set the healing process on its way.'

He dropped back as they passed through the gate and then cantered for a few strides to catch up. 'The doctor did not give me anything,' Hester said doubtfully.

'I am sure I have the bottle still, it was only last year. It was Dr Forrest himself who prescribed it, merely a mild extract of poppy juice, you know. You can check with him,' Sir Lewis added comfortably. 'I can certainly recommend it. Good day, my lord!'

Hester looked to her right with a start to see the earl emerging from the vicarage driveway on his bay hack. Sir Lewis was already reining in, but she dropped her hands and the cob broke into a canter, sweeping her past Lord Buckland. She raised her whip in a neat salute as she passed and simply drove on until Sir Lewis caught her up.

Hester knew her colour was up and wondered what she could say to Sir Lewis to explain away her snub to Lord Buckland. She glanced across and caught a look of amusement on his face. She smiled ruefully in return.

'Ah ha!' he said in a rallying tone. 'Have I discovered someone who is not one of his lordship's numerous admirers?'

His look was so quizzical that she laughed. 'Not at all; the earl has been all that is kind. It is just that he feels I should remove from the Moon House and I am not inclined to oblige him.'

She expected Sir Lewis to assume that worries about Jethro's accident and the rumours about the house were behind this concern. Instead he looked serious. 'Then he still wishes to purchase it? With the benefit of hindsight, I wish he had been before you in applying to my father.'

'You know? Oh, but of course you must.' Hester reined back to a walk.

'His agent contacted my father only days after he had agreed the sale to you. Naturally he sent a refusal, but the man persisted, most strongly, asking for your name and direction.

'Of course my father refused to disclose such details, particularly as a lady was involved, and soon after that he died. At the time we were in no mood to be harassed by such matters and I wrote to say there would be no further correspondence on the subject. Obviously the man was over-eager on behalf of his employer; I am sure the earl would not press in such a manner.'

'No,' Hester agreed thoughtfully. 'No, of course he would not.' But it seemed he had known when she was intending to move down to Winterbourne St Swithin and had taken care to arrive a few days before her.

She was still biting her lip thoughtfully when they arrived in front of Winterbourne Hall. Sir Lewis directed her round to the stables where he called over a taciturn red-haired man in gaiters and explained her problem.

'Yes, sir, I'll get right on it. Happen you're right about the butt and the downpipe.' He knuckled his forehead to Hester and strode away to a group of labourers who were grouped round a pile of bricks in one corner.

'We're always building,' Sir Lewis remarked, helping Hester down. 'Place seems to need constant attention; sometimes I wonder if I'll ever get on top of it.'

Now he had drawn her attention to it, Hester could indeed see that the Hall was in poor repair. There was a long crack across one wall, a tarpaulin covered the roof of part of the stables and the paintwork on the windows of the main façade left much to be desired.

'It is very charming,' she said politely. 'Is it Queen Anne?'

The baronet was explaining the history as he ushered Hester into the hall. 'Now, where has Sarah got to? I left her engrossed in a book in the library.'

'Miss Sarah is still in the bookroom, Sir Lewis.' The butler took Hester's gloves and pelisse. 'Shall I send to say you are home, sir?'

'No, we will go in.' He opened the door on to a pleasant panelled chamber, its walls lined with shelves. 'Sarah? We have a visitor.'

Miss Nugent appeared from an embrasure, a book in one hand and a parchment in the other. Her reaction on seeing who was at her brother's side was startling.

'Miss Lattimer! Oh, no! How can I tell you…oh my goodness!' She sank down on a *chaise*, fluttering the parchment before her face.

'Tell me what?' Hester demanded with more sharpness than was strictly polite. 'Please, do not distress yourself, Miss Nugent. Here, try this.' She searched in her reticule and thrust a smelling bottle under the afflicted lady's nose, producing a sharp recoil and an end to the posturings.

'Lewis, look, see what I have found in this old book.' Sarah thrust a volume into her brother's hands. 'I was looking up the family histories in an attempt to find more about the hauntings at the Moon House and this parchment fell out. You see, it says the evil grows with the waxing of the moon—the thing that walks by night in search of its lost love, hating all that are happy and live, strewing its love tokens as it passes. And then at the full moon…'

Love tokens? The roses? 'Well?' Hester demanded, looking at Lewis's face as he studied the worn scrap in his hand. 'At the full moon?'

'At the full moon…' his voice shook slightly '…at the full moon death walks and—'

'And what? What about death?'

'I do not know.' He handed her the paper. 'It is torn at that point.'

'And the moon is waxing,' Sarah said, her eyes enormous.

CHAPTER TEN

'Local legends—how amusing,' Hester said lightly, resisting the urge to tear up the parchment in her hand. It felt unpleasant: old, dirty, strangely gritty. She handed it back to Sir Lewis with an attempt at a bright smile. 'You must not lose this from your archives, Sir Lewis. One of the family was obviously a collector of antiquarian lore.'

'Great-uncle William, I believe.' He frowned at his sister. 'You should not be alarming Miss Lattimer with this nonsense, Sarah.'

'I am not at all alarmed.' Hester eyed Miss Nugent warily. From suspecting her of having airs to be interesting, she was now wondering if the girl was of a hysterical nature; she was certainly flushed and her eyes glittered. 'But I appreciate Miss Nugent's concern and I think this discussion is distressing her.'

Far from eliciting a sympathetic response from Sir Lewis, he said sharply, 'Sarah, you will make yourself ill; leave these musty books and this foolish superstition. Fresh air will do you good—the day is fine, why not show Miss Lattimer around the gardens?'

'I would not dream of inconveniencing…'

'How could you?' Sarah flared at him. Hester took a step

back. 'How can you forget and call this foolish? Father sold the Moon House and look what happened to him.'

'It was an accident. He was unwell and slipped.'

'He was unwell from the moment he signed the deeds away. And an accident? To slip on the steps in full moonlight? And where did the rose come from, pray?' She broke off panting, staring defiantly at her brother, who appeared lost for words.

'Rose?' Hester queried, not wanting to hear the answer.

'There was a dead rose in his hand,' Sarah burst out and ran from the room.

'I…' Sir Lewis gave himself a little shake. 'I apologise. Allow me to offer you some refreshment while my sister composes herself.'

'No, please, I would not dream of imposing upon your time when Miss Nugent is unwell. Please give her my apologies for not waiting to take my leave of her.' Hester felt she was babbling and added, as she stepped into the hall, 'You must both come to dinner one evening when she is feeling more herself.'

'Let me walk you back to the stables.' He fell into step beside her in awkward silence. Finally he said, 'I am sorry if Sarah alarmed you. She is distressed because her betrothed is kept longer than expected on his plantations in the West Indies. She misses him and, of course, the wedding had to be postponed anyway because of our bereavement. She reads too much to pass the time and broods on what she has read. If I had my way, I would burn every Gothic novel ever written!'

'She has a vivid imagination.' Hester struggled to find something helpful to say. 'I am sure she is very sensitive.'

'The trouble is,' Sir Lewis said grimly, 'it is not all her imagination. I do my best to play down her fears and the strange stories, but something is very wrong with that house; I hope you will be careful, Miss Lattimer.'

'Perhaps I should sell to the earl after all.' Hester brushed her fingertips together to try and get rid of the unpleasant gritty feel of the parchment before pulling on her gloves. 'I am sure he could rout the spectre.'

'I do wish you would decide to sell, and that you would sell it to me.' Lewis Nugent halted her with one hand on her arm. 'I feel it is the only honourable thing to do. I would not wish you put in fear, nor to transfer the curse or whatever it is to anyone else; this seems to be a problem for the Nugent family.'

Hester looked up into his handsome, anxious face. 'No, Sir Lewis. I thank you, but the Moon House is my home now and I am not going to be scared out of it by ghostly or human agency.'

He let her go then with renewed pressure to reconsider and an offer to send a groom with her, both of which Hester refused firmly. She was just guiding Hector past the front door again when he ran out, a brown medicine bottle in his hand. It was half-full of a thick liquid and, as he held it up to her Hester could see a label in a thin hand attached to the neck. 'Do try this; it will help the lad sleep and give you all some much-needed rest as a consequence.'

Thanking him, Hester drove thoughtfully home. It was difficult to imagine the sort of dangerous spectre that Sarah Nugent conjured up on this brisk, sunny day. Poor girl—she had judged her too harshly. Perhaps it was no wonder she thirsted after attention and excitement, what with the loss of her father and her betrothed's prolonged absence. A gentleman with plantations in the West Indies seemed a good catch for a country baronet's sister and she could be excused for wishing to have the knot tied as soon as may be.

Hester could see no sign of Susan when she arrived home, so she unhitched Hector herself and carried the sleeping draught across the yard. She would see what Maria thought about using it.

To her surprise she met Parrott at the kitchen door. He doffed the hat he had just assumed and opened her own door for her. 'Good day, Miss Lattimer. I took the liberty of calling to see young Ackland. I had promised to speak to him, if you recall, and I thought it might help keep him entertained.'

Hester stamped firmly on her immediate, heated reaction, which was to ask if his lordship thought she needed a minder, and smiled. She was surely misjudging the butler. 'Thank you, Parrott.' Jethro would have thoroughly enjoyed such a visit and it was kind of Parrott to have remembered his promise. 'That was most thoughtful. I appreciate you sparing the time.'

'A well-run household needs but the lightest touch, Miss Lattimer,' Parrott said serenely. 'Is there any way in which I may assist you while I am here?'

Nothing except to carry out a quick exorcism, she thought wildly. 'No, nothing, thank you, Parrott.'

With a bow he left, shutting the door behind him, and Hester went upstairs to see whether his visit had left Jethro overexcited and running a temperature.

She found him sitting up looking pale and bright-eyed, but with no sign of a fever. Across the landing she glimpsed Susan in her room with the door open, a basket of mending at her feet. From Miss Prudhome's chamber a faint bubbling snore made itself heard.

He tried to sit up more when he saw her, but the effort made him wince and he fell back again. 'Do have a care, Jethro, you must take pains not to strain your shoulder.' Hester laid a hand on his forehead—it was cool enough. 'How are you feeling? I see you had a visitor.'

'I'm fit as a flea, Miss Hester. Mr Parrott stayed a whole hour and he told me so much! All about how he started off as a boot boy to Sir Jasper Ings and worked his way up. He says it's a matter of strategy and planning and one can't just wait for a post to come up. He says he used to listen in the clubs—did you know footmen and butlers have clubs in London, Miss Hester?—and work out where the next vacancy was likely to be and then read up all about the household.'

'Well, we had better start our research,' Hester said lightly. 'Where do you want to start?'

'I can't leave you, Miss Hester!' Jethro sounded scandalised. 'I just mean that when you…when you don't need me, like…then I know all about finding a new job.'

'And when will that be?'

'When you get married, of course, Miss Hester.' Jethro was bending over a book, which was lying on the covers, and missed Hester's blush of confusion.

Bless the boy, who does he think is going to marry me with my reputation and lack of a fortune?

'And see what Mr Parrott lent me, it's called the *Household Vedey Meckum* or some such and it's all about everything you need to know to run a big household.'

'*Vade mecum.*' Hester took the big book and opened it at the title page. 'It's Latin, Jethro, it means it's a useful companion full of all sorts of knowledge.'

His eyes widened in awe. 'Will I have to learn Latin to read it, then? He didn't say anything about Latin.'

Hester set his mind at rest and left him doggedly ploughing his way through page one, his tongue protruding slightly in concentration.

Susan, nodding over her needlework, confessed that she had left the butler and the boy together and had gone to have a bread and cheese luncheon so she had no idea what they had talked about. Seeing her suppressing a yawn, Hester packed her off to bed and went to make a meal for herself and Jethro which he ate with one hand while precariously balancing the book on his knees.

When Maria emerged looking the better for her nap Hester showed her the sleeping draught. 'It is Dr Forrest's handwriting, I recognise it from the notes he left me on making up a saline mixture. It says one wineglass before retiring, but that was for a grown man. Perhaps it wouldn't do him any harm just to have half a glass, the sleep would do him good, Hester. When he's so restless he tosses and turns and that can't help his back and shoulder.'

In the event, by bedtime Jethro was looking flushed and uncomfortable and put up only a token resistance to the medicine. His three weary nursemaids gathered on the landing outside his room, each with their chamber stick in hand, and exchanged relieved looks at the sound of heavy breathing from within.

'I've doublechecked round all the locks and catches,' Susan said. 'The groom from over the road has been to see to Hector and the lanterns are safely out in the stables.'

'What are you holding?' Hester peered at the object Susan was attempting to conceal in her skirts.

'The kitchen poker. I'd like to see any headless ghoul get the better of that!'

Smiling faintly at the puzzle of where one hit a headless apparition with a poker, Hester took herself off to bed. A thin line of moonlight fell across the floorboards and she went across to look at it out of the window. 'The waxing crescent,' she murmured, looking out at the pure beauty of the sickle of white pinned on the black velvet of the sky. 'What nonsense to attribute evil to that.'

She paused, her hand on the crumbling silk curtain, looking across at the darkened house opposite. Strange that it should be so quiet so early. Perhaps Guy had gone away. That would be a comfort, she told herself stoutly. No one to endanger her reputation in the eyes of local society, no one to lure her into behaving in an immodest and reckless manner, and it would certainly remove the only person who wanted her house. *The only person I* know *who wants it*, she corrected herself.

Not that physical proximity would stop whoever it was; whatever she might suspect Guy of, it was not personally creeping about the Moon House depositing dead roses.

Hester climbed into bed and settled herself to sleep by watching the faint shimmer of twigs from the climbing roses outside her window thrown into silhouette on her bedchamber walls by the cold moonlight.

She woke some hours later feeling uncomfortably thirsty. The baked gammon at supper had been rather salty and she had not thought to bring a glass of water to bed with her. Hester lay half-dozing, hoping she would go back to sleep, but the discomfort persisted and, as the longcase clock in the hall struck two, she gave up and scrambled out of bed and into her dressing gown.

It did not occur to her to trouble lighting her chamber stick; the old house was so familiar now that she could have walked around it with her eyes closed, and, in any case, the moonlight cast the faintest of light through uncurtained windows.

Her bare feet were on the lowest step of the stairs before her sleepy brain roused sufficiently to suggest to her that this was not a sensible thing to be doing. Hester took another, cautious, step down so that she was standing on the cold hall floor and listened intently, thirst forgotten.

Silence. Or at least, as her ears strained, the silence of any house at night. A stair creaked where she had just trodden on it, the longcase clock ticked heavily, outside an owl hooted and the ivy scratched against a window pane. Then the lightest of draughts touched her cheek, and with it came the suggestion of the scent of roses.

Hester smiled, then became still at the realisation that all the windows downstairs should be closed. Where was that stir of air coming from? Even as her mind formed the question and her hand tightened on the newel post, she heard the breathing.

It was right beside her, the faintest whisper on the air, the sound of someone keeping very, very still. Waiting. Watching her from the shadows in the drawing room.

She had already made a mistake in standing still for so long, surely they would suspect she knew they were there? Could she make it to the kitchen before they attacked her? There were knives there, the rolling pin—but not the poker, which Susan had taken to bed with her.

And there was also, she recalled with a sudden flash of relief, her father's sword propped up by the front door. She had put it there that morning to remind herself to drive a nail in to the long wall opposite the clock and hang it up.

To reach it she would have to leave the stairs and cross in front of that half-open door. The breathing was so faint she wondered if she was imagining it, then a board creaked as though someone had shifted their weight. No, that was not imagination.

Fighting the urge to run upstairs screaming her head off, Hester stepped briskly into the hall, half-turned as though to go towards the kitchen then spun round, reaching for the sword. Her hand found the hilt and her fingers closed round it with the ease of long familiarity. How many times had she cleaned it for Papa? She dragged the blade free, letting the scabbard clatter to the marble, and swung round to face the door.

The sword was heavy and she had to use both hands to hold the point up at waist height.

'Come out. I know you are there.' Her voice sounded surprisingly level and determined in her own ears.

The door swung wider, slowly revealing a tall silhouette. Hester raised the sword. 'Out.'

The shadowy man stepped forward, then with a speed that completely wrong-footed her, side-stepped the blade, caught her wrist in one hand and dragged her into the room and against his body.

'Quiet!' he hissed. The voice was instantly recognisable.

'You!' Hester struggled in Guy's grip. 'How *could* you?'

CHAPTER ELEVEN

'You...you *bastard*.' Hester struggled to free herself.

'Language, my dear Miss Lattimer.' Guy was not letting her go and her efforts to free her wrist only succeeded in tightening his grip. 'Please let go of that sword before you run me through or I will have to hurt you.'

'I *mean* to run you through,' she gasped, attempting to kick him, but finding that in bare feet all she was doing was stubbing her toes, despite the fact that he appeared not to be wearing boots. 'I *wanted* to trust you and now I know I was right not to—but how you could—'

He let go of her suddenly, then used both hands to twist the sword in her grip. With a gasp Hester let it go and heard it land with a soft thud on the *chaise* as he tossed it away.

'I'm sorry, but one of us was going to get hurt.' She found herself gathered tightly against Guy's chest. 'Now please, stop struggling and be quiet. Do you want to wake the household?'

'Yes!' She stamped hard on his stockinged foot. 'Brute! You treacherous, lying, deceitful brute. Jethro will be down with a shotgun in a moment—'

'No, he will not. He was snoring his head off when I climbed through his window; in fact, everyone was snoring, except you, and you were making enchanting whiffling noises. Look, if I let you go, will you stop kicking me and come and sit on the *chaise*?'

'No, I will not! Whiffling? I do not *whiffle*.' She broke off and stared up at what she could see of his face in the faint light. 'Why were you climbing through Jethro's window? You couldn't know he had taken a sleeping draught.'

'Parrott and he thought it was best if I came in that way, because of course we wanted Susan to lock and bolt everything downstairs as usual.' He relaxed his hold. 'Be still, just for one moment, and tell me if this looks like the actions of a man who is set on haunting your house with dead roses.' Guy stepped away from her and there was a sudden narrow beam of light that fell on the *chaise*. Blinking, Hester realised he had partly opened the slide on a dark lantern.

On the *chaise* was a pillow. On the floor beside it his discarded boots and a long-barrelled pistol contrasted incongruously with a bottle and a napkin open to reveal what appeared to be a ham sandwich.

The dark lantern clicked shut. 'Now, come and sit down. We do not appear to have woken Susan or Miss Prudhome, but I suggest we keep our voices down. I have no wish to be taken to task by your chaperon for having a tryst with you in your nightgown.'

'It would more likely be Susan brandishing the kitchen poker.' Hester felt confused and relieved in equal parts but she let herself be steered to the *chaise*. Guy put the sword on the floor and sat down beside her. 'I am sorry I kicked you—but what are you doing here?'

'Setting a trap for your night-time visitor, although I imagine if he is within fifty yards of the place he will have fled by now.' She could see no more of him than his outline against the faint light from the window, but the sense of being protected was so strong that it was an effort not to throw her arms around his neck and cling to him. She had been wrong about Guy and suddenly the knowledge that he was innocent was all that mattered.

'And Jethro knows?'

'I was worried about you all, so I sent Parrott over. He was coming anyway to talk to the lad. They spent a cosy afternoon plotting and Jethro promised to leave his window open for me.'

'But how did you get up to it? We have no ladder long enough.' The image of Guy making his way stealthily across the road encumbered by a ladder almost provoked a giggle and she stifled it hastily. Hysteria seemed rather too close for comfort.

'On to the water butt, along the penthouse roof over the scullery, up a somewhat poorly attached rainwater pipe and in through the window.'

'Your clothes must be filthy.'

'My valet sent me out in my second-best housebreaking outfit,' he assured her in a solemn whisper.

This time the giggle did escape. 'Oh, Guy, I am so glad it is not you,' Hester managed to gasp between faint hiccups of mirth.

'Are you? Why?'

'I felt in my heart…I mean, I felt instinctively that you would not do such a thing, but my head told me to be sensible and mistrustful.' At least he could not see her blushing in the darkness—why had she mentioned her heart? 'I felt you were my friend—those few moments when I was convinced I was wrong were horrible.'

'Well, I *am* your friend, although I give you fair warning that I still intend trying to persuade you to sell to me. Why did you cut me dead this morning?'

Hester sniffed. 'I did not want another prosy lecture on what I ought to do.'

'Prosy?' Guy sounded indignant. He reached out in the dim light and tweaked a lock of Hester's straying hair. 'I was merely being careful on your account. As I should be now—go to bed, Hester.'

'Do you think I would get a wink of sleep?' she demanded. 'I am staying here.' To emphasise the point she curled up against the pillow at the head of the *chaise* and tucked her feet under her. Nothing was going to dislodge her now. Reverting to his previous remark, she added, 'And I did not cut you, I waved my whip.'

'Ah, yes, to make sure I noticed that you were with my rival for your affections.'

Hester gave an inelegant snort. 'What nonsense! Sir Lewis was merely escorting me to visit with his sister, and in any case, surely I am allowed more than one friend?'

'He is very good looking—or so the other ladies seem to think,' Guy remarked pensively.

'He is indeed. *Very* good looking,' Hester teased, determined not to pander to Guy's vanity by pointing out that he, too, was an attractive man. 'It is odd,' she added, suddenly serious, 'but whenever I see him I am reminded of someone, but I cannot think who.'

'Are you? Now that is interesting. I wonder if anyone else has noticed the likeness?'

'To whom? Guy, you are being deliberately provoking and mysterious. I must tell you that now I have another prospective purchaser for the Moon House I can safely cut your acquaintance unless you stop teasing.' It was so unreal in the moonlight and shadows that it felt safe to talk this nonsense, scandalously alone with a man.

'Who has offered to buy it?' He was all at once serious.

'Why, Sir Lewis. Miss Nugent was telling me the most ridiculous stories from some old family collection of legends and he said that, if I was suffering from haunting at the Moon House, he would feel honour bound to buy it back.'

* * *

That made sense. Guy stared into the darkness that was the hall. Miss Nugent does her best to scare Hester with ghost stories and her brother makes an offer for the house. But why would the father sell the house and the children want it back—especially if they were the ones behind the hauntings? What could they possibly want so badly? It was obvious that Hester knew nothing of their motives. He knew things about their connection with the house that she had no idea of, and he was not about to enlighten her.

It was disturbing, yet curiously restful, to be sitting in the darkness next to Hester. She was curled up like a cat against the head of the *chaise*, so close he could feel the warmth of her. He moved his hand and it brushed her bare foot.

'Your feet are freezing; here, put my coat over them.' He reached behind the seat and found his coat by touch, tucking it around her legs and over her feet.

'Thank you. I should have thought to put on my slippers, but I was so sleepy and thirsty that I didn't think of it.' She was smiling, he could hear it in her voice, despite the fact they were whispering. Now, if there was ever a moment, was the time to intensify his flirtation with her. Moonlight, intimacy—if he could not win her over to doing what he wanted by the end of the night, then he was losing his touch with women.

As he thought it Guy felt a stab of distaste. He did not want to flirt, or to persuade Hester into anything she did not want to do. He wanted…what? She wanted to be friends, she already considered him one, hence her furious sense of betrayal when she found him here. Was friendship enough?

Hester shifted slightly, but was quiet. She had a quality of repose which was attractive. It seemed she felt no need to chatter or to display her fears in order to attract attention. Guy smiled, recalling Hester's courage and quick wits as she drew the sword on him. No, he wanted more than friendship—it seemed he wanted to court her.

Taken by surprise at his own thoughts, Guy shifted away to the other end of the *chaise*. Hester murmured, 'Thank you,' obviously thinking he had moved to give her more room.

Am I in love with her? He took a startled look at the question and made himself consider it, never having suspected himself of such an emotion before. *She is delightful to look at*, but then so were all the high-fliers and bits of muslin he had enjoyed an association with from time to time. *She is quick-witted, unusual, direct*, never qualities he had looked for in a woman before. *And she is brave, to say nothing of stubborn, proud and secretive.* How did that add up to love? If love *was* this feeling that was a mixture of desire, tenderness, protectiveness and sheer terror and he wasn't simply suffering from brain fever.

After all, Guy reasoned with himself, *you came here on an errand that could only be described as quixotic and romantic, perhaps you are just in the mood to fancy yourself in love*.

'Can you smell roses?' he whispered. 'I've only just noticed it—but surely there cannot be any in bloom now, or smelling at this time of night, come to that.'

'You can smell them too?' she asked eagerly. 'I thought it was only me. I smell them when I am happy, or when I am thinking about the house. I sometimes think that scent is the only ghost the Moon House holds. There are a few sodden blooms in the garden, but of course—'

'Quiet,' he murmured, putting his fingers over her mouth. Was he imagining it? No, there was the sound of movement from the hall, the merest brush of unshod feet on the marble, the almost imperceptible stirring of the air. 'Stay here.' He used one hand to press her down on to the *chaise*, with the other he reached for the sword. The thought of bullets flying in the darkness with Hester there chilled him.

Almost holding his breath, he drifted towards the door. The intruder was closer now, at the foot of the stairs. Guy lunged out of the door and a figure whirled around, cloak swirling as it did so. Guy took in only that it was fast, clad all in black and that it had no face, then his mind caught up with his imagination and he realised it was masked.

'Stand! I am armed.'

The figure seemed to waver in the faint light, then something swept towards his face. Instinctively Guy threw up his left arm to protect his eyes and stabbed forward with the sword as pain lanced through his face. For a moment he thought the intruder had thrown a cat and it was clawing at him, then his hand closed around hard, thorny stems and crisp, dead leaves and he realised it was roses.

He swept them aside and drove towards his attacker again, lunging forward in a fencer's attack. His foot came down, not on flat marble but something hard and rounded, slipped as the scabbard moved on the polished stone, and, completely off-balance, he began to fall. As he went down he dropped the sword and hit out with his right fist, to feel it connect with a satisfying thud on the masked face.

Then he was on the floor, scrambling to regain balance to spring to his feet as someone tripped over him with a cry of dismay. His reaching hands found themselves full of fine cotton and the warm female form beneath. 'Hester!' Unceremoniously he rolled her off on to the floor behind him and got to his feet. The hall was empty, the house silent. Where the hell had it gone?

The stillness lasted only seconds, then there was an outburst of cries and opening doors from upstairs and light from two candles illuminated the staircase.

'Hester! What's happening? Oh, you brute!' Miss Prudhome, uncaring of curl papers, flannel nightgown and bare feet, flew down the stairs to Hester's side where she rounded on Guy, one trembling hand holding a chamber stick, the other clenched to wave under his nose. 'Hurry, Susan, bring the poker—the beast has tried to ravish her—see how she has scratched him!'

The maid was hard on her heels, poker in raised hand, her candle waving wildly.

'Quiet!' It was Hester, managing a voice of absolute authority despite being in the middle of scrambling to her feet with her hair in a tangle, her feet bare and her nightgown hitched up to her knees. A wave of pride in her washed over him, warring with a stab of lust. 'Be quiet, everyone—we found the ghost and now it's gone and we have to search.'

Guy took the opportunity to remove the poker from Susan's grip and scoop up the scabbard from the floor before it tripped anyone else up. 'Stay behind me, please—and, as Miss Lattimer says—be quiet!' He took Miss Prudhome's candle and glanced into the dining room. Empty. That left the kitchen, although by now a troop of cavalry could have unbolted the door and made their escape.

But not only was the kitchen empty, but the bolts were shut, the door still firmly locked, the windows closed and latched. The only sign of the intruder was the trail down the hall of dead roses and the drops of Guy's blood that marked the way it had fled towards the kitchen.

Guy, with Susan dogged at his heels, searched the dining room again, looked in every nook and cranny of the kitchen and scullery, even opened the door of the longcase clock and peered inside, but he found nothing. But then he had not expected to—whoever was getting into the Moon House, they were not coming in through the door.

* * *

Hester left them to search, instead filling a kettle from the scullery pump and banging it down on the range. 'Fetch the poker from his lordship, would you, please, Maria? I don't know about you, but I need a cup of tea.'

By the time the searchers returned, predictably empty handed, the tea was brewing and Maria was buttering bread. 'Bread and butter is very soothing in a crisis, I always find.'

Guy made a noise that sounded suspiciously like a snort of amusement, but Hester was too concerned with the state of him to join in the joke. Now they had lit all the kitchen candles his face, covered in scratches and streaked with blood, looked horrifying.

'Guy, your face! Come and sit down and let me sponge it.' Hester tipped hot water from the kettle into a bowl, seized a petticoat that had been drying by the fire, ripped a handful of cloth from it and advanced on him. 'Now, sit down here and let me see. Did anything go in your eyes?' She bent over him, tipping his chin up in one determined hand in much the same way as she would have with Jethro.

'No, ma'am,' he said with unaccustomed meekness.

'Are you sure? Are you hurt anywhere else? Your breathing sounds very heavy.' She tipped his face up some more, and carefully inspected the scratches, their noses almost touching. Now there was no mistaking the wicked twinkle in his eyes.

'I am labouring under a great deal of stress, Miss Lattimer.'

Hester dropped the cloth back in the bowl and handed him a dry piece with a reproving look. Her own heart rate had accelerated to an uncomfortable degree.

'Have a cup of tea, my lord,' Maria urged, mercifully missing the by-play. 'I am sure that will make you feel better. Then I will fetch the basilicum powder.'

'Thank you, Miss Prudhome.' He gave the chaperon a look of such docility that Hester could have boxed his ears.

'There are only ten tonight,' Susan said, dumping an armful of roses on the kitchen table. 'Fourteen the first night, twelve the next…'

'It started with the new moon.' Hester made her voice steady with a struggle. 'It happens every second night, and each time there are two fewer. By the time of the full moon there will be none. And at the full moon—' She broke off, unable to repeat the nonsense Miss Nugent had spouted.

'At the full moon, what?' Susan was wide eyed.

'Nothing, just some nonsense Miss Nugent says she found in an old manuscript.'

'Tell us,' Guy commanded. He glanced round at the other women. 'I suspect that Sir Lewis and Miss Nugent may be hoping to alarm Miss Lattimer into reselling the house to them. I would like to hear what taradiddles they have concocted.'

'You think they are breaking into the house?' Hester found it incredible as soon as she said it. 'Respectable members of local society?'

'I am respectable, and you had no trouble believing me the culprit,' Guy pointed out with a grin. 'Now, what is supposed to happen at the full moon?'

'The evil in the house will wax with the moon, and then when it is full… Oh, this is such fustian, it isn't worth repeating!'

'Go on, Miss Hester,' Susan urged. 'You can't not tell us now, imagining is much worse.'

'Very well, if you must have it. When the moon is full, Death walks.'

There was silence as the four of them absorbed this. Then into the stillness they heard the dragging footsteps coming down the hall. Four pairs of eyes turned to the door, which slowly began to creak open.

Guy got to his feet, gesturing with his hand for silence.

With a muffled squeak Miss Prudhome clutched Susan and Hester found herself standing, her hand on Guy's arm.

The door opened to reveal a white-clad figure and, with a sigh, Miss Prudhome slid to the floor in a dead faint.

CHAPTER TWELVE

'Jethro!' Hester released her hold on Guy's arm and went to take the unsteady figure by the elbow. 'What on earth are you doing down here at this hour in the morning? You scared us all to death! Oh dear, Susan, is Miss Prudhome all right?'

'She will be if I can just find some feathers to burn under her nose.' Susan struggled to get the wilting companion into a sitting position, only to find his lordship bending at her side.

'Here, let me, I think she is coming round.' He scooped up Miss Prudhome, almost dropping her again at the screech of alarm she let out when she realised she was in the arms of a man. He hastily seated her in a Windsor chair by the range and retreated to assist Hester, who was urging Jethro to take the seat opposite.

'I heard the to-do, Miss Hester,' Jethro explained, wincing as the hard chair back met his shoulder. 'But I didn't reckon on being so shaky on my feet. It took me near ten minutes to get out of bed. I'm sorry, my lord.' He turned his pale face towards Guy, 'I should have been more alert-like, ready to help.'

'It's a very good thing you did not, Jethro, there were enough of us falling all over the place—I am afraid I let your ghost go.'

'I think we need a council of war,' Hester announced,

marching back into the room with the brandy decanter in her hand. 'Susan, brew some coffee, please. Tea is simply not stimulating enough.' She placed the decanter on the table. 'Now, who would like brandy in their coffee and who would like it in a glass?'

'Oh, if anyone should see us,' Miss Prudhome lamented. 'Drinking brandy at three in the morning with a *man* in the house.'

Guy unstoppered the decanter, sniffed, then reached for one of the glasses Hester put on the table. 'It would be a crime to mix this with coffee.' He poured five glasses and pushed them around the table. 'Is the rest of your wine cellar up to this standard, Miss Lattimer?'

Off guard she replied, 'Oh, yes, all of it is very good, although I have not dared look at the clarets yet after their jolting on the carrier's cart.'

'You must introduce me to your wine merchant.' Guy took an appreciative sip. 'I imagine we are too far from the sea here for it to be run brandy.'

'I inherited it,' Hester admitted. 'Unusual, I know…'

'Your father had excellent taste.' Of course, that was the obvious conclusion, there was no need to fear he would guess the truth.

Hester smiled brightly. 'Thank you. Maria, are you feeling a little recovered?'

'Yes, indeed.' In fact, Miss Prudhome was faintly flushed, and Hester noticed that she was taking rather more sips from the glass than from her cup. 'This is very reviving, although naturally I do not approve of spirits except in a medicinal capacity.'

'Good. Now, what are we going to do?' Hester looked round the kitchen table at her supporters. One nervous lady's companion, one feisty maidservant, a boy with a damaged shoulder and a nobleman who most certainly shouldn't be there. 'We know whoever is doing this is flesh and blood; Lord Buckland hit him.'

'Hard enough to bruise.' Guy rubbed his knuckles.

'So we must watch out for men with a bruised cheek or a black eye. We know they can get in and out of here without using the doors and windows.'

'Which is strange, in a house of this age,' Maria remarked. She was sitting up, looking much recovered, a faint flush on her cheeks. 'I mean, it is not as though it is some ancient mansion where you might expect priest holes and secret passages, is it?'

'The ghost has therefore taken time to prepare something before your arrival,' Guy mused. 'Or the secret entrance was built at the same time as the house. The latter, I imagine.'

Hester shot him a suspicious glance. There was something about the tone of his voice that made her suspect he was putting two and two together—and that the clues he was adding up were unknown to her.

'And that entrance is in this kitchen, or the scullery,' Susan added. 'That would make sense—this is the back of the house and shielded from passers-by.'

'And the only person, other than his lordship, who has expressed a desire to buy the house is Sir Lewis.' Hester shook her head in disbelief. 'He has not pressed me about it, only said that if I was alarmed he felt it was his duty to buy it back. I cannot imagine that would be easy for him, his own home is in poor repair.'

'You think him short of funds?' Guy twirled the stem of his glass between his fingers. 'If he does indeed want this house, then it must represent an investment of some kind to him, but what I cannot imagine.'

'Someone was here at night, several times just before I arrived.' Hester recounted the village gossip. 'Lights were seen.

But if they were searching, there was no trace of it. The Nugents could well have retained keys, of course—the back door was not bolted when we arrived. But why should they? It is only a short while since their father sold it to me; if there were some secret, something of value, surely both father and son would know about it, and it would have been removed before the house was sold.'

'If Lewis *did* know. I wonder just how sudden his father's death was.'

'He was unwell—Miss Nugent would have it that he became so when he signed the bill of sale—but the end was sudden, following a fall, and, according to her, the moon was full and a dead rose was found.'

'A nice piece of embroidery,' Guy observed cynically. 'Perhaps I am misjudging them and Sir Lewis is straightforward and Miss Nugent has a taste for melodrama, but I will call on them the day after tomorrow and see if Sir Lewis's handsome features have become marred in any way. It will be as well to allow the bruise time to develop.'

'Of course! That will settle it.' Hester felt a flood of relief at the thought of such tangible proof. 'It has just occurred to me,' she added slowly. 'Sir Lewis gave me the sleeping draught for Jethro. What better way of making sure that no one was sitting up with him.'

'Hmm, you could well be right. I will send a footman over every night to sleep here in the kitchen, with a lantern lit. That should stop any attempt to enter.' Guy raised an eyebrow at Hester, daring her to refuse his help again.

'Thank you, Lord Buckland,' she responded meekly. It seemed the most prudent thing, and the man would be in no danger if the ghost saw that the room was occupied.

'Then I suggest you all make your way back to bed. The clock has just struck four; I will stay here another hour, which is probably as long as I can risk it without being seen leaving by some passing yokel on his way to the milking. Ackland, do you need helping to your room?'

Jethro got to his feet with a wince, but shook his head. 'No, my lord, I'll do if I go slowly.'

Hester watched as Susan and Maria left, fussing after the boy, then turned to Guy with a rueful smile. 'Thank you. I am sorry I suspected you, and I am sorry I was so cavalier with your offers of help.'

He smiled. 'So long as you trust me now. But you will be careful, Hester—promise me? That character was at the foot of the stairs, I am sure on his way up. I suspect you would have woken to find those roses on the threshold of your bedchamber.'

'Yes, I promise.' She got to her feet, bone weary now the excitement was all over. 'May I come with you to Winterbourne Hall? Two of us may observe more than one, and I have the excuse of enquiring after Miss Nugent's health.'

'A good idea. I will collect you—I said the day after to-morrow, but it is already almost morning, so it will be tomorrow—about two, if that is convenient.'

Hester nodded her agreement, smothering a cracking yawn behind both hands. 'Oh, I beg your pardon! I am so tired.'

'Goodnight, Hester.' Guy gathered her into his arms and bent his head to kiss her brow, smoothing back the tumbled hair with a gentle hand. She let herself rest against him within the circle of his arm, safe and warm. Her body, unfettered by stays or petticoats, fitted against his hard, lean frame as if it had been made to measure for his embrace. This was so right. Against her closed lids the darkness was velvety black and she was sinking.

'Up you come, sweetheart.' Hester was sleepily aware of being lifted and snuggled against Guy's chest. She uttered a muffled mutter of protest. He should put her down, of course, this was outrageous, surely she was too heavy to be carried upstairs like this.

'*My lord!*' That was Maria, she thought dreamily with a smile, turning her face into the soft linen of his shirt. 'You cannot go in there!' It seemed Guy was taking no notice, for she was deposited on to her own bed and the covers pulled up snugly around her shoulders. 'Out this minute!' A hand brushed her hair with a light caress.

'Go'night,' she murmured, but the door closed with a click and sleep claimed her.

It was late when she woke that morning; the sun was streaming through the unshuttered window and the house was silent. In the road outside she heard the passing of a herd of cattle, their complaining lowing punctuated by the sharp barking of the dogs.

Hester pushed her hair out of her eyes, and sat up against the pillows. Distantly she heard the church clock strike nine.

Why did she feel so very happy? She let her mind wander over the events of the previous night. It should have been terrifying, but as she recalled it she was aware that her mouth was curved in a smile and her heart was warm with contentment.

Guy was innocent of the ingenious persecution that had so puzzled and frightened her. She had an ally, a friend. The smile deepened as she recalled those last, sleepy moments as he carried her up to bed so tenderly; the trust she had felt, curled up on the *chaise* in the dark room, talking with him in whispers.

But it was more than tenderness that Guy Westrope was capable of. Hester's own hands fisted on the edge of the sheet as she remembered the strength with which he had disarmed her, the explosion of controlled force as he attacked the intruder.

Hester shivered, closed her eyes. If they had been alone in

the house last night, alone as he had carried her up to her bed—would she have felt so very sleepy then? Or would she have pulled him down beside her? The bed seemed to dip, her hands unclenched and reached out. 'Guy.'

'Hester dear.' The tapping at her door jerked her rudely out of the dream.

'What? I mean, come in, Maria.' Her companion peeped round the door and Hester, rubbing the sleep, and the disturbing dream, out of her eyes, reflected that she looked exactly like a nervous hen peering out of the coop to make sure the fox had gone. She came right into the room and Hester saw she was fully dressed, although she still wore her nightcap with curl papers protruding at the front.

'Are you awake, dear?'

'Yes, just. We have been lie-abeds, Maria, but I think we may be excused after last night's excitement. Is Susan up yet?'

'She has just gone down to make up the range and to see the drawing room is as it should be in case we get any morning callers. Jethro is still asleep, I am glad to say.' She went to look out of the window at the ugly red bulk of the Old Manor opposite. 'His lordship is a most determined gentleman, is he not? I do not feel I was firm enough with him last night, but what can one do?'

'And he is so very large, is he not?' Hester added mischievously, recalling Miss Prudhome's diminutive frame against Guy's height.

'Exactly! When he was carrying you upstairs last night— so very shocking, but he took not the slightest notice of me— I felt a positive thrill of awe at his strength. It was just like a medieval romance, or one of Sir Walter Scott's stirring poems.'

'Why, Maria, I do declare you are half in love with our noble neighbour,' Hester teased, laughing at her companion's look of outrage. 'Oh, I am sorry, that was a most improper observation.'

Miss Prudhome's expression softened. 'It would be an unfeeling woman indeed who did not admire such a man at the height of his powers, providing he is a Christian, gallant gentleman. And it is so very comforting to have such a capable champion to hand, given our troubles.' She put her hand on the door knob. 'Shall I ask Susan to bring up hot water now?'

'Yes, please.' Alone again, Hester sat up and curled her arms around her knees. She had been jesting with Maria, but she had an uncomfortable suspicion that someone in the house was in danger of falling in love with the Earl of Buckland and that person was staring back at her from the reflection in the cheval glass in the corner of the bedchamber.

Susan bustled in with the ewer. 'Good morning, Miss Hester. Which gown would you like this morning?'

'Oh, just the dimity for now. I think I might drive into Tring this afternoon—I never did buy Maria's wool and I expect there are a number of other things we need.' Hester hopped out of bed, feeling invigorated by the thought of some shopping, even though she suspected the small town would have few really tempting shops.

As she stepped out on to the landing she could hear a vigorous altercation coming from the spare room. She pushed the door open to find Miss Prudhome, one finger raised to wag under Jethro's nose and the lad himself, somewhat white but determined, with one leg in his breeches and one out. His large shirt covered him with perfect decency, but he still blushed scarlet at the sight of Hester.

'Jethro, what are you doing out of bed? Get back this instant.'

'That is exactly what I have been telling him, Hester.' Maria sounded thoroughly flustered. 'But he insists.'

'Do you want us to *put* you back to bed?' Hester threatened, advancing on the lad who managed to negotiate the other leg of his breeches and backed away from her.

'Miss Hester, my shoulder feels better if I'm not lying down, honest it does,' he protested.

'The doctor said you were to rest for a week.'

'I can do that downstairs. Please, Miss Hester, I'm going out of my mind, stuck up here. I can sit in the kitchen, quiet-like, and read my book.'

'Very well, but only if you promise that if Miss Prudhome thinks you look tired or unwell and orders you back to bed, you go with no argument. Now, is that a promise?'

'Yes, Miss Hester.'

'Then finish getting dressed.'

'Only if you ladies go out. I'm not seven, Miss Hester!'

'Er, no. Of course not. Come along, Maria, and leave Jethro to finish dressing.' Hester managed to keep a straight face until they were out of the door. 'Poor Jethro, I do feel he has a hard life sometimes in a household of women. Perhaps Parrott will not mind if he walks over to the Old Manor one day soon for another talk.'

They reached the kitchen to find Ben Aston the handyman propping up the door into the yard and chatting to Susan. He straightened up as Hester entered and knuckled his forehead. 'I came round in case there was anything you needed doing, Miss Lattimer, what with last night an' all.'

'What about last night?' Hester kept her voice calm with an effort.

'All the lights on back here, thought perhaps you'd had the burglars or som'at.'

'Burglars? Goodness, no. Young Ackland was very unwell in the night and we were up for most of it brewing hot possets and warming bricks and I don't know what else. But it is good of you to be concerned, Aston. How come you were around at such an hour?'

'Up early to a sick cow, Miss Lattimer,' he answered glibly.

Poaching, Hester translated to herself. It just went to show how difficult it was to keep anything secret in a village.

'Now you are here, you can finish turning out the sheds in the yard. Let me have a look at everything you find, but I expect most of it will have to be burned. Then sweep them out and check the roofs for leaks, if you will please.'

They were finishing their belated breakfast to the sound of thumps as Aston tossed a seemingly endless mountain of junk out into the yard when Mrs Dalling arrived for her day's work at the Moon House. Hester had come to an arrangement with the two village women recommended by Mrs Bunting that they would take it in turns to come in daily on five days of the week for the rough cleaning, the washing, to prepare vegetables for meals and to make bread. In this way, most of the heavy work was taken care of and the household had their privacy by the evening.

Hester and Maria took themselves off to the drawing room, leaving Susan organising Mrs Dalling and Jethro seated in the big Windsor chair by the range with a cushion behind his back and Mr Parrott's book on his knee.

Hester picked up a pile of bills and her accounts book and Maria started to rearrange a winter bouquet of evergreens on the mantel. But she seemed disinclined to concentrate on the task.

'What do you think Lord Buckland will do if he finds Sir Lewis with a black eye?'

Hester frowned at the butcher's account. 'Is it possible we consume so much stewing steak? Sir Lewis? I have no idea; presumably his lordship has arrived at some plan.'

'Will he call him out, do you think?' Miss Prudhome stood, one limp ivy frond in her hand, an excited glint in her eye.

'I have no idea, Maria. Probably he will do nothing to disclose our suspicions. Now, please, do let me concentrate on these accounts.'

'Perhaps he will hit him again.' This seemed to gratify the genteel companion to a surprising degree. 'He most certainly deserves it.'

'Yes.' Hester nibbled the end of her quill abstractedly. The image of Guy, standing over a cowed and beaten foe who had been felled to the ground after a spirited flurry of blows, was a stimulating one. The fantasy developed rapidly to the point where the earl strode over and took Miss Lattimer in his arms, passionately embracing her and raining kisses upon her up-turned face.

Hester pulled herself together to find a large blot on her account book. This must stop. It was dangerous folly she was deluding herself with—the one thing that was certain in the life of Miss Hester Lattimer was that no respectable alliance with any gentleman was possible. To fall in love with an earl could have only two endings: heartbreak or the acceptance of a *carte blanche*.

CHAPTER THIRTEEN

Hester was still feeling somewhat subdued when luncheon was finished. Although she would have been quite happy to take bread, cheese and ale at the kitchen table, Susan and Maria were both shocked at the thought.

'Not with *outside* staff present,' Miss Prudhome pronounced and Susan sniffed and nodded her agreement.

Hester supposed they were right; it was all part of appearing to be the upright, conventional spinster that she must now portray herself as being. Doubtless news of any unconventional behaviour would be all around the village in no time and would soon reach the ears of Mrs Redland and Mrs Bunting.

So she and Maria sat down in the dining room and partook of exactly the same meal, only off china and glass instead of earthenware and pewter, served by Susan wearing a crisp white apron.

'That Ben Aston's fishing to know if anything odd's been happening,' she reported as she cleared the plates and brought in a bowl of fruit. 'I told him that Jethro near breaking his neck was more than enough oddity for us and none of us held with nonsense about ghosts and he didn't ask any more.' She glanced towards the door. 'I reckon the whole village is waiting to find out if the stories about the strange goings-on are true.'

This aspect of village curiosity had not occurred to Hester and she tapped her fruit knife thoughtfully against her plate as she considered it. 'I don't think having Aston and the women here will do any harm, providing we are all discreet. Everyone will soon get bored if they don't hear of any strange happenings, and beside anything else, they will be able to observe that there is no truth in all that nonsense you heard at the Bird in Hand about his lordship.'

'Not if they know he was here at three in the morning,' Susan observed pertly, whisking out of the door before Hester could retort.

She finished her apple and got to her feet. 'Would you care to come into Tring with me, Maria?'

'Thank you, but I promised Mrs Bunting I would help her with the church flowers this afternoon.' She broke off with one of her anxious twittering noises. 'Oh, but Jethro cannot accompany you—should I send to let Mrs Bunting know I cannot join her after all?'

'No, there is no need for that, I am sure; this is hardly London, Maria. I am sure a lady can shop in a small market town without any fear of causing comment.' And it would be pleasant to be alone for a few hours, she mused as she collected the list of things Susan had thought of that could not be purchased at the village shop.

Ben Aston harnessed Hector and she set off in the gig, feeling quite adventurous. She had often driven alone when in Portugal, but never in England, and, although the roads were far superior, the traffic was heavier. For the first time she could not rely on having Jethro to jump down and take Hector's head, or check for her that she was not too close to the kerb on narrow streets.

Halfway down the length of the Green she came upon Annabelle Redland, strolling along, her bonnet dangling by its strings from one negligent hand, an expression of dissatisfaction on her face.

'Good afternoon.' Hester reined in. 'A pleasant day for a walk, is it not?'

'I suppose so,' Annabelle agreed, 'providing that is what one *wishes* to do.'

'And you do not?'

'No. Mama said we could go for a drive, but now there is the most dreadful row over the downstairs maid who is…' she lowered her voice, although there was not another person within fifty yards '…in an unfortunate condition.'

'Oh dear,' Hester said sympathetically. 'Is the father willing to marry her?'

'She will not say who it is, that is why there is such a dreadful row,' confided Miss Redland. 'Mama is threatening to call in the vicar and I am not supposed to know anything about it so I have to go out for a walk.'

'Would you care to come into Tring with me?' Hester offered. 'I only have a rather tiresome shopping list, but it would be a change of scene.'

'Yes, please.' Miss Redland was up on the seat beside Hester without a second's thought.

'I will just turn back and ask Ben Aston to take a message to your mother to let her know where you are.' Hester executed a turn she felt quietly pleased with and urged Hector to trot back.

'There is a very good drapers in Tring,' Annabelle confided. 'And a confectioners where one can get hot chocolate and ices.'

Ben Aston listened to the message and agreed to call at the Redlands' house on his way back home. 'I was just finishing up, Miss Lattimer. I've put all the bits and bobs young Ackland thought you'd want to look at back in the first shed, and I'll have a bonfire of the rest just as soon as the wind's turned a bit westerly, otherwise all the washing'll get smudgy.' He crammed his hat back on his head and strode off.

'They say he's a terrible poacher,' Annabelle confided as they set off down the Green again. 'But he's a hard worker, everyone agrees. And very reliable.' After this observation she fell silent, then enquired artlessly, 'Have you seen much of Lord Buckland?'

Hester turned on to the turnpike road. 'One cannot help it as he lives opposite, but socially, no, not since Mrs Bunting's At Home. He has been very kind in lending us staff since Jethro fell down the stairs.'

'Oh.' Annabelle sounded disappointed. 'I thought perhaps you might be having a dinner party or something soon.'

'I can hardly do such a thing as a single lady,' Hester pointed out. 'Perhaps your mother is planning some entertainment and you will meet him again then.' Rather mischievously she added, 'I expect, like all of us, you are interested by the mystery his presence here poses.'

'I do not care in the slightest why he is here, only that he stays,' Miss Redland declared frankly. 'He is so glamorous, do you not think, Miss Lattimer?'

'Glamorous?' Hester considered the question, a not unpleasant excuse to think about Guy Westrope. 'I suppose he is very sophisticated for village society.'

'And so good looking, and rich and *unmarried*,' Annabelle uttered reverently.

'He may well have an attachment we know nothing of,' Hester said firmly, as much to herself as to her companion.

'Oh.' Annabelle subsided, momentarily deflated, then rallied. 'Well, if he has not, do not forget that you and I are the only eligible young ladies in the village.'

'I am certainly not looking for a husband,' Hester stated

flatly. 'And perhaps your mama would wish you to have done your London Season before you do so.'

'I am sure I would meet no one so handsome or eligible.'

Hester was inclined to agree, but felt it more than time to change the topic of conversation to something less painful. 'I understand that Miss Nugent is betrothed. What a pity that her fiancé should be out of the country and not here to support her after the death of her father.'

'Hmm,' Miss Redland observed cryptically, then, the urge to gossip overcoming her discretion, added, 'If he still is her fiancé, of course.'

'Really?' If it had been anyone else but Sarah Nugent, Hester would have turned the conversation, but anything about the family was of interest now. 'I was given to understand by Sir Lewis only recently that she was betrothed.'

'Well, where is he, then?' Annabelle demanded rhetorically. 'In the West Indies on his big plantation, that's where—and showing no sign of coming back to England to marry her. I heard that she put herself into a position where he compromised her and *had* to offer for her. But now he's all that way away, why should he bother?'

Why indeed? Hester knew perfectly well that she should not be having this conversation with another unmarried girl, but the gossip was too intriguing to ignore. 'Whatever did she do to compromise herself?' she asked.

'I overheard Mrs Piper telling Mama. She heard it from her second cousin who was at this ball in London and *she* said that Sarah was found in the conservatory with this Mr Bedford, in his arms, with her bodice all disarrayed and her hair half down. Mama was very much shocked, but as he promptly proposed, and local society is so restricted, she thought that everyone should just pretend they hadn't heard the story.'

'Perhaps it *is* just a story.' Hester guided the cob into the crowded High Street. 'Do you know which is the best inn to leave the gig?'

'The Rose and Crown is where Mama always stops.' Annabelle pointed down the road. 'See, on the left. I don't believe it is a story, you know, it is just the sort of thing Sarah would do, she was always scheming and plotting to get her own way, even when we were little. I used to try not to have to play with her: she always wanted to win.'

That was an interesting glimpse of Sarah Nugent's character. Hester stowed it away to tell Guy and concentrated on turning into the inn yard without mishap.

The ladies spent a pleasant afternoon, even though most of Hester's shopping consisted of such dull items as darning wool, grate cleaner, two mousetraps and a length of white cotton to replace the petticoat she had sacrificed to swab Guy's scratched face.

Annabelle pressed her nose to the window of the milliner's in the High Street and was only persuaded away by Hester denying all intention of going in to try on a hat and her own lack of funds. They did, however, both succumb to the lure of a new consignment of lace trimmings in the draper's while Hester was buying her length of cotton.

'I will pay you back tomorrow,' Miss Redland promised as they loaded their parcels into the gig and went off in search of the confectioner's shop and ices. 'I did not think when I went out for my walk that I would need any money.'

They had the refreshment area of the emporium almost to themselves; once their chocolate and vanilla ices were served, Hester observed, 'You know the Nugents very well, then?'

'Oh, yes, we all grew up together.'

'And what is Sir Lewis like?'

Annabelle wrinkled her nose. 'Very good looking, of course, but I do not know...if I am to be sensible he has not the character I would look for in a husband. He was always too much influenced by Sarah, in my opinion, which is odd, because she is younger than he is. Mind you, their father was a horrid old man.' She broke off, seeing Hester's raised eyebrows. 'I am sorry, Miss Lattimer, but he *was*. Always cross and all starched up. Poor Lewis never could do anything right, and I overheard Mama saying that he is not making much of a fist of it now.'

It occurred to Hester that Miss Redland had rather sharp ears altogether and that she should not encourage her predilection for gossip. 'I thought the Hall looked somewhat shabby when I called the other day,' she remarked, ignoring her conscience.

'Exactly, although that is not Lewis's fault. Mama says that his paternal grandfather was a wealthy man, but all the money just seemed to vanish and Lewis's father never recovered either it or his spirits.'

Altogether a full basket of interesting facts to recount to Guy, Hester decided as they drove home. She just hoped he would make more sense of them than she could.

She refused Annabelle's pressing invitation to come in to take tea, reflecting that Mrs Redland would prefer not to have guests if the drama of the unfortunate maid had not resolved itself, and was just in time to wave to Mrs Dalling as she took herself off, apron bundled into her basket, coal-scuttle bonnet tied firmly on her head.

Her household had little to report. Jethro had sensibly retired to bed for a nap after luncheon; Susan was pleased with Mrs Dalling's work; Sir Lewis's estate manager had been down and looked at the damp cupboard, promising to return with a plumber to divert the leaky guttering, which he considered the source of the problem, and Maria had spent a profitable afternoon, helping fill the church vases with evergreens from the garden and listening to parish news.

Hester unloaded her purchases on to the kitchen table, scrubbed white at last as a result of Mrs Dalling's efforts, and observed, 'Do you think it is right of us to accept the help of Sir Lewis with our damp problem as we suspect him of being our intruder?'

'If he is, then he owes you at least that, and if we are wrong, then he will never know we suspected him,' Susan said comfortably. 'I like this lace, and the cotton is good quality. That's a relief, I thought we were going to have to go into Aylesbury for all our shopping.'

Hester decided she was refining too much upon the possibility of misjudging Sir Lewis, firmly told herself that there was no excuse to write Guy a note and ask him to come over and hear what Annabelle Redland had told her and settled instead to cutting out her new petticoat and whipping the seams. It was an occupation that kept her hands busy and allowed her all too much time to think.

It was chastening to realise that being firm with oneself, facing the facts squarely and not deluding oneself had no effect at all upon an unruly imagination. Hester's hands stilled on the seam and the fabric, which she had tucked under her arm to maintain the tension, sagged unregarded. It was as though she was incapable of thinking about anything but Guy Westrope. She recalled the feel of his body against hers, the pressure of his lips on her mouth, the wicked twinkle in his eyes when they shared a joke. How much longer was he going to stay in Winterbourne and torment her? And would the torment be any less if he were not here?

The notion of life without Guy was not one she had considered before and it was unexpectedly distressing. 'I *am* in love with him,' she murmured to herself. And all that this admission brought her was the same painful choice once more: to try and forget him once he left or, if it was offered, to surrender all her principles and yield to an immoral liaison. Hester was shaken to realise that she could even consider such a choice; it seemed she was less resolute than she had believed.

The next day found her no calmer and eager to bury her disconcerting thoughts in a discussion of clothes with Susan.

'This walking dress?' The maid pulled out a rather practical garment and shook the skirts free of wrinkles. 'It should be fine for climbing up and down from that high-perch seat if his lordship's using the curricle.'

'No, not that one. I want to look particularly well dressed this afternoon. I do not want to give the slightest impression that I have been worrying about a mystery or dealing with alarums and excursions.'

'But his lordship knows you have.' Susan put back the rejected gown and began to rummage.

'Not for his lordship, for the Nugents. If they are behind this I do not want to give them the satisfaction of appearing in any way anxious or distracted.' She began to lift out folded garments. 'What do you think to the amber walking dress with the frogging? And the kid half-boots and the deeper brown bonnet with the grosgrain ribbons?'

'Very smart,' Susan approved. 'And his lordship will like it,' she added as Hester poured hot water into the washbasin.

Hester told herself that she would not dignify this observation by a reply, then, as she was washing her face, admitted to herself that she probably could not muster a convincing one in any case. Susan appeared to be reading her state of mind very clearly which was an uncomfortable thought.

* * *

It was an elegantly attired and somewhat sobered lady who stepped out of her front door as the curricle drew up at her gate. Some ruthless self-examination had convinced Hester that whatever the temptation to abandon her principles she would not yield to it. She already knew what the stigma of being labelled as a fallen woman was like—she had no intention of justifying that description. And, in any case, she was probably refining too much upon the possibility that Guy would make her such an offer.

'Good day, Miss Lattimer.' Guy helped her up on to the high seat and waited until the groom took himself back to the Old Manor's stable yard. 'You look very fine, Hester; not intending to give the Nugents the satisfaction of thinking they have rattled you, I presume?'

'Precisely.' Hester settled herself on the seat and looked admiringly at the pair of matched greys that were fretting at their bits. 'That is a fine team.'

Guy looked at her again, wondering what it was that had changed about her. Or perhaps the change was in him and the way he felt about Hester Lattimer. On an impulse he asked, 'Would you care to drive them later?'

'Truly? I have never driven a pair before, I must confess.' Her eyes sparkled, the intriguing flecks of gold he looked for to gauge her mood showing quite clearly, then they vanished, almost as quickly as they had appeared. Something was oppressing her, he could sense it. Was it simply the mysterious persecution hanging over her household?

'Yes, truly. They are spirited, but good mannered, and once they have shaken the fidgets out they will give you a good drive. How is everything at the Moon House?'

'Very well.' Hester settled down to recount the news of the day before and Guy could tell that, if it were not for the mystery, Hester was more and more at home in the house. He listened with half his mind. Did he really need to buy it, now he knew it was in safe hands, owned by a woman who loved it as much as its first occupant must have done?

But he could not walk away from it without telling her the story of the house, of his involvement—and to do that he would have to ask for Georgiana's consent for that secret to be revealed. Would his sister agree? Somehow he doubted it.

And could he walk away from Hester Lattimer? That too was something he was beginning to doubt.

'…Sarah. Guy, are you listening to me?' she demanded.

'No,' he admitted with a smile to deflect her wrath. 'But I was thinking about you.' The blush that coloured her cheeks was delicious and renewed his hopes that she was not indifferent to him. Surprised by the pleasure the thought gave him, he pursued it. Just what did he hope for from Hester Lattimer? He was not given to trifling with well-bred virgins—any virgins, come to that—nor had he any plans to settle down, but Miss Lattimer was shaking that certainty.

'Guy! *Now* what are you thinking about?'

'I was still thinking about you, but—' he threw up one hand as if to ward off a blow '—you now have all my attention. Tell me all the gossip about Sarah Nugent.'

CHAPTER FOURTEEN

To recount all of Annabelle Redland's gossip about the Nugents took until the curricle reached the gates of the Hall. Guy reined in the greys and regarded Hester thoughtfully.

'It sounds as though Miss Nugent is the stronger character of the two, and not above chicanery, if the tale of her unfortunate fiancé is true. I wonder if he has decided to stay safely in the West Indies and break off the engagement by letter. If they were relying upon his wealth to restore their fortunes, that may well account for them taking desperate action.'

'But it still does not account for the desperate action taking the form of scaring me out of my home,' Hester pointed out.

'No, indeed it does not. Remind me, what excuse do we have for this call?'

'I am enquiring about Miss Nugent's health and you have kindly agreed to drive me.'

'Yes, that is perfectly plausible, but I wonder if I cannot manage to explore further.' Guy let the greys walk on and regarded the front of Winterbourne Hall critically. 'I am glad that is not my brickwork or my roof,' he remarked. 'I wonder if the work you observed was to repair the house or simply to get it into good enough condition to sell. It all depends on what their debts are and where they come from, I presume.'

No one materialised when they halted at the front door so Guy drove on round to the stables. Hester remained meekly in the background while he embarked on a lengthy conversation with the groom who took the horses, making no complaint until he finally joined her and began to walk round to the front door again.

'You certainly have the knack of extracting information,' she said admiringly. 'Sir Lewis has been selling horses, the work on the repairs to the rear elevation has stopped and I could swear that man was within an inch of asking you if you had any vacancies in your stables.'

Guy accepted the compliment with a smile that caused Hester's heart to contract. It was extremely unfair of him to have such expressive eyes that seemed to speak to her without any need of words. 'It begins to fill out the picture. I will ask my London agent to make enquiries about Sir Lewis and see if we can garner any information about his debts.'

The butler opened the door to their knocking and appeared to be on the point of saying that the Nugents were not at home when Hester skipped briskly past Guy and into the hall. 'Dear Miss Nugent,' she gushed. 'I know she would not deny me for I have called to enquire after her health. I could not bear to think of my new friend being unwell and—oh, good afternoon, Sir Lewis.'

He appeared from the library into the shadowed hall so silently that Hester jumped. 'Good afternoon, Miss Lattimer, Westrope. How kind of you to call, but I am afraid Sarah is from home, staying with an aunt in Aylesbury to recover from having a tooth pulled.'

To Hester's frustration he showed no sign of either stepping forward into the better light, or of inviting them in. 'How dreadful! No wonder she was feeling so low the other day when I was here if she had toothache. Was it an abscess?'

'Yes, rather a bad one.' Lewis appeared to hesitate and Hester was very conscious of the difference between his attitude now and when she had visited alone. 'Perhaps you would care to take tea?'

At last! 'That would be delightful—'

'But I am afraid we have an appointment elsewhere,' Guy interjected smoothly. 'However, I do wonder if I might trespass on your hospitality and ask for the loan of one of your books of local history and antiquarian lore? I find the subject fascinating and Miss Lattimer happened to mention that you had a collection of works by a relative—' He broke off and simply stood there, radiating a willingness to encumber the Nugents' hallway for as long as it took to get what he wanted.

Hester bit her lips to prevent herself smiling. It was refreshing to see someone else on the receiving end of Guy's technique. 'Your great-uncle William, was it not?' she added helpfully.

'Yes, of course.' Lewis appeared to pull himself together and accept their presence. 'I'll just go and find you something.' He turned back through the library door with his uninvited guests hard on his heels.

'*Such* a charming room,' Hester gushed.

'And such a well-lit one,' Guy added, his eyes fixed on his host's head.

Lewis turned, the morning sun streaming through the casements and directly on to his face, its smooth, handsome planes unmarked by so much as a shaving scratch.

Hester felt her breath leave her throat in a sigh which, just in time, she turned into a cough. She knew she could not meet Guy's eyes.

'Yes, it is one of my favourite rooms.' Lewis turned, almost at the door, and stepped across to a section of shelves, lifting down several books and offering them to Guy, who pulled off his gloves before taking them. Across the knuckles of his outstretched right hand the skin was reddened and sore and Lewis's eyebrows rose.

'You have been indulging in fisticuffs?'

'It was nothing, merely a rogue I ran across.'

'Doubtless the rogue will be sporting at least an equal injury.' Lewis's voice was quite neutral, but Hester thought she glimpsed a flash of anger in his eyes.

'One hopes so. Thank you.' Guy took two of the proffered volumes and began to examine them, apparently impervious to Lewis, who seemed quite willing for him to take the entire pile.

Hester glanced around the room while the men were occupied. Under the *chaise* in front of the crackling fire was a box giving every appearance of having been thrust there in a hurry. One stray leaf of paper lay forgotten under the low table by the side of the seat. With an eye on Lewis, who was urging Guy to take the whole collection, she wandered over to the *chaise* and sat down, insinuating one booted foot under the table until it rested on the corner of the paper which she could draw out into the open.

It seemed to be a letter, the ink faded, the writing a flamboyant, characterful, rather old-fashioned hand that was difficult to read. Hester squinted, bent as low as she dared and finally managed to make out the words '…Moon House… precious…so fearful…we have to hide it…'

'Miss Lattimer?' It was Lewis's voice and Hester almost dropped her reticule as she tried to suppress her guilty start.

'I am so sorry, were you speaking to me? I thought I had a loose button on my boot. Are you ready, Lord Buckland? My goodness, what a lot of books, I should imagine that will totally satisfy your antiquarian zeal, my lord.' She stood up as she prattled, holding Sir Lewis's gaze with hers while she nudged the letter back under the *chaise* with her toe. 'Please give my kindest regards to poor Miss Nugent. I do hope she feels very much better soon. Now we must be off, for I am sure we have trespassed upon your hospitality far too long.'

Once the library door was closed behind them again, Sir Lewis appeared to regain his normal character, speaking of holding a small entertainment before Christmas if his sister felt better able to emerge a little from her mourning. Hester, shaking hands as she took her leave, found herself almost doubting the impression she had had of a secretive, frightened man. And the fact remained: no one had hit Sir Lewis Nugent in the face with enough force to damage their own knuckles in the past few days.

He walked with them back to the stables, assisted Hester up on to her seat, complimented Guy on the greys and waved them goodbye. 'Very determined to see us off the premises,' Guy remarked as he waved back cheerfully.

Instead of turning right to go back into the village he turned towards the downs and drove in silence up through the beech woods, their greenish-grey trunks and branches interlaced over the deep drifts of copper-coloured leaves. At length they emerged on to the open, sheep-cropped tops. He turned off the road on to the first reasonably dry track they came to and drove on a little way to where a tangle of hawthorn bushes gave shelter against the wind and the view over the Vale of Aylesbury opened up in front of them.

'I'm sorry, I had promised that you could drive.' Guy climbed down, tossed the reins over a bush and helped Hester down from the high seat.

'I do not think I could have done,' she confessed with an attempt at a laugh, holding out her shaking hands to show him. 'I had not expected it to be so tense and strange.' Guy reached behind the seat, found a lap rug and shook it out around her shoulders. Hester stood, rather blankly staring out over the Vale. 'Guy, he did not have a mark *anywhere* on his face.'

'No, and that does have me puzzled. I have been trying to remember what the ghost smelt of, and the answer is, of nothing but plain Castile soap.'

'Which is expensive.' Hester caught his meaning at once. 'So it is not a groom, or some local criminal paid to break in.'

Guy leaned against the carriage beside her. His body sheltered her and she glanced up at him from under her lashes, letting herself think only about him and her feelings for him for the first time that day. The air was chill and her toes cold, but inside something burned warm and constant, a glow of trust and attraction and, she was beginning to fear, of wanting.

'And what were you up to, sitting demurely on the *chaise*?'

'There was a box which had been pushed hastily under it; all I could see were bundles of papers, and what looked like journals. But one sheet was on the floor under the table. I think it was a letter in old-fashioned handwriting. The ink was faded.' She wrinkled her brow in an effort to recall the words and told him.

'*Moon House*, *precious* and *hide*,' Guy repeated slowly. 'That confirms what we suspect, that there is something of value hidden there which their father did not know of and they discovered too late. And their only hope is to find and remove it before you do, or to scare you into selling the house back to them so they can pillage it at their leisure.'

Hester sighed, suddenly depressed by the whole coil. She had so much wanted peace and quiet, the chance to start afresh with her reputation intact. Now she had fallen impossibly in love and the home of her dreams was tainted by some strange mystery.

'You are tired and frustrated by our lack of progress.' Guy put an arm around her shoulders and pulled her against his side. She went with the movement without conscious thought, aware only of the comfort of his body and the gentleness in his voice. 'I wish I could take you away from this, take you somewhere peaceful where you could relax, sleep, forget all about it.'

'That sounds so good,' Hester murmured, turning her face up to smile into his. 'Peace, sleep.' She did not finish the thought. Guy shifted position, until he was standing facing her, pressing her back against the carriage, so close she could see the pulse in his throat above his neckcloth. He had pulled off his gloves and with gentle, bruised fingers began to untie her bonnet ribbons. 'Guy…' The bonnet came off and was tossed up on to the seat.

'Mmm?' He was trailing kisses across her forehead now, down the line where her hair grew at her temple, down her neck and up again to nibble at her ear.

'Guy, you should not.' *I should not…we should not…* Hester felt her body arch instinctively against his, moulding itself to his larger, stronger frame. Despite their heavy winter clothes she felt heat from him, knew her own breath was coming in little gasps to cloud the still air.

'Why not?' The murmured question seemed to burr against her ear. 'The sun is shining, we are alone and quiet and this is a sort of heaven.'

Hester put up her hands to push him away, turned her head to look him in the eye and sternly order that he stop this outrageous, immoral, scandalous behaviour immediately. Instead her fingers clenched on Guy's lapels, her lips sought his mouth and without conscious volition she found herself kissing him.

This was not like that kiss in her dining room when she suspected he was sending her a warning as much as taking a liberty. This was a slow, gentle, mutual exploration of scent and taste and sensation as his tongue teased and caressed, his lips gentled hers into surrender and his teeth made her gasp with sudden, delicate nips. She was aware of the sunlight on her closed lids, of the cold scent of dead leaves all around them, of the harsh cry of a pheasant and the thud of a heartbeat—hers or Guy's she could not tell and did not care.

Her fingers moved, reached for the strong shoulders above her, found the lean, muscled column of his neck, locked into the springing, virile hair at his nape. *This* was the man she loved, this was how his weight felt against her, how his arms held her, how his hands and mouth and murmuring voice caressed her. The man she loved.

Reality came back and with it the memory of those hours spent facing the choices before her, the memory of the decision she had made. Marriage was out of the question for her, and that left only a choice which went hand in hand with the ostracism and humiliation she had experienced before and a shame that this time she would have earned.

'No!' Hester twisted her head away. 'No.' Furious with herself, she pushed harder than she intended, her hand slipped and she fetched Guy a glancing blow on the side of his head. Startled blue eyes met hers, then he had stepped back and was standing five feet away.

'Hester, it was not my intention to frighten you, I am sorry.'

'I am not frightened.' She knew she was snapping and could not help herself. 'I am *angry*.' Guy threw up a hand in the fencer's gesture of surrender, turned on his heel and walked away from the carriage, away from her. 'No!' she shouted after him. 'Not with you. Guy, come back.'

Somehow she was moving across the springy turf, a faint scent rising from the cold thyme underfoot as she ran towards him. 'Angry with *me*, not with you.'

'Why?' He turned back, his eyes dark. 'Be angry with me, I should have known what would happen. I just wanted to be alone with you, hold you. Hester, my feelings for you are—'

'Much better left unsaid,' she interjected hastily, walking past him so she was looking out over the Vale and not at his face. 'Nothing is possible between us other than friendship. It seems there is an attraction as well. I cannot allow that to continue, not and live the sort of life I have set out for myself.'

Where the words, and the strength to say them, came from she had no idea. Hester blinked back what felt treacherously like tears and focused hard on the village lying below her, the white line of the post road snaking past it, the glitter of water marking the canal beyond. This was home now, the only fixed thing in her life.

He had moved silently behind her; the first she knew of it were his hands on her shoulders. They rested there, heavy but undemanding. 'Do you believe I was intending to offer you a *carte blanche*?'

'I do not know,' she replied in as calm a voice as Guy was using. 'But I know that I should not act in such a manner that you could be forgiven for believing such an offer would be acceptable. It would not be.' She spun round and he dropped his hands. 'Ever.'

His eyes had gone from dark to stormy and with a shock Hester recognised anger to match her own. Anger, and, although it was hard to believe, uncertainty, almost vulnerability. She did not want him to be vulnerable or uncertain. She wanted a rock, a supporter, a friend—and had foolishly believed she could have all that and keep her feelings hidden. What Guy's feelings were she had hardly stopped to consider, she realised with a pang of guilt.

'I can assure you that, whatever my intentions, offering you a position as my mistress was not one of them. You may have my word that I never will.'

His anger sparked hers into fire again. Guilt, the knowledge that she was behaving badly, the tensions of the mystery that enveloped them, flared.

'Good. In fact, excellent. We now know exactly where we both stand. And let me assure you that I will never sell you the Moon House, whatever you offer me, and you can therefore cut your losses and leave Winterbourne. If I experience any further trouble, believe me, I will call upon the local magistrate.'

Guy half turned as he stalked back to the curricle. 'The local magistrate may well be Sir Lewis Nugent.' He gathered up the reins and waited in silence until she reached his side, handed her her hat, then helped her up on to the seat.

Hester sat down with a thump. 'Then I will take on Ben Aston as a bodyguard and hire a Bow Street Runner. Will you please drive me home, my lord?'

'Very well, Miss Lattimer.' He set the curricle in motion, his weight shifting easily as it bumped over the rough track.

Hester jammed her bonnet back on her head, yanked the ribbons together and sat fuming. By the time they reached the bottom of the hill she was feeling ashamed of herself, at the point where they passed the gates of Winterbourne Hall she realised that the pair of them staring fixedly at the road in front must present a ludicrous picture and by the time the church tower was in sight her sense of the ridiculous had got the better of her and she had to suppress a wry smile.

'My lord?'

'Yes, Miss Lattimer?'

'I apologise, my lord.'

'So do I, Miss Lattimer. I presume it has occurred to you, as it has to me, that attempting to have a row in a curricle is both impractical and undignified.'

Hester gave a little gasp of amusement that was half genuine, half the unsafe laughter of tension and excitement.

'I trust we have not been presenting a spectacle of the sulks for any passing yokels.'

'I never sulk. I may exhibit a brooding silence, it is quite another thing.' This time her gurgle of amusement was wholly genuine. 'Do you think we might revert to Christian names, Miss Lattimer?'

'I believe so, my lord.'

She flashed a glancing smile at him and saw the storm clouds had gone from his eyes and the twist of amusement that so charmed her was back at the corner of his lips. But she was shaken; she had never aroused such passion in a man, never had her own passions aroused in such a way. To the knowledge that she loved Guy Westrope she had to add the realisation that she desired him in every possible way and that, whatever his feelings or intentions, he felt that desire also.

As the curricle drew up in front of the Moon House the door swung open and Hester's small household appeared.

'Oh, Hester dear, thank goodness you are safe!' Maria almost ran down the path.

'Why ever should I not be?' Hester demanded. She climbed down and was startled to find herself clutched to Miss Prudhome's skinny bosom.

'Because there are more roses and we did not know where you were,' Susan said bluntly, meeting them as they came up the path. 'Sir Lewis called in with a book he said he had forgotten to give you and seemed surprised you had not returned. You've been gone three hours, Miss Hester.'

'We have been for a drive.' Hester felt flustered at having to account for her movements, but even more so by the obvious alarm of Maria, Susan and Jethro. 'Jethro, what has happened? You said more roses?'

'Come upstairs.' He led the way, but in the hall Guy strode past him and took the stairs two at a time.

'Stay there, Hester.'

Stubbornly Hester mounted the stairs in his wake. Whatever had occurred, seeing it could not be worse than imagining it. Guy was standing on the landing outside her room, looking at the floor. A trail of evenly spaced roses led halfway across the landing.

With a calm she was far from feeling, Hester stooped and picked up the flowers. 'Eight,' she counted. 'He keeps to his pattern, does he not? And they are where you predicted—approaching my door.'

'He is thinking as I would if I wanted to frighten you,' Guy remarked dispassionately, standing hand on hips surveying the corridor. 'I will send a footman over this evening to spend the night in the kitchen again, but I think he will have a peaceful time—after this you should be safe for a night and a day.'

Guy opened the chamber door and raised an eyebrow at Hester. 'May I? I would feel more comfortable if I checked the room.'

Hester nodded and followed him in. His tall figure in boots and riding coat seemed to overpower the feminine room and she was almost more conscious of him as a male creature than she had been in his arms on the downs.

She waited, standing quietly while he checked under the bed, in the dressing room, flicked back the bedclothes to run a hand over the sheets, lifted the pillows.

'All clear, it seems.' He paused, his hand on the door knob. 'And Nugent was here this afternoon. I wonder if he has been just a little too clever this time. Let us go and see what your gallant household observed.'

Hester nodded, wishing she felt as gallant. Guy took the roses that she was still holding. 'The kitchen range for these.' He touched her lips lightly with one finger. 'You are a soldier's daughter, Hester. Your father would have been proud of you.'

CHAPTER FIFTEEN

Hester led the way into the kitchen. Somehow the warmth of the range, the homely gleam of pewter and brass and the scrubbed simplicity of the long table were a comfort. What her neighbours would think of her entertaining an earl there she could only imagine.

Guy tossed the roses on the fire and watched them sombrely as they crackled and burned. 'What happened when Sir Lewis called? Was he alone at any time, Ackland?'

'No, my lord.' Jethro shifted his arm in its sling and concentrated. 'He came to the front door and knocked. I answered it and he said he had a book he had forgotten to give you this morning. I thanked him and said that Miss Hester was not at home. When I told him that he looked very serious and said that surely you would have returned by that time.'

'Then I came out of the front room,' Miss Prudhome chimed in. 'And I invited him in for tea, which he accepted. So I rang for Susan…'

'You were all in the front room by this point?'

'Yes.' Jethro closed his eyes the better to picture the scene. 'I stepped in to clear the tea table, which Miss Prudhome had been using for her sewing things. Susan came in to ask what Miss Prudhome required.'

'And I was sitting by the hearth with Sir Lewis opposite,' Maria finished.

'Not long,' Hester observed. 'But I suppose long enough for someone to come in through the secret way and hide in the dining room. From there they could go upstairs as soon as Jethro and Susan went back to the kitchen.'

'And that would explain why he brought the book to you,' Guy added. Hester smiled at him, enjoying the bittersweet sensation of shared thoughts, of watching him thinking and reasoning and joining her mind with his in this puzzle. 'I had asked for the books—the only reason not to take it to the Old Manor would be to distract the household here.'

'And if he knew about the footman in the kitchen he would know he could not get in at night. He must be getting desperate,' Hester added.

'I'll give him desperate,' Susan muttered.

'We need to catch him red-handed,' Miss Prudhome announced, her face grim. Beside her Jethro picked up the vegetable paring knife and ran a thumb thoughtfully down the blade.

'Well, unless we sit here all day and night, that may be easier said than done.' Hester smiled at her bloodthirsty allies. 'I think you are going to have to withdraw your footman from the kitchen at night and give the ghost a clear run, my lord.'

Guy fought down his instinctive retort that, on the contrary, he would also install a groom with a blunderbuss in the hallway and told himself to stop thinking with his heart and instead to apply his head. Miss Hester Lattimer was turning both his resolve and his intellect head over heels. She was right— another trap was the only way of resolving this, but somehow it had to be contrived without putting her in danger. An idea was stirring at the back of his mind.

Susan gave the burning roses a vicious poke and set the kettle down on the range with a thump while, without speaking,

Miss Prudhome began to gather up the teapot and caddy and measure out tea. Guy suppressed a smile. The automatic reaction of the household to any emergency appeared to be to put the kettle on.

The desire to smile faded as he looked at Hester. She had cast off her outer clothes and was sitting speaking quietly with Jethro about his shoulder. Any casual visitor would have noticed nothing amiss, but to his eyes there were clear signs of strain.

The delicate skin under her eyes looked bruised and almost fragile, her natural grace held something of a braced alertness now and her hands were clasped, the long, elegant fingers more eloquent in their rigid stillness than if she had been twisting them in anguish.

Since that moment of revelation, when they had sat in the darkened front room waiting for the ghost, he had wrestled with his feelings for her. Desire, of course. Affection, admiration, and frequently exasperation—all those certainly. But this new, unsettling feeling, this awareness of her and what she was thinking, the spark of understanding when their eyes met, this desire to tell her his thoughts and his hopes without reservation—this was something else. This, he was coming to realise, was love.

Was it possible that Hester felt it too? She fought what she quite frankly admitted was a physical attraction, she was outspoken enough to inform him she would not accept a *carte blanche*—but then she was a gently bred young lady with undoubtedly firm moral principles.

Guy Westrope had never before considered making a declaration of marriage. He considered it now, sitting at the scrubbed kitchen table, a mug of tea in his hand and the love of his life seated opposite briskly persuading her adolescent butler that balancing hot oil on top of half-open doors or sawing halfway through stair treads were not stratagems likely to succeed. It was not, he readily admitted, the sort of environment in which earls normally contemplated marriage. Which, he supposed, only went to show that it must, indeed, be love he was feeling.

'Why are you smiling, my lord?' Hester had finally convinced Jethro that his schemes were likely to be more dangerous to the household than to any intruder and was regarding Guy like an alert robin, head on one side, brown eyes twinkling. The strain and fatigue were gone, or, at least, well under control. Once more admiration for her courage gripped him and the desire to pulverise Lewis Nugent hardened into a hard knot of fury.

'I was enjoying Ackland's imagination.' Now, even if he could get her alone, was not the time for protestations of love. Her eyes said quite plainly that she did not believe him and that she suspected him of something, if only of teasing her.

'I think…' Hester said slowly, sipping her tea, 'I think we have been too much on the defensive. If something of value is hidden here, then we can find it as well as the Nugents. Where, my lord, do you think it could be?'

Guy found himself transfixed by that intelligent brown gaze once more. 'I have no idea, Miss Lattimer.'

'No, my lord, that will not wash.' She put down the mug firmly. 'You know something about this house you have not told me, else why would you wish to buy it?'

Guy was conscious of four pairs of eyes fixed intently on him and was thankful for years of card playing and the ability to maintain a straight face. 'I know who used to live here after it was built, that is all. I have no more knowledge of treasure or hiding places than you, I swear it. And before you ask me, I cannot tell you who that occupant was.' And as soon as he could speak to Georgiana and secure her consent to tell Hester everything, the happier he would be.

'Then we will search,' Hester announced with determination. 'Starting on Monday, from attics to scullery. A least we have no cellars to worry about.'

'I will help if I can,' Guy offered, 'but tomorrow I must go back to London to escort my sister Lady Broome who is set on visiting me—chiefly to convince me to accompany her and her family to Broome Hall in Essex for Christmas, which she knows I have not the slightest intention of doing!'

Georgy would have at last two other aims in mind, of that he was sure. One was to distract him from what she considered his dangerous obsession with the Moon House and its possibilities for family scandal and the other was doubtless to introduce him to yet another 'suitable' young lady. Miss Lattimer, he was only too well aware, she would regard as anything but suitable—no title, no 'family', no wealth.

He rose with a word of farewell and was not surprised when Hester followed him through into the front hall with a word to Jethro to stay where he was.

'I will send over a footman again tonight. No—' he held up a hand when she opened her mouth to protest '—if you do not let him into the kitchen then he will have to sit outside the back door all night and I am sure you would not inflict that on him in this weather.'

Hester glared at him, then let her mouth relax into a reluctant smile. 'Very well, thank you, Guy. But we are never going to trap the ghost this way.'

'You may be right, but I have an idea. What is it your intention to do at Christmas? Will you visit relatives?'

'I have none,' Hester admitted simply. 'We will stay here and have a quiet holiday, I expect. I had not given it much thought.'

'I think you should have an evening party—say, on the twenty-second. Carols and buttered rum punch—a conversable evening around the fire with all your new friends and neighbours, including, of course, the Nugents. And I think there should also be some seasonal story telling. Do you not agree?'

'Ghost stories?' Hester asked, trying to read Guy's face as he nodded. 'Have you a plan?'

'I think I have.' He smiled wickedly. 'A lot depends on the Nugents accepting. Goodbye, Hester, and take care of yourself.' He paused, looking down at her, and Hester fought back the impulse to stand on tiptoe and press her lips to his. 'Take care,' he repeated and was gone.

Hester went back into the kitchen, counting on her fingers. 'Do you realise it is only twelve days to Christmas? It has just crept up on me this year and we haven't made any preparations for it at all!'

The others looked up from their various tasks and Hester could see the thought of the holiday was a welcome diversion from the other preoccupations they had been wrestling with.

'Mrs Bunting asked me to help in decorating the church,' Maria remarked.

'I had best order a goose and I don't know what else.' Susan reached for a scrap of paper and a pencil and began to scratch a list. 'Plum puddings.'

'I'll get Aston to cut more logs and the silver'll need polishing,' was Jethro's contribution.

'I think I will hold a party here,' Hester announced. 'On the twenty-second. Something quite informal…a supper party, probably. We must have the piano tuned and I will make a guest list.'

By the time the Moon House party trooped over to the church next morning, Hester had made her list and written her invitations. Fortunately her acquaintance was still not large, for, if everyone accepted, the front rooms would hardly hold the company.

Both Nugents could be glimpsed in their front pew and Hester timed her exit from the church to catch them as they shook Mr Bunting's hand.

'Miss Nugent! How do you go on? I was so sorry to hear about your tooth.'

The slender figure turned, a fine, dense veil shielding her face. 'Miss Lattimer, good day. I am much better, thank you. Only rather sore still and the bruising has still not gone down.'

Her brother hovered protectively at her side and Hester turned her smile on him. 'And Sir Lewis—thank you for delivering that other book. I have passed it on to his lordship, who is doubtless finding it most interesting.' She fell in beside them as they made their way down the churchyard path to the lych-gate.

'Has anything else strange happened recently?' Miss Nugent's voice seemed rather muffled, doubtless by the painful results of the extraction and Hester glanced at her just as a gust of wind caught the edge of her veil. There was a glimpse of her face before she snatched at the hem and had it under control again. The cheek revealed was quite definitely swollen and there was indeed a fading bruise—a bruise that showed clearly the marks of four knuckles.

Sarah Nugent was the ghost. Hester got both her face and voice under control and made a rapid decision.

'Yes. Yes, something very worrying has happened,' she confided, making her tone anxious. 'May I tell you in confidence?' They both nodded earnestly and Hester cast a rapid glance round before whispering, 'Someone is getting into the house and leaving…dead roses.'

Sarah gave a little shriek of alarm, which, if she had not seen her bruised face, would have convinced Hester of her surprise. 'Roses! I knew it—the curse. My dear Miss Lattimer, I beg you, reconsider and accept Lewis's offer to buy back the Moon House before it is too late.'

'I do not know.' Hester hoped she was sounding undecided yet unnerved. 'It is such a lovely house and yet…now I feel so uneasy there. Perhaps I am being over-imaginative. I am reluctant to make any decision before the Christmas season is over. Which reminds me…' She took an invitation out of her reticule and handed it to Sarah. 'I am having a small party on the twenty-second; just a sociable evening at home with supper and perhaps singing carols around the piano. I do hope you can come.'

There was a perceptible pause. What were they thinking? 'That would be delightful, thank you, Miss Lattimer,' Sarah said at last. 'We had made no plans ourselves because of our sad loss, but an evening with friends would be most welcome.'

Sir Lewis took her hand and squeezed it. Hester repressed the urge to snatch it away and box his ears and instead gazed trustingly into his green eyes. 'If at any time you come to a decision to sell, Miss Lattimer, you have only to say.'

Hester watched them climb into their carriage and turned back grimly to distribute invitations to others of her acquaintance who were leaving the church. A gratifyingly large number expressed their immediate acceptance and Hester made her way back home, mentally writing lists and reviewing her wine cellar. As they reached the front gate she glanced across at the Old Manor standing red and forbidding across the lane.

Where was Guy now? He had not been gone a day and already she missed him with a dull ache. She wanted to talk to him, tell him about Sarah Nugent, confide that she had risked speaking about the roses. And more than that, she wanted to be held in his arms, feel the strength of him under her hands, against her body. She wanted him to make love to her.

'Miss Hester?' It was Jethro, obviously wondering why she was standing on the front step with the door wide open letting the heat out. 'Miss Hester, I was talking to one of the footmen from the Hall up in the church gallery and he says that every Christmas the Nugents used to have theatrical parties.'

'Did they, indeed?' Hester stepped briskly inside and closed the door. 'What else did he say?'

Jethro took her heavy cloak and gloves, favouring his right side where the muscles were still paining him. 'That Sir Lewis was a good actor, but Miss Nugent was even better and that she organised everything and made up the plays and Sir Lewis just does what she says.'

Hester went into the sitting room, calling the others after her. 'Miss Nugent is our ghost; I saw the bruises from Lord Buckland's knuckles plain on her cheek under that veil. And if Sarah is such an accomplished actor, no wonder she has been able to spin all these tales about ghosts and a curse and appear so distressed.'

'Shall we start to search the house?' Jethro was already rolling up his sleeves, only to be interrupted by a scandalised cluck from Miss Prudhome.

'Not on a Sunday, Jethro!'

'His lordship has been travelling on a Sunday,' he muttered mutinously.

'We can discuss how we are going to search and where,' Hester suggested placatingly. 'And we can think about our Christmas plans. I cannot recall when I have been so behindhand with that.'

An hour later, nibbling the tip of her quill before the sitting room fire, Hester thought back to Christmases past. English Yuletides with her parents were a distant memory; fresher were the colourful, often chaotic celebrations in

Portugal with roast ribs of beef acquired by dubious means, the mix of uniforms adding to the festive scene and the sun shining in a way it never did in England in December.

Then, two years ago, returning to England, bereaved, desolate, shivering in an English winter, her only sanctuary the house of an old friend of her father, invalided out of the army two years previously. The house where she expected to spend her first English Christmas for many years.

Hester had found the address in Mount Street and handed the gaunt, crippled man who lived there her father's letter addressed to him. Colonel Sir John Norton had read it while she had watched him, shaken that a contemporary of her father's should look so much older. Major Lattimer had referred to a shoulder wound that would have soon healed, but the man before her was suffering from far worse than that.

But shaken as she was by the appearance of her host, she was even more confused by the letter he handed to her which had been contained within his own.

...as we have spoken of before now, if you find yourself alone you will have gone to my good friend John Norton...he and I agreed...make provision for you...best for you to marry him, for there is no one else I can send you to...

She had had to read the letter twice before she could take it in. Her father and his old friend had hatched a plot for her protection, which involved her marrying the colonel if her father was killed.

She had looked up, startled, and had met the kind, tired eyes that were watching her.

'I was not such a wreck when he and I parted,' he explained wryly. 'An operation went wrong, I contracted a rheumatic fever that affected my heart. The quacks give me a year.'

'I am so sorry.' She had tried to smile bravely. 'I cannot

possibly impose on you, that is obvious. Perhaps you can suggest a respectable hotel—'

She had got no further. Sir John pointed out with a forcefulness, which left him breathless, that if she married him she would have a home, the protection of his name and would, very shortly, become a wealthy widow.

Hester had refused point blank and the battle between the mortally ill man and the homeless young woman had raged for two days before she had agreed to stay and he had agreed to respect her determination not to marry him.

She soon realised that, as well as being ill, he was lonely. His servants were adequate, but no substitute for family or friends, and his relatives, with whom he had had little contact or sympathy while he was in good health, saw no need to seek him out now. Hester settled into the role of companion-housekeeper within days and a strange, warm friendship grew up between the dying man and the bereaved girl.

When John had died she had felt bereaved all over again as though she had lost a second father. Facing the prospect of homelessness and genteel poverty on the small portion she had inherited, she had been touched and deeply grateful that at the reading of the will it transpired that the colonel had left her a respectable competence as well as his wine cellar. And with it the chance to remake her own life away from London.

Hester tossed down her quill and got to her feet to stare out of the window at the uncompromising red-brick wall on the other side of the road. Now, here in the Moon House, she was determined to build a future on what John and her father had given her. The past was behind her.

She turned back from the window with a shiver, the thin sunlight throwing her silhouette in front of her across the boards. It seemed like a warning, a reminder that what was behind you could cast a long shadow into the here and now.

CHAPTER SIXTEEN

The next morning Hester rallied her troops and set them searching.

'Jethro, see what you can find in the kitchen and scullery. Somehow someone is getting in, so look from the outside first. The rest of us will search for this treasure. Susan, you take the ground floor, Maria, the bedrooms, and I will search the attics.'

She had to scrub a rag over the tiny windows in the eaves and light two lanterns, but at last Hester could see to explore the attics. Unfortunately it was also sufficient to reveal some very large spiders. The contents were disappointingly sparse, almost all broken and most had never been of any value at all. Nor could she see any possible hiding places, despite carefully tapping and pressing every piece of woodwork and prodding each loose brick or slate.

Straightening her back, she called downstairs to Maria and Susan, but they too reported not so much as a painted-over cupboard to give any hope. Hester eyed the dust-smeared floorboards. 'I suppose you are the obvious place,' she muttered at them resentfully. 'What a good thing I never liked this gown overmuch.'

Lantern in one hand, she inched across the floor on her

knees, trying to lift the boards at the ends, prodding the knot holes. Nothing. And then, in the furthest corner, her hand brushed against a change of level. She held up the lantern and revealed a painting, thick with dust. Hester pulled it out and lifted it, showering herself with dirt and what seemed to be a mass of ribbons. It was the canvas, sliced and torn into shreds, which still clung to the frame where the edges of the canvas remained intact.

Hester knelt there, her arms aching with the effort of supporting it and felt the cold horror of violence that had filled her when she first saw the ravaged dressing room. To have done this spoke of bitter anger and spite and a fanatical desire to despoil.

Wishing she could take it straight to Guy, she got to her feet, blew out her lanterns and carried the frame and its fluttering tatters downstairs. Maria emerged from the unoccupied back bedroom, shaking her head. 'I've had all the rugs up, pulled the shutters right out of their boxes—nothing. My goodness, what is that?'

'Come downstairs and I will show you. Susan!'

Hester carried on down to the dining room where she lowered the frame on to the table. 'Do you recall that sheet of glass we found in the shed? If you can fetch that, I will use it to lay out the canvas and we can see—' She broke off at a cry of triumph from the kitchen. 'Jethro?'

'I've found it!'

They hurried in to see the lad standing triumphantly in the doorway of the unused cupboard. 'Look—no wonder it was damp in here, there is a hidden doorway in the bricks at the side and it does not quite meet the ground. See?'

Susan and Maria squashed into the cupboard after Hester, exclaiming at the ingenuity of the secret door, ducking outside into the recess that had seemed blocked by the overflowing water butt and the pile of old hurdles. 'No wonder Sir Lewis did not want you sending for a builder, Miss Hester.' Jethro pushed the door closed and brushed up the dead weeds against it. 'We'd never see this, but any craftsman checking the brickwork couldn't help but find it.'

'And his man came down, looked all round here and said nothing. More evidence for the magistrate,' Hester said triumphantly. However much her head had told her there was a malevolent human agency behind the appearance of the roses, it was still a relief to see tangible proof of it. 'Try and leave everything as it was, Jethro, we do not want to frighten off the Nugents. Not yet. Brr, I am cold, let us go in.'

'Miss Lattimer? I knocked at the front door and could not make myself heard.' It was Guy. Hester scrambled over the hurdles with more speed than grace and caught his hand, the cold forgotten in the comfort of feeling that strong, warm clasp.

'We have found it! Come and see. I am so glad you are returned.'

He paused, closing his hand tight around hers, and looked down into her face. 'So am I.' Hester felt the yard go quiet around her. Somewhere behind her the voices of Maria and Susan were a faint twittering like birds in a distant tree. Her cold hands and feet ceased to have any feeling. All she was conscious of was the warmth in Guy's eyes, the meaning in his voice, the sensual curve of his lips.

The edge of a hurdle cracked under her foot and the moment was gone. Feeling as though she had woken from a deep sleep, Hester blinked. 'Jethro found the door. Look.'

Guy climbed over the barrier and helped her back. Together they examined the door, its carefully disguised hinges, the slight angle that the wall was set at which hid it utterly unless one was face-on to it. 'As I suspected, this was built as part of the house, not added later.'

'So it must be part of the original secret, the same secret as the treasure?' Hester speculated as they regained the kitchen.

'Yes. If there ever was a treasure. I am beginning to wonder about that. And you know, those old family books of legends make no mention of any dead roses or of this house at all.'

'The Nugents think there is a treasure, or why else are they doing this? Oh, yes, and I forgot to tell you—Miss Nugent is our ghost, I caught a glimpse under her veil yesterday and she has the bruises of your knuckles on her cheek, plain as day. She is also a good actress, according to Jethro's sources.'

'Is she, indeed?' Guy regarded his knuckles. 'I have never hit a woman—I cannot say it gives me any great pleasure, whatever she has been about. As for the "treasure", they may be misinterpreting some clue—that letter you glimpsed, for example.' Guy leaned against the kitchen table and looked around the room. 'This is a home, this place. I cannot see it as some kind of treasure house, can you?' Hester shook her head, intrigued that he seemed to experience the same kind of feelings as she did for the Moon House. 'It is feminine, warm. A house for a man to come to and relax, sit by the fire, enjoy a woman's company.'

His gaze rested on Hester as he spoke and she found her lips curving into a smile of recognition at the picture he was painting. She could see herself seated by the fire, or curled up on the *chaise* in her bedchamber, holding out a hand to Guy as he came through the door in the candlelight. She would pull him down beside her in the firelight while the snow swirled against the window panes…

'Why, then, would he need to sneak in through a secret opening?' Hester wondered aloud. 'An assignation?' Jethro, Susan and Maria had all vanished from the kitchen. She wondered why, then supposed they had all gone to wash hands and faces after their dusty explorations.

Guy shifted position suddenly as though to snap himself out of his flight of fancy. 'Perhaps. I need to read that box of documents.'

'But how?' Hester felt she could watch the play of expression on his face for hours. In company he shielded his thoughts and emotions and one saw only what he wanted you to see. But lately she felt he let his guard down with her—or perhaps, being in love with him, she could read him more clearly.

'What is it, Hester?' Guy reached out a hand across the table and she put hers into it with a smile, surprised once more at how right his touch seemed.

She must have looked startled at his question, for he added, 'You were staring at me. Have I a smudge on my face?'

'No, no…I was wool-gathering.'

'Well, you have—a smudge, I mean. And cobwebs in your hair. In fact, I think you are even grubbier than the first time I saw you.'

Guy watched the emotions chase across Hester's face, then mischief won over indignation. 'Wretch! To remind me of that is most unfair.'

'I thought you made a very fetching parlourmaid,' he commented, wondering how much longer he could hold her hand before she became self-conscious and snatched it away.

He very much wanted to do more than hold her hand. If he was honest with himself, the thought of kissing her again, holding her in his arms, making love to her, was beginning to obsess him. Up there on the chilly downs he had thought for a dizzy moment that she returned his feelings, but it seemed that all she felt was friendship—and *attraction*. In the tone she had used, that was the sort of word which was usually preceded by *unfortunate*.

The vehemence with which she rejected the idea of a *carte blanche* puzzled him. Of course any well-bred young lady would be appalled at the thought, but her reaction was more intense, more personal. And the fact that it had occurred to her at all, significant. Had someone tried to force his attentions on her in the period after her father's death when she had been alone and not yet safely employed?

Whatever her secret was, he did not intend cajoling or tricking it out of her. If she trusted him, she would tell him when she was ready, and if she did not trust him, then this was pointless anyway. A patient man, Guy settled himself to play a long game, but for the first time he found himself apprehensive about whether he would win it.

He must have been lost in thought for long enough to make her uncomfortable for Hester coloured and, extracting her hand from his grasp, stood up. 'I am keeping you from your sister. I am sorry, I should have asked you if she had a comfortable journey.'

'She had a very comfortable journey, I thank you. During the course of it she sprung the news upon me that her husband has gone north to County Durham to visit a very sick greatuncle of his, leaving her to amuse herself as best she can over the festive season. Being Georgy she has decided that descending upon me and causing me to celebrate Christmas in style would entertain her best.

'By this I imagine she expects me to decorate that hideous house with evergreens, dispense mince pies and punch to tuneless wassailers, issue invitations to the local society and generally behave in a manner that is best calculated to drive me back to London to shut myself up in one of my clubs until it is all over.'

He could not suppress the grin that Hester's gurgle of amusement provoked. 'Oh, *poor* Guy! And you such a curmudgeonly recluse—entertaining will obviously go right against the grain with you. Is Lady Broome explaining all this to Parrott at the moment?'

'No, fortunately she decided she would call upon her very dear friend Lady Redbourn who lives in Watford, so I was able to drop her off for a couple of days of exhausting gossip and character assassination before she comes on here.'

He saw Hester was looking dubious in the face of such a frank description. 'I adore my sister, and at a distance of twenty miles we get on excellently well. I think about a sennight will be delightful, after that I will not vouch for the Christmas spirit enduring.' He regarded Hester who was looking somewhat relieved. 'I think she will like you. At least, should we manage to keep you from looking like a chimney sweep. Here, stand in the light.'

The smudge on the end of her nose was irresistible. Guy proffered one corner of his pocket handkerchief and Hester obediently licked it. The pink, pointed tongue darting from between her lips was so erotic he almost dropped the handkerchief. Instead he dabbed carefully at the end of her nose. 'There. Now the one on your forehead.' She was standing very still, looking at him solemnly with those great brown eyes. Guy could feel his heart thudding. His hand shook slightly; was it the effort not to snatch her into his arms or was there something in her gaze that was making him vulnerable?

Another glimpse of that tongue would undo him. Guy dipped the cloth in a bowl of water standing in the sink. He dabbed at the line of dirt on Hester's cheekbone and stopped, his hand upraised, his eyes locked with hers. 'Those gold flecks are back again. Are you angry or happy?'

She blinked at him and then said tartly, 'Chilly, my lord. There is cold water dribbling down my cheek.' The dimple at the corner of her mouth showed she was feigning anger, but

Guy knew he was close to overstepping whatever invisible boundary she had set between them.

'I am sorry. Here.' He handed her the towel, which hung on the back of the door, making no attempt to wipe the water away himself. Suddenly he could not trust himself to touch her.

Hester knew she was making rather a business of drying her face. It was ridiculous, if Guy had the slightest idea of the effect he could have on her with such a simple gesture as washing away a trace of dirt, he would imagine she was fevered. In an effort to control her hectic imagination, which had him taking her masterfully in his arms and heeding not the slightest her maidenly pleas to desist, she dragged her mind back to the last sensible thing they had spoken of.

'You did not tell me how you intended examining the box of documents in the library at Winterbourne Hall.'

'Let us just say that the Nugents do not have the monopoly on breaking and entering around here.'

His expression spoke of nothing but a thoroughly masculine delight in doing something dangerous, reckless and foolhardy. Hester found her anxiety surfacing in a rush of anger. 'Are you all about in the head? Housebreaking? Breaking into a magistrate's house at that? No one would think the worse of him if he took a shotgun to an intruder. And what if he doesn't shoot you? What is the penalty for breaking and entering? Hanging? Of all the stupid, ill thought out...*male* things to be contemplating—'

She broke off, panting, as Guy held up both hands placatingly and leaned against the edge of the kitchen table. 'It is not ill thought out. I know exactly how and where to do it and have not the slightest intention of being caught.' He held up his hand again as she opened her mouth to disabuse him of any delusion that this was a comforting assurance. 'And as for being a *male* thing to do, well, I am a man.'

'I had noticed,' Hester snapped.

'I am gratified,' he responded smoothly, apparently intent on provoking her into reaching for the skillet, which stood temptingly to hand. 'Now, I will send over a footman again tonight at about ten o'clock. I imagine your people will be in and out of the kitchen until then. We do not want to show our hand yet by securing the secret door. In fact, tonight is the night when six roses are due, is it not? That should keep the Nugents suitably distracted, trying to find a way to deposit them. Do you not like the idea of paying them back in their own coin, sweetheart?'

Hester was too cross for the endearment to register. She was also, she realised, very chilly. 'It is freezing in here. The front door must be open. Susan!'

The front door was indeed open. Hester pushed it to. 'You must have left it open when you came in. Oh, no, I was forgetting, you came round the side because we were all at the back. Where are they all? They must have gone out and not pulled it shut.'

'I can hear voices in the kitchen.' Guy put his hand on the door handle. 'I must be off, but before I go, how is young Ackland's shoulder?'

'Much better. It seemed to heal all of a sudden, although he still favours it a little and I will not let him lift anything heavy.'

'Ah, the benefits of youth. Goodbye, my dear.' And he was gone, leaving Hester prey to a very mixed bag of emotions indeed.

She mulled them over as she closed the door behind him and walked back to the kitchen. Anxiety over his plan to break into Winterbourne Hall warred with a warm, selfish glow of happiness that his sister was not staying with him yet and she had a few more days of his company.

The three members of her household were busying themselves with an air that Hester could not help but find suspicious. It was not until Susan said casually, 'His lordship's gone, then?' that the penny dropped. They had gone off, leaving her alone with him quite intentionally.

'Yes, he has,' she responded robustly. 'And where did you all vanish to, might I ask? Maria, you are supposed to be chaperoning me—did you think you were matchmaking?'

That reduced Miss Prudhome to blushing incoherence and Jethro simply to blushes. Susan, however, stood up for herself. 'And what if we were? He's a fine gentleman and he likes you very well indeed.'

'And you know—and Jethro knows— exactly why I cannot think about marrying a gentleman, ever. Do you not?'

'What do you mean, Hester dear?' Maria emerged from behind her hands where she had retreated in guilty confusion. 'An earl would be a very splendid match, but not out of the question for a gentlewoman and the daughter of a distinguished officer.'

Hester sank down at the table, her legs suddenly too weary to support her. It was time to tell Maria the truth and if she decided she could no longer act as companion to someone with Hester's reputation, then that was simply a judgment upon her for not being frank at the outset.

'Let us go into the sitting room, Maria.' Somehow this warm kitchen was too informal for the confession she was about to make. 'Susan and Jethro know what I am going to tell you; I can only reproach myself for not having been frank with you from the outset.'

Bemused, Miss Prudhome followed her employer and sat in the chair opposite Hester's, her hands clasped anxiously in her lap, the flickering firelight sparking off the jet brooch she wore.

'When my father died I came back to England,' Hester began painfully. She had never had to tell this story to anyone and it felt as though it were being wrenched from her now. 'He was not able to leave me well endowed, and I had no surviving relatives, but he had left me instructions to go to an old army friend of his, Colonel Sir John Norton, in London. I went, hoping he would be able to recommend me to a suitable employer so I could become a companion.'

She told the story, seeing her own emotions reflected in Maria's face: pity and shock at the realisation of the colonel's condition; amazement, then rejection of his proposal and finally approval of the compromise they had reached together.

'John only had a few relatives, and they had neglected him for many years, obviously feeling that a dying man, however gallant, was no concern of theirs. With no other heirs, they had no reason to fear he would leave his money elsewhere.

'But after my arrival, it took only days for those distant relatives to scent my presence and descend upon Mount Street. The ensuing row was an epic and Sir John's cousin, her husband, her two sons and their wives swept out of the house, having convinced themselves that he had fallen prey to a fortune-hunting hussy and that I had settled into the house as his mistress with an eye to his money.'

She sighed, wondering yet again if there was anything that could have been done at the time to stop the damage. But she had been too proud, and John too furious, to beg their understanding.

'If they had taken themselves back to the country it might not have mattered so very much, but instead they settled in their town house and proceeded to spread the news of the colonel's shocking liaison.

'I found myself pointed out in the lending library and the few callers Sir John had been used to fell away abruptly. At

the fashionable milliner's where I had begun to take my cus-
tom I found they had too much work on to oblige me and the
ladies of households where I called to take up letters of introduction from my father's commanding officer were never at
home to me.'

Maria gasped in outrage. 'How bigoted, how unjustified!'

Hester shrugged. 'Can I blame them? I do not know.
Reputation is such a fragile thing. My world closed in to the
Mount Street house and my companionship with Sir John. I
tried not to think about what I would do when he died, for my
portion was small and the scandal had put paid to any hopes
of becoming companion to anyone else.

'But I should have known better. He left me a legacy in his
will. Not a fortune, for most of his wealth was entailed on his
cousin's son, but a very respectable competence, which, with
what my father had left me, means I am able to support the
appearance of a gentlewoman.' She broke off and smiled.
'Where, that is, no one knows of my reputation.'

'And because of that reputation, even if it is quite undeserved,
you cannot accept an offer from a gentleman,' Maria stated sadly.

'Not an honourable offer, that is for sure,' Hester added
wryly. 'But I should have told you at the beginning, Maria; it
was wrong of me not to. You might well have decided you did
not wish to be associated with me—you may still feel that way.'

'Never!' Miss Prudhome leapt to her feet and hastened to
hug her startled employer. 'You *are* a gentlewoman, but even
if these unkind rumours were true, I hope I can recognise true
kindness and quality when I meet it.' She sat down with a decided thump and blew her nose briskly.

Hester found she could not speak and contented herself
with leaning over and squeezing Maria's hand gratefully. The
little spinster was so kind. If only she thought Guy would be
as understanding if she told him frankly of her past. But, of

course, that was asking too much. He was a leading member of society, a man with a reputation and a standing. He might take someone with a besmirched reputation as a mistress, but never as a wi—as a *friend*, Hester corrected herself hastily.

What am I thinking of? She turned and gazed into the flames, her eyes unfocused. *Because I love him, because he has been a good friend to me and has shown he is attracted to me physically, that does not mean he would have any thoughts of marriage.* When this puzzle was wound up she felt certain in her heart that he would cease to try and buy the Moon House for whatever mysterious reason motivated him. And then he would go, back to London, back to society, out of her life.

CHAPTER SEVENTEEN

Hester had enough self-perception to know when she was thoroughly blue devilled and likely to spend the rest of the day moping by the fire. And she knew that only some brisk activity or something else to concentrate upon would snap her out of the megrims. A walk was out of the question; a chill mist had descended, bringing with it a promise of frost later according to Jethro, summoning up the knowledge from the rural upbringing Hester suspected he had experienced.

After luncheon she cleaned the pane of glass rescued from the shed, mixed herself up a bowl of flour paste, cut the canvas free of its frame and with camel hair brushes set to reconstruct it. She dusted the tattered fragments of the picture and carefully laid each strip on to the glass, securing them with the paste.

Gradually the picture took shape as the portrait of a lady shown from the waist up. Her hair tumbled in unpowdered blonde curls around her bare shoulders, her gown was of leaf green satin in the elaborate style of perhaps fifty years before and around her neck was a long rope of exquisitely graded pearls matching the drops in her ears.

As the first of the pearls appeared under the gentle brush strokes Hester stopped wondering why the lady was not *en poudre* as the fashion of the time dictated and stared instead at the necklace. Could it be the same one that now lay un-strung on her dressing table? The lustre of the pearls gleamed with a glow that matched the satin, catching the green reflection of the fabric. The quality was certainly as good.

She realised her hands were trembling and took a hold on herself. This portrait was as much a focus of the blind hatred that had invaded this lovely house as the dressing room had been; of course the pearls were the same ones.

The picture built up slowly, for it was difficult to coax the fragile, brittle pieces to lie flat and to ease slashed edges devoid of paint under their neighbouring strips.

The light was fading fast as she smoothed a soft cloth over the last piece; as she did it, Susan entered, lamp in hand, ready to set a taper to the candles.

'Why, who would have thought you could have done anything with that dirty old thing, Miss Hester?' she remarked comfortably, bustling round the room. The candles lit, she came to peer over Hester's shoulder.

'Oh, my Gawd!'

'Indeed,' Hester agreed shakily, too startled by the effect of the candlelight on the completed image to reprove Susan's language.

'It's his sister, surely?' Hester could see the resemblance too plainly to enquire whose sister her maid meant. The hair colour, the modelling of the face, an indefinable *something* in the smile that played about the lady's lips—all spoke of a relationship to Guy. A close relationship.

'It cannot be his sister, Lady Broome. See how dated the gown is. I doubt it could be his mother either.' Hester tried to do calculations in her head. 'If Guy is about thirty, it means he was born in '84. This was painted when? About 1750, perhaps—and the lady is in her early twenties, which means she was born in about 1726 or '27 which would make her—' She broke off, her brow furrowed. 'In her late fifties when he was born.'

'His grandmother, then?'

'That is more likely. But see how green her eyes are, not blue like Lord Buckland's.'

'They look familiar.' It was Susan's turn to wrinkle her brow. 'No, I give up. Will you show him?'

'No.' The negative emerged with more vehemence than Hester had intended. 'Take it up to my dressing room, please, Susan, and set it up on that shelf next to the dressing table. It will be safe there. No, on second thoughts, ask Jethro to carry it, it is too unwieldy and you'll need to open doors.'

Hester hardly noticed Jethro's exclamation of surprise as he came in and carried the picture away, and certainly did not register Susan's murmured explanations and speculations as she led the way up the stairs. The portrait had affected her deeply, she realised. 'Guy,' she murmured out loud, running her fingers along the frayed edge of the empty frame as though touching his hair.

It was a glimpse into his secrets and an insight into the reasons he had not felt able to share with her for his interest in the Moon House. It began to explain why he was so determined to buy it, but it did not explain who the woman was or why she had been the focus for such hate.

Susan's shriek tore through her thoughts and she was on her feet and running for the foot of the stairs before a low-voiced stream of swear words from Jethro and Susan's furious exclamations reassured her that the two of them were safe.

'What is it?' Then she saw without having to wait for their reply. Propped up carefully against the door of her bedchamber was another bunch of dead roses, only this time their stems were caught together with a trailing bow of black satin.

'Six, of course.' She edged past Jethro, who was standing

in the middle of the landing taking up a considerable amount of room with his hands spread wide to carry the portrait, scooped up the bunch and pushed open the door. All within was exactly as she had left it.

'I do not think they came in here.' Hester opened the dressing-room door for Jethro to set his burden on the shelf.

'But how did they get into the house?' Susan demanded, checking the windows as though the 'ghost' could have scaled the front of the house in broad daylight.

'Through the front door, I suspect,' Hester said. 'I found it open when I showed Lord Buckland out. I assumed you had left it ajar when you all *tactfully* removed yourselves.'

Susan had the grace to blush, but Jethro protested, 'I know I shut it behind us—it is too cold to leave doors open.'

'Well, if this is the Nugents, no doubt they have a key and would have no trouble with an unbolted door.' Hester went to the window and looked out. It was dark now and the cold panes gave her back only her own reflection.

Then the stable-yard gate opposite opened, letting light flood out, and a rider on a black horse emerged. Hester stared. Who on earth would be riding out on this dark, freezing night? The mist had cleared and the moon was not yet up. Then the horse backed and fidgeted and was brought under immediate control as the rider, a shadow in black, bent to speak to the groom who had opened the gate. Guy, of course. His style was somehow unmistakable. But why—and where?

'Shall I go and tell his lordship?'

'No.' Hester snapped the answer. Of course, this was what Guy had meant when he said the Nugents did not have the monopoly on breaking and entering. He could be walking straight into danger.

'No. His lordship has gone out—and so must I. Jethro…' She eyed him up and down in a way that had him backing nervously towards the door, convinced that his usually immaculate clothing was all awry. 'Yes, they should fit. Go and fetch me a pair of your breeches, a thick shirt and a jacket, if you please, and then saddle up Hector. Use your saddle, not mine. Susan, please find me my riding boots, gloves, my whip and a dark shawl.'

'Saddle Hector, Miss Hester? Will he stand to be ridden?'

'So the man who sold him to me said. I shall doubtless find out. Susan?'

'You mean to ride him *astride*? What will Miss Prudhome say?'

'Nothing to any effect if she is still dozing by the drawing-room fire and you do not wake her. Now hurry and get those clothes from Jethro.'

It took perhaps twenty minutes before Hester was standing in the yard, tying the shawl around her shoulders in an attempt to find some extra warmth. Hector seemed to take being saddled well, but Jethro was still protesting.

'But, Miss Hester, you can't ride astride and how am I going to keep up?'

'I rode astride in Portugal, and you, Jethro, are staying here to look after Miss Prudhome and Susan. Now, give me a leg up.'

'Where are you going?' Susan wailed as Hester turned Hector's head to the gate and urged him into a trot.

'Winterbourne Hall.'

The trot soon turned into a walk, for the road was far too dark for her to make out more than a trace of the verge, but the cob seemed both happy to be ridden and confident to stride out in the dark. Even so, the way seemed endless and Hester was beginning to lose sense of both time and place when she reached the barn that she remembered from her visits to the Hall.

It loomed, a dark bulk beside the road, and Hector slowed, turned his head towards it and whinnied.

'Shh!' Then another horse answered from the barn. Hester slid down from the saddle and led Hector in. Sure enough there was a shape of a large, dark animal tethered inside. She tied Hector up beside it, leaving the two to exchange cautious sniffs, and made her way out.

The moon was rising, the waxing crescent bold and solid in the sky now. Hester found the entrance to the grounds and began to jog up the hard surface of the driveway, racking her brains to remember whether there were any potholes. There were. Her foot cracked a thin skin of ice on a puddle and she fell, jarring her arms and, tearing through the thin leather of her gloves, skinning her outstretched palms.

'Oh…*stay laces!*' Hester got to her feet, her hands stinging, cold wetness all down one leg, her nose and ears freezing, and contemplated sitting down on the grass and giving way to hysterics. One couldn't, of course, but the moment she got her hands on that pig-headed, arrogant, reckless man she was going to box his ears.

If, that is, she worried as she started to trudge more cautiously up the drive, *if he has not already been caught and Lewis Nugent is not enjoying himself gloating over a housebreaker.*

She had left the house, followed Guy on an impulse. Now she realised how much her boy's raiment restricted her options. She could hardly walk up to the front door and create a diversion dressed like this! Ruefully she acknowledged that she had been inspired by something akin to envy of a man's freedom to act.

The old house loomed before her, a dark shape against greater darkness. Either no one was at home or they were at the back. Where was the library in relation to the rest of the house? Hester tried to stop worrying and think. Around the back, of course. She set off, managed to find her way at the expense of only two collisions with walls and one with a tree and found herself on a gravelled terrace, which, she recalled, overlooked the gardens. Light showed from the windows sunk half below ground level—the servants' hall, no doubt. The stones crunched under her feet, the sound like musket fire in the cold, still air. She might as well march along banging a big drum.

The moonlight caught the edge of a low brick wall edging the terrace and Hester tiptoed to it, climbed up and began to balance cautiously along. She was almost level with what she thought must be the library window when a sudden flash of light from within streaked across the terrace and was gone. Someone inside was using a dark lantern.

So Guy had got in, and had done so without, apparently, being heard. Hester closed her eyes on the darkness and tried to recall what she had seen in that flash of light. *Yes*, a flagged path across the terrace.

She reached the library windows, holding her breath, and ran a hand lightly along the casements until she found one that was ajar. Within the room was dark, then she realised that the curtains must be drawn. Slowly she eased back the window until it stood wide and ran her hand down the wall below it. As she had hoped, there was a point where the brickwork stepped out. With one foot on that, both hands on the window frame and ignoring the pain in her grazed palms, Hester hauled herself up until she could straddle the opening and climb down inside.

She found herself nose to fabric with thick curtains and eased them apart. Darkness. Where was he? Perhaps this was the wrong room. Hester stopped and thought. Guy would have forced the window, climbed in and then drawn the curtains to—that was when she saw the flash of light as he checked they were closed. She assumed he would then open up the light and start his search, but there was no—

'Aargh…umph!' Her gasp of alarm was stifled as a hand clamped over her mouth and another spun her round to pinion her tight against rough frieze cloth. 'Lemmego!' she mumbled. The broad, hard chest she was tight against was unmistakeably Guy's, the scent of him was Guy, but the hard, unforgiving hands were not at all familiar in their ruthlessness.

'Be quiet.' The almost soundless whisper in her ear was an order. Hester nodded, as far as she was able, and was released. 'Are you mad?' the voice hissed.

'No, I am not, but I think you must be,' she hissed back. 'What are you going to do if you are found?'

'Run like hell—which will be a damn sight more difficult with you here, you little fool. Why *are* you here?'

'To stop you.'

'It's a bit late now.'

'Yes, I had noticed that.' It was difficult to be sarcastic in a whisper. 'Can't you open the lantern?'

'Wait there.' Hester waited for what seemed like half an hour, her ears straining to follow Guy's almost soundless progress across the room. When the dark lantern shutter was opened he was standing by the door, dropping a sofa cushion on to the floor. Then he walked back, keeping to the carpet, and motioning her into the middle of the room. Hester realised the cushions effectively blocked any glimmer of light that might escape under the door and raised an eyebrow. 'Do you do this sort of thing often?'

Guy ignored the question, and eyed Hester critically. 'What the devil are you wearing?'

'Jethro's breeches. I wasn't about to ride about the countryside side saddle. If I fell off I'd never get back on.'

Guy's critical gaze ran slowly down her body to her filthy

knees and soaked stockings. 'Your seat on a horse appears poor enough astride.'

'I fell running up the driveway,' Hester retorted furiously, fuming even more as Guy simply rolled his eyes. She kept her damaged hands carefully behind her back, unwilling to give her head for a further washing.

'We cannot do anything about that now.'

'I don't *want* you to do anything. Nothing hurts if you don't keep reminding me.' They glared at each other for a moment, then Hester whispered, 'Have you found anything yet?'

'Hardly, I've been too busy dealing with you. Where was that box you saw?'

Muttering to herself, Hester tiptoed over to the *chaise* and knelt down, trying not to wince as her knees met the floor. Apparently they were bruised too. 'Here, pushed right back with a lid on.'

Guy bent, picked up the *chaise* and moved it bodily to one side. Hester blinked, decided not to pander to male pride by showing admiration for his strength, and tried to lift the lid. 'It's locked.'

Somehow she was hardly surprised when Guy produced a bunch of spindly metal objects from his pocket and began to pick the lock.

'Where did you get those?' she hissed in his ear.

'One of my footmen has a colourful past. Shh, I'm listening.'

The lock yielded easily. Hester could not decide whether it was beginner's luck or long practice, but she was at Guy's shoulder as the lid lifted, her fingers already delving into the contents. 'Look, here's that letter.'

Guy took it and began to read while Hester delved deeper. 'Accounts for building the Moon House dated 1760, a journal for…' she squinted at the faded writing in the poor light '…July 31, 1764. *I have never felt the need to write before*

but now, now all my happiness and hope of support has—I
cannot read this word, *gone*, I think—*I will set it down, for
to whom can I*…possibly this is *confide*…yes, it is. *Darling
Allegra*… No, the rest of the pages are water-stained and mil-
dewed.'

Hester glanced at Guy, but his face was set hard and unreadable and she sensed he had erected a wall to guard his emotions. She could not ask questions, not here. Turning away, she
began to dig under what seemed to be loose sheets of accounts, a page of music and reached the bottom of the box.

'There is nothing more. No, wait.' Her fingers touched a
chain and, pulling it, revealed a locket. It flicked open under
the pressure of a fingernail and there, smiling up in the flickering light of the lantern, was the blonde lady from the slashed
portrait on one side and on the other a small child, hardly two,
all unformed chubby cheeks, a mop of blonde curls and eyes
of blue which blazed from the tiny portrait as intensely as
those of the man who lifted it slowly from Hester's lax fingers.

'This goes with me.' His voice was still a whisper, but
Hester's breath caught at the emotion in those few husky words.

'What about the letter?'

'That can go back. It is no wonder they thought there was
something of great worth within the walls of the Moon House.
It is full of references to treasure, something valued, precious,
to be kept safe and protected.'

Hester reached out and took the paper from his hand, letting her own fingertips brush across his in a silent caress. 'Do
you know it all now?' she whispered and received a nod in
return.

A twist of the picklocks and the box was shut. Hester
pushed it back carefully until it fitted its old mark on the carpet, then helped Guy position the *chaise* so it too fitted into
the dents its feet had left. She held the lantern barely open

while he retrieved the cushions, then let herself be swung down into the flowerbed while he followed her, closing the window soundlessly behind.

It seemed they were safe.

Guy clenched his teeth firmly shut and drew a long, steadying breath of freezing air in through his nose. His head was spinning with tension, concentration, fury with Hester and churning emotion over the discoveries in that box.

First things first, he told himself, keeping one hand firmly on Hester's shoulder and guiding her towards the low wall. 'Go along the wall.'

'I know,' she snapped back, low voiced. 'How do you think I got here?'

'By broomstick,' Guy muttered and was almost caught off balance as she swung round furiously to face him.

'That was unkind, unjustified—'

'Look out!' Guy seized Hester as she swayed on the wall and the terrace was suddenly lit by a flood of light from the central room facing on to it. This was more than one candle: someone had lit every light in the room and then thrown the curtains back.

Caught like an actor in the stage lights Guy froze, Hester clasped in his arms, and looked at the scene within. Lewis was standing with his back to the window, having obviously just flung back the curtains, his sister, untying the ribbons of her bonnet, was walking towards him. At any moment they would look out on to the terrace and see the figures on the wall, petrified like two statues.

CHAPTER EIGHTEEN

'Run!' he urged and Hester did, straight as an arrow, sure-footed on the narrow wall, unhesitating until she got to the end where she caught hold of a branch and swung herself quietly down on to the betraying gravel. Despite his anger with her Guy felt a wave of pride wash through him. Foolish and stubborn she might be, but Hester had courage and quick wits, which filled him with admiration.

Not, he thought grimly as he took her arm and marched her unceremoniously around the house and down the drive, *not that I am going to hesitate for one moment in turning her over my knee and tanning her backside just as soon as we are somewhere safe.*

To be afraid on his own behalf had not occurred to him; one assessed the risks, took precautions, had a strategy for escape if necessary. But to find the woman he loved careering around in the darkness, plunging herself into danger in a house occupied by people whom she knew to wish her no good—that had shaken him.

And Guy Westrope was not accustomed to being shaken, decidedly unused to people flouting his wishes and, most of all, a complete stranger to having his mind and will taken over by a brown-haired chit of a girl with golden flecks in her eyes.

They turned out on to the road and he unshuttered the 'glim', as Stuttle, the third footman, called it. The small crowbar—or 'bess', according to Stuttle—was wedged uncomfortably in the waistband of his trousers. It had proved extremely effective; Guy resolved to slip the man a half-sovereign. Besides rewarding him for his assistance, it would do no harm to keep him loyal. Men with Stuttle's skills were better on the inside than on the outside with a 'bess' in their hands.

The grim smile this thought provoked must have lingered on his lips, for as soon as they reached the barn and Hester tugged her arm free of his grip, she demanded, 'And what is so amusing?'

'Nothing whatsoever.' Guy checked on his hunter, who was nose to nose with Hector, then set the lantern down on a ledge. 'There is no humour whatsoever in a well-bred young lady galloping around the countryside, unconvincingly dressed as a boy and attempting breaking and entering.'

'I more than attempted it, I succeeded,' Hester snapped back, a not-unattractive flush colouring her cheeks. 'And the breeches are simply because I needed to be able to ride easily, I was not attempting to convince anyone I was a boy.'

'Well, that's a mercy,' Guy drawled, allowing his gaze to wander from the feminine curves filling Jethro's breeches to the angry thrust of her bosom. *God, how he longed to push her down on to that heap of hay, kiss that angry mouth with its full lower lip, caress those long, shapely, provocatively displayed limbs.*

'Why you…you rake!' Hester took an impetuous step forward, hand raised. 'How dare you ogle me like that?'

'I am merely…Hester, what have you done to your hands?' He caught her wrists, turning her hands palm up and pulling her towards the lantern, lust and anger turned instantly to concern. The cuffs of her shirt had blood and dirt on them, the gloves were shredded and grazed, cut skin showed through the tears. 'Hester.' Words would not come.

Somehow, through all the mysteries and alarms at the Moon House, he had managed to keep his apprehension for her within bounds, to be rational about it, to assess the dangers and put what precautions he could in place without giving way to his instincts to simply march in, drag her out to a carriage and drive her away somewhere safe.

But these ugly grazes on her soft skin, the way she had ignored what he knew must be painful while he had dragged her out of the house and down the drive, made his heart stop. 'Hester,' he said again, gently turning back the cuffs of the gloves and drawing them off her hands. 'Oh, my poor darling.' He lifted them, one by one, and kissed the inside of her wrists, clear of the grazes. Under his lips her pulse fluttered beneath the blue-veined skin.

'Guy?' He looked up and saw her eyes were clouded with tears.

'Sweetheart, I've hurt you, I'm sorry. And I dragged you out of there, frogmarched you down the drive, shouted at you.'

'Hissed at me, you mean.' She was smiling at him, rather mistily. 'You didn't hurt me, and I know why you were angry, it was the same reason I was so cross with you. We were frightened for each other, that was all.'

'You were frightened for me?' Holding her wrists so her hands were kept free at her sides, he drew her towards him until he could bend his head to rest his forehead against hers. On the cold air she smelt faintly of her distinctive, mossy scent. 'I love you, Hester.'

'I love you too, Guy.' The words escaped from her lips before she could recall them, before his declaration registered with her mind rather than her heart. 'You said—you said that you love me?'

'Yes. Love you, want you, desire you. I have been afraid to put it to the touch. Somehow I thought you regarded me more in the light of a friend than a husband.' His lips pressed against her forehead, her eyelids, down to her mouth.

Husband? His kiss silenced her protest, making her head spin with a sensual onslaught even as she tried to be rational, tried to think. How was it possible to move from absolute happiness to despair in the flight of a second? Could she tell him about her ruined reputation? Even if he believed her, would she ever be confident that he was not simply honouring his offer to marry her when, if he had known from the beginning, he would never have offered for her?

He must have sensed her inner turmoil, for he lifted his head, keeping her in his arms as he looked down into her face with a wry smile. 'My poor darling. I must win some sort of prize for the most wretchedly timed proposal ever. You are cold, shaken, hurt and we are standing in a filthy barn at midnight. I think I must take you home, call again and attempt to do this once more in form.'

'Guy, I cannot marry you.' The words were forced from between stiff lips, but she had to try to convince him, not let him go through a night believing she would accept him.

'I understand.' He went to check Hector's girth, then to hold the stirrup for her. 'Come, up you get before you are too chilled to sit a horse. Do you need a leg up?'

'No. What do you mean, you understand?' Bemused, Hester took the reins, then winced.

'Damn, I had forgotten your hands. Here.' Guy removed two handkerchiefs from his coat pockets and wrapped them tenderly around each palm. 'My valet believes a gentleman can never have too many clean handkerchiefs.'

Hester settled into the saddle and gathered the reins in her swathed hands. 'You have not answered my question.'

Guy reached down, picked up the lantern, blew out the light and fixed it to his saddlebow. 'I know why you feel you cannot marry me. It is of no matter; I do not regard it and neither should you. Now, come, home before Miss Prudhome sends the village constable and a search party.'

He *knew*? Hester rode automatically, her mind reeling. How could he know? Then she remembered him saying he would put investigations in train into the Nugents' finances and debts. At the same time he must have had her own background looked into. So he had known for days about the scandal and her role in John's life. But what did he know? The truth or the rumour?

Hester tried not to look at Guy's shadowy figure as he rode, one hand relaxed on his thigh, his back erect, his breath clouding the freezing air. But she could not keep her eyes off him and the heat of his kisses glowed as though she had a hot brick snuggled under her shawl.

He loves me, he wants me, wants to marry me, even though he knows about John. Hector plodded on and Hester let herself slip into a sort of contented doze on his broad back. *Where will we be married? Will his family like me? His sister sounds formidable. I will be a countess, of all the improbable things.* A little gasp of laughter escaped Hester's lips.

'What are you laughing about, my love? You are home, come now, let me help you down.' She let herself slip down into Guy's arms. Her legs really did not want to support her, it was so safe and *right* to be held close against his chest. 'Come on…' she could hear the amusement in his voice '…you are asleep on your feet, but we need to get Jethro out here to look after Hector and I need to distract my footman who most certainly must not see you coming home at this hour wearing breeches!'

'My lord, is she with you?' The back door swung open and Jethro came out, lantern in hand. 'There you are, Miss Hester! Where have you been? We've been worried sick, Miss Prudhome's had the vapours and Susan was all set to send for the village constable.'

'Miss Hester is quite safe, Ackland, although I think the sooner she's in her bed the better. Where is my man?'

Hester found herself pushed gently into Susan's arms as the maid appeared from behind Jethro, clucking with mingled anxiety and scolding. 'You're frozen, Miss Hester! You come along in, I've got the water on the range for a nice bath.'

Stumbling, Hester let herself be led inside, vaguely aware that Jethro was explaining that he'd sent a message to Parrott to keep the footman away. 'Didn't want him seeing Miss Hester coming back dressed like that, my lord.'

Susan pressed her down into a chair by the fire and went to heft a jug of water off the range. 'You just sit there a minute while I fill your bath. I don't know, what goings-on…' she muttered on her way out into the hall. By the time she had lugged three jugs upstairs Hester was hearing the scolding through a warm mist of exhaustion, but she roused herself to smile sleepily at Guy when he came into the kitchen with Jethro on his heels.

He lifted her out of the chair as easily as though she were a child and carried her through the hall. 'I seem to be making a habit of this, sweetheart,' he murmured and she turned her head into the angle of his neck with a soft sigh of agreement. 'And I have no doubt I'll be chased out of your bedchamber just as briskly this time. Which is a pity.' He lowered his voice and whispered, 'Just when I would like to stay.'

Maria met them at the bedchamber door with the predicted outraged cluckings. 'How could you allow her to do this sort of thing, my lord?' she demanded.

Guy negotiated the steaming hip bath in the middle of the

floor and lowered Hester on to the *chaise*. 'If you have any suggestions for controlling Miss Lattimer, I would be most glad to hear them, ma'am. I have so far failed to discover anything that stops her doing precisely what she wants, the minute it occurs to her. Meanwhile, might I point out that her hands require cleaning and the application of some salve.'

Guy dropped to one knee beside Hester and took her hands gently in his. 'I will send the footman over; they are overdue with the six roses.'

Hester shook her head. 'No, they were here, propped against my door and tied with black ribbon. I have not had a chance to tell you.'

His lips set into a hard line and Hester shivered, grateful that she had not done anything to earn his enmity. 'I must go tomorrow and collect my sister. I should be back by evening at the latest, my love.' Heedless of the gasp of outrage from behind him, he kissed Hester rapidly on the lips, then stood. 'Ladies, I bid you goodnight.'

There was a long silence as the sound of his booted feet echoed up from the hall, then, 'He kissed you, he called you his love! Miss Hester, are you going to *marry* Lord Buckland?'

'I am certainly not going to enter into any other sort of relationship with him,' Hester roused herself sufficiently to retort. 'Susan, please help me with these clothes or I declare I am going to fall into that bath fully clad.'

'But…does he *know*?' Miss Prudhome, who had been clutching the bedpost in shocked silence, finally found her voice.

'About the colonel? Apparently he does. Oh, that is so good.' Hester sank into the warm water, not even wincing as her grazed hands were submerged. 'So very good.'

Guy walked the short distance to the Old Manor, reins loosely grasped in one hand. 'Of all the cackhanded ways of proposing marriage, that just about takes the biscuit,' he remarked to the big horse which twitched one ear in response. 'Seems to have worked, though.' He realised he was smiling in what was no doubt a thoroughly fatuous manner and got his face under control before his groom saw him.

He handed over the reins to the man and turned on his heel to look up at the lighted bedroom window in the Moon House. His imagination conjured up the image of a naked Hester, warm and sleepy, soaping herself languorously in the hip bath before the crackling fire. Despite the cold and his own weariness the thought was powerfully arousing and he stood for a moment, his eyes fixed on the window, letting the cold sap the heat from his body before going in.

Parrott was waiting, his face expressionless. Guy wondered, not for the first time, what he would have to do to crack that composure. 'Send James over to the Moon House if you will, Parrott.'

'Yes, my lord. The study fire is lit and I have put the decanters out. Was there anything else you require, my lord?'

'No, thank you, Parrott.' *Nothing that I can have tonight, at least.* 'Was there something else?' It was unlike Parrott to lurk, but that was the only description Guy could apply to his butler.

'I was only wondering, my lord, if you will pardon the liberty, whether your lordship was intending to make any changes to the household in the light of…' The man hesitated and Guy watched, fascinated by the phenomenon of Parrott lost for a word. The butler regained his poise. 'Recent events, my lord.'

'You refer to my imminent marriage, I collect?'

'Yes, my lord. Permit me to offer my congratulations, my lord.'

'And permit me to offer mine on your perspicacity, Parrott. You are the first to know of this and I would be obliged if you would keep it secret for the time being.'

Parrott inclined his head majestically and removed himself, leaving Guy to wonder just how transparent he was being. He poured himself a glass of brandy and settled in the leather chair before the fire. No, it would not do to have talk of this marriage bandied about until he had overcome Hester's scruples. Of course she was reluctant, he knew she would be sensitive to what she might expect people to say about the daughter of a country gentleman-soldier marrying an earl.

But it made not the slightest difference to him. He loved her and that was more than enough. But he must move carefully, secure Georgy's support and, once he had that, introduce Hester to various relations whom he had confidence would welcome her into the family. Not for anything would he have his Hester feel slighted or uncomfortable in her new role.

His Hester. He felt the grin curve his lips again and then let it slowly fade as he thought of the Nugents. The locket was still in his pocket and he pulled it out, letting it spin in the firelight. He already had a score to settle with that family, one that was near fifty years old. Now he had another to add to it. Lewis Nugent was going to discover that delving into the past would bring him not treasure, but the vengeance of a man who was more than capable of protecting his own.

CHAPTER NINETEEN

An entire day at least to fill without Guy. Twenty-four hours without seeing him, without being held in his arms, without hearing that deep, flexible voice change from teasing to loving in the space of a breath.

Could he really love her? It seemed that he could and with enough passion to ignore her spotted past, ignore her relatively humble origins and make her his countess. Was it possible to be this happy and yet sit quite still, quite quiet and eat one's breakfast just as one did every morning? Hester glanced across the table at Maria, who was attempting to read the *Buckinghamshire Gazette* while disguising the fact that she was sending anxious glances at her employer.

'What is it, Maria?' Hester asked, suppressing a smile.

'His lordship has truly made you an offer?' She put down the newspaper and sighed gustily. 'It is wonderful.'

'He has indeed, and I agree, it is so wonderful I feel I must pinch myself to ensure I am waking not dreaming. I only hope I meet with the approval of his sister, Lady Broome, who sounds most formidable. She is spending Christmas with Lord Buckland, you know.'

Miss Prudhome appeared daunted. 'I do hope she will consider me a suitable chaperon for you. Oh, and what about gowns? Do you have the right gowns, for you are sure to be attending many social events in the next few weeks now, surely?'

'I suppose so.' Hester bit her underlip in thought. 'I expect Guy will wish to introduce me to various relations.' She was feeling as daunted as Maria looked. 'I think my gowns will pass muster, but I must purchase new gloves and stockings, some more evening slippers, perhaps a fur tippet—why, all manner of things, now I think of it. And I have done nothing about Christmas presents or the party we are to hold. And I am short of ready cash. Maria, I think we must make an expedition to Aylesbury tomorrow to make the acquaintance of my new bank manager and to do our shopping.'

Maria frowned. 'More roses are due then. Should we leave Susan and Jethro?'

'I am really becoming quite bored with those dratted roses,' Hester exclaimed, cutting into a piece of toast with some vigour. 'Now we know who is behind them, they no longer have any mystery. I suppose the best thing is just to give the Nugents easy access to the house so they can deposit them—it will be four this time. On the other hand, I do not want them thinking they have the run of the place. Let me think.'

Hester brooded while Maria flicked through the pages of the paper, exclaiming from time to time over snippets of news or advertisements. 'It says here that three murderers are to be hanged from the balcony of the Town Hall next Tuesday and their bodies cut down and anatomised! How frightful. Signor Olivetti, famed silhouette artist, wishes it to be known that he has established a studio in Aylesbury. A new silk warehouse advertises the fashionable and elegant silks at a price to please the most discerning lady. Oh dear, look at this, a child has lost his puppy and the parents advertise for its safe return.'

'I know! Jethro!'

Jethro appeared, green baize apron wrapped firmly round his skinny midriff, one of Hester's few pieces of good silver in his hand. 'Yes, Miss Hester?'

'Did you not say that Hector needed shoeing?' Jethro nodded. 'Very well, can you take him tomorrow, and Susan can go with you and do the marketing. Miss Prudhome and I are going into Aylesbury and I think it would be convenient to give the ghost the opportunity of an empty house to deposit the day's roses without too much trouble.'

'How will they know?'

'I intend calling in and enquiring kindly if I can carry out any little commission for Miss Nugent whilst I am in Aylesbury. I will let drop what you are doing while I am about it.'

'Driving what, Miss Hester?'

'Oh, how foolish! I never thought. Well, there is nothing for it, Jethro, you will have to go over and ask Parrott if I might borrow a horse. His lordship must have something suitable for a gig, surely?'

'Very well, Miss Hester.'

He returned ten minutes later, looking uncommonly flushed. 'Mr Parrott says that, on his lordship's behalf, he could not possibly lend us a horse for the gig as his lordship would not like you driving yourself all that way. He says he will have his lordship's second carriage and a team sent round at ten tomorrow morning, Miss Hester, with two grooms and a footman.' Jethro grinned. 'I wish I could learn the way he has of talking, Miss Hester. He said he hopes he knows what is due to your consequence, even if I do not!'

'Well! My consequence indeed!'

'Perhaps he knows,' Miss Prudhome ventured.

'Mr Parrott knows *everything*, so I expect he knows about *that*,' Jethro opined firmly, taking himself off to the kitchen to tell Susan the news.

Feeling very fine indeed, Hester found some amusement next morning at the expression on the face of the butler at the Hall when he saw the carriage, and even more at the hastily concealed expressions of surprise on Lewis and Sarah's faces as she swept in, all smiles and chatter.

'...so I thought, if you are perhaps not feeling quite yourself still, Miss Nugent, that there might be some small commission I might perform for you in Aylesbury. Embroidery silks, rouge, that sort of thing. Is it not kind of his lordship to lend me a carriage? I foolishly forgot that Jethro has to take the cob to the smithy this morning and Susan has to go marketing, so you may imagine what a boon the loan of a footman is as well.'

Five minutes later she remarked to Maria, 'That was a very fat and obvious fly to cast in front of a trout, but I do not think they suspect I know what they are up to. Now, let us look over our lists and think how to make the best of our time.'

Hester eased her hands cautiously out of her tight gloves, smoothed down the lint that protected her grazed palms and took out her tablets and pencil. 'It is a lowering thought, Maria, but shopping for presents and fripperies is a delightful way to make one forget almost everything.'

Not that any amount of list writing could drive the thought of Guy from her mind—or the worry of what to buy him for Christmas. What did a young lady buy an earl? What did one buy a man doubtless too rich to want for anything? It was too late to embroider slippers, which was one of the few unexceptional items she had once been told would be allowable as a gift to a man. Not that she could imagine Guy wearing slippers.

Her smile of pure mischief at the thought of him sitting before the fire, pretending to be at ease in a pair of embroidered slippers, faded as the picture led her imagination further, deeper, into much more disturbing byways. Guy with bare feet, Guy wearing an exotic dressing gown of heavy silk—and nothing else.

Hester felt her cheeks burning and fanned herself surreptitiously with her pocket notebook. He was so very male, frighteningly so for a young lady with no experience whatsoever, and the demanding passion of his kisses on the downs and in the barn that night promised something far beyond her experience. But not, she realised, her cheeks burning hotter, beyond her desiring. Her body responded now when she thought of him, recalled his caresses. It was as though she was aware of every inch of bare skin where it touched her clothes, of her breasts, strangely heavier and fuller, of an ache deep in her abdomen.

'This is a comfort,' Maria remarked, jolting her out of her heated imaginings. 'I was dreading the journey in a closed carriage, but this is nothing like that frightful post *chaise*. You will live in such luxury—there are so many advantages to this marriage.'

'Indeed, yes,' Hester agreed, resolutely suppressing the thought of some of them.

They arrived back from their expedition weary, satisfied and more than grateful for the attentions of the footman who had stoically marched behind them all day, gradually vanishing under a mountain of shopping.

Hester felt the day had gone well. The bank manager had been attentive; she had distracted Maria long enough to buy her a fine Paisley shawl for Christmas; a pretty dimity dress length and three yards of lace were wrapped up for Susan and she had even managed to find a copy of the book of household management that Jethro coveted.

But her idea for a present for Guy was inspired, she felt, touching the hard package in her reticule that contained a silhouette of her profile, expertly cut by Signor Olivetti.

As for stockings, gloves and slippers, she could not help but feel she had been somewhat extravagant; but, as Maria pointed out, it would not do to present an off appearance and embarrass Guy when she met his relatives.

Susan and Jethro reported a quiet day after their return from the forge. A bunch of four roses had been duly found, although it had taken some searching, Susan reported. 'They were in one of the clothes presses in your dressing room. It's taken me an age to get all that nasty crumbly dead leaf out of the linen.'

'Clever,' Hester acknowledged. 'If we hadn't been expecting them, it would have been a while before they were found and we would not have known when they were put there. I cannot but feel they are only going through the motions now. I hinted that I was unsettled enough to consider what to do after Christmas, so perhaps they will stop when they run out of roses.'

Despite her calm words, Hester feared she was being optimistic—surely the closer the waxing moon came to being full, the more dramatic the Nugents' hauntings would become. And if they were badly in need of whatever treasure they had convinced themselves was concealed within these walls, then they would want to turn her vague expressions of uneasiness into a desperate desire to sell up and leave.

What would they do when they learned of her engagement to Guy? Hester gave a little shiver of excitement at the thought of it. Would she ever become used to the knowledge that he loved her?

'Is Lord Buckland returned yet?'

Jethro shook his head. 'Mr Parrott says he does not expect him until dinner time at the earliest.'

Hester went upstairs to put away her purchases, then drifted over to the *chaise* where she could curl up and watch the road for the return of Guy's carriage. It still seemed a waking dream, one that would not be real again until he was here and holding her in his arms. Then she could talk to him, find out how her life would change as his wife, begin a lifetime of learning about the man she loved. The early winter darkness fell, still with no sign of him, and at last Hester went downstairs.

Ben Aston was in the kitchen, dumping an armload of logs into the basket beside the range. He knuckled his forehead as Hester came in and remarked that it was looking like being a powerfully cold frost that night before nodding abruptly to Susan and taking himself off through the back door.

'A man of few words,' Hester observed.

'He's chatty enough.' Susan tossed a log on to the fire. Her cheeks were red and Hester wondered what she had been cooking to keep her so close to the heat. 'Is there any sign of his lordship yet?'

'No, not yet. Susan, when I am married, I do hope you will stay on as my lady's maid.'

'Oh!' Now what was the matter with her? The girl was looking positively flustered. 'That's very kind of you, Miss Hester, but won't his lordship expect you to have a smart London dresser?'

'Then we will have to disagree upon it, because the last thing I want is a haughty dresser looking down her nose at me—I hear they are usually quite oppressively genteel.'

'What about Miss Prudhome?' Susan began busying herself with the pans of vegetables.

'I hope with Lord Buckland's connections I can find her a

good position as a companion. As for Jethro, we will have to see what his lordship can suggest.'

A knock on the front door sent her hurrying down the hall. As she had hoped, it was Guy, his breath steaming in the frosty air, his lips cold as he swept her into a kiss.

'Guy! For shame, kissing me on the doorstep—come in before half the village sees you.' But she was laughing as she said it, her heart singing as she pulled him across the threshold and closed the door behind him.

'Mmm.' He buried his face in her hair, holding her tight. 'So warm, so…edible.' His teeth were grazing wickedly down her throat, making her want to sigh and giggle all at once. 'Have you missed me?'

'So much.' Reluctantly she moved out of his embrace, ridiculously pleased when he simply turned her into the shelter of his arm and held her against him as they entered the drawing room. 'Guy, I really do have to talk to you.' It was no use simply assuming he had found out all about John— how could he know everything? It had to be discussed, for she doubted he realised the extent of the gossip about her.

'Are you going to tell me all over again that you cannot marry me?' His eyes were tender on her face and Hester found herself lost for words. It did not seem possible that he felt like this about her. 'I have to tell you, Miss Lattimer, that to kiss a man as you have just kissed me and then refuse to marry him is quite shockingly forward.'

'No, but, Guy—'

She broke off at a tap on the door and Maria peeped around it, her colour high with the embarrassment of interrupting what Hester suspected she would characterise as a *tender interlude*.

'Yes, Maria? As you see, Lord Buckland has returned safely from his journey. I should have asked you at once, my lord, did you find Lady Broome well?'

'Very well, thank you. Thoroughly revitalised by a few days of gossip and more than ready to organise my Christmas social life. She is, naturally, most eager to meet you, my love.'

Hester swallowed. 'You told her?'

'That I had met the love of my life and that she had accepted me? Yes. Georgy expressed herself gratified that I was at last settling down and amazed that I had found a lady foolish enough to take me on.'

Hester snorted, earning a cluck of censure from Miss Prudhome. 'I imagine there are any number of ladies willing to do that, my lord. Should I call tomorrow?'

'No, if I may, I will bring Georgy to call upon you. Shall we say half past ten?'

'My lord.' Maria, who had been fidgeting just inside the door, interrupted apologetically. 'Your footman has just arrived and says that Mr Parrott sends his apologies, but believes that your lordship's return to the Old Manor would be highly advisable.'

'Oh, lord! That means that Georgy has already started trying to organise Parrott—and that bids fair to be a fight to the death.' He bent and kissed Hester rapidly on the cheek. 'Until tomorrow morning, my love. Sleep well.'

Ten-thirty the next day seemed to take forever to arrive, but eventually it came, finding Hester once again waiting in the drawing room with Maria, as they had on Guy's first visit to the Moon House. Only now, Hester was gratified to know, the room was furnished in some style, a fire blazed brightly in the grate and, thanks to Ben Aston's efforts, she could tug the bell pull with absolute confidence to summon refreshments.

Hester picked up her embroidery frame with its unfinished pew kneeler and tried to set a stitch or two. *What are you worrying about?* she chided herself. *Lady Broome is Guy's sis-*

ter, she will be like him. You are certain to like her and she will become a sister and a friend.

'They are coming up the front path,' Maria whispered, as though she could be heard outside. 'Lady Broome has a prodigiously fine bonnet.'

The knocker could be heard, then a murmur of voices in the hall. Jethro, in his striped waistcoat, would be doing his very best impersonation of Parrott. Hester felt her lips relax from the stiff smile of welcome she had assumed; everything would be all right.

'Lady Broome, Miss Lattimer. Lord Buckland.'

Hester got to her feet and took a step forward, to greet the woman who would be her sister-in-law. Then she froze. Walking towards her was the woman from the slashed portrait—modern bonnet and furs did nothing to hide the perfect resemblance. Hester found the words of welcome drying up in her throat and felt the blood ebbing out of her cheeks before she collected herself. Of course, she had seen the resemblance to Guy—in a woman the likeness would be even more pronounced. But she could see from Guy's expression that her shocked reaction must be noticeable and he stepped forward to retrieve the situation, directing a reassuring smile towards Hester.

'Georgiana, allow me to introduce Miss Lattimer. Hester, this is my sister, Lady Broome.'

Lady Broome was staring at her, stony faced, her wide blue eyes, so like Guy's, fixed on Hester's face. 'Miss Lattimer? Late of Mount Street and the household of Colonel Sir John Norton?'

The floor seemed to shake under Hester's feet and behind her she heard Maria's gasp. She could not move her eyes from the accusing blue ones in front of her, could not look at Guy. *But he said he knew*—why did he not then speak?

The silence seemed to stretch on for minutes until Hester found her voice. 'Yes, I did reside in Sir John's house in Mount Street.'

'I thought I recognised the name,' Lady Broome said grimly. 'But I could not believe my brother would so debase the family name by offering marriage to a kept woman.'

'What?'

Hester dragged her eyes away from her accuser and stammered, 'You said you knew. I tried to tell you and you said you knew.' Guy's face was rigid, but there was something in his eyes that she did not recognise and which filled her with dread.

'No, I did not know,' he said softly, 'and I did not guess.'

'How should you have?' Lady Broome demanded, her colour high. 'I would never have suspected if my friend Mrs Norton had not pointed her out to me as the hussy who insinuated herself into the colonel's home and his bed and caused such an estrangement between him and his family. Butter would not melt in her mouth to look at her.'

Hester kept her eyes fixed on Guy. To look away, to let herself listen to his sister, would be to let her world spin out of control, to shatter into nothing. If he did not trust her, then nothing mattered.

'Hester—*why*? Tell me. Why were you his mistress?'

It seemed the worst had happened and somehow she was still standing there and the room was still as it was. But the shock and the pain were being replaced—no, she realised, not replaced, drowned—by a rush of anger so intense she thought for a moment she could not speak.

'This is unjust, untrue!' Miss Prudhome, red blotches disfiguring her sallow cheeks, took a step forward and confronted Lady Broome. 'You do not know—'

'Thank you, Maria, that will do! Kindly ring for Ackland. Lady Broome, you are correct, my living with Sir John did cause a rift with his family, which lasted until his death. Lord Buckland, while I was ready to lay before you the truth of my relationship with Colonel Norton, I am most certainly not now going to justify myself to a man who is prepared to protest his love for me, but who does not trust me.' The door opened and she cut across the words Guy was beginning to speak.

'Ackland, please show Lady Broome and Lord Buckland out. I am not at home to either of them at any time in the future.' Ignoring Guy's hand outstretched to stop her, Hester swept out of the room, past a startled Jethro and up the stairs to her room. She shut the door and turned the key, leaning back against it until the muffled sounds from the hall below died away.

Someone was tapping on the door. 'Hester dear, let me in.'

'No, Maria, not now. Leave me alone.'

'Please, Hester.'

'No.'

Footsteps pattered off down the landing and all was silent again. So it had happened. She had been right to believe her happiness could not last, right to tell herself that she had no future other than as a single woman. He had believed what his sister had said; not even protested, only asked her flatly, *why?*

The anger that had taken her out of the room and had given her strength to climb the stairs ebbed as fast as it had come, leaving her legs unsteady. Hester sank down on to the bed, wondering that this pain could be as sharp, as physical as the pain of bereavement. But of course, it was a death, the death of love and trust.

Suddenly the tears came and she curled up on the bed and wept. *Guy, oh, Guy, I love you, I do love you.*

She must have fallen asleep. Several times there had been a scratching at the door, the soft, anxious voices of Susan and

Maria, but she had buried her face in the damp pillow and shut them out. Now it was night. Hester sat up, pushing the hair back out of her face and looked around her. The room was full of a chill, pure light. Unsteadily she went to the *chaise* where she could look out at the moon.

Its full orb cut only by the merest sliver of darkness, it glowed cold and white and serene, touching the frosted darkness below with an edge of silver. So beautiful, so cold, so utterly uncaring. *I love him*, Hester murmured, resting her hand on the icy glass as though to touch the circle of white through the pane. *He said he loved me, but he does not trust me and now he never can.*

CHAPTER TWENTY

'Guy, I am so sorry, but the shock of seeing her—and she must have recognised me as a friend of Anne Norton's. Did you see the expression of guilt on her face when I walked in?'

'I saw a woman who looked as though she had seen a ghost, not one who had a guilty secret.' Guy held the front door open for Georgy and shut his lips tight as Parrott came forward to take their coats. 'We will be in the library, Parrott, and do not wish to be disturbed.'

He shut the door behind them and leaned back against it, unconsciously echoing Hester's own movements. 'I am a bloody fool.' This was hurting, damnably, but it was hurting Hester a sight more, of that he was certain.

'You cannot blame yourself for being taken in.' His sister, a handsome woman in her mid-thirties, came and took his arm, urging him towards a chair. Guy cooperated, too intent on his thoughts to resist. 'She looks so respectable, so well bred.'

'I was not taken in, and she is all you have just said. I should learn to think before I speak. Georgy, I have kissed her, held her in my arms, and if Hester Lattimer is not a virgin then I am the Prince Regent.' He had made his sister blush, he saw with a kind of bitter amusement.

'But perhaps she is a very good actress. Mrs Norton said—'

'How well do you know Mrs Norton?'

'Well enough, for acquaintances.'

'And had she any expectations from the colonel? Something that his relationship, whatever it was, with Hester could have jeopardised?'

'I do not know.' Georgiana sat silent, her lower lip caught between her teeth. Guy regarded the fire and wondered if there was any way in which he could have handled that scene any worse. Probably not.

'They were cousins,' Georgy said suddenly. 'And he was unmarried. I think her son must have been his heir. You think that was it?' She looked at him, eyes wide and anxious. 'Have I made a terrible mistake?'

'No, you have made an understandable mistake, my dear. I have made one which might be unforgivable. Will you excuse me? I think if I do not go out and ride hard and long I will yield to the temptation to go right back across to the Moon House and that will probably make things a hundred times worse.'

'Can you make it better?' Georgy was watching him with a troubled expression quite unlike her normal confidence.

'I do not know. I only know that I love her, and that is suddenly not enough.'

He took a hunter from the stables and rode, as he had promised, both hard and long. Riding blind he found himself up on the downs where he had held Hester in his arms and where she had reacted with what, he now realised, was understandable revulsion to her suspicion that he was offering her a *carte blanche*. Then on, along the crest of the hills in the teeth of the bitter wind until at last he dropped down again, through the beech woods to a village whose name he did not trouble to ask.

An inn called the Valiant Trooper furnished him with punch

and bread and cheese and left him undisturbed by the blazing fire while the day lengthened and the sky became darker. At last, Guy stood up and stretched. He had a plan, of sorts, he had his bitter anger at himself under control and he had some hope. Hope that Hester loved him as much as he thought she might, hope that her anger and bitter sense of betrayal was a measure of just how much.

As he settled up the tapster pointed out the pike road that led to Winterbourne and Guy rode back through the gathering darkness to the gates of the Moon House.

Some instinct made him look up and there, lit faintly by a candle, he could see Hester, her head bowed, one hand resting splayed against the glass as though to touch the moon that was reflected there.

'Hester, I love you. I will make it right, I promise you.'

'My lord?' A groom was swinging the gates open.

'What? Oh, nothing, just thinking aloud. Thank you, Wilkins. Give him a good rub down and extra oats, he's done well today.'

Hester came down to breakfast the next morning filled with a kind of bitter energy that cowed her household into silence. As she met their anxious eyes her resolve almost faltered, then she took a deep breath and sat down. 'I am not going to discuss what happened yesterday. You all know the truth, but I forbid you to offer any kind of explanation to Lord Buckland or his sister. You will not speak or have any kind of communication with them. Neither they, nor any of their servants, will set foot in this house. Do I make myself plain?'

'But, Hester, if he knew the truth…' Maria faltered with what Hester realised was considerable courage. Explaining felt like running a knife into her heart, but she knew she owed them that.

'If I, or you, tell him the truth, how will I ever know he trusts me? If he cannot tell what and who I am, then I do not want him, or his love.'

'Bastard,' Jethro muttered, his face red with emotion. Hester could tell he was close to tears.

'I am sorry, we will have to find you another mentor in place of Mr Parrott,' she said gently.

'I don't care. If he works for *him*, I don't want his advice, not no how.'

Silence fell, broken only by Susan mechanically lifting eggs out of the skillet on to a plate and Miss Prudhome tearfully making tea.

'Are we going to move away?' Susan ventured at last as they sat down and began to eat. Hester found that she could. It seemed that hunger, or at least hunger stimulated by the smell of frying bacon, could overcome even a broken heart. From somewhere a small, twisted gleam of humour tried to raise its head.

'What? Cut and run? I think not. We have a party to prepare for and most of the gentry for two miles around invited to it. There will be two fewer guests than I had planned upon; we will not regard that.' She looked around at their startled faces. 'I have done nothing wrong. I do not intend skulking off like a pariah, especially after I have offered hospitality to friends.'

'And to the Nugents,' Susan reminded her. 'Lord Buckland had a plan to send them rightabouts. What about that?'

The pain that lanced through her at the mention of his name took Hester by surprise. For a moment she could not reply. 'I can do nothing about that. All I can hope is to show them a confident face. Surely they will know soon enough they cannot scare me away?'

'There are two roses due tonight,' Susan pointed out. The

others began immediately to discuss what was to be done, a babble of voices that Hester realised was due to relief at not having to talk, or think, about her ruined romance.

She shrugged. 'Let them deliver them. Unless they attach a gunpowder charge to them, what harm will it do?' At the moment she would almost welcome it. Then pride took over and she straightened her back. She had lived through bereavement, insecurity, scandal and opprobrium—one man and his lack of trust, his failure of love, was not going to defeat her now.

'It's the full moon.' Susan sounded uneasy.

'Well, if Death stalks the house with a scythe, you will just have to take to him with the poker,' Hester said, realising that she had almost shocked them by making the feeble joke. 'I am not such a poor honey as to be cast down by one man,' she said, trying to convince herself. 'And we are not going to be terrorised by two greedy people. Now, let us make some toast because I warn you, we are going to have a busy day today and this afternoon I am going to go for a drive.'

'*What?*' Maria gaped at her like a stranded fish. 'Drive out after what happened yesterday?'

'You think I should skulk inside like a shamed woman? We will make lists, clean the house and plan our entertainment. There are only three days and one of them is Sunday.'

Physical hard work was a therapy, Hester realised as she chivvied Maria and Susan about the house with beeswax polish, long feather dusters and black lead. For minutes at a time she could focus only upon removing every last dull patch from the drawing-room fender or vigorously scrubbing at the window panes with scrunched-up brown paper and vinegar. But then, just when she least expected it, a memory would hit her: the scent of Guy's skin, the feel of his hair under her seeking fingers, the heat of his mouth on her breast, his words of love, his words of doubt and distrust.

Then the pain lanced through her as though she had been stabbed and she was hard put not to cry out, stopping what she was doing to push her clenched fist hard against her stomach as if to crush the pain out of existence. A strong woman, a woman of resolution and pride, would dismiss him as unworthy of her. 'But I love him,' Hester murmured to herself. 'I love him.'

Over luncheon they made lists, argued about the food and drink they would need and debated whether it would be possible to buy sheet music in Tring or whether a trip on Saturday to Aylesbury would be necessary.

'Had we better not try the piano?' Miss Prudhome ventured. 'I do not think it has been played since we arrived.'

A few minutes later Hester grimaced at the sound and agreed that a piano tuner had best be summoned as soon as may be. 'Add that to the list for Tring tomorrow,' she decided. 'He can come on Monday. Now, I am going for a drive. Jethro, please harness Hector. Who would like to come with me?'

'I will.' They all spoke at once and Hester could have hugged them all. How would she be coping if she did not have friends and loyal supporters like this?

'I will,' Jethro said firmly. 'I will bring the gig round to the front, Miss Hester. Mr Parrott may not think I know what is due to your position, but I do.' He stalked off, looking determined, and Hester went upstairs to change into a walking dress and find her warmest coat, bonnet and muff.

She hesitated over a bonnet with a veil, the one she usually wore to church, then tossed it aside in favour of a frivolous confection in green velvet she had not considered suitable for the country. Guy would probably neither know, nor care, what she looked like, but it was suddenly very important to defy him, his sister, and, in spirit, those judgmental gossips who had dragged her name through the mire in London.

Jethro had drawn the gig up before the front gate and was sitting there in his best greatcoat, cockaded hat gleaming, whip cocked at a stylish angle. When Hester came out he jumped down and helped her up with ceremony before handing her the reins and sitting upright, arms folded and with an expression of great solemnity on his face.

Hester did not know whether to laugh or cry. In Jethro's mind he was sitting on the box of the most fashionable barouche in Piccadilly and his mistress was the equal of the cream of the *ton*. Impulsively she leaned over and kissed him on the cheek. 'Jethro, I have never regretted for an instant bringing you home that day. It was one of the best things I ever did. I hope you realise that.'

His Adam's apple bobbed frantically with his efforts to keep some sort of control. When he spoke his voice cracked as though it was breaking all over again. 'And I love you, Miss Hester, and I want to kill anyone who hurts you.'

'Please don't, Jethro, I need you too much to see you hanged. Now, I had better drive on before we both disgrace ourselves on the public highway.'

The air was crisp and frosty and, if one was in the mood, it was a delightful afternoon for a short drive. For Hester it was like stepping into a crowded room wearing a placard reading 'Fallen Woman'. What if Lady Broome had already spread the news of her disgrace around the neighbourhood? Or perhaps she had not yet made the acquaintance of local society and this was the last time Hester could go out with her reputation intact.

She saw Mrs Bunting being driven in her dog cart by her groom and the two carriages drew up alongside to exchange greetings. The vicar's wife beamed at her and Hester found she had been holding her breath. 'Good day, Miss Lattimer! I must tell you that the vicar and I are much looking forward to your evening party on Monday. Such a pleasant way to begin the Christmas festivities.'

'I'm so glad, ma'am.' Hester managed to smile and drove on, a new dread forming. What if they all found out before the party and she did not discover it until she found herself with no guests? *I'm mad to persist with this, they'll find out sooner or later, I must leave...*

She almost completed her circuit of the Green, then, at random, took one of the side lanes. Rounding a corner, she had to rein in sharply to avoid a little group standing almost in the middle of the roadway. Mrs and Miss Redland were in conversation with Guy and Lady Broome.

There was no escape short of turning the gig in the narrow lane in front of their eyes. Hester looked only at Mrs Redland and could not suppress a gasp of relief as she stepped forward with a smile.

'My dear Miss Lattimer, how are you?'

'Very well, ma'am.' Somehow Hester got enough breath back to respond. She could feel the eyes of the others burning into her like a brand. 'I must not keep you standing here in the cold; I am looking forward to seeing you on Monday.' She raised her whip in what she hoped Mrs Redland would interpret as a general leavetaking of the group and trotted on.

'Phew.' Jethro sent her a sideways glance as soon as they were safely around the corner. 'Do you think they'll say anything to her?'

'I don't know. I don't think Lord Buckland would, even if he is *very* angry with me. But Lady Broome may feel it her duty.'

'Then she's a nasty, interfering old cat,' Jethro said with some vehemence. 'Will it not look strange that they are not at the party?'

'Very, I fear. That in itself may be enough to start talk.' It was easier to discuss the party, with all its uncertainties, than to think about that glimpse of Guy. She wanted to go back, jump down from the gig and throw herself into his arms, say, *You are wrong about me, let me explain.* But if he believed that she had been another man's mistress and had been prepared to hide that from him, he simply did not feel for her as she thought he did. And that was an end to it.

Guy had spent hours following the confrontation between Hester and Georgiana in a state of indecision such as he had never experienced before. He had hurt Hester abominably, he knew that. It took him some time to face the fact that she had hurt him by not telling him the truth, and then longer yet admitting to himself that he had stopped her when she had tried to explain.

I love her, none of it matters. But it did matter, it was not a little thing; and the scandal it would cause in London if he married her was no little thing either. Going to her until he was clear about what he had to say would only make things worse and that glimpse of her, chin high, the colour flying in her cheeks as she came upon them in the lane, haunted him.

Then there was the problem of the roses. He checked his almanac: tonight was the full moon. Two roses were due and heaven knew what else. He rang for Parrott.

'Parrott.'

'Yes, my lord?' Parrott enquired after a good minute of silence.

'I am not, at the moment, on speaking terms with Miss Lattimer.'

'So I gather, my lord.'

How the hell does he know? Then Guy dismissed the question: Parrott knew everything. 'I am concerned about the safety of her household.'

'Quite so, my lord. The last two roses are due tonight.'

'Exactly.' Sometimes Guy wondered if it would be easier just to allow Parrott to carry on without orders. Possibly he could do his courting for him. He could hardly make more of a mull of it.

'I have already spoken to Ackland, my lord. He informed me that his orders were not to communicate with anyone in this household and certainly not to accept any assistance.'

With that he had to be content, although a near-sleepless night spent sitting at his bedchamber window watching the Moon House for any sign of disturbance or lights did nothing for his state of mind the next morning.

Parrott, who was winding the longcase clock in the hall and setting the hands to twenty-five to seven, allowed one eyebrow to rise by an infinitesimal amount when he saw his master descending the stairs. 'Good morning, my lord. I regret that preparations for breakfast have only just been commenced. Would you wish me to have something prepared immediately?'

'Hmm? No, thank you, Parrott. I will go out for a walk.'

'And then call upon Miss Lattimer?'

'If I can think what best to say to her, yes, Parrott. I got the devil's own sleep last night.'

'The lady is somewhat up in the boughs, I collect.'

'You may well say so, Parrott. Miss Lattimer has a number of things to throw in my dish, of which tactlessness is probably the least of it.'

'But surely you will not be calling at this hour?'

'I imagine it will take me two hours to arrive at my tactics.' Guy grimaced with an attempt at humour he was far from feeling. Somehow he had to make it up to Hester. 'I have no idea what I am going to say. If she has been as miserable as I these past forty-eight hours, then perhaps I have a hope—but who knows?'

'Tsk. Miss Lattimer has always seemed a lady of acute common sense to me, my lord.'

'Exactly what I am afraid of!'

'I will find your lordship's heavier coat; it will not do to arrive upon her doorstep with your teeth chattering.'

Guy walked out of the gate into the frosty early morning gloom and turned to pass the front of the Moon House, heading for the expanse of the Green. An hour's brisk walk to the canal and back, followed by breakfast at the Bird in Hand, which he could eat without interrogation from Georgy, should at least clear his head.

He looked up at Hester's room as he passed, seeing it in darkness, wondering what her reaction would be if he stood in the garden like a lovesick fool—*which I am*—and threw pebbles at her windows. 'A jug of cold water off the nightstand, I imagine, if I know my Hester,' he answered his own musings.

Then something fluttering on the front door caught his eye and he slowed. A Christmas garland? That boded well for the mood of the household if someone had spent the time making decorations. Then, as he came closer, he saw it had no festive air about it, but instead hung heavy and dark, its ribbons black.

Surely it was not what it appeared? It was the lack of light, that was all, but Guy opened the gate and strode up the front path.

Then he saw it was a funeral wreath fashioned of yew and ivy, tied with black ribbons and with two dead roses at its centre. A card, inscribed *H.L. Requiat in Pace* in Gothic script was secured at the top. Fear for Hester, a superstitious dread he would have sworn he was incapable of feeling, swept through him, leaving an icy clutch around his heart. *A knife in the dark? A soundless attack on Hester, leaving the household unaware? Or poison and they were all lying there...*

With hands that shook he wrenched the wreath from the

door and hammered the knocker on its base plate. Ten more seconds and he would break a window.

There was a fumbling sound as the bolts were drawn back. Jethro opened the door, saw who it was and began to close it, alarm on his face. Guy simply threw his shoulder against the panels and knocked the boy back into the hall with the power of his entry. 'Where is she? Is she safe?'

CHAPTER TWENTY-ONE

'You cannot come in here, my lord!' Jethro was white-faced and clutching his shoulder. In some part of his brain Guy realised he must have hit the boy's bad side and was sorry for it, but that would have to wait.

'Have you seen Miss Hester yet this morning? Is she awake?'

'What? Do you know what time it is?' Jethro demanded, shocked out of any semblance of good manners or deference by surprise and pain. 'Of course she's not up yet, Susan said to let her sleep in.'

The door from the kitchen opened and Susan appeared, looking irritated. 'Jethro, what's this racket? You'll wake Miss Hester and she needs all the sleep she can— You! Miss Hester said as how we weren't to let you in, nor even speak to you, my lord. What can you be wanting at this hour?'

'This was hanging on the front door.' He thrust the wreath at them. 'See? That says "H.L. Rest in Peace".' He was taking the stairs two at a time before they caught his meaning and began to run after him.

'Oh, no,' Susan was repeating over and over. 'Oh, no, no one could have got in last night…'

Ignoring them, Guy threw open the door of Hester's bedchamber and crossed to the bed in two long strides. She was lying on her back, eyes shut, one arm flung back on the pillow, her face pale. For a second that seemed to last a year he thought she was not breathing, then she drew a long breath and stirred. Her eyes flickered open, blinked and she gasped when she saw who was looking down at her.

'No!' She scrambled back against the pillows. 'No!' She covered her eyes with her hands and shook her head violently. 'This is a dream, I'm going mad.'

'No, no, you are not.' Guy rounded on Susan and Jethro, who were wringing their hands in the doorway. 'Out!' He took a step towards them and they jumped back instinctively, giving him time to slam the door shut and turn the key in the lock. He had enough to do to cope with his emotions over Hester, let alone listen to their exclamations.

Ignoring the pounding on the door and the rattling of the handle, he turned back to Hester, who was wide awake and sitting bolt upright in bed. Her eyes were wide, her hair streamed down her back and her body was clad only in the flimsiest of nightgowns.

It raised no feeling of desire in him, only a horror at how fragile she looked, how white her skin, how delicate her shoulders and arms seemed. He had thought he had lost her and fury swept through him, anger with the Nugents, anger with himself for not protecting her better, anger at her for making him feel this way. It silenced him and he filled the empty space by stooping to touch a taper to the smouldering fire in the grate and light the candles.

'I thought you were a nightmare.' Her voice shook and she got it back under control; he realised her anger matched his, although it was much simpler, much more justified. 'What possible reason can you have for bursting in here like this? Let my people in this minute.'

'There was a wreath on your door. A funeral wreath. It said "H.L. Rest in Peace".' There was silence while she absorbed it, then went pale.

'But we are all right. No one got in last night. Why should you leap to conclusions?'

'*Leap?* After what has been happening here? I thought I would find you all poisoned in your beds.' He was pacing angrily, fighting the urge to go and shake her until she admitted he was right to be frantic about her. Hester swung her legs out of bed and stalked over to confront him, quite unconscious of the transparency of her nightgown. A wave of desire lanced through the anger. It didn't help.

'What nonsense,' she declared scornfully. 'No one could poison our food.'

'No? Where does Susan keep your milk and butter and cheese to make sure it is cold? Where is your meat safe? In that lean-to by the back door, that is where, and if I know that you may be sure half the village knows, let alone anyone putting their mind to doing you harm.' He kept his eyes locked with hers, if nothing else it kept them away from the tantalising rise and fall of her breasts, the shadow of the nipples through the fine lawn. He recognised the primitive source of his anger even as he chose to ignore it—this was *his* woman, he would fight to the death for her and he wanted nothing more than to make love to her when he had done so.

'Could you not have sent Susan upstairs to check on Miss Prudhome and me?' she enquired, her voice sinking to a dangerously reasonable level. 'Why all these dramatics?'

Guy could feel his teeth grinding. 'Because I was frantic with worry about you, that is why.'

'Indeed?' She was positively icy now. 'You have no justification, no business, to be concerned about me.' She glanced down, realised what she was wearing and coloured, turning away.

'Hester, I asked you to be my wife.'

'Yes, you did,' she agreed, pulling on her dressing gown and making rather a business of tying the cord before turning back to him. 'However, now you are aware I am another man's leavings, that is irrelevant.'

'I do not want *another man's leavings*,' he snarled in savage echo of her words. As soon as he spoke he knew it had not sounded as he meant it.

'Quite.' Hester was white with anger now. 'You made that abundantly clear the other day, it is unnecessary to repeat it.'

The thud at the window made Hester start and Guy swing round with an oath. Against the lightening sky, Jethro could be seen peering in through the window. He banged on it.

With an exclamation Hester brushed past Guy and dragged up the lower casement. 'It is all right, Jethro, you can climb down. Oh! Be careful!'

There was a cry from Jethro and the sound of the ladder hitting the flags below. Grimly the youth scrambled over the window ledge with Hester tugging on his jacket. With a darkling look at Guy, he stalked over to the door, turned the key and opened it. Miss Prudhome was on the threshold, poker in hand, Susan at her shoulder.

'Monster!' she declaimed, entering dramatically, an effect somewhat marred by curl papers and a red flannel dressing gown.

Guy made a desperate attempt to find his sense of humour and removed the poker from her grip. 'Now, Miss Prudhome, we have been all through this before, have we not, on the night I slept in the drawing room—and with the poker too?' She glared at him. 'And we established then that I am not a monster and I am not here to ravish Miss Lattimer.' He waited and was rewarded by a grudging nod.

'Good. Now, I freely admit that this is very early in the morning and I should not be in Miss Lattimer's bedchamber, but I was very concerned about her. I also admit,' he got in rapidly as she opened her mouth, 'we were having a blazing row, which is not something that a gentleman should be doing with a lady under any circumstances, so I will remove myself and wait downstairs until Miss Lattimer recovers the tone of her spirits and we can continue our discussion in more acceptable surroundings.'

He was halfway out of the door before Hester flared, 'I have nothing to speak to you about, my lord.'

Guy turned back. 'There is the party.'

'That is no concern of yours.' God, she looked lovely, her colour high, her bosom heaving, her eyes flashing. All the anger drained away, leaving nothing but pure, aching desire.

'We agreed to trap the Nugents, did we not? Have you forgotten they could have killed Jethro in that fall down the stairs? I will wait downstairs.'

Hester stared at the closed door until Susan said, 'Shall I fetch your water now, Miss Hester?'

'Oh, what? I am sorry, I forgot you were there. Yes, please, Susan.'

She was standing there when the maid came back with the steaming jug. 'He's still in love with you, you know,' Susan observed, pouring the water. 'Come along now, do, Miss Hester or he'll come up here again looking for you.'

'Yes.' Hester untied her robe and began to wash. Everything felt rather numb. 'It isn't as easy to fall out of love as people say. I can't fall out of love with him just because he hurt me, and perhaps he can't fall out of love with me just because he thinks I was a kept woman and a trollop.' She rubbed her face with the towel. 'I expect he'll manage it soon enough.'

'But why not try again?' Susan demanded, shaking out a petticoat.

'What, with a man whose first reaction on hearing his betrothed accused of being an Impure is not to refuse to believe it, not to defend her, but to ask *why*?'

But, oh, she did still love him, did still want him so very, very badly. What would she have done if he had taken her in his arms just now and kissed her? Struggled? Perhaps not. It was a mortifying thought, but then she had seen the desire in his eyes. It had burned hot, hotter than she had ever seen, and yet he had been quite capable of not acting upon it. But of course, he would not want to touch *another man's leavings*.

Buoyed up by angry pride, Hester came downstairs and found Guy standing in the kitchen with Jethro rather stiffly laying the table for five and Maria rattling pans on the stove.

'I thought a council of war over breakfast might be a good idea.'

'Indeed? I am sure you would be more comfortable in your own dining room. May I help you with anything, Maria?'

'I have a great deal to do today that depends upon your agreement, and would prefer an early start.' Frustrated by Maria, who was hastily disclaiming any need for assistance and able to see that Guy might have a point, Hester sat down and waited with what composure she could muster.

Guy took the chair at the other end of the table and watched her steadily from blue eyes that seemed shadowed, perhaps by sleeplessness. *Poor darling.* She wanted to go to him, smooth her fingers over his brow and temple, pull his head back until it rested on her breast and kiss away that expression. What was he thinking? That he wanted this over and done so he could leave and forget her?

And what would he want to do about the Moon House once the Nugents were dealt with? His sister had delivered the perfect way to make her sell it to him. Once the word was round in the village about her reputation, she would have no option but to leave.

At last they were all seated. Hester found she was ravenous, tried to remember what she had eaten for dinner and failed. It seemed losing one's temper had an invigorating effect on one's appetite. She took a sip of coffee and decided that attack was the best defence.

'You are assuming there will be a party, my lord.'

'You no longer wish to hold it? It will be the safest way to deal with the Nugents, you know.'

'I may wish to hold it, but if my neighbours stay away in droves then it will be pointless.'

He picked up her meaning without her having to spell it out. 'Georgiana has said nothing to anyone about your previous life.'

Ignoring Maria's muttered 'So I should hope', Hester swallowed hard. The intense relief made her feel quite dizzy, but it would not do to show her emotions. She raised an eyebrow.

'I assume she will not be attending?' She half-hoped to goad him, but she was not succeeding.

'My sister will not be among your guests, that is for sure, and in fact, although she has met Mrs Redland and Mrs Bunting, she is unlikely to go about much in the next few days. She will probably miss church tomorrow, a fact that will lend conviction to my explanation on Monday that she is suffering from a severe head cold.'

'I see.' Hester tried to hide her intense relief. It was going to be hateful enough to have to entertain a house full of guests while pretending to be on good terms with Guy without having his sister there, regarding her as a fallen woman. But doubtless she had refused to cross the threshold and Guy simply did not wish to say so.

'What is your plan, my lord?' Maria enquired frostily.

'Some of it I can tell you all now, some I will only tell Susan and Jethro because on your reaction, Hester—and yours, Miss Prudhome—much of the success of this scheme lies. I want you to be as surprised and mystified as any of the guests.

'Now, I will bring two other gentlemen with me. They will be strangers to you, and, I hope, to all the guests. Please accept them as though they were friends of mine you had kindly invited.'

'Very well.' Hester nodded her agreement, deciding that to try to second guess any of this would only reduce the element of surprise. She felt more comfortable with Guy now, and tried to stiffen her resolution. It would do no good to let down her guard, forget what had happened.

'I imagine you will be using both front rooms and one of the bedrooms for cloaks.'

'Yes. I was going to lay out a buffet in the dining room with the table against the wall and chairs and little tables scattered around. Then more chairs in the drawing room. All the surplus furniture except the piano will have to go out in the sheds. Will you lend me chairs?' She had been worrying about how she was to manage, having cut herself off from Guy's practical help, and had decided she would have to approach Mrs Bunting for the loan of chairs and china.

'Yes. Ackland, speak to Parrott about whatever you need— chairs, tables, china and glass. You can use the Old Manor kitchens as well if that will help. I need to take up quite a bit of room in yours.'

'But what for? A squad of Bow Street Runners?'

'That is a thought.' The smile Guy sent her was one of affectionate amusement and she found herself smiling back until they both realised what was happening. Guy's face became impassive, Hester coughed and poured herself some more coffee. 'Now, I imagine the earlier part of the evening will be simply social mingling with people eating, then carols and festive songs around the piano?'

'Yes, that was my intention.'

'After a few songs one of my friends will begin to speak of ghost stories and how telling them is another Christmas tradition. When that happens, simply follow my lead. Someone will suggest we repair to the kitchen—fall in with whatever I, or my friends, suggest.'

'Very well.' It seemed he was taking over her home and her party with his typical assumption of authority and she had nothing to say to it. Well, if it cooked the Nugents' goose and served to hasten his own departure from the village, so much the better.

'If there is nothing else you would like to eat, my lord?' Anger also appeared to have sharpened Guy's appetite—the platter was bare. 'I am sure we have at least some bread remaining if you would like toast and preserves?'

One eyebrow quirked at the sarcasm in her voice. 'I would not dream of inconveniencing you, Miss Lattimer, and will take my leave. An excellent meal, Miss Prudhome; you are a notable cook, if I may say so.'

Maria simpered, recalled that she was out of all measure cross with him, and turned the gesture into a sniff. Guy crossed to the door and then turned back as a thought struck him. 'If you see the Nugents in church tomorrow it will do no harm to repeat your unease with the house. If you can think up some manifestation other than what we know they are responsible for, something to suggest to them that they have…awoken something, that would be useful. But nothing definite, just vague impressions.'

Hester began to gain an inkling of what he was about. 'I will think of something.'

'I will warn Parrott to place my household at Ackland's disposal from first thing on Monday, then.' He smiled fleetingly and was gone.

'Mr Parrott putting his household at *my* disposal!' Jethro considered this glorious prospect. 'Me! If that don't bear the bell, I don't know what would.'

'You had better begin to make lists, Jethro,' Hester suggested drily. 'It would never do to let Parrott find you unprepared or indecisive.'

Saturday passed strangely, a mixture of list-making, marketing, planning and moments when she felt all alone in the midst of her household, as though cut off by thick glass or swirling snow from reality. Then all she could think about was Guy, his words, his anger, his desire. And knew she was never, ever, going to be free of loving him.

Sunday dawned fair and frosty and the household were rosy with cold and rather breathless from walking fast when they arrived at church. For several minutes Hester was worried that the Nugents would not be attending, but they came in, just reaching their pew as the organist struck up and the choirboys trooped in.

In the Old Manor pew Hester could make out the crown of an impressive green velvet bonnet with plumes beside Guy's dark head. Lady Broome had come to church after all. Hester felt herself sliding lower on her seat as though to bring her own head below the level of the panelling, then caught herself and sat up straight. *I have done nothing to be ashamed*

of, whatever she thinks. But it was not Lady Broome's opinion that mattered, only Guy's.

'Let us pray.' Obediently Hester knelt, fixed her mind on
what Mr Bunting was saying and tried to forget her sore heart.

She timed her exit from the church with care and was relieved to see Guy helping his sister up into the carriage. Lady
Broome was heavily veiled and, as Hester watched, lifted the
gauze slightly to press a handkerchief to her nose. Setting the
scene for her head cold tomorrow night, no doubt.

The Nugents, having arrived in a rush, now seemed more
relaxed and both brother and sister turned to Hester and Miss
Prudhome as they approached.

'We are looking forward to your party very much, Miss
Lattimer,' Sarah said with a smile that seemed charming, but
somehow did not reach her eyes. Hester read calculation and
an almost cruel watchfulness. She felt like a wounded bird
being watched by a stoat, which was trying to decide if she
were weak enough yet for it to pounce.

'I am glad,' she replied with what she hoped was a nervous
smile. 'I have to confess I look forward to having company in
the house with noise and chatter and music. You will say it is
foolish of me, but lately I have felt oppressed and nervous there.'

The Nugents made indeterminate soothing noises. 'There
has been a repetition of those strange happenings?' Lewis
prompted. 'Some sort of roses being left, did you say?'

'Yes, that, of course.' She produced a shaky laugh. 'We had
got almost used to that. No, there is something else. As though
something is in the house, something we cannot see. A presence that seems somehow restless and angry.'

'Oh.' Sarah Nugent appeared startled. 'How very…odd.'

'It is horrible! Horrible,' Miss Prudhome burst out shrilly,
then clapped her handkerchief to her face and hurried down the
path to the lych-gate where Susan and Jethro were waiting.

'My goodness,' Hester congratulated Maria once they were safely out of sight down the lane. 'That *was* an effective outburst.'

'It was that or accuse her to her lying face,' Maria declared vehemently. 'Odious girl. I could not stand to speak to her a moment longer.'

Hester would not countenance any heavy work on a Sunday, but they spent much of the day helping Susan produce little comfits and sweetmeats and making bows out of the crimson and silver ribbon Hester had found in the haberdashers. 'If we cut evergreens tomorrow, we can make garlands and swags for the stairs and door cases and mantelshelves. Set about with candles and these bows, I think it will look very pretty.'

But try as she might, stuffing marchpane into dates, sifting sugar over tartlets and cutting lengths of ribbon were no way to keep the mind occupied. Hester caught herself daydreaming about Guy and only pulled herself together by recalling every damning word he had said about her relationship with John. This made her so angry that she cut six dates completely in half before Miss Prudhome removed the knife from her sticky fingers and advised her to wash her hands and try tying bows for a change.

The clock striking five recalled her to herself to find the others clearing the kitchen table and only three bows in the basket at her feet. The crackle of the fire in the range was conducive to dreaming and the silky slip of the satin over her fingers recalled only too vividly the feel of Guy's skin under her spread hands.

Hester found from the heat in her cheeks that she was blushing and frantically tried to recall what she had been thinking about. The answer was all too humiliating: Guy's kisses and how his mouth had felt on hers, how strong his arms were around her, how she wished she had pulled him down on to the spread hay and incited him to take her there in the cold barn that night.

And that would have proved him correct about you, would it not, Hester Lattimer? she told herself savagely, tossing the scissors into the basket and jumping to her feet. 'Shall we have an early supper and be early to bed? There is much to do tomorrow and we will be up late.'

It was, therefore, only nine o'clock when Susan carried the first of the warming pans upstairs. When she came down again and stood in the doorway it was her silence that arrested their attention. Jethro put down the platter he was polishing, Miss Prudhome her hemming and Hester laid down the book she was trying to concentrate on.

'What is it, Susan?' The maid was white as a sheet.

'Je…Jethro,' Susan managed, hanging on to the door handle as if to a lifeline. 'Upstairs…Miss Hester's bed.'

Hester was on her feet, supporting Susan as Jethro pushed past and ran down the hall. 'Jethro, wait, I'll come with you. Maria, help Susan.'

'No!' Susan's hand closed painfully around her wrist. 'No, you do not want to see it.'

There was the sound of Jethro's returning footsteps, dragging now, then the lad himself carrying a long glove box. Over it he had draped a linen hand towel.

'Jethro?'

He moved to put it on the kitchen table, obviously thought better of it and put it on a barrel that was doing duty as a candle stand in one corner. His face was an unhealthy greenish white.

'Jethro, what is it?' Hester stretched out a hand and he caught it, echoing Susan's words.

'You really do not want to see this, Miss Hester.'

'If I do not, I swear I am going to scream with suspense.' Half-expecting some unpleasantness like a dead bird, she shook off Jethro's hand and flicked off the linen cover.

Lying in the box were the delicate bleached bones of a human hand. Caught in the brittle finger tips was a gauze handkerchief, brown with age, and loose on one finger was a simple pearl ring. Hester dropped the cloth back and managed to drag in a breath. 'A woman's hand.' How was she managing to keep her voice so steady? 'This is an abomination— are they grave robbing now?' It was anger, she realised, that was stopping her fainting or screaming or any of the other things Jethro and Susan feared.

Susan was helping an appalled Miss Prudhome to her chair. They were all too horrified at the desecration to be afraid. 'Jethro, please go and fetch Mr Bunting. If nothing else, this should be lying in the church until we find out where it has been stolen from.'

It seemed an age until the vicar came, grave and anxious beside Jethro. The women sat and waited, eyes averted while he examined the box.

'This is a truly dreadful thing for anyone to do,' he said at last, 'but you may at least rest assured that whoever perpetrated this revolting trick has not committed an act of sacrilege. This, unless I am much mistaken, is part of a skeleton that was stolen from Dr Forrest's library last week. It is of the kind that every medical student uses to study anatomy. The bones of some poor criminal, I very much fear.'

'Will you return it to him, Vicar?' Hester asked. 'And can I ask you not to say anything of this to anyone other than the doctor? Ask him to keep silent too, if you please. Lord Buckland knows who has been perpetrating a series of unpleasant tricks on this household and is preparing to unmask them. It would not do to give them warning.'

The vicar left at last, bearing the grisly relic and murmuring his distress at such wickedness in his parish. Hester regarded her solemn household. 'This truly is the limit of what one could imagine those wretches to commit, but they will be unmasked tomorrow. Please do not say anything to Lord Buckland, there is nothing he can do and—' Her voice broke and she regained control with an effort. 'Quite frankly, I cannot cope with either his anger or his solicitude if he should discover it.'

CHAPTER TWENTY-TWO

'Where are the pearls, Susan?' Hester twisted round on her dressing table stool and regarded the maid with an worried frown.

'Oh, I put them away safely,' Susan reassured her. 'Now, you are quite sure about the fern green crepe and not the rose pink satin?'

'Definitely the fern green.' Hester rummaged in her jewellery box and lifted out the small box with her diamond ear bobs. 'And the dark green slippers and the silver drawn-thread scarf.' She began to brush out her hair, watching Susan in the mirror. 'Will you take some time to sit down and rest in a minute? I can help Miss Prudhome.'

Susan nodded. 'I will do. But we'll be fine once the guests start arriving, it is just that we've hardly stopped all day. Now, if you'll just stand up…'

The gown was slipped on and both young women peered at the neckline. 'Tighter,' Susan pronounced, tugging firmly on Hester's stay-laces until her bosom swelled above the soft floss edging of the low-cut neckline.

'Oh, yes,' Susan said with a decided nod. 'Now that'll make him sorry!'

She did not have to say who 'he' was.

* * *

There was already a small crowd making their way up the front path of the Moon House when Guy walked across with his two guests. He felt unaccountably on edge and spent the few minutes it took to get to the front door to run through his preparations. Nothing had been omitted, everything was as ready as it could be, he was backed up by two very senior magistrates and all the support they could possibly need. So what was he worrying about?

The answer hit him as he came through the front door in the wake of the curate and the Buntings. Hester.

She was standing in the hall directly under the lantern and the light sparked off her diamonds and burnished her hair. Her gown swathed her in a column of green so that she looked fresh and spring-like amidst the darker green of the swags. He had never seen her look lovelier and when she saw him her pale skin became rosy with a soft and charming blush. Should he really despair if he could make her colour like that? Surely she felt something for him still?

Her eyes, when he was close enough to take her hand, were expressive too: wide and brown and with the dangerous golden glint in them that warned him she was on her mettle and by no means ready to trust him tonight.

'Good evening, my lord.' Her voice held just the right degree of warmth and welcome and not one iota more.

'Good evening, Miss Lattimer.' He bowed over her hand saying, low voiced, as he straightened, 'I have never seen you in greater beauty.'

If he had hoped to soften her, to prolong that delicate blush, he was mistaken. 'Indeed, my lord? Then I must conclude that all my efforts were worthwhile, must I not?'

'Viper,' he returned, amused, and saw her eyes glint even brighter. 'Please allow me to present my friends, Sir Jeremy Evelyn and Mr Earle. Gentlemen, Miss Lattimer.'

Sir Jeremy, rotund, jovial and a man who looked as if he spent his time acting as a model for Toby jugs rather than wrestling with difficult cases at Bow Street, bowed low over Hester's hand. 'Ma'am, we are in your debt. To be invited, as complete strangers, to share such charming festivities is a pleasure indeed.'

He was supplanted by Mr Earle, thin, cheerful and apparently, from his highly fashionable outfit and numerous dangling fobs, an amiable nonentity. This illusion served him well and it had taken him many years to perfect it.

Having greeted their hostess and yielded top coats and gloves to Jethro, resplendent in striped waistcoat and a tail coat only slightly too large for him, the gentlemen drifted through to the drawing room, which was already humming with company. Guy set himself to introduce his friends while mentally ticking off a list of who was there. Possibly half the expected company—and no sign of the Nugents. Too early to be concerned yet, they had a way to come.

Having chatted to the Redlands, met two new neighbours and congratulated Mrs Bunting on the results of her latest battles with the choirmaster, Guy moved across the hall to see who was in the dining room. Most of the young people, he noticed with amusement. The young men with half an eye on the buffet and half on the young ladies, the young ladies with no interest at all in the food and pretending complete indifference to the boys.

Smiling, he was about to turn and observe as much to Sir Jeremy when the picture propped on the mantel shelf caught his eye. He stared for a long moment, then strode up to it and studied it more closely. Where the *hell* had she found this?

'Is that not strange, my lord?' The voice, with nervous giggle, belonged to Miss Redland. 'I mean, it has been slashed to shreds and just stuck back together. But the lady is very lovely, is she not?'

'Very,' Guy agreed, staring back at the image, so hauntingly like his sister. *I am going to strangle Hester.*

'Do you admire the lady from the attic?' Hester spoke, cutting across his thought, ushering the Nugents into the warmth of the room. Guy turned, narrowing his eyes at her, furious he could not express his anger in such company—and then realised just what a masterstroke it was.

Both brother and sister had gone white to the lips, staring at the ravaged portrait. Of course, they would recognise Diana from the locket in the box. He fingered the golden oval that lay in his pocket.

'Whoever is it, and what *has* become of it?' It was Sarah Nugent speaking, recovering far faster than her brother, as Guy might have expected. She would be the hardest of the two to break, he knew that.

'Yes,' Guy chimed in, peering at the picture with every appearance of interest. 'Do tell us about this, Miss Lattimer.'

'Why, I know nothing,' Hester said lightly with a shrug. 'I found it in the attic in a terrible condition. I mended it as best I could, but she remains a mystery.'

'I wonder you should care to have such a damaged thing on display, Miss Lattimer.' Sarah Nugent's brittle laugh made heads turn and several other people strolled over to look.

'In a way I do not,' Hester was saying, a troubled look in her eyes as she stared at the portrait. 'But I felt…compelled. The thing positively haunts me.'

'Fascinating.' It was Sir Jeremy, braving the fire to stand as close as possible to study the scarred face.

'Fascinating,' Sir Lewis echoed, edging away. 'Come, Sarah, there is Marcus Holding, and you recall he was interested in buying that mare of yours.'

'Well done, Miss Lattimer,' Sir Jeremy murmured. 'I see you have a talent for intrigue.'

'Hester.' Guy took her arm and steered her as far away from the other guests as he could. 'What are you about? That could have been dangerous.'

She smiled at him, maddening him and arousing him at the same time. 'She looks so lovely from across the room. She used to hang there, I am quite sure. Do you think you will be able to get her properly restored?'

'Me? But she is yours.'

'Oh, no.' Hester shook her head. 'Do you think me blind? She is your grandmother, I assume.' Without waiting for an answer she moved away to speak to other guests, leaving Guy staring after her.

Hester was soon too busy with her guests to worry overmuch about Guy's inimical stare upon her or what the Nugents might be up to. The front rooms were filled to the point where she could be confident that this party would go down as a thorough-going success and she was in constant demand to chat to old friends and more recent acquaintances.

Then the footmen borrowed from Parrott began to carry through the hot savouries and the guests flowed into and out of the dining room, carrying plates of food, brimming glasses and finding themselves places at the numerous little tables she had managed to fit in.

'So delightfully informal,' said a laughing voice and Hester realised with amazement that it was Mrs Redland and she appeared to be flirting, just a little, with Mr Earle. She looked away, caught Guy's eye and raised an amused eyebrow. He smiled back and she was lost.

It was not simply that he looked so handsome, although he most certainly did in his elegantly simple evening clothes, with his air of assurance and poise and just the hint of controlled, dangerous power under all the civilised trappings. No, she was back at the moment when she first saw him in her drawing room and recognised her ideal. Her heart seemed to move in her chest and her skin felt hypersensitive as though she was naked and exposed to thousands of tiny, prickling ice crystals.

He is mine, and I love him. And I want him. Oh, how much she wanted him. Hester could feel the colour rising under her skin and dragged her gaze away. But there was no escape while she was in the same room. She moved through the throng of guests into the relative quiet of the hall and turned instinctively towards the kitchen.

'You can't go in there, Miss Hester.' It was Susan, bustling back with a stack of dirty plates. 'Honestly, what a pickle; we're having to just stack everything in the scullery, can't do a thing in the kitchen.'

Back in the drawing room the more mature guests had finished eating and were sitting back with glasses of wine, chatting comfortably. Hester opened the piano and, as she expected, several mamas were not slow to urge their daughters forward. Lucy Piper sat and began to play and three of her friends grouped round and started to sing. Hester found the curate and he needed little persuasion to add his pleasant baritone to the chorus; she suspected he was somewhat enamoured of Lucy.

Half an hour passed pleasantly with a cheerful selection of seasonal songs and carols. Hester, moving from group to group in the dining room, chatting and passing sweetmeats, tried to see what Guy and his two friends were doing, but it seemed that they had nothing on their minds other than conversation. She waited until Guy looked in her direction, then raised her eyebrows in interrogation; he merely nodded almost imperceptibly towards Sir Jeremy, who was talking to a wide-eyed Annabelle Redland.

'Ooh, Sir Jeremy! What a good idea!' Annabelle craned her neck and located Hester. 'Miss Lattimer, Sir Jeremy was telling me that it is a tradition in many houses to tell ghost stories before Christmas—might we do so, do you think? It sounds such fun, and so scary.' She shuddered dramatically and batted her eyelashes at Sir Jeremy.

'What do you say, Miss Lattimer?' he appealed to her. By now all the guests in the dining room were watching for her reply, and, by their animated expressions, it appeared they favoured the suggestion.

'It seems an entertaining idea,' she conceded with a smile, then looked around the room. 'But we cannot all sit in one chamber and it would be a pity to split the party up so definitely.'

'How about the kitchen?' It was Mr Earle. 'Might I go and see?' Before she could reply he was out of the room.

'Very impulsive, but means well,' Sir Jeremy remarked, at which point his friend reappeared.

'Plenty of room,' he announced. 'If you will just allow me to organise this, Miss Lattimer? I would not put you out for the world, but I do so enjoy a ghost story.' He vanished again, Jethro at his heels, leaving an anticipatory buzz behind him. Already people were discussing good stories and Mr Bunting was being urged to tell the one about the monk in black said to haunt the woods around his previous church.

Hester went back into the drawing room to find that Guy had effectively halted the carol singing by the simple expedient of flirting with the young ladies who had been singing. Jethro and two footmen were removing all the spare chairs to the kitchen and word of the impromptu entertainment was being received with good humour by the matrons.

Hester saw the Nugents standing back in a corner in earnest discussion and went across with an anxious smile. 'Not, perhaps, the subject I would have raised, given the strange happenings here lately, but I do not think I can divert Mr Earle. I count on you both to support me.' She linked her arm through Miss Nugent's, ignoring the lack of enthusiasm with which this was greeted. 'Just telling stories can do no harm, can it, Sir Lewis?'

He seemed pale, but nodded encouragingly. 'No, of course not. You must not let these occurrences unsettle you, Miss Lattimer.'

By the time Mr Earle had reappeared and begun ushering her guests towards the kitchen, Hester was prey to rising nerves. Tension seemed to flow from Miss Nugent until Hester felt quite sick with it. She looked around for Guy and failed to see him. What to expect? In the event she found the kitchen spick and span, the table pushed back to the wall, chairs arranged in several half-circles facing the rear wall and the back door and the two cupboard doors hung with black cloth, apparently to keep the draught out.

Candles burned brightly all around the big room and the range was screened by the metal fire shield to keep the heat from scorching the complexions of the ladies nearest it.

Guy was helping people to their chairs and Hester with her reluctant companions found herself in the middle of the front row. She released Sarah Nugent's arm and Guy touched her wrist as he straightened her chair. Hester looked up at him, but his eyes held no message for her and she shivered.

Mr Earle had assumed the role of master of ceremonies. Hester wondered what, exactly, his occupation was, for in the pleasantest manner possible he had them all in the palm of his hand.

'Now, then,' he announced from the Windsor chair he had pulled to the front so that he sat facing the audience with his back to the shrouded back door. 'Who is to be our first story-teller? A little bird has told me that the vicar has a scary tale to tell.'

Amid much encouragement Mr Bunting came to the front and took the chair while Mr Earle effaced himself. With the aplomb one might expect of an experienced preacher, he told a simple tale with spine-tingling effectiveness and was much applauded as he returned to his seat.

'Who next?' Mr Earle invited. Glancing round, Hester wondered if anyone else had noticed that Susan had snuffed some of the candles and the room was perceptibly darker, with deepening shadows in the corners.

'Mama,' Annabelle was saying, 'do tell the tale of Black Shuck.'

Mrs Redland was demurring, but her son joined in his sister's persuasion and in the end she gave in. 'This is a tale from Suffolk where I grew up,' she began as she took the seat facing the audience. 'The tale of the great black hound of death, which travellers find behind them on the road at night.'

Hester found herself quite caught up. Mrs Redland's dry, well-bred manner threw the tale into stark relief and made it all the more frightening. Little gasps rose from the young ladies and even the gentlemen were sitting forwards in their chairs, paying rapt attention. The applause was vigorous, almost as if people found relief in the noise, Hester thought, noticing that even more candles had been snuffed.

'Who next?' Mr Earle enquired. 'Lord Buckland? How about that tale you hinted at at luncheon today? A story that could hardly be more apposite for this occasion.'

Guy moved out of the shadows and looked towards

Hester quite openly. 'Perhaps Miss Lattimer would find it uncomfortable.'

Hester laid her hand on Sarah's as though seeking support and replied, 'What do you mean, my lord?'

'As you know, thanks to the kind loan of books from his collection by Sir Lewis, I have been reading about local antiquarian lore, and the story of this house in particular. I did not tell you, Miss Lattimer, and I think I was remiss in not doing so, but this led me to investigate further into the story of the Moon House. It is certainly a tale fit for this evening's entertainment, but you must tell me if it is too intrusive.'

'I...I would be sorry not to hear it now, for I am sure we are all intrigued by that introduction, my lord. Please, tell the tale.' Hester was pleased with her own acting. She flattered herself that she sounded slightly alarmed, certainly uneasy, but too polite to tell her guest not to continue. Sarah Nugent moved her forearm restlessly under Hester's palm.

Guy took his time settling himself and, while all eyes were on him, Hester noticed more lights being doused. The room was in semi-darkness now, lit by the glow of the fire that gave the whitewashed ceiling a red flush and by two branches of candles at the back with one on a barrel by Guy's side. He had moved the chair slightly and now the black-draped door of the cupboard containing the secret entrance was on his left-hand side as he sat facing the audience.

How was he going to manage this? Hester found herself watching the man she loved as though he were a stranger. The candles underlit his face, giving him a saturnine and sinister look, but his stance was easy, as elegant as though he was taking tea in a fashionable salon. When he spoke his voice was conversational with no attempt to inject unease or horror; he could have been reporting any item of local gossip.

'This house is haunted,' Guy said and a ripple of anticipation ran around the room. He had them all in the palm of his hand. 'But, to begin at the beginning, we have to begin with a scandal.'

CHAPTER TWENTY-THREE

Guy swept the room with his eyes, using his silence to gather the attention of everyone there. At the back he could see Susan, candle snuffer in hand, waiting for her next cue. To one side young Ackland watched the Nugents, his grey eyes hardly wavering.

Sir Jeremy was just behind them and John Earle was on the other side to Ackland, but his eyes, like Guy's, had come to rest on the still figure of Hester Lattimer, poised and lovely in her green gown, the silver of her wrap and the glitter of her diamonds the only signs of her agitation as they flickered in the candlelight.

God, he wanted this over, he wanted her out of danger, clear of the Nugents and their schemes. And he wanted her alone so he could rebuild what was between them, make up for the hurt he had given her, make her his wife if she would ever agree to that now. The remarkable brown eyes, which were haunting his dreams, were fixed on his face. Her expression was one of polite anticipation, but her gaze held questions, and a trust that he only hoped he could fulfil.

Time to begin. 'Fifty-four years ago a local gentleman had a cottage on this site demolished in order to build the house we are guests in this evening. It was to be a speculative venture apparently, for not long after it was finished a young widow moved in as a tenant. She was expecting a child and soon gained the sympathy of her neighbours with her tragic story, for her husband, a merchant, had been lost at sea during a voyage to the West Indies. She was retiring and well bred and, although very beautiful, she repulsed tactfully the hopeful advances of a number of local bachelors. This enhanced her standing amongst the matrons of the village.' A murmur of amusement ran around the room.

Guy dropped his voice a fraction so that they had to concentrate to hear. 'No one appeared to notice the strange coincidence that the lady, Mrs Parrish, should be called Diana when the house carried the sign of the moon above the door. The sign of Diana the huntress. Her daughter was born in January of the next year, a child promising to be as lovely as her mother, and was welcomed into local life as was her mother. It could not have been a more respectable little household and it was noted how very discreet Mrs Parrish was, for the only gentleman ever seen to enter the house alone was the vicar.

'What was not seen, however, was that her landlord was also her lover and entered the house nightly by a secret entrance that had been built in from the beginning. For the name of the house was no coincidence and the local gentleman, far from being the complacent husband of a difficult and sickly wife, had been carrying on an affair with Mrs Parrish, a talented actress, for more than four years.' Was this going to be too shocking for the strict mamas in the audience? Guy watched Mrs Redland for her reaction, but saw only fascination and a dawning awareness on her angular face.

'All went well. Diana was discreet, her child grew lovelier by the day and her lover managed his double life with such skill that his family never suspected a thing. His only failing was to forget that all men, even those in love, are mortal. His death at the age of forty of a seizure, one day before his daughter's third birthday, was utterly unexpected. His grieving widow left all matters in the hands of her son, an arrogant cub of seventeen who lost no time in going through his father's papers where he discovered ample proof of just what the older man had meant by calling the the Moon House an investment.

'Accompanied by three grooms, he descended on the Moon House and forced his way into Diana's dressing room, where she was sitting at her dressing table clad in only her night rail. Imagine if you can her state of mind that morning.' Again he dropped his voice a little. The audience was leaning forward in its chairs, he could feel the intensity of Hester's gaze on him, but dared not look at her and risk losing his thread.

'Three days ago her lover, a man she loved deeply, her only source of support, had died without warning, leaving her with a child and her only possession of value, a wonderful rope of pearls which she always wore. She had just twisted it about her neck: perhaps she was stroking it, remembering the night he gave it to her, remembering the words he had spoken.

'Then her door was forced open. With her child screaming with fear, her maid brutally forced from the room, she had the pearls torn from her neck, the nightgown ripped from her body, leaving her naked and humiliated in front of those men. Her lover's son gave her an hour to pack and leave, his henchmen threw her clothes on to the floor so she had to scrabble on her hands and knees to gather up what she could, her baby hanging around her neck, terrified, seeing violence and hearing raised voices for the first time in her life.

'They threw her out of the house with her child, the clothes they stood up in and one valise. She had two sovereigns in her reticule. The snow was thick on the ground, the wind harsh. Behind her she could hear the sounds of men wrecking her home; perhaps even the sound of a knife ripping through the canvas of her portrait, which hung over the fireplace in the dining room.'

There were gasps as people remembered the picture that Hester had restored, then Mrs Bunting said, 'The poor creature. Whatever became of her?'

'She caught the stagecoach to London, that much is known. Then, who can say?'

There was the sound of a sob—Miss Redland had a softer heart than her frivolous exterior betrayed. Hester, when he risked a glance at her, was white to the lips.

'The Moon House stayed empty for many years. Around it grew up a mystery and tales of tragedy, for no one beyond the family of Diana's lover knew what had happened. A story of haunting grew, and strange details were added to the legend; many swore that the scent of roses lingered around the house, even when the flowers were not in bloom, for in Diana's day the house was surrounded by a garden of great charm, filled with her favourite roses.

'Then the grandchildren of her lover inherited, but by then the house had been sold.' A small gasp interrupted him: at last they were thinking about what he was saying, not as a story but as history, and the identity of Diana's lover must be obvious to everyone. 'These heirs found the papers telling of the building of the house and found the secret way in. They also found love letters referring to a treasure hidden in the house, a secret known only to Diana and her lover. They needed money and they were greedy. Lights were seen in the days before Miss Lattimer moved in, but nothing was found and now she was in residence: how could they search?'

Somehow he was holding their attention. No one spoke, although eyes were turning towards the Nugents, who sat like statues in the front row. 'Their only hope was to force Miss Lattimer to leave, but she would not sell. She must be scared away, and so a new haunting of the Moon House began. They almost killed Miss Lattimer's butler in the process, they terrified her companion and maidservant, they harassed her beyond what any lady might be expected to stand and they told a tale of tragedy and death walking, coming closer with the changing phases of the moon.'

He paused, counting heartbeats. One…two…three…four. 'But they disturbed something with their blasphemous meddling, and now, it seems, Diana's spirit has returned in truth. The moon is waning…'

As he spoke the room was suddenly filled with the scent of roses, as shocking as it was lovely, wreathing through the air like a summer's evening in deepest December. Mrs Bunting gave a sudden gasp and all the candles but the branch by Guy's side went out. His cue. *Now*. He started to his feet, 'What the hell?'

A cold wind blew through the room, sending the candle flames guttering and the flames in the fire dancing, their reflection casting a devilish glow across frightened faces. Then the heavy curtains over the door at his side fluttered as though they were merely gauze and parted and a figure appeared. All in white, its long golden hair falling in ringlets around its shoulders, a great rope of pearls falling across its milky pale bosom, it turned slowly to face the audience and stretched out a hand.

The scream when it came wrenched Hester from her state of shock. By her side Sarah Nugent was on her feet, but it was not she who had uttered that ghastly noise, it was her brother. Sir Lewis had his hands thrown up to ward off the spectre, his face was contorted in the strange light, but everyone heard his voice.

'You're dead, you whore, you're dead…get away from me…it's ours, all the money's ours, he bled the family dry for you, you whore. If she had only seen sense, only sold—'

The vicious slap his sister cracked across his cheek silenced him and he recoiled from her, his hands still to his face. Hester stared round the room; the audience was transfixed, the spectre of Diana had vanished as silently as it had appeared. 'You fool!' Sarah snarled. 'Now get us out of this!'

She seized Hester's arm, spinning her into Lewis's arms and he grabbed hold of her with the strength of desperation. Hester struggled, then she was pushed away as a small figure hurtled into Sir Lewis like a terrier on a rabbit. There was a thump, a cry and the baronet was doubled up, retching and clutching his groin.

'Are you all right, Miss Hester?' Jethro caught her and held her. 'I kicked him in the gingambobs, he won't be going anywhere now.'

'I know you did, Jethro, well done. Thank you.' Hester turned in his embrace and stared at the chaos that her kitchen had become.

A group of thickset men erupted from the cupboard where the ghost had come from and held the Nugents firmly between them while one repelled Mrs Bunting, who seemed intent on doing physical harm to both of her neighbours. 'Wicked, wicked,' she was repeating. Miss Redland had fainted neatly into the arms of the curate, but for once her mother was paying no attention, instead listening, as they all were, to Sir Jeremy Evelyn.

'...powers invested in me as magistrate I arrest you, Lewis Nugent, and you, Sarah Nugent, for breaking and entering, assault, causing grievous bodily harm...yes, Vicar—?' he broke off to listen to Mr Bunting's agitated whisper '—theft and the improper disposal of human remains. These constables will take you to Aylesbury where you will await trial.'

'I demand a lawyer.' Sarah was not yielding one inch, although at her side her brother was sobbing now.

'Certainly, ma'am.' Mr Earle stepped forward. 'I am at your disposal. You are going to need all the help you can get.' His smile was not reassuring.

As they were bundled out of the door, Hester looked round for Guy and found him interrogating Mr Bunting. His face when he came over to her was stiff with anger. 'Why did you not tell me about the hand?'

'There was nothing you could do about it.' She felt too tired now to explain.

'It was in your bed?'

Why was he so angry with her? She had not put the sad, grisly relic there. 'Yes, on the pillow. Guy, please, I am sorry to be ungrateful, but I wish you would just go away and take all these people with you.'

There was a long silence while he stood looking at her, the anger still hot in his eyes. 'Very well, Hester. I will go away and leave you in peace.' To her surprise he did not argue but did just that, taking Sir Jeremy and the remaining constable with him.

'Oh.' Hester sank down on her chair, prey to a feeling of complete anticlimax. Susan was lighting the candles again and Maria, showing far more firmness that usual, was ushering people out of the room and sending Jethro and the footmen to retrieve wraps and coats. 'Such a shock for all of us, I know you will forgive us for ending the evening so abruptly.'

Her voice faded away as the door shut and Hester leaned back, blinking at the firelight. So it was all over now. The ghost laid, the Nugents routed and Guy at last ready to leave and forget her. She closed her lids; how foolish to stare into the glow like that, it had made her eyes water. *I will feel better soon*, she told herself, *not so tired, better able to manage. This is just shock making me feel so dizzy.*

Hester opened her eyes and found the ghost of Diana

Parrish standing looking down at her. 'Hello,' said the ghost wearily, revealing herself to be Georgiana Broome. 'Men are very good at this sort of drama, are they not? But not very expert at managing the aftermath. Has my brother gone?'

'Yes.' Hester gestured at the chair next to her, too disorientated to ask why Georgiana no longer appeared to think her a scarlet woman. 'He is angry with me.' She explained about the skeletal hand.

Lady Broome sighed and sat down, extending a hand to the flames. 'That cupboard is freezing. I wonder how long it will take the smell to go away—that was an entire bottle of rose essence which went on to the fire. Oh, let me give you these back.' She lifted the pearls from round her neck and handed them to Hester.

'Thank you, but I could not possibly take them, they are so valuable—and, in any case I rather think they are yours. You are her granddaughter, are you not?'

'Yes.' Georgiana continued to hold out the rope of milky orbs. 'I insist, please take them. She would have liked you to have it, you have her sort of courage.'

'What happened to her and her child?' Hester took the pearls reluctantly and let them run through her fingers, thinking of the woman who had once owned them. It was strange to be sitting here at peace in a sort of exhausted truce with the woman who had crushed her hopes of love and happiness with a few words.

'The child was our mother Allegra. Diana struggled to stay alive in London. Mama could remember very little of that, other than being cold and hungry and it always being noisy. Then, when Allegra was eight, Diana found employment in the home of Lady Theodora Westrope. She soon rose to become a trusted companion and Allegra was brought up with Theodora's favourite nephew, our father, who in the fullness of time became the Earl of Buckland and married his child-hood playmate.

'We knew nothing of this until my mother was dying, then she called us both to her and told us everything, gave us the papers Diana had left. Like a fool I wanted to leave things as they were, not admit to having an actress for a grandmother and a mother born out of wedlock, but Guy wanted the Moon House—I think as a sort of reparation for what had happened to Diana, to bring it back to the woman it was intended for.'

'And he could not tell me why he wanted to buy it because it was your story too and he knew you would not want it known.'

The two women sat in silence for a while, then Georgiana said, 'I am more sorry than I can say about blurting out the scandal of your position with Colonel Norton. Miss Prudhome came to see me and told me the truth.'

'What?' Hester was startled out of her exhaustion. 'How dare she?'

'She dared because she loves you,' Lady Broome replied. 'And she made me promise not to tell Guy. She said that my opinion did not matter provided I did not spread the rumour, but that if he did not come to disbelieve it of his own accord there was no hope for the two of you.'

That was true. How brave of Maria to dare her wrath and the scorn of the haughty Lady Broome. Who was apparently not so haughty after all. 'Does he believe it?'

'I think perhaps he must after all,' Georgiana replied sadly. 'Otherwise, why does he not come and speak to you about it?'

There was a scratch on the door and Jethro came in with a folded note on a salver. Hester recognised the bold, black handwriting and reached out her hand, but he shook his head. 'For Lady Broome, Miss Hester.'

Politely Hester stood up and moved away, leaving

Georgiana to read the message. 'Have they all gone, Jethro? What were they saying?' It was possible to carry on, even through a haze of shock and exhaustion, even if your heart was quite broken.

'Yes, Miss Hester. They were all very shocked, of course, but I don't believe, once they started thinking about it, that they were very surprised.'

There was an exclamation from Lady Broome who was holding two sheets of notepaper covered in Guy's sprawling hand and looking at Hester with an expression she could not read. 'He has gone to London.' She looked down at the letter again and murmured, 'Will there be enough time?'

'For you to carry out the Christmas preparations in his absence? I am sure you can leave it all to Parrott,' Hester assured her. 'Parrott can manage anything.' Did she imagine it, or did Lady Broome mutter, *But not this?*

CHAPTER TWENTY-FOUR

The Moon House was easy enough to set to rights after the party, but local society was in a turmoil that apparently would not be calmed without endless repetition, and exaggeration, of the facts.

Hester, wanting nothing more than to sit and mourn Guy's loss, found herself receiving one visitor after another, each intent on telling her how brave she had been and how they had never trusted the Nugents. Even the villagers had their own way of finding out what was going on and Ben Aston seemed to have no other work than to hang around chopping wood and bringing in kindling for Susan.

'Christmas Eve tomorrow,' Hester said brightly, far more brightly than she felt. She was no worse off than she had been before Guy Westrope had entered her life, she told herself robustly, so why was she feeling so very sorry for herself now when she was secure in her home and all danger was past? 'We must wrap our presents and find a Yule log and do as much cooking as we can so that Christmas Day is a holiday.'

'I did promise Lady Broome that I would spend some time with her tomorrow, if that is all right, Hester dear?' Maria looked anxious and faintly agitated, and Hester had not the heart to point out there was plenty to keep her occupied at home. If this new friendship helped bring Maria out of her shell, so much the better. She had already spent several hours at the Old Manor. Hester had said nothing about her breach of confidence: much good had come from it and she had shown more perception than Hester had credited her with in not telling Guy the truth.

Oh, why was she thinking about him again? The entire village seemed empty without him, she felt lonely and abandoned, yet she knew where he was—in London, doubtless on important business—and his whereabouts should be of no concern to her now in any case.

Put it off as she might, bedtime came round with a horrible inevitability and Hester took herself upstairs reluctantly, knowing she was facing another night when sleep would prove elusive. Susan tucked her up, muttering something about some laundry she must set to soak overnight and Hester was left alone in the flickering light of the fire to watch the waning moon through her uncurtained window. *I really must do something about the shutters and some curtains*, she thought. That at least was a practical thing to occupy her mind as she lay awake in the dark. Repair the shutters, of course, but what about the curtains? Silk again, or would dimity be pretty?

The clock struck twelve. Had Susan gone to bed yet? She hadn't heard her. Then the tread at the top of the stair creaked and she could hear footsteps along the landing. At last. Susan must be tired, she had worked so hard on the party, and then today, clearing up.

Her bedchamber door opened. Bless the girl, she was checking on her.

But the shadow that fell across the floor was male and the footsteps, now they were in the room, were of booted feet. Hester scooted upright in bed with a gasp as Guy walked in and shut the door behind him. He touched the candle he was holding to the branch on the mantel shelf and smiled at her.

'God, it is cold out there. The air seems to be freezing into ice crystals.' And, indeed, she could see the frost melting on his greatcoat. He shrugged it off, tossed it over a chair and sat down, starting to tug off one boot.

'What do you think you are doing? Where have you come from?' This was some sort of hallucination, she was so over-wrought that she had made herself ill.

'Taking off my boots.' His left boot came off, and he tossed it aside and began to tug at the right. 'And I've been in London, I told you. At least, I told Georgy.'

'But why? No, I do not mean, why did you go,' she protested as he pulled a thick, folded document tied in red tape from his pocket and tossed it on to the table. 'I mean, what are you doing here?'

'Thawing out.' He stood up with a grunt and rubbed his hands into the small of his back. 'That is a long drive in these conditions.'

'You can thaw out at home,' Hester protested.

'And get cold again coming back?' His coat joined the greatcoat.

Hester stared at the shirt-sleeved figure. 'How did you get in?' This was like one of those infuriating parlour games where one had only a limited number of questions to ascertain whether the person who was It was Wellington, the vicar or the Empress Josephine.

'Through the secret door.' Guy was tugging his neckcloth loose now.

'Well, you must go back immediately.' Hester tried to assume a calm manner, keeping her voice level as though she was dealing with an unpredictable lunatic. 'And go quietly or you will wake Maria and Susan.'

'Maria is snoring her head off at the far end of the landing and Susan was leaving by the secret door in the cupboard as I was coming in.'

'*What?*'

'To meet Ben Aston. Surely you knew about that?'

Hester felt her mouth drop open and shut it with a snap. 'No, I did not! You mean they are courting?'

'Certainly they are. I enquired about his intentions last week—I thought it best to make sure he hasn't a wife somewhere—and they seem perfectly honourable.' Guy strolled across and leaned on the bed post.

'You asked him? Why did you not tell me?'

'I assumed you would want to hear about it from Susan; meanwhile, it seemed wise to let him know someone had her interests at heart.' He was watching her from under heavy lidded eyes, bruised by tiredness, but Hester was not fooled into thinking Guy Westrope was the slightest bit sleepy.

'Thank you.' This situation was so unreal. Hester fell back on common civility to guide her. 'And thank you for dealing so effectively with the Nugents.'

'Ah, yes, my delinquent cousins. Georgy told you all about that, I presume.'

Hester nodded. 'She was very kind. What have you discovered about them?' She really wanted to know, but not at midnight with a man in her bedchamber.

'That they are very deeply in debt and there seems to be some suggestion of fraud involving Sarah's erstwhile fiancé.'

'What will happen to them?' Hester pulled the counterpane up around her shoulders.

'I will let them sweat a little and then buy the house on the condition they leave the country. Provided you drop charges and Jethro and the doctor do not want to pursue their claims, they will be free to leave.'

'Oh, yes, anything to be rid of them.' Hester tried for a firm note. 'Thank you for letting me know, I hope you are warm enough to go home now.'

'Not nearly warm enough.' His voice was a husky drawl and Hester gasped.

'You have come over here thinking that, because I was one man's mistress, I will take you into my bed? Get out this minute!' She pointed furiously at the door. 'Go on.'

'Hester, I came to apologise for making you think I was judging you, condemning you.' Guy sat down on the end of the bed and she withdrew her feet sharply. He was far too close, far too male and, now his waistcoat joined his coat on the chair, wearing far too little. 'I was very clumsy and I did not know how to make things right between us.'

'You mean you do not believe I was John's mistress?' Had Maria or Lady Broome said something after all, or was this the declaration of trust she had been praying for?

'I mean that I do not know. If you were, then either you were deeply in love with the man and for some reason could not marry him—and if that were the case, it would be rampant hypocrisy on my part to condemn you, knowing what I do about my own grandmother—or you were forced into that position against your will, in which case, what blame is there in that?'

Guy was watching her face, his own serious as he spoke. Hester could feel the colour ebb and flow under her skin as her emotions struggled to keep pace with what he was saying.

'You mean you do not *care*?'

'Of course I care.' He reached for her hand and she snatched it away. 'I care if you have lost someone you love, I care if you were forced into a relationship you did not want, I care if you were the object of gossip and scandal whatever the circumstances.' He moved swiftly and captured both her hands before she could evade him and pulled her gently towards him. 'Hester, what I am trying to tell you is that I love you. I love you now, as you are, whatever or whoever you are. I was not part of your past, but I want to be your future.'

The room fell silent, so still that Hester could hear the crackling as ice crystals formed and brushed against the window panes. 'But…I thought all men wanted to marry virgins.'

Guy smiled, lifting her hand to brush it against his cheek. 'That would be very hard on widows if it were the case.'

'Do not jest with me.' She should pull her hand free, but it felt so good against his cold cheek, rubbing against the stubble that was darkening his jaw.

'Hester, I hurt you, firing out questions when what you needed was for me to take your side against my sister instantly, without explanations. I did side with you, but too late, when I was alone with her. I believe I put enough questions in her mind about why such a scandal broth should have been stirred in the first place.'

'She knows the truth,' Hester said stiffly. Something was hurting inside—did a broken heart mending hurt like this? 'I had better tell you.'

'Only if you want to.' Guy released her hands and ran his palm caressingly down her hair. 'Hester, I asked *why* because I hurt for you, wanted to know so I could protect you. I am not looking for an explanation, or for you to justify yourself to me.'

Hester swallowed. The pain was an ache now, a fading ache. Hearts did mend after all and it seemed it was possible to smile. The change in his expression when he saw that tremulous curl of her lips made something inside her jolt. Slowly she began to explain, watching Guy's face, seeing the comprehension in his eyes as the tale unfolded.

'I did love him,' she finished at last. 'I loved him like an uncle or a much older brother, but never in any other way. It would have been wrong to marry him simply to provide for myself. I accepted the legacy he left me because I knew he truly wanted me to have it and it would have worried him so much if he thought I would not. His is the wine you have been admiring.'

'Then I will drink to his memory when next we open a bottle of it. He sounds a good man. It is a tragedy that his last months were made miserable by the spite and the greed of his relatives.'

'But that spite remains,' Hester pointed out, doggedly determined to drag out into the light every festering element of the scandal. 'I should never have agreed to marry you, and I should have explained why at once. Think of the scandal if you marry me now.'

'If Georgy knows the truth, then believe me, her influence in London society utterly eclipses that of Sir John's cousins. By the time you reappear in London at my side, there will be no scandal.'

'Guy, do you really want to marry me? We were thrown together, you were emotionally involved with this house, you felt you had to protect me. I would understand if you find you were mistaken…' Her voice trailed off as he rose from the bed and moved away towards the fire. *It was the right thing to say*, she told herself, wondering if she would manage not to cry until he left the room.

Instead of picking up his clothing as she expected, Guy took the document from the table and handed it to her. 'So far am I certain that I have driven to London and back to obtain this from Doctors' Commons.'

'Doctors' Commons?' Hester unfolded the stiff parchment and read. 'The Faculty Office? Guy, this is a special licence!'

'Well, I sincerely hope I have not picked up the

Archbishop's laundry list in error.' He was standing, hands on hips, looking down at her. 'Hester, will you believe I love you and I want to marry you, because I am not sure what else I can do to convince you and I really do not want to have to throw you over my shoulder and carry you off to church on Christmas morning.'

'Oh.' Hester stared at the document in her hands, then up at the man waiting so patiently at her bedside. 'Oh, yes, Guy, I—'

She got no further before she was in his arms, being held so tightly she thought she might faint. His face was buried in her hair; through a haze of happiness and desire she could feel his mouth moving as he murmured words of love into the thick brown curls.

Everything inside her seemed to be liquid, hot, aching. Hester wriggled until she could hug him in return, flatten her palms against the muscled back through the thin linen of his shirt, inhale the spicy male scent of him, nuzzle her lips along the line where his hair curled into his frost-cold nape. 'I love you.'

'I love you.' He pulled back to look at her. 'May I show you how much?'

There was no doubt and no hesitation, although she could feel the colour rising in her cheeks as she moved across the bed to make room for him. Guy shucked off his shirt and began to unbutton his breeches. Hester closed her eyes, cracked them open a fraction, took one look and then closed them again with a little gasp. The reality of an unclothed, aroused man in one's bedroom far exceeded anything her fevered dreams had conjured up.

The bed dipped, the covers flipped back over her and she was pulled down against a long, hard body. There was a second of breathless stillness then Hester gave an outraged shriek and recoiled. 'Your feet are freezing!'

Guy regarded her solemnly, only the faintest twitch at the corner of his lips betraying his amusement. 'You know, Hester, in the frequent, heated and very detailed fantasies I had entertained of making love to you, the need for a hot brick in flannel or a pair of bed socks never occurred to me.'

Hester collapsed on his chest, helpless with giggles. 'I...could...find a brick,' she managed to gasp only to find herself rolled over in a very masterful way.

'Never mind,' Guy growled in her ear, 'I will simply have to find a way to heat my blood up.'

After that she found she had little opportunity, or breath, for giggling. His lips were slow and tormenting on hers, demanding, teasing, nibbling until she was gasping for some sort of release. Even then he kept his mouth on hers, biting gently on her full lower lip as his hands caressed down over her breasts, pushing away the thin lawn that covered them.

Hester arched to meet him, her own hands clinging, kneading, stroking down the long back muscles, down over the narrow waist to the flat hips, up to the curve of his buttocks.

He rolled her again, holding her for a moment balanced on his body as he pulled the nightgown free to float disregarded to the floor. Her whole body pressed against his, every inch of it hot now, every inch of it frighteningly, magnificently male.

'Don't be frightened, sweetheart.' His voice was soft in her ear, coming from a long way off as she felt his weight on her, found herself parting instinctively for him, gasping in shocked wonderment as he entered her.

She had not expected it to be like this. Not to feel utterly one with him, certainly not to be swept up in a ravel of overwhelming sensation that was winding tighter and tighter until she felt she could not bear it any more until it burst and she cried out against his mouth, only to feel it swallowed in his own cry of triumphant release.

It was not possible to move. She did not want to move, except that she did not think she could breathe. How long had they lain here, tangled within the cradle of each other's limbs? 'Guy?'

'Mmm?'

'Can you move, just a little bit?'

'Mmm.' He rolled on to his side, bringing her with him to lie in the crook of his arm. His breath tickled her ear as he nuzzled gently along the soft skin of her temple. 'You taste of vanilla and cream and woman.'

Hester stretched as best she could, then snuggled back. 'You taste of cinnamon and dark honey and man.'

'Sounds like a recipe for syllabub,' he murmured. 'My feet are warm. Shall we try that again? I feel that practice is essential and I am sure there must be at least six places on your body I have not kissed yet.'

'Again?' Hester opened her eyes and blinked at him in the candlelight. His eyes were heavy with a dark heat that stirred new longings deep inside her. 'Again, tonight?'

'And again, and again and again.' Guy's dark head dipped below the edge of the bedcovers. 'So soft…'

Hester woke in the clear light of morning and lay unmoving, listening. But there was no one else breathing in the room, and when she stretched out a questing arm the bed beside her was empty. But the hollow in the mattress was still warm and the pillow, when she rolled over and buried her face in it, smelled of cinnamon and dark honey and Guy.

There was a scratch at the door and Susan came in with a cup of chocolate. The two young women eyed each other uncertainly.

'About last night…' they began together.

'I was going to tell you about Ben Aston,' Susan blurted out, setting the cup down and going to find Hester's dressing gown to put round her shoulders. 'Only I thought he ought to come and tell you himself and he said he was bashful.'

'Bashful? Aston? Well, if you say so, Susan. Do you love him?' A vehement nod of the head. 'And he wants to marry you?' Another nod. 'Where will you live?'

'He has a fine cottage, Miss Hester, and a smallholding with a cow and a pig and a good flock of chickens and a large vegetable garden. And he's a hard worker.'

'The vicar vouches for him and his lordship has spoken to him and seems satisfied he is good enough for you, which is what matters to me. Oh, come here and stop looking as though you expected me to ring a peel over you for courting! A fine case of the pot calling the kettle black that would be.'

Emerging pink cheeked from Hester's embrace, Susan perched on the edge of the bed. Hester could feel herself blushing under the clear regard, but she met her maid's eyes squarely. She might ache oddly, feel quite light-headed and still be half-persuaded that she was dreaming it all, but she was not going to apologise for loving Guy.

'Is it all right, Miss Hester? I mean, his lordship pinched my cheek on his way out through the kitchen this morning and said I was to look to my needle, but I didn't like to ask.'

'Lord! What time did he leave? Maria and Jethro didn't see him, did they?'

'No,' Susan reassured her. 'Miss Prudhome's just getting up and I sent Jethro off down to Ben's for more eggs. Mr Parrott's looking after most of the wedding breakfast, but I did think as how I ought to make the cake at least.'

'Wedding breakfast?' A hazy memory of Guy saying something about Christmas Day floated into Hester's mind. 'He isn't thinking of marrying me on Christmas Day, is he? That's tomorrow!'

'You had better get up.' Susan paused at the door. 'We had

all of yesterday to plan things and Lady Broome and Miss Prudhome have had that smart *modiste* from Aylesbury settled in over the way sewing your dress.'

'But that means he knew I'd say yes even before the party!' But Susan had vanished and Hester was left staring at the door. She gulped the chocolate, jumped out of bed and then back in again when she realised she was stark naked. By the time Susan came back with the hot water she was out of bed, wrapped in her dressing gown and attempting to think coherently—not that that was helped by finding Guy's cravat on the floor, tangled with her discarded nightgown. If Guy really believed she could be ready to marry him by tomorrow, he must be made to see reason. It was impossible.

But she came downstairs to find Lady Broome already ensconced in the drawing room with the *modiste*, Parrott and Jethro in earnest consultation in the kitchen and Annabelle Redland and Maria in the dining room creating a bouquet and decorations for the church. It seemed that she, as bride, had nothing to do other than to approve a gown of cream silk with a spencer of holly green, and submit to endless fittings.

'Now, I have brought some gold velvet, and I could make that up in a trice, if you would prefer, Miss Lattimer,' Madame Lefevre offered through a mouthful of pins. 'Although the green does look charmingly.'

'I found bonnets to match either choice and kid half-boots,' Lady Broome added from her position at the side of the chair upon which Hester was standing for the hem to be pinned. 'Oh, yes, and gloves and a veil. Now if you are sure about the green, I think this twisted floss trim at the hem would be best.'

Hester agreed to the green and waited before the *modiste* had left the room before jumping down and taking Lady Broome's hands in hers. 'Thank you so much! Do you truly not mind me marrying Guy? Only I love him so much—'

'I am *delighted*, I could not hope for a better wife for him. I have had my heart in my mouth ever since I read his note where he told me what he was going to do. He had to tell the Buntings, of course, but I only told Mrs Redland and Annabelle this morning because I knew we'd need some help with the flowers.'

'I keep pinching myself,' Hester confessed. 'I know Guy is inclined to take charge and just get his own way, but this leaves me breathless.' She bit her lip, then decided to risk asking. 'Lady Broome, would you be my matron of honour?'

'My dear, of course, and you must call me Georgy. Now, what about bridesmaids?'

Hester cast a glance at the other room where Annabelle could be heard talking nineteen to the dozen. 'I think I have just the two.' The mound of greenery on the table was being ruthlessly ordered into wreaths by Maria, who looked up with an anxious smile when she saw Hester. 'Do you think these will be all right for the pew ends?'

'Delightful,' Hester assured her. 'I came to ask if you, Maria, and you, Annabelle, would be my bridesmaids.' Maria promptly burst into tears, but Annabelle cast down the bow she was fashioning from gold gauze and hugged Hester.

'Oh, yes, I would love it above all things! Oh, please don't cry, Miss Prudhome, we have almost finished here and then we can decide what to wear. Isn't this wonderful?'

Hester turned back to find Jethro in the hall, Parrott looming behind him. 'We've found another turkey, Miss Hester, and a goose, a fine piece of beef and a pickled salmon.'

Hester looked around the chaos that was the Moon House and smiled. 'It seems I have a wedding breakfast, bridesmaids, a wedding gown and flowers. Now all I need is my bridegroom.'

CHAPTER TWENTY-FIVE

Guy stood at the altar rail and tried to recall if he had ever felt quite so nervous in his life before. Beside him Major Neil Carew, the friend who had braved the weather in answer to a plea delivered *en route* to Doctors' Commons only two days before, murmured, 'Stop worrying.'

'Have you got the ring?'

'In the same pocket it was in when you asked me ten minutes ago.'

'Is my cravat straight?'

'Immaculate.'

'She's changed her mind.'

'All brides are late, it is traditional.'

Guy cast a harassed glance around the congregation. The entire village seemed to have turned out in their festive best, red faces beaming amidst the garlanded pillars and pews where berried holly and trailing ivy were crowned with flickering candles.

Then there was a stir at the west door, the unmistakable tones of his sister organising someone, a squeak of dismay from Miss Prudhome, which made Susan, standing a few pews back next to a well-scrubbed Ben Aston, grin and the organist struck up.

Guy closed his eyes for a moment. When he opened them Major Piper was walking steadily down the aisle with a slender figure in cream and green on his arm. *Hester.*

Her face was hidden by a fine veil, but he would have known her anywhere as she trod towards him with the confidence of a woman who knew exactly what she was doing. Her hands were still as she held a bouquet of mistletoe and gilded ivy, its stems bound with trailing ribbons of gold gauze. His hands were shaking with awe and love and disbelief that he was this fortunate.

Then she reached his side and he turned to face Mr Bunting as Hester handed her bouquet to his sister and pulled off her green kid gloves to reveal long, white fingers, bare to receive his ring.

'Dearly beloved,' the vicar began as the organ sank into silence, and Guy found his hands were quite steady.

'You may kiss the bride.'

Hester turned to face Guy and caught her breath as he gently raised the edge of her veil and placed it back over her bonnet. He was still white, almost as white as he had been when she had walked down the aisle towards him. Seeing him, she had known with a surge of love and confidence that this was utterly right. That feeling would never leave her now, she knew that.

She gazed up at him, a tender little smile on her lips, and waited while he looked down at her. Then he smiled back and kissed her, gently, possessively and as though he would never stop. Hester stood on tiptoe, put her hand on his shoulder and returned the kiss while the blood sang in her veins. When they finally broke apart, she knew she was blushing, Guy's eyes were bright and a sentimental sigh swept through the congregation.

She took her bouquet and let Guy lead her down the aisle,

past the smiling faces, down to the west door. Parrott was standing there, a cloak over his arm.

'My lady, I believe you may need this.' The ancient door swung open and Hester stepped out into a world of dazzling whiteness. The great soft flakes of snow fell gently. Above them the Christmas bells peeled out from a tower almost hidden in the snow, sending joy for the season and joy for this wedding echoing across the village.

Guy bent to take a sprig of mistletoe from her bouquet and fixed it in his hat band. 'All the better to kiss you with,' he whispered as, laughing, she turned to throw the bunch. It soared up through the snowflakes and fell neatly into Susan's reaching hands.

Guy lifted her in his arms and carried her down the churchyard path through the untrodden whiteness to the waiting carriage. Inside he began to tuck a fur wrap over her knees, but Hester threw it back and curled up on his knees, her arms around his neck, her face buried in the warmth of his neck.

'I do not need a fur to keep me warm,' she murmured and was rewarded by his long fingers finding her chin, tipping up her face to meet his kiss.

'I came here to Winterbourne to find the truth about an old love story,' Guy said as the coach wheeled away from the church and began the short journey back to the Moon House. 'I never expected to discover what love meant.'

'And I came to learn to live alone,' Hester answered, curling an arm around his neck and snuggling close. 'I never expected to discover the one person I cannot live without.'

His lips closing on hers seemed the only possible reply.

Make your Christmas wish list – and check it twice! ★

Watch out for these very special holiday stories – all featuring the incomparable charm and romance of the Christmas season.

By Jasmine Cresswell, Tara Taylor Quinn and Kate Hoffmann
On sale 21st October 2005

By Lynnette Kent and Sherry Lewis
On sale 21st October 2005

By Lucy Monroe and Louise Allen
On sale 4th November 2005

By Heather Graham,
Lindsay McKenna, Marilyn
Pappano and Annette Broadrick
On sale 18th November 2005

By Marion Lennox, Josie Metcalfe
and Kate Hardy
On sale 2nd December 2005

By Margaret Moore, Terri Brisbin
and Gail Ranstrom
On sale 2nd December 2005

By Lisa Jackson, Barbara Boswell
and Linda Turner
On sale 18th November 2005

MILLS & BOON®   1105/03b V2

Live the emotion

_Medical
romance™

THE NOBLE DOCTOR *by Gill Sanderson*

From the moment she meets gorgeous Dr Marc
Duvallier, midwife Lucy Stephens is sure he's The
One – and he's just as sure, just as quickly! But
Marc isn't only a doctor, he's also the Comte de
Montreval. Soon he must return home – can he ask
Lucy to leave her life behind for him?

DELL OWEN MATERNITY: Midwives, doctors, babies
– at the heart of a Liverpool hospital

A SURGEON WORTH WAITING FOR *by Melanie Milburne*

Trauma surgeon Jack Colcannon and adorable
Dr Becky Baxter have a difficult relationship
– their brief affair ten years ago only adds to the
complication of them working together. Then Becky
becomes the target of terrifying threats and only
Jack can keep her safe – day and night…

A&E DRAMA: Pulses are racing in these
fast-paced dramatic stories

CHRISTMAS-DAY FIANCÉE *by Lucy Clark*

Dr Marty Williams, the new paediatric registrar,
is causing quite a stir – he's an excellent doctor,
gorgeous, funny and single – and he intends to stay
that way! Until Dr Natalie Fox re-enters his life.
Marty knows her better than anyone – and he also
knows why she has never let herself fall in love…

On sale 2nd December 2005

Available at most branches of WHSmith, Tesco, ASDA,
Borders, Eason, Sainsbury's and most bookshops

Visit www.millsandboon.co.uk